*Advanced*

# Root That Mountain

Evan Balkan

BROTHER MOCKINGBIRD

For my mom

EVAN BALKAN

# CHAPTER ONE

It's an unspeakable smell. The smell of death. The ripping open of animal to let out the demons, loosing the jumble of organ and bone and tissue and exposing it to open air where microbe and maggot and mosquito can do their work.

Black piles of waste swarming with insects fill clearings in the woods, just beyond the demarcated perimeter where decrepit buildings totter in the heat. Two scraggly roosters barely muster up the energy to chase each other in languid circles amidst food wrappers and beer cans. Muddy men wearing flip-flops cradle tattered playing cards and AK-47s.

A voice booms from inside the long, flat building: "Hey! Hey! Hey!" over and over like a wicked hymn. A shirtless man emerges. Stretching from his right shoulder to his belly button is a long purple scar. The belly button protrudes like a tiny appendage. His arms are outstretched, and unlike the other men, he has a nice potbelly.

He stands with hands on hips, surveying. Slowly, he moves in little circles like an airplane, his arms straight at his sides. He stops, smiles. What's left of his chiseled and cracked teeth is canary yellow, matching the tincture in his eyes. The smile drops from his face as he slowly crouches toward the ground, eyeing, measuring, hunting. One eyebrow sinks low; he squints at his prey.

He picks up a rock and then straightens himself to his

full height. He hurls the rock at a man dozing against a tree.

The rock explodes an inch above the man's right ear, chipping the tree trunk. He jumps up and falls into the dirt. He gets up again, grabs his gun and points—at nothing, no one, everyone and everything. He sees like a man coming out of drunkenness; the world sheds its rough corners and sharpens. He sees who has thrown the rock. He lowers the gun, allows its metal to clang against his kneecap, drawing pearls of blood, and then runs off behind a building.

"Now we go," the big man orders, laughing—a low growl of a laugh.

Two rebels with guns obey and push another man along a muddy path. A frayed rope binds his wrists. The twine digs in, searing the skin with each step and etching the tissue until the twine stays with tendon. The man hardly registers this pain. It is nothing. It is a pain he knows he will wish for in the days and years to follow. He prefers this be his last day, his last hour, his last minute. The end of this world is a blessing.

They stop at the wide stump of a once mighty tree, pocked now with numerous blade chops and stained a berry purple. The rebels push the handcuffed man to the ground and then pull him into a kneeling position in front of the stump.

The big man with the purple scar and protruding belly button spits in the wet grass. "Short sleeve or long sleeve?"

The man looks up, sputters, cries, pleads a gurgle of protest.

The big man leans down, kisses the other man tenderly just below his right eye, takes the salt of his tears and tastes it on his lips. He moves those lips to the man's ear and whispers, as if to a crying babe: "Short sleeve or long sleeve?" He places his hand gingerly on the back of the man's head as he asks this.

The tears come faster now, like the slow uncorking of a rusty and underused spigot. He opens his mouth to answer, the future before him an unwinding of terrible consequence. He tries to answer, but vomit fills his mouth, escapes his lips, drops to the log.

The big man grabs his arm, loosens the chord, and forces his forearm onto the log. "Now!" he roars.

The machete drops, taking the right hand above the wrist in one clean sweep.

The big man grabs his other arm and forces it onto the log. "Go!"

They can hear this order above the man's screams, dark unceasing howls that rattle the jungle and send the few birds and monkeys yet to have quit this place scurrying off for safer lands.

The machete comes down, but the angle is not precise and the hard bone does its good work of deflection so that the hand is not severed but rather broken, hanging and lifeless. The man stands, sees the dangling hand thumping against his forearm, and he crumples. The others hold him up, forcing him back to the stump. He does not resist, but rather helps by unfolding his legs and coming to rest on his knees. It's as if there has been some terrible mistake and they all work together now to fix it. All of them precise and concerned. They take the arm and place it against the stump. The hand dangles over and one of the men grabs it and pulls it so that the tendon is stretched taut, clear, and clean. The machete comes down and severs.

Success. The tension gone now. Everyone stands in satisfaction. One of the men grabs the hands and tosses them into a pile. They twirl—the hands—they wave, giving one final salute to the world as they spin through the air, blood trickling from the wrists.

The man knows to hold his arms up, but he's having trouble. The others remind him, grabbing his arms above the elbow and pointing the fresh stumps to the heavens. The veins have recoiled, snaking back toward the heart, their tension released like ripcords.

"Hold them up," they remind him. "Hold them up or you will bleed to death."

He wishes to bleed to death. It is all he wants. And yet he listens to their instructions. He relies upon them. He stumbles down the trail, his arms pointing upward. He approaches the next group: three more men with another being dragged down the trail, arms tied behind his back with a plastic chord. The soldiers laugh. They joke that "the surgeon" is done with him and is ready for his next patient. When he sees the man without hands come toward them, the man with his hands tied kicks and squeals and screams and fights. The others wrestle with him. But he is strong and he kicks one in the groin and gnashes his teeth until he catches another in the cheek and he butts his woolly head against another until blood pours from his nose, and then the third man takes a snub nosed pistol from his belt and shoots the man in the head so that they all are covered with blood and brain matter and they have to angrily wipe it away and they turn on each other and scream and yell as if doing so will allow them to decide whose fault this all is anyway and why it is they live in a world of jungle and death and things that they long ago decided are just not right and yet because they are so wrong they must have some natural place in the world, a certain rightness more true than all the right in the world combined.

Their argument is a kind of music, a discordant jangle of things limned into the music of the living and the dreams of the newly dead.

In the capital, Freetown, hundreds of miles away, the rebels walk together like an army. They don't slide on their bellies like their jungle brethren, out in the Kono hinterlands cutting off limbs. They don't hide behind trees or behind broken cars, their windshields shattered, wipers dead and useless across the dashboards.

Those who have guns carry them with both hands, palms on the underside of the faux wood, near the banana curve of the clip. The others, most of them, have machetes.

The people are moving away, shielding children, not looking the rebel men in the eyes. Moving away quickly, but not running. Panic, they reason, will only inflame the rebel men, like wild beasts that attack only after they see a person turn and run.

The men continue their march through the streets of Freetown, past Siaka Stevens Stadium, taking the Main Motor Road toward Aberdeen Bridge, then march north toward White Man's Bay, crisscrossing a series of filthy streams, fetid ravines, sprawling shanties.

They reach the entrance to the Amputees Camp. A satellite dish. A lone palm tree, its fronds stilled in the motionless blister of mid-afternoon. The white and blue sign, "Vulnerable Group Feeding Programme." Under the sign, propped against the left pole, a discarded prosthetic leg.

Inside the camp, a man on crutches makes his way over a rutted gash full of dirty water in front of tents covered in plastic sheeting spread out in haphazard rows, each the same dreary off-white interrupted by thin horizontal blue lines. Figures line the dirt pathways. If they have hands, they wave halfheartedly at flies. A group of children, all missing one body part or another—hand, leg, nose, lips—playing a game with stones, throwing or pushing or blowing them into a circle drawn in the dirt.

Inside the tents: A woman bathing a boy in a plastic tub, his right arm gone to the shoulder. A nurse holding the hook of an artificial arm while the owner tries to write with a pencil, but dropping it instead onto the page. He shakes his head when he drops the pencil; hopeless, his head shake says. A girl, a double amputee, on a bed asleep, the ends of her stumps looking like they've been pulled with drawstrings. A teenage boy, the sunlight glistening off his stumps tied off like sausage ends. A man in front of a mirror, moving his one remaining arm up and down, back and forth, a plastic limb sitting behind the glass.

A boy in a tattered white shirt is the first to see the rebels. Frays of white thread from the end of his cutoff jeans hang limp in the air above where his right leg used to be. He's been left with only one finger on each of his hands, a perpetual pointing over the rubber handles of his crutches. He just stares at the men with machetes; he has little left to lose.

Some of the nurses see. They run. But one nurse confronts the men. A man with a machete intercepts her and thrusts his machete into her stomach. He pulls up and then down, a jagged line like the lion's mane of hills outside the city that gives this country its name. When he pulls out his machete, her bowels spill to the ground.

Now everyone runs.

But Francis Laszlo, the white man in Tent No.3, does not run. He does not know what's happening outside the pinstriped sheets of nylon that make up the walls of his new home. But he will know soon. It will be the last thing he will know.

# CHAPTER TWO

It looks cold. Soulless blocks of limestone piled one on top of the other in unimaginative squares like a stale wedding cake. Four gigantic columnar teeth protrude from above the entrance, a tumbledown amalgam of squat columns and flat rectangular roofs. As if the building is swallowing her whole as she enters.

Rosemarie Laszlo inhales, sucking in resolve. Enough of the crying. Enough of the hysterics.

She enters the State Department's lobby and piles her belongings into the tray before walking through the metal detector. The police officer looks bored. He doesn't help as she collects her purse and coins and the envelope she's brought with her. She doesn't want to ask him where to go.

She walks the hallway looking for clues. She opens the envelope and pulls out the letter, unfolding its well-worn edges, and reads it again: "We provide guidance to grieving family members on how to make arrangements for local burial or return of the remains to the U.S. The disposition of remains is affected by local laws, customs, and facilities, which are often vastly different from those in the U.S."

She can't stand it. It gets her every time, and she reads it several times a day even though she knows the words by heart.

"'Vastly different from those in the U.S.,'" she snorts, pretending to be lost in her own world, hoping someone will hear, sympathize, agree, spout outrages at an unfair world. "Of course they are. Those people are animals."

A woman approaches. "Can I help you ma'am?"

"My husband was murdered in an Amputees Camp in Freetown."

"I'm so sorry . . . Freetown?"

"Sierra Leone."

The woman nods.

No one ever seems to know, or know for sure. She nods sympathetically. "You want the Office of American Citizens Services. That's Room 4817."

Rosemarie folds the letter again, running a finger along the edge, and puts it back in her purse. Tears well in her eyes, but she blinks them away.

She takes the stairs.

Mr. Hank Peters is the man who will need to assist in this. He is the American consular officer in Freetown, Rosemarie is told.

Is he a sympathetic man, she asks.

Of course, of course, she is told, and is led to another office.

She meets with a State Department officer, who speaks at her: "Jewelry. Apparel. Personal documents and papers. Convertible assets. Mr. Peters will prepare an inventory of the deceased's effects and we will follow your instructions concerning those effects." He adds: "I understand the deceased had no identification on his person, that he was identified by a French doctor working in the camp?" He looks on a piece of paper and struggles out the name: *Alexandre Grillet*, though he Anglicizes it, saying, "Alexand-er Grill-it."

"Is this Grill-it a family member?" he asks.

"Of course not. I have no idea who he is."

The officer looks at his pen. He taps it against his teeth. "What we need . . . what would make this process much smoother . . . is if next-of-kin identifies the deceased."

"But the deceased is in Africa."

"Yes, ma'am. Freetown."

Rosemarie stares at him blankly. "You're telling me he can't come home until I go there and identify him?"

He nods, sympathetically. A difficult job, one a person has trouble getting used to.

"So if I don't go get the body . . . My husband forever in that horrid African country?"

He nods. Taps his teeth again. "Next-of-kin. You? Perhaps an offspring?"

"They don't know the man they have," Rosemarie says.

"I understand. It's just that, well . . . there have been instances. Occasions. What we don't want . . . what this office tries to avoid . . . is to have the wrong person . . ."

She stares. She sees in his face his struggle for the right words. She doesn't care. *Let someone else squirm for once.*

"I understand he was murdered."

She nods. The tears are coming back. The burn in the throat, the viperous squeeze in the chest.

"That can complicate . . . there are cases sometimes when the deceased, as a consequence of the tragedy . . ."

"The deceased is unidentifiable," she whispers.

"Sometimes mistakes can be made. We need to be sure," he says, fixing her with a stare directly into her red-rimmed eyes.

She nods. She's tired. Very, very tired. She hears the rest, but it hardly registers:

" . . . this office can help with Letters Testamentary, Letters of Administration, and Affidavits of Next-of-Kin . . . we will be in contact . . . Mr. Peters in Freetown . . . U.S. consular mortuary certificate . . . orderly shipment of remains to facilitate U.S. Customs clearance."

She nods again, hating this man, hating Hank Peters, hating, most of all, Dr. James Albert. This is his fault, she thinks. Dr. Albert was supposed to be a friend. But he is the reason her husband went to Sierra Leone. He's the reason, she is sure.

The officer is speaking quickly now, finding refuge in well-worn bureaucratic grooves: ". . . Mr. Peters will ensure that the foreign death certificate, affidavit of the foreign funeral director, and transit permit, together with the consular mortuary certificate, accompany the remains to the United States. But . . ." and this is where Rosemarie hears him again because this is what complicates everything, what will ultimately change her world even more than it already has: " . . . all this first requires a positive identification."

There is nothing positive about this, she laughs. But it's not a real laugh and he knows it. So he doesn't laugh back, only pauses before he gets back on with it: "As I said, Mr. Peters in Freetown will ensure that the foreign death certificate, affidavit of the foreign funeral director, and transit permit, together with the consular mortuary certificate, accompany the remains to the United States . . ."

And then Rosemarie is out in the overcast day, and

little that has transpired over the past forty-eight minutes has registered.

So she makes her way blindly to the restaurant where she's to meet her son.

When Felix flew back to Baltimore from Paris, his mother wasn't at the airport. She had proposed they meet for lunch in D.C., as she'd been spending all of her time at the State Department. Their first meeting being a public one is designed to be a deliberate guard against potential hysterics.

When he enters the restaurant, she's sitting alone at a small table, her elbows resting on two menus. She stares out the window. Her hair, usually a perfectly coiffed masterpiece of layers and wings, has fallen flat across her forehead. Her eyes sink into a nest of purple wrinkles. She looks as if she's on the edge of breaking.

Felix walks to the table and kisses her cheek.

"Hello, darling," she says, clutching his elbow.

"You look good," he lies.

She smiles—a sad, unconvincing smile.

"How was Europe?"

"It was good. I took lots of pictures."

She nods. "I'll want to see them. Did you love Paris?"

"Yeah, I did."

"Your father and I—"

"I know. Your honeymoon. You don't have to, Mom."

She takes a tissue to her eyes. "It's this awful weather. So sad," she says.

"It was like this in Paris."

"You think it's sunny in Freetown?"

"Maybe." Felix picks up the menu, scanning. But little

sinks in. His mind flashes to the moment when he got the news. He was in Jausiers at the time, a little ski village in the French Alps near the Italian border. Word came the old-fashioned way—by telegram, via three separate taxis—from Marseille to Gap to Barcelonette to Jausiers. The property manager delivered it.

*"Je regrette, monsieur. Je regrette,"* she said over and over as Felix threw his things into his bag and took the same waiting taxi into a succession of larger towns until he got a train out of Marseille. He called his mother from Orly before he boarded his plane; she wasn't yet grieving, but was instead harried by crazed attempts at sorting through the details. But this much was clear: he had been murdered, shot in the chest at the Doctors Without Borders Amputees Camp in Freetown.

They're silent. Felix has surprised himself with his composure and realizes the intelligence in meeting this public way. He'd pretty well sobbed himself dry the past forty-eight hours.

He reaches across the table and places his hand on his mother's. But as soon as he does, she retracts, stiffens up, and takes a deep breath. "They say that his body has to be identified before they send him home."

"What about his passport? He had some ID, I'm sure."

"He was naked . . . the animals stripped him of everything. A woman, too. She was naked also."

His dad was found with a woman and they were naked? Felix searches his mother's face for hints of being betrayed, but there's nothing. Perhaps she's in denial. Or maybe she has thought about it, but one shock is more than enough. The notion that she might have lost her husband twice—once to another woman, and once to those "animals"—is simply too much to bear.

"What about Dr. Albert? Couldn't he identify Dad?"

"He's in the jungle . . . Some friend, huh? Lures your father to Africa and then slips off into the jungle to watch his elephants while your father gets murdered."

"Dad wasn't 'lured.'"

"It's rotten, if you ask me. His body sits in Freetown while that man is off taking his photos and dung samples. There's no one else, Felix. Those Africans are hopeless."

There's no gravid pause, no grand moment of consideration, before Felix says: "Why don't I go get him myself?" As if there is no more natural solution in the world.

Her features tighten. Tears hang on the precipice of her swollen lids and then at once fall to the table.

The waiter approaches and asks if they're ready to order. "Ped Pad King," Felix says even though he isn't hungry. "Mom?"

"Just water."

The waiter takes the menus and walks off.

"No," she whispers. Then she adds, loudly, "Absolutely not, Felix. I'm not going to lose my son the way I lost my husband." She puts her hand, palm down, on the table.

"I'll identify him and bring him home. We can bury him like a real human being. I can't stand him being there, in that place. You can't either."

"No, Felix. No."

"So, what? He's just going to stay there forever?"

"Those animals don't know the man they have," she says. She grabs a napkin from the holder on the middle of the table and pats her eyes.

"Let me get him then."

"How would you?" she asks. "You don't even know anyone."

"I can contact someone in Doctors Without Borders."

"Those cowards. They let him die. He was one of their own and they let him die."

"I'm not sure what they could have done."

"They vacated after the attack. There's no one."

The waiter brings two waters and Felix gulps at his while his mother's sits untouched.

"What about Dr. Albert?" Felix asks.

"He's a thousand miles away."

"But maybe he can arrange something. He has to know people."

Rosemarie looks out the window. She stares for a long time. So long Felix turns around to see what she's looking at, but sees only a sheath of rain coating the glass. "Do you know that he called the house?" she says finally. "Dr. Albert. He called from Bangui. After the coup attempt last year. The government could no longer guarantee his security. The university was calling him back. Do you know what that man did?"

Felix shakes his head.

"He stayed anyway. Arranged private security. Some Australian guy. I don't understand how one man can be such big security." She heaves a big sigh and picks up her water glass.

"So? That sounds pretty impressive to me."

She puts her glass down and stares at Felix as if trying to divine who he is, some sudden stranger masquerading as her son.

"I can't believe it. You are your father, Felix."

"Is that a bad thing?"

"He reacted the same way. Very impressed. Do you know that he moped around the house for a week, even worse than usual? Then he woke me up in the middle of the night. He was out of his mind. He kept calling himself a coward. There was James, in the jungle, in a country where people were being killed in the capital, but he was out there anyway. 'And where am I?' he asked. I said, 'Baltimore.' I meant that as a good thing. 'James Albert is crazy and you're not.' But all he said was, 'Exactly,' and he went downstairs. I caught him the next morning with that damn atlas. He was making arrangements to go to Africa that very week."

"It's what he wanted, Mom."

"James Albert is no friend of this family."

Felix wants to protest; he'd always admired Dr. Albert. But he knows better. This is not the time to defend the old guy. So the rest of their meeting consists mostly of Felix picking at his food and his mother watching him. Soon, they part, with nothing settled. He kisses her check, promises to call in the morning.

Felix goes home to get some sleep, only to be awakened just after midnight by insistent pounding on his apartment door. It's his mother. She sweeps her mussed hair from her face. Two thin blue streaks run from her eyes. Her cheeks are very red, as if she'd been slapped.

"Are you okay?"

"I want you to go," she says.

They move to the couch and he pushes aside his duffel, still unpacked from Europe. A dozen canisters of film roll out. "I spoke to James," she says.

"Dr. Albert?"

Despite her deep misgivings, in an extraordinary act

of courage—or desperation—she'd reached Dr. Albert that evening and asked him if he'd take her son to Sierra Leone.

"If you're going to Freetown, you're not going to do it alone. You'll go to the Central African Republic first," she says.

"That's not real close to Freetown."

"Meet Dr. Albert in Bangui and then the two of you will go to Sierra Leone together. It's the only way. Those idiots at the State Department . . . I need him home, Felix . . ."

And so, home from Europe barely one full day, Felix readies himself for a trip to Bangui, Central African Republic.

## CHAPTER THREE

Felix shuffles through the familiar terminals at BWI, the international departure wing once again, and takes his place on board. He promptly falls asleep, then wakes at JFK before the long haul into Bangui with a one-night layover in Accra.

Despite his fatigue, he's unable to sleep on the voyage across the ocean. His thoughts run interminably to Lizzy. He can't explain the sour taste in his mouth. She's done nothing wrong, of course. It was not her fault that he'd gone to Europe by himself, that he'd allowed their relationship to simply dissolve before he took off, so imbued with a sense of freedom, feeling—erroneously, ridiculously—that the trip would last forever and the real world would remain out of reach somewhere, suspended, condemning only others to its rules and demands and responsibilities. None of this was her fault—not that his father is dead, not that he's by himself heading to Africa. The irony of this, and her absence, is not lost on him.

He'd wanted to go to Africa after college. When he told Lizzy this, she looked at him blankly and asked, "Why Africa?" Hearing her trepidation, he had visions of being stranded in Addis Ababa or Dar Es Salaam, waiting for broken down buses and Lizzy sitting silently nearby while he berated himself for getting them into such a mess. So he changed the trip to Europe, a more palatable destination, ostensibly for her. But he did all the planning himself, stopped consulting her. And of course she didn't come. She had a new teaching job to start. So he went alone. And now he'd come back, three months later, been home a day, hadn't called her, and now—leaving again.

And now that he's in Africa, heading by taxi from the airport to his hotel, under the most inauspicious circumstances, he thinks again about her, about what a fool he is. About her justified anger when she learns that he'd been home from Europe, that he hadn't even called her to tell her about his dad—in the three years Felix and Lizzy had been together, Lizzy and Felix's father had developed a close relationship with one another—or that he'd taken off again.

What he'd give now to talk to her, to touch her, to hold her. Never so alone in his entire life as this.

He wishes it weren't so, but this aloneness isn't entirely to do with just Lizzy. It's as much to do with fright. He can silently condemn his mother for what he assumes is her lack of imagination, for her view of Africa as nothing more than one enormous killing machine full of savages; he knows the ignorance in this. And yet it's only a thin barrier that keeps him from falling prey to a similar line of thinking.

Its genesis runs back all the way to elementary school, when his third grade class watched a *National Geographic* film about Ubangi tribesmen, great black men carrying spears and wearing poles through their lips and noses. Most of the kids in the class laughed and spoke in gibberish in imitation. They couldn't stop cracking up—it was an obvious and easy joke and while their teacher tried to impress them with the culture and history of the Ubangi people, they only laughed more. "Do you Bang-ee?" they asked each other. "You better believe I Bang-ee," was the rote response, a joke that never got tired. It was different for Felix—the women standing in dignified poses, babies tied to their backs and large, flat plates extending their lower lips—they mesmerized him.

Still, that night in a dream, he saw Ubangi men dancing around fires and shrieking, their fierce white eyes rolling around in their pitch faces. Nearby, Felix peeked through a stand of tall reeds as the men danced around the fire, their pendulous penises swinging like ropes. Then, all at once, they stopped. They turned toward him, their eyes flashing at the blind where he hoped he'd become invisible. He wanted to scream, but no sound. Just the eyes—savage eyes that spotted him, eyes moving within heads that would soon communicate guttural instructions to tie Felix to a spit and roast him over a fire. Then he woke, his heart pounding. Ignorance and boyhood fright had created that dream. But now, as he is edging ever closer to those people, where these real live human beings actually live, it is no mere nightmare, no silly joke. The sensation titillates him, titillates by terrifying him.

Worse, he has actually been to Africa once before, very recently in fact, and, he is forced to admit to himself, it hadn't gone well. During his Europe trip. In southern Spain, he'd hopped the ferry at Algeciras to Tangier. As Felix walked to the front desk of his hotel, a tall thin man with dark, bushy hair marched past. He stopped at the arched threshold and turned to Felix.

"I'd get the hell out, mate," he said. "This city is full of beggars and thieves. Fifteen months away from New Zealand, and it's one day in Morocco that I lose all my things. I'd get out now, while you still have your gear." Felix shrugged and walked past him, eager to see the place for himself, to accrue some great stories to bring back to his dad. This was real adventure travel—so much more exciting than tame Europe—and he thrilled in the foreignness, the hint of danger. He knew: his dad would love it.

He headed to the city center, following the narrow streets as they widened near a blue-tiled mosque. Women clutched the ends of their burnooses and shielded their faces. The men, all wearing small, rounded caps, ignored him. Kids in western t-shirts followed, yelling that for a small fee they would be his guide. They each grabbed a hold of his hand and tugged him in different directions until one—he looked to be about sixteen and the oldest among them—pushed the other kids away. He pulled Felix aside and whispered conspiratorially, "I am guide. I take you. You see Paul Bowles' house?"

Felix shook his head.

"The Rolling Stones? Timothy Leary? William Burroughs. Naked Lunch. Heroin?"

"No, thank you," he said and turned to walk away.

"Tune in, man. Turn on." He smiled and held out his hands. "Drop out, my fren."

It was getting dark and the merchants were packing up, so Felix grabbed two skewers of grilled chicken and some oranges and made for his hotel. But he soon realized that he'd turned down the wrong street. He thought he recognized a bank, so he turned down the street where it sat at the corner, but that wasn't right either. It was almost completely dark.

Felix tried a few more streets and wound up in an alley that ended at a sandstone wall. When he turned around, he saw the figure of a man outlined by a faint stretch of lamplight. Felix walked over to him. The man didn't move. "Hello?" Felix said. He mumbled something. Felix came closer. The shadows moved across the man's face, covering his forehead and eyes. Felix could see half his face clearly now, his little chin bobbing up and down as if he was gumming a meal. Gray and black whiskers stood erect on his jaw. Felix came closer and the light shifted to reveal two dead eyes—cold, blue, and sightless—scanning back and forth.

Felix took off, running full speed down every deserted street, searching desperately for the yellow arch of his hotel. A solitary cat prowled by, but it fled at Felix's approach. Disembodied voices floated out of a thousand television sets, chasing him through the city, its sagging roofs sporting a multitude of satellite dishes.

Finally, he reached the hotel. He'd run past it several times; darkness had turned the yellow arch into the color of a bruise. He retreated to his room and locked the door. Sweat raced in rivulets down his face. He sat in the darkness for a long time, waiting for his heart to resume a normal pace before he went to the window to let in some air, hoping to chase away the oppressive heat. He pulled back the flimsy white shade and saw a man there, staring at him. The man's hands rested inside the pockets of his jeans; a crumpled cigarette hung from the corner of his mouth below a thick black mustache.

Felix and the man stared at each other. The only movement between them the slow escape of a stream of gray smoke from the man's nostrils. Felix grabbed the stick that had been left in the windowsill and wedged it between the jamb and the top of the window. Then he let the shade drop and felt his way through the dark toward his pack. Rifling through the front pocket, he pulled out his Swiss Army knife. He sat with his back against the wall, the knife opened to its largest blade and resting on his palm.

He drifted in and out of sleep throughout the night,

waking to a dim idea that the man in the courtyard was trying to kill him, that it was his dark eye that was the object in the crack of space between the shade and the windowsill. Then, scratching at the doorknob. Felix watched in the darkness as the knob revolved slight quarter turns, opening his eyes as widely as possible and then squinting as hard as he could, trying to decide if what he was seeing was real or some trick of the shadows.

Slowly, on tiptoes, Felix moved to the door and bent to the keyhole. He pressed his eye there and saw only darkness. He stared for a long time until he saw two clearly discernible rows of eyelashes closing. He could see everything—the way the lashes clasped one another in a perfect embrace, the slow lifting to reveal a black pupil.

Felix sprang from the door and onto the bed. Holding the knife straight up in front of him, he sat up the rest of the night until dawn announced itself in shades of pink through the sash. He looked outside—there was no man waiting to kill him, no phantoms, no apparitions regarding him with blind and evil intent. Had the entire thing simply been his overheated imagination?

Whatever it was, Felix was sufficiently spooked. He grabbed his bag and headed to the lobby where, on his way out, he passed the Kiwi describing to a bored policeman what it was that had been stolen. By mid-morning, he was on the return ferry to Spain.

Embarrassed, he wouldn't tell his father that he'd gone to Africa and then promptly turned around.

# CHAPTER FOUR

Lizzy Rose stands in front of her full-length mirror. She removes her t-shirt and underwear and studies the lines and curves of her naked body. She began doing this when she was eleven, studying then the straight lines like a boy's, turning to see her profile. Not the slightest hint of a rise at the breasts. Just two little pink nipples erect in the cold of morning. She had an older cousin who'd begun to wear bras and her hips had flared a bit so that when she walked the two halves of her bottom seemed to move independently of one another. And the boys had started to shower her with attention. Lizzy wanted the same, a blessed compartment to shuttle her thoughts away from the one dominant place they had been ever since the dissolution of her parents' marriage.

Now, at twenty-two, the body is as near to the perfect conception of womanhood she had conceived more than a decade earlier when she was just a girl and had no real sense of what being a woman meant, only that it meant something. That when you no longer look like a boy, when your body starts to move and bounce, then suddenly the world values you in a different way than before. That people look at you. The only question: what then?

She and Felix met in college. Dating him was easy. He was thoughtful and respectful of her. He made her laugh.

When they made love, he lingered over her as if it was the very first time he'd been with a woman, imbibing her, telling her over and over how much he loved her. He touched her body with wonder and gratitude and a bubbling desire he barely managed to suppress. He was different in this way; every boy before him treated her body as if it was his personal playground, inserting and pumping and feeling satisfied only when finished. Felix's first consideration, always, was her. Her pleasure. It was with him that she realized the wonders of her own body. It was in his reactions to her nakedness, to the soft rise of her breasts and the valleys of her sex, that she remembered the promise in those days before puberty, when she stood in front of the mirror and guessed what it would all mean when she no longer looked like a boy.

She wonders if she'll ever see him again. The "break-up" had been strange, more a slow disbanding than anything else. As for the Europe trip, they agreed that he'd go and she'd stay behind. By the time he got back, she'd be knee deep in her new teaching job. They could each get on with their lives and they had the ready excuse of his being half a world away. Allow the inertia and then the restlessness for something new take over and swallow the relationship whole. There was a nebulous agreement: they'd talk when he got back.

They spoke only once while he was in Europe. A strained call from a phone booth in Slovakia while rain pounded on the glass. It was Lizzy's birthday and she was heading out to celebrate with friends, people from her work, people Felix didn't know, people—no doubt—who wondered why this beautiful blonde woman was celebrating her birthday in Baltimore while her boyfriend drank beer with strangers in Bratislava. The phone connection had a delay and it crackled with bursts of static. It was, in a way, a relief. The awkwardness between them could be blamed on the line instead of the great divide that had nothing to do with countries and oceans.

But it wasn't just that, wasn't just Europe for three months. Now, apparently, it's Africa. And she knows only that he's going to see some friend of his father's somewhere—in the jungle? She's not sure—and then he'll be going to Sierra Leone. All this she'd gotten from Rosemarie, who, after Felix left, called Lizzy and explained what had happened. But it was all so rushed and confusing. *Sierra Leone.* She'd never even heard of the place. Something to do with lions and mountains? When you mashed the words together, it sounded like an Italian dish.

Lizzy insisted that she come right over, to provide comfort and to grieve together. But Rosemarie told her to wait, that she was just too busy with everything now, that they'd get together soon.

"Can I help you? Please? With whatever you have to do?" Lizzy asked.

"Thank you, dear. Thank you. But . . . I need to . . . I'll call you. Okay?"

Lizzy hung up the phone and cried for an hour straight. She wanted to be of use. She hated being rebuffed. But she considered that maybe her presence at this moment, with all its attendant memories and associations, might make things harder for Rosemarie. But Lizzy had loved Mr. Laszlo. And she felt very close to Rosemarie, too. It was paralyzing, waiting for something, doing nothing.

And so she stares at herself in the mirror, mortified by the fact that she's doing such a silly, pointless thing. And yet . . .

She turns to look at her profile. The thin arms. The naked breasts that feel like something more than simple utility only when he touched her. The short stretch of torso she always wished was longer. The tuft of hair she had planned on trimming, but for what?

She pulls on her clothes. The idea would have horrified her cousin or her mother or her own feminist sense of herself, but her naked body seems a superfluous thing without him. It feels incomplete. As if she is eleven years old again. Little different than a boy.

She'll see him again. They had simply been too intertwined for too long to never see one another again. If nothing else, she wants him to know she's sorry and she's thinking of him, that he can maybe find some solace somewhere. But who knows when he'll be home? And when he does come home, what then? And how?

# CHAPTER FIVE

"What brings you to Accra?" the concierge asks. His eyes are tinged at the edges with a malarial hue.

Felix looks at him, considers the question, puzzles out how to answer, settles on: I'm heading to Bangui.

The concierge raises an eyebrow. *Who goes to Bangui? Not white kids like this,* his expression says.

"I'm meeting someone. A friend. And then we're going to Freetown."

The concierge nods again, but looks bemused. No one goes to Freetown. People *leave* Freetown. If they can.

"I'll knock you up in the morning."

Felix nods, hands him a small stack of cedis.

The room is small—a bed, a table and lamp, and in the corner a metal bucket with water. Felix sits down on the bed. It doesn't give at all, like a tombstone.

Alone. He runs his hands through his hair. The thoughts crowd him, coming at him one against another so that none forms as a whole.

*Is his body bullet-riddled? Covered in flies, rotting away in some malarial sickroom?*

He goes to the lobby, tries Dr. Albert, but with no luck. It has all been arranged, so he tells himself he shouldn't worry; he'll meet Dr. Albert at the airport in Bangui. Still, there's trepidation. They haven't yet even spoken. He knows that Dr. Albert has been off deep in the bush, doing his field work in the Dzanga-Sangha Reserve and that he's promised to be back in time to meet Felix. But what if something happens? What will he do alone in the airport in Bangui?

It's out of his hands, confirmed for him by the sound of the hard plastic cradle receiving the phone after a dozen rings and nothing else.

Back in his room, he stares at the ineffectual fan on the ceiling, watching the slow pointless circles. A Sisyphean journey. He's endured a succession of flights already and there are more to come. And when it's all done, and he's landing once again in Baltimore, he will have a world without a reference point. A place where he can no longer pick up the phone and tell his father that he's gone somewhere, traveled around the world as his father had done, hear him sigh with satisfaction because, in the end, his boy is just like he is—or was.

He lifts himself off the bed and looks out the window. A parade of soap bubbles bobs across the frame of the window before popping into oblivion before an impenetrable mosaic of brown roofs. An occasional splash of blue on the side of a house or door. A woman in a long yellow and black dress cinched around her waist lifts a small child by the arm and wraps him in a sling across her chest.

With a rising and startling intensity, Felix feels fury toward his mother. It surprises him. *What did she do to drive him away?* he wonders but then pushes away these thoughts, feels guilty for having them.

He pulls the crank for the window. It groans in protest before it gives with a pop. He pushes the glass. Stretches his finger and bursts a bubble.

Felix turns back to the darkness of his room and collapses on the stone bed. The fan blades slow, then stop. The heat descends like a curse, full and enveloping. It's blessed exhaustion that allows him to sleep. And sleep he does, uninterrupted and deep and dark, straight through the evening until the pink of an Accra dawn announces itself at the window. Felix freshens up best he's able with his bucket of water. Despite more than twelve hours of sleep, he's still wracked with fatigue. And it's going to be a long day heading to the Central African Republic.

He tries Bangui again from the airport. This time he catches Dr. Albert.

"I'm sorry about your father, Felix," he says. "It was probably my stories of this place that brought him here. I used to kid him about that placid practice of his. The suburbs of Baltimore—man, they're nothing like the heart of Africa."

"You can't blame yourself, Dr. Albert."

"I'm not. Your dad was a grown man, a smart man, fully aware of himself."

In his place in Bangui, Dr. Albert looks at the framed photograph of the baby elephant he snapped last time out. The trunk extended, an imitation of what it believes it means to be an adult. "I'm just not sure he was fully aware of what he was getting into," he continues. He wraps the cord around his finger, looks into the sky, sunny now after a morning shower. A few moments of freshness before the onslaught of diesel and dust. "But spending time lamenting it does the old man a disservice." He pauses. "So, how are you?"

"I'm okay. I miss him." This is true, of course, but going to retrieve him makes him feel somehow alive to Felix. He agrees with Dr. Albert; his dad wouldn't want mourning. He'd chosen to go to Sierra Leone, Felix is sure, partly for the excitement, the potential of danger.

"I've got one more trip out to the jungle," Dr. Albert says. "You'll come with me, and we'll go to Freetown when we get back."

"The jungle?"

"I'm not finished my work here. Besides, it will be good for you. For the both of us."

"What about my dad's body?"

"He's not lying out on the sidewalk. He'll be fine. The Toraja people in Indonesia keep bodies preserved for months before they do anything with them. The guys working for State can do it just as well. Trust me."

Felix doesn't much care about the Toraja—whoever they are—but he *does* trust Dr. Albert.

"Okay," he says. "I'll see you soon."

"Godspeed, son."

Felix hangs up.

He looks out the window, beyond the runway, the sky a mottle of clouds. The central African jungle: it promises precisely the type of adventure he knows his dad would have loved.

He will go, Felix decides, as his dad's surrogate.

# CHAPTER SIX

Dr. Albert has kept it together admirably. He's barely been home an hour, fresh from the killing. While on the phone with Felix, he'd managed to push away his own private grief, conceal the horror, concentrating on Felix whose grief, no doubt, is much worse than his own.

That morning, as he had done every day the previous two weeks, he'd crouched on the edge of the Dzanga Bai, watching eleven pygmy elephants congregate in three small groups in the center of the watering hole. Pockets and small rivulets snaked to the edge of the forest, the clearing mostly mud. But some medium size pools remained. Here is where the elephants milled. The sun poured over, speckling the full trees with their spindly trunks at the far end of the watering hole. The elephants alternated in gray and white as they lumbered into and out of sun spots and shadows.

Dr. Albert put his binoculars to his eyes, studying the marbled folds and creases. Caressing them with his eyes like they were Pieta marble.

They left the hole together and walked the slight rise to the forest where they disappeared. They may have smelled him. He put the binoculars down and watched them.

He thought about his old friend, dead now. Murdered. Rosemarie had caught him on his one day back in Bangui, a supply run between field surveys. Her voice was controlled. All business. She never had much use for him, he knew.

It hadn't been but a year since the last time he saw her, when Dr. Albert had been at the Laszlo home in Baltimore, sitting on the edge of the lazy chair in the living room while the Laszlo men listened with wide eyes. Rosemarie sipped impassively at her Scotch and soda, the ice jingling a little too loudly in the glass. "It's not like the safaris in Kenya and Tanzania," he told them. "These wonderful creatures, they actually *disappear* into the woods. You can hear them, you can even smell them. You sure as hell can sense them, but you can't actually see them. Then suddenly, an eye, or a tusk, or a trunk. It's indescribable."

*Loxodonta pumilio.* "Pygmy elephants."

"The conventional wisdom is that it is a distinct species of elephant—distinct from its savanna cousins," he continued. "But I say not. They're only smaller because they have no natural enemies—it's too remote even for the poachers. It's a question of evolutionary biology." His hands flailed around to mimic the size and scope of the subject—though when he said "pygmy elephants," he cupped his hands like he was holding a mouse. "And the plants . . . There's one called euphorbia, looks like a cactus—hurts like hell to touch it, too. But if you do touch it, the plant is virtually destroyed and it won't grow back for years. It's the dichotomy. There's this wild area, full of things that'll kill you. But it's so fragile, too. It's beautiful. Just beautiful."

And it was beautiful, there in the bush, on the edge of the bai, watching the most extraordinary creatures on the planet. He'd packed away his materials, sliding a thumb across the top of the binoculars to get the mud off, and said a silent goodbye to the elephants. It was time to get back to Bangui. Felix was on his way.

He turned and the heel of his left boot slid in the mud. His knee arrested his fall, but the mud grabbed his foot like a tentacle. He gripped the gnarl of an exposed root and hoisted himself up and that was when he heard the gunshot. Then another. High-powered rifles. Several of them, firing away all at once. 30-06s, maybe.

When an elephant falls, it makes a thunderous sound. Trees crack and splinter. The animal releases a trumpet. The other elephants crashing through the forest to escape are like a Panzer division.

Dr. Albert lay still. He put his cheek to the muddy coolness, dark brown mud on the lashes of his right eye. Very slowly he took the binoculars to his eyes and scanned the far edge of the forest. He picked up the little rivers of water, their soft petering out, and the slight rise into the trees, pocked with the impress of the elephants.

And there it was. The tail flickered twice and then stilled. His eyes moved over the body. No rise and fall, no inhalation or exhalation. He followed the humped lines to the head, where the ear lay folded back, almost like a blanket, against the shoulder. The eye with the dark line running from it like streaks of tears from a hysterical child who has only recently stopped crying.

Three men approached cautiously. They inspected the elephant. Satisfied, they lay down their guns and got to work. They pulled long knives from their belts and grabbed the tusks, yanking the head as best they could into position.

Dr. Albert couldn't watch.

He collected himself, stifled a shriek of protest. He knew that if they spotted him he'd be next. He slid into the grass. Satisfied that he had tree cover, he rose and half walked, half ran, waist bent and moving at a trot. After a mile or so, he walked upright, toward the spot, several miles away, where the truck would take him to the helicopter back to the fetid capital, the center of this wonderful, horrible place. He didn't want to cry, but he couldn't help it. The tears ran down his face as he walked. Felix was on his way, and the boy had his own murdered loved one. Dr. Albert needed to be strong for him. It wouldn't be easy, but he resolved to do his best.

They'll go to Freetown together, but not before Dr. Albert goes back into the bush. His team is there now, cleaning up the mess, redoubling security. He'll have to go back, reclaim the place for himself and for the elephants. He'll take Felix, but he won't tell him why he's heading back. Felix has enough to contend with.

# CHAPTER SEVEN

Felix's flight to Bangui stops at what Dr. Albert had described as "every piss-ant capital in West Africa." Cockpit announcements punctuate each landing: "Aeria welcomes you to Boigny International Airport, the 'Hub of West Africa,'" "Welcome to Togo. Enjoy your visit to Tokoin Airport," "You have reached Yaounde-Nsimalen." At every stop, one or two people get off; no one gets on.

The only distinguishing view during the flights is an empty brown beach and whitecaps outside Lomé. Felix watches the striking blue water crash against the continent. But then it's unbroken forest again, stretching into forever until punctured by the approach of Cameroon's capital—a city coming out of the darkness, out of nothing but trees: Yaoundé, with its diamond-shaped buildings and wide roads, hemmed by jungle.

On descent to Bangui's Mpoko Airport, the plane banks sharply. All Felix can see is blue sky. He grips the armrest. A sickening sensation flashes through his stomach. Several passengers gasp. Then, the pockmarked tarmac of an airport whips by the window. He closes his eyes and holds his stomach as the plane bounces around before screeching to a stop on the rough strip amidst a burst of passenger applause.

The terminal is a two-story building with a balcony crammed with people looking over the new arrivals. Inside, women wear loose tops and brightly colored cloth around their waists. The men wear small round hats and what look like pajamas—tie-dyed and batiked prints from head to toe. A series of low fluorescent lights buzz overhead, casting a terrible shine on the tile floor. A dense heat covers everything. Little flies buzz Felix's ears. He swats and fans to drive them away, but no one else seems bothered by them. One motionless man, sitting on the floor with his back against the wall, has flies crawling on his face.

Felix navigates customs without incident or delay. The clerk behind the wooden booth looks half asleep, or half dead, his jaundiced eyes sunken in his skull. He points to a conveyor, the only luggage belt in the airport. Felix goes upstairs to the balcony to look for Dr. Albert while several kids rush over selling chewing gum and cigarettes. He waves them off and heads to a food stall, where he points to a banana floating in a gooey brown sauce.

"*Une, s'il vous plaît*," Felix says to the man behind the counter.

"*Une mille C.F.A.*"

Pulling out a dollar bill, Felix looks for a change bureau.

The vendor grabs the dollar and stuffs it in his pocket.

The soft mash of the fruit along with the sweet tang of the sauce is delicious. Felix points to a big jug filled with a milky, clouded liquid.

"*Peke*," the man says. "*Vin de palme*."

Palm wine. "*Une, s'il vous plaît*." Again, Felix gives the man a dollar and he waves the back of his hand as if shooing him away.

"*Merci*," he manages as he starts to walk away.

"Hey, *la verre reste ici*."

"The glass? Oh." He downs the *peke*. It tastes like Schnapps gone bad.

"Felix!"

It's Dr. Albert.

He looks just as he had the last time Felix had seen him at the house in Baltimore. He has the same thin gray beard, the same gray eyes. But the equatorial sun has turned his skin bronze, making him look healthy and strong.

"Your flight okay? You tired?"

"I'm fine," Felix says.

The same group of kids assault Dr. Albert, but he cuts a line through them, holding his hands at his pockets and saying, "*Non. Non.*"

Outside, people hug and kiss, grabbing bags and heading toward waiting cars. One man drops his bag and dark brown hunks of something spill onto the floor.

"Dried goat," Dr. Albert says.

They walk past a line of four taxis to a row of parked cars. "Here we go," Dr. Albert says, leading Felix toward a yellow Citröen.

He drives off, circling a low bank of mango trees and speeding past the other vehicles on the road. A river and thick forested hills bind the city. Shacks and low-slung buildings begin their gradual rise toward the city center. "Bangui's a real rat's nest," Dr. Albert says, driving way too quickly for the poor conditions of the brown, rutted roads.

"It doesn't look so bad from here. The river—"

"The Ubangi? Twenty seconds in that soup, you'll be crawling with malaria and bilharzias." They smash through a pothole.

Ubangi. That word—the music of it, the terror of it.

The dreams. The nightmares.

A large off-white arch looms ahead. "What's that?" Felix asks.

"That asshole Bokassa had it built. If only it lasted as short a time as he did. Ever since then, nothing's been built at all—we're talking twenty years here, Felix. The stadium walls are crumbling and weed-choked. The government buildings are falling apart. Every couple of months, a few people are killed by chunks of falling roof."

*Killed.* The word is enough.

"Can you tell me what happened? With my dad?"

"I can't tell you because I wasn't there."

"I thought you would have known."

"I didn't get the wire, Felix."

He suspects that Dr. Albert knows more than he lets on, but just as quickly realizes that he really couldn't have known. He was five countries away. Or even if he does know, there's probably a good reason he isn't saying. Perhaps to protect Felix from the sordid details—details he really won't want to hear. Or maybe he harbors some guilt, the very guilt Felix's mother suggests he should have and, according to her, does not.

"Thank you for all this," Felix says. "For taking me in. I really appreciate it. And my mom does, too."

"Rosemarie doesn't care too much for me."

Felix doesn't bother denying it.

Dr. Albert takes his hand from the gear shift and runs it along his face, stroking his beard, before he places his hand back on the stick, thrusting it with too much force into a downshift. "She's got a right. I'm sure she blames me for your dad. I don't think she ever quite understood his need to leave.

It was never anything to do with her. This is a difficult thing
for a wife to understand." He exhales. "She has a right to her
anger."

Felix feels a sudden respect for his mother. It had to
have been wrenching for her to call Dr. Albert. He'd probably come across as glib or flip. But he knows Dr. Albert isn't
one for sentimentality—unless it comes to the elephants. So
perhaps it isn't really respect that Felix suddenly feels for his
mother, he realizes. Instead, it's complete and unabashed sympathy. Felix's being here, in the place where her husband had
gone off and never come home, must be excruciating for her.
In her view, this really is a heart of darkness. The old cliché
living on well past the reality. This massive continent no doubt
functions in her imagination as nothing more than a slaugh-
terhouse.

Dr. Albert downshifts, approaching the city center.
"Never get used to the smell," he says. It's a sickly potpourri
of rotting fruit, diesel exhaust, urine—a pungent tang of rawness, of life ripped bare.

Plumes of black smoke rise from piles of burning garbage. Old women shoo flies from ears of grilling corn in front
of broken-down shacks and conical huts. A man guiding a
wheelbarrow darts in front of the car, bloody carcasses overflowing the cart.

Felix's eyes go wide. Dr. Albert looks at him, smiles.
"Don't worry. I know where to eat," he says.

Groups of men sit on the curb, their bare feet in the
road only inches from the Citroën's tires. The route keeps
them on the tarred and potholed roads, but red dirt streets ra-
diate in every direction. Glancing down these earthen streets
is like peeking into another world, like lifting the corner off

the city: markets, women in traditional dress, head cargoes. A girl with green, yellow, orange, and red flowers decorating her black dress holding a tin plate overflowing with full heads of lettuce. Men dancing in front of large boom boxes, throwing dice against the side of a building. A man in cutoff jeans feeding bricks into the side of a gray wall, glowing orange like hell fire in the hole at the bottom. Around every corner tin-roofed shacks, electricity wires nowhere in sight.

Dr. Albert drives along the Avenue Boganda and turns onto Avenue David Dacko. Old French villas stand like decrepit castles. They pass the American Embassy, barricaded and lonely-looking, like a rich man in a slum—guilty, stealthy, oddly out of place but tolerated. The American flag hangs limp on its rusted pole. Nearby, a group of men and women mill in front of a dilapidated building.

Dr. Albert comes to a traffic jam, idling amidst a fleet of European cars. He toots the horn, realizes the futility, sits back. "A damned populace that can't even afford a horse cart, but enough cars here to fill New York."

Two women take advantage of the jam and approach. They're wearing tight one-piece dresses, one stark white, the other a leopard print. They have the same hairstyle—long, thin braids falling to their breasts—but one has hers dyed gold, the other red. They also have the same smile: perfect teeth, red gums, too much lip-gloss.

"Don't bother with them."

"Who are they?" Felix asks.

"HIV and AIDS carriers. More disease riddled than the Ubangi. Keep it in your pants while you're here."

Three white men in uniforms carrying guns walk toward the girls. They whistle, leer, cop feels with their eyes.

"French *militaire*," Dr. Albert says. "Looking down their frog-gy noses at their old subjects. 'Special relationship,' they call it."

The girls walk away, the French soldiers step behind them swinging their hips.

A young boy sticks his face in the side window closest to Felix. "*Mon ami*. Buy arrow. Babinga Pygmy." He holds up bows and arrows. When Felix doesn't say anything—doesn't really know how to respond—the boy shoves the bows and arrows in his face. Soon, other boys join him. They hold up woodcarvings, stools, dried butterflies—massive, beautiful affairs with blue and orange wings—thrusting them toward and into the open window. Dr. Albert remains indifferent to the whole assault.

"We leave first thing in the morning," he says when they finally get going. "Damned guerillas in the jungles near Gabon. They shoot at planes just for target practice. So the route is changed from the way I usually go."

"What are we doing out there?"

"I've got to wrap up. It won't take long . . ." He says nothing about the poachers. "You hungry?"

"I ate some banana in the airport."

"We'll get you a real dinner, yeah? Those stalls you see with the jugs: ginger beer and banana wine. The beer's usually okay. Just don't touch the *peke*, the palm wine."

"Why not?"

"The water they use is often contaminated."

"With what? I had a glass of it in the airport."

"If it was, you're liable to get pretty sick."

"Why? What's in it?"

"You'll be okay. It'll be stomach cramps at worst."

A bubble worms its way through Felix's intestinal track like an admonition. Felix burps it away, doesn't say anything. Dr. Albert is taking him into the jungle; Felix wants to show him, show his dad somehow, that he can take it. He can take a little tainted palm wine.

Dr. Albert pulls up to a beige house with peeling plaster and a barbed wire fence around the perimeter. Three men approach as if they've been waiting for Dr. Albert's arrival. One pulls a small knife out of the waistband of his pants. "*Donnez nous l'auto, tubab,*" he says.

Dr. Albert remains calm. "Fuck you," he says. He turns to the back of the car, where he pops the trunk and grabs Felix's bag.

"*Maintenant!*" the man with the knife screams, his eyes wild and bulging.

The front door of the house tears open. A white man runs out, charging toward them and screaming in a language incomprehensible to Felix.

The three thieves run in opposite directions, each looking over his shoulder to make sure the crazy white man isn't following. Their sandals slap against their soles and their clothes flap in the rush of their escape.

The white man doesn't follow them; instead, he stands and watches before wrapping his massive arms around Dr. Albert. Felix stares at him puzzling out what's so strange about him until he realizes that the man's missing his right ear. In its place remains a mottled patch of skin with a perfectly circular, dime-sized hole in the middle.

"Felix, this is Wesley. Just in from the west."

Wesley has the body and face of a drill instructor: cool blue eyes, beefy brown mustache, shaved head with pulsating vein, broad shoulders, barrel chest. A prominent brow hangs over his eyes.

"Nice to meet you." His Australian accent makes it sound something like, "Noice ta meetcha." He lights a cigarette with an elaborately designed lighter engraved with a chessboard knight, producing the flame with a flourish and snap of his wrist.

Felix's heart has not ceased its pounding. "Who was that?"

Dr. Albert waves off the question as if it's an inconsequential gnat. "Gangs. Wannabe gangs. Locals are scared as hell of Wesley." Dr. Albert smiles. "All over the continent. Isn't that right, my boy?"

Wesley winks but does not smile.

"I'm the only foreigner who lives anywhere near K-Cinq," Dr. Albert says. "They generally don't mess with me so long as Wesley is around."

"What language was that?"

"Songha," Wesley says. "I'm the only white bloke around who knows it. Even Doc here don't know it."

"I can't wrap my mouth around it. It's like a bird that you track—you get close and then it flies off. You think you're asking a local for water and they give you turtle shit. I stick with French."

Dr. Albert winks and he and Wesley pass between them what looks to Felix like some sort of conspiracy. But this rumination is soon lost, engulfed by a strange twinge in the pit of Felix's stomach, radiating from his lower abdomen, something foreign and threatening.

"You want to go get something to eat?" Dr. Albert asks. "Then to bed. Early morning tomorrow."

Felix nods. Wesley takes his bag inside as Felix and Dr. Albert head off.

"What's with Wesley's ear?" Felix asks, trying to disregard his gut; the sensation in his stomach has turned into pins and needles dancing all the way to his groin.

"Sawed off in Uzbekistan. He's a wild one, the only protection I need. He's got a reputation. I'm going to miss the guy."

"He's going away?"

"Wesley doesn't come with me into the jungle. Once you and I are back from Dzanga-Sangha, I return to Baltimore, show the folks at Johns Hopkins what I've got to show for their rather large investment. This is after we go to Freetown, of course."

"What does Wesley do then?"

"Off to Guinea. Wesley's a mercenary. He's been hired to help put down a growing insurrection there. It's confined to the jungles now, but they don't want it getting any larger than it already is, obviously. Wesley first came to Africa as part of a military outfit for hire out of South Africa. They were in Sierra Leone to help rout the Revolutionary United Front rebels. He got injured, had to go back home to Australia to recover, and then the ceasefire came to Freetown before he could get back. But there was no doubt he was coming back. Doesn't know any other way of life."

The men arrive at K-Cinq—stalls loaded with coffee and sweet milk, bread and huge slabs of butter. Mangoes, bananas, spices, oils, cotton, metal buckets and utensils, huge bowls overflowing with nuts. Massive flies shuttle back and forth over pig ears and tongues. Women pour milky, opaque water from bowls of rice.

Dr. Albert grabs bread and coffee. He eats his quickly but Felix only nibbles on the bread.

"I think this is all I want. I don't feel so great," he says.

During the walk back to Dr. Albert's house, Felix takes deep breaths to relax his tightening stomach, which is beginning to feel like a clamp seizing his midsection.

Dr. Albert shows him around the house, the living room first: an orange and black couch with blankets on it and piles of books and newspapers scattered around. The floor a slightly moist brown concrete. Two small bedrooms in the back of the house. Beyond that a kitchenette and a door off the kitchen leading to the back yard surrounded by a tall concrete wall. There, tiny shards of glass reflect the last of the day's sun. There's no grass in the yard, only the same dead russet that covers most of the city. A big bucket with a hose attached hangs in the low branch of a tree. Next to that stands a small concrete hovel with a wooden door: the bathroom.

Felix gets settled on the couch in the living room and quickly fades, the travel and the heat and the foreignness working together like a narcotic. He hears Dr. Albert and Wesley whispering in the kitchen over coffee and then he falls asleep.

When he wakes, the room is black. He shivers, his stomach on fire.

Urged to movement, like a prod, he stumbles to the back of the house, past the kitchenette, and outside.

The hinged door of the bathroom slams behind him. It's dark inside and stinks terribly, something acidic and decaying. He holds himself with his arms against the cold and perspiring wall, remaining in that expectant position for a long time, waiting for whatever's in his stomach to come hurtling violently into the hole. The sensation is indistinct, a mixture of pain and nausea. He leans against the wall and rests his head against the cool concrete but then pitches forward from the cramping.

He rests against the wall again, savoring the coolness. Something scurries across his forehead. But alarm requires strength. A hazy light creeps through the space above the door. It grows into a flaming red ray that makes the wall look like it's on fire. As the light intensifies and begins to illuminate the inside of the bathroom, Felix slowly makes out the contents of the toilet, indistinct gray piles covered with flies and spiders. Waste of the world and its parasites.

Vomit sprays the walls. Felix hangs his head over the hole, repulsed by the smells of human insides—his own and others. He vomits again, as violently as before.

He instinctively looks for a handle to flush, but there's only a dank hole half-covered by a beaten up wooden plank. He rubs his hand across his forehead. Soaking wet. He shivers violently. The feeling in his stomach turns to a hollowness, a welcome pause in the violence of constriction and effort.

Felix leaves the bathroom and starts toward the house. The sun is fully up now and the heat has already descended with malice. But he shivers again, an internal frostiness pushing its way out of him as if his very soul is frozen.

A sudden spearing pain in his gut seizes him. He doesn't have time to turn around before he throws up again. He finishes, wipes his chin and forehead and sits in the dirt, throat burning with acid, his eyes filled with tears. He scoots across the dirt and leans against the outside of the bathroom wall, drawing his knees up to his chest and pinning them there as tightly as he can. The joints in his legs throb.

He slowly rocks back and forth. No way he's going into the jungle with Dr. Albert. This realization is in some respects a relief. But without this trip, he knows, all he'll have in the end is his father's coffin.

He stands up, determined to shake the illness, get cleaned up, gather his things, head out. But when he straightens, the pain in his midsection causes him to pitch forward again. It's an evil, malignant thing coiling inside him and it's not yet ready to let him free.

When Dr. Albert comes out of the house, he looks at Felix as if his hair is on fire.

"I got sick."

"No kidding. You look awful."

"I feel awful."

"Well, get yourself together. We're leaving in twenty minutes."

"I don't know if I can make it, Dr. Albert. I think it was that palm wine."

"It'll pass, Felix."

He brings himself to his fullest stretched position, something approximating a hunched over S. "I don't think I can do it."

Dr. Albert rubs his palm over his face and looks off into the brightening sky. "What did you expect here? Pellegrino and filet mignon? Of course you're sick. Everyone gets sick when they first come here. It'll pass."

Dr. Albert turns toward the house, toward the uncomfortable and dangerous place where he lives while he pursues his life's work. He's quiet for a while, regarding Felix, studying him like he no doubt does his elephants. Finally, he says, "I'll arrange for Wesley to take you to Freetown. Maybe you can't handle the jungle now."

"I'm sorry."

He puts his hands on Felix's shoulders, bends down, and looks him in the eye. "You've got a tough thing to do, Felix. Going to get your dad. That is going to be extremely unpleasant. I could have gone to the jungle by myself, but I brought you out here because I want you to see some of what makes this place beautiful. Africa is a real fucker, son. It kills people. We're not supposed to say that anymore, not supposed to continue to refer to all of Africa as some monolithic thing that's little more than sickness and autocrats and hopelessness. But you know what? By and large that's the case. No matter whose fault it is: the white man, colonialism, something inherent in Africa, in Africans. It doesn't matter. Most of this place is sick. And it kills indiscriminately. It killed your dad. But . . . well, I just wanted you to see some of the beauty, too. Because, believe me, there's beauty here like nowhere else on the planet." He pulls his hands away and looks out toward the horizon where a shimmering orange ball has taken full shape over the far green hills.

Felix looks at Dr. Albert's worn boots and wills away another spray of vomit.

Then he manages to look up. The sun has struck the left side of Dr. Albert's face, illuminating his gray beard and eyes and turning his eyelashes and the tips of his hair into little splinters of yellow and orange.

"I'm sorry."

Dr. Albert snaps his palms onto his side. "I'll tell Wesley."

Twenty minutes later, as Dr. Albert gathers his field bags, he goes over the final details: "It's a bitch flight," he says to Felix, fingering a Michelin map of West Africa. "It goes north through Cameroon and Chad and then west to Niamey. Monrovia from there. Then from Monrovia you get the flight to Freetown. Real roundabout, but it'll get you there. Wesley will hang out for a few days after you arrive in Sierra Leone. He'll help get everything square before heading off to Guinea. By that time, I'll have arrived in Freetown and we'll fly back to the U.S. together. Ok?"

Felix can only nod.

A few minutes later, he watches from the window as Dr. Albert loads his truck and drives off, his one chance to go into the jungle gone. But just as Felix considers running off down the street and catching Dr. Albert, he instead sprints to the bathroom to get sick again. When he's done, he crawls back onto the couch. Despite the thick heat, he pulls a blanket over himself until the house darkens.

There's no sign of Wesley, but as Felix floats in and out of sleep, he thinks he hears him—or someone—a dozen or so times. He opens his eyes, but he doesn't have the strength to sit up or call out. Lips chapped. Throat burning. The effort of getting up and getting water doesn't seem worth it. Only when his legs are pinned against his torso does the pain in his stomach subside to a tolerable level.

Middle of the night, Felix wakes to the sounds of people screwing in the back room. He assumes that Wesley's gotten himself a hooker, maybe one of the HIV-carriers that Dr. Albert had warned about. The house fills with groans and grunts and what Felix assumes are explicit instructions in a language he can't understand.

His father with another woman? The thought comes back to Felix. Had he really been having an affair? Understandable enough, he figures, if his father had in fact been in the middle of making love to someone when the rebels burst in. He pictures a beautiful, young French nurse—an irresistible, live body in a place filled with moving corpses. How could his father resist? He pictures him shielding her, telling those rebels to go fuck themselves even as they charged at him with guns drawn.

With the lurid soundtrack of Wesley and his woman filling the house, Felix stares at the moving pattern on his blanket, a plaid patchwork that takes on the shapes and outlines of countries—countries with porous borders delineated by jungle and shifting river, where people spill back and forth to escape massacres and famine. Slipping in and out of consciousness, he watches geopolitics and local grudges play out just below his chin, folding the blanket this way and that, merging one line to another, feeling like God with the power to quell these conflicts and bring people together. But the lines manage to stay firm.

He throws the blanket onto the floor as the room quivers in a dull haze. He stares at the shifting gray masses near the hallway leading to the back rooms. It takes some squinting, but he soon enough realizes what he's seeing: elephants in a lakeside field.

The elephants are silent, serene, feeding on sedges and grasses. Flocks of little white birds alight on their backs, picking at insects. A crocodile's snout emerges on the water's surface, bobbing lazily. A low bank of black trees sways in a breeze.

Dr. Albert crouches on the edge of a small watering hole watching the elephants. He creeps over, finger to his mouth, and beckons Felix off the couch. He follows and soon

they're crawling along in the mud. Felix has a notepad in his
hands and a pencil in his mouth. They skulk along method-
ically, brushing aside the crane flowers and slinking through
the mud. Dr. Albert points. There, in a small clearing, near a
water hole, he spots the herd.

The elephants mill, chewing grasses and drinking wa-
ter. One lifts its trunk into the air. It raises its ears and lets out
a great bellow. The earth moves. Felix wants to get closer, but
Dr. Albert puts his hand on Felix's arm.

The elephants disperse. One elephant, an ancient ma-
triarch, lags in the rear. It limps, falling farther and farther
behind as the other elephants, one by one, disappear into the
woods.

"She's old," Dr. Albert says. "She's got little time left."

The sight of that old elephant, struggling to keep up
with the herd, her skin draped over her ribcage, makes Felix sob. Dr. Albert touches his shoulder, points. Felix sees his
father in the middle of the field, sitting in his favorite brown
chair, an open book on his lap. He's wearing a white lab coat.
Suddenly, the elephants race from the woods and charge toward him. His hands and feet are bound to the chair. He's
saying something, his lips moving, looking right at Felix, but
Felix can't hear over the rumble. He gets up to run, to grab
his beloved father and save him from the herd, but Dr. Albert
holds him back. The ground shakes as he's held, as he struggles. "No, Felix. You can't save him," Dr. Albert says, over and
over.

And over and over.

And it's "You can't save him," that is ringing through
Felix's head when he wakes, alone on a couch in Bangui.

## CHAPTER EIGHT

Issa Manzo and his men stare at the television: Niger's President Mamadou Tandja—the cavernous lines creasing his face, clear delineations between mouth and cheek, two deep ravines splitting the forehead and running to the specs perched on his wide nose. The hair clipped short and high on the forehead.

"I am making an urgent appeal to all those involved in this adventure to return immediately to their respective units in the interest of peace and tranquility in our country." His brow furrows, his gaze just slightly off camera center.

"The attempt on the barracks here in Niamey has been repelled by forces loyal to the freely elected government. Nothing can justify or make us accept these senseless acts, whose undisclosed motive is to undermine our country's political and economic stability."

*And what about us! What about our stability? Our families?*

Issa quiets the men in French. Shut up, he says, *ferme ta bouche*, signaling the television.

"This behavior tarnishes Niger's credibility and threatens our democracy. Exemplary sanctions will be taken against all those found to be directly or indirectly responsible for these events."

Issa smiles. He does not worry about such threatened sanctions. He is a bigger man than the President. The President has asked the leadership in Nigeria to help return the one hundred soldiers who had fled across the border into Niger. He is ineffective. Issa makes calls, and the soldiers are on their way back to Diffa. The prefect and the N'Guigmi canton head have been released from Diffa as well, also on Issa's orders.

The image waves, splitting Tandja in two. His ears leap into diagonals, then meet, then spread far from one another again. The colors fade and then spring back, Technicolor and tinted in crazed hues. Issa doesn't bang the top of the television. The men wait. The picture will restore itself.

". . . press freedom to which we continue to be deeply attached cannot justify certain lapses likely to undermine the very foundations of the Republic . . ."

The television snaps off.

"Okay. I am going now," Issa says.

He walks to his Jeep, rolling his sleeves over his elbows, the fabric tensing under his biceps. His glittering, diamond-encrusted wristwatch catches the sunlight.

He climbs into the truck and points it toward Diffa. After that hell-hole, it will be all the way to Sierra Leone. That sickness of a place. To deal with insubordinates, undisciplined kids who cannot control themselves, whose drug-fueled craziness has fed the world images of kids with amputated limbs—almost brought the Western world in to stop the madness. Alas, it is Africa; the regimes across the continent know that the West will not concern itself in any meaningful or lasting way. Too messy, too hopeless, no strategic gains to be had by intervention.

But attacking a refugee camp? Killing a Western doctor in the process? Maybe that *would* be too much for the West.

There had been some discussion, yes. But killing a Western doctor? *Idiots.* Idiots who invite unwanted attention. When Issa arrives in Diffa, he skids his Willys to a stop in the sand. The rebels run to meet him, each with a gun and each wearing a differing approximation of a uniform. Some have full regalia, head to toe: hat to shirt to pants to boots, all of it government issue and still, incredibly, possessing the cleanliness of a new enlistee. Others wear nothing signifying company—they have flip-flops and t-shirts emblazoned with Michael Jordan or Brittney Spears. They assemble in a line as straight as a crooked arrow. Some put a hand to their head in salute; at least one drops his gun onto the ground to do so. Others stand with both hands cradling the gun. Two smoke. No one seems sure what to do. Issa lifts himself out of the Jeep without opening the door. He approaches. Behind him, his boot prints leave a presence, no small matter in a world of wind and sand.

"*Hommes,*" he shouts as he moves toward the make-shift soldiers. *Men,* he calls them, even though several of them are fifteen, sixteen at most. He has a big shock of afro, upon which tilts a black beret. Issa is in his early forties, a physical prime. He's easily six foot four or five. His olive green uniform strains under his muscular chest and shoulders as he moves toward his "men."

The assembled take this as a sign to lock themselves into whatever varied poses they strike. Lips chomp down on cigarettes and hold. Hands held in salute tighten, the veins popping up and over the knuckles.

*You are not* my *men,* he tells them. *You do not belong to me or to yourself or even to your God. You belong to your coun-*

*try. You belong to Niger. And it is to Niger that you will serve.*

*There is an airplane coming,* he tells them. *It will be here day after tomorrow. And when it arrives, we will commandeer it. We will let those aboard know that they now belong to us. We will let them understand that they, too, have become servants in the great fight for the liberation of Niger. Do you understand me?* he asks. He knows what this scene is supposed to look like, in places like America, in many of the countries his men know nothing about. Several of them look to those on either side for clues. But they do not know what to do or what to say. Several respond, *"Oui. Oui."* They are young and they are inexperienced and soon they will have hostages. And they won't know what to do with them. Will they kill them? Will they be expected to rape and torture? They know only that they will look to Issa Manzo. He will know what to do. They can tell as much as that. All it takes is one look at him to tell that Issa knows what to do. That much, they do know.

# CHAPTER 9

For the next day and a half, Felix lay tethered to the couch emitting the remaining fumes of his illness. At dawn, he hears roosters in a nearby courtyard, their incessant wailing spearing the base of his aching skull.

Every now and again, Wesley comes in to check on him. He pinches his nostrils and waves his hand across his face. "Christ, mate," he says. "You smell like yer dyin.'"

But soon enough, Felix is able to eat again. Wesley triple bolts the door, walks down to K-Cinq, and returns with food. Rice at first. Then goat stew and mangoes. He won't let Felix go there by himself. "I made a promise to Dr. Albert," he says. "You go without me, I'll find you and take you within an inch of your bloody life. Once you're out of my charge, you can get yourself sliced and diced for all I care."

Felix just wants to get on already, to never see Bangui again, in this life or any other. So he's thrilled when it's time to leave. Wesley drives a badly dented red pickup to the airport to meet their charter flight, the only plane on the tarmac. "Rumor has it that the President's plane is coming in soon from Niamey," he says.

Felix nods.

"The capital of Niger," Wesley says. "You Americans and your pathetic geography."

"I know where Niamey is," Felix says, except that he doesn't know where it is and has never heard of it. "When we get to Freetown, do we just go to the ambassador's office?" he asks.

Wesley shrugs. "I suspect Doc has made arrangements. He's a thoroughly thorough chap."

Nine other passengers, French tourists scouring the old colonial haunts, cram in knee to knee in the plane. A thin curtain hangs outside the cockpit, but it isn't closed, giving Felix view to all of the plane's little lights and gadgets.

The plane taxies and sets off and soon they pass over a massive plantation of some kind. Then, nothing but unbroken forest; a feral, untamed landscape. Felix imagines Dr. Albert out there and regrets again not being with him. Here, in this tiny plane instead of there, in the great wilderness, he has to face up to his own coming wilderness, a world without a compass point, a world without his father. He has no sense of what's really waiting for him apart from the body that has helped give him life, itself now lifeless and cold. What mechanisms will be in the way of his retrieval, his reunion? What monstrous bureaucracies, populated by little men, will stand in his way? How much longer will he be dependent upon Wesley, this man he's come to dislike very much? Will Dr. Albert be there?

And what of Lizzy? And his mother? Of the two women in his life who feel irreparably distant to him, as if he may never see either one of them again?

Wesley slaps down a very large and detailed map of northwest Africa and runs a finger along their route—north and west away from Bangui, traversing the southwest corner of Chad, over the upraised thumb of Cameroon. One refueling stop in Diffa, Niger, near the Chadian border. A circuitous route to Freetown.

Felix takes his finger and slashes it across the landscape. "Why don't we just shoot straight west, to Sierra Leone?"

"That's impossible."

"Why's that?"

By way of answer, Wesley closes his eyes and settles in his seat. He has that rare ability that some large men possess of being able to make themselves comfortable in spaces far too small for them. Felix keeps his gaze on him, for a long time, still waiting for an answer, an explanation.

Getting nothing, he takes the map.

From the Mediterranean, he traces his finger over the sea and into Algeria, following it to where the town names and the red lines of highway disappear into the great brown expanse of the Sahara. Down through Mali to Burkina Faso and its sing-song capital Ouagadougou, where the brown slowly turns to green in the Sahel, slicing westward through the jungles of Côte D'Ivoire and Guinea until the Grain Coast of the Atlantic Ocean, in Freetown, the capital of Sierra Leone. The unlikeliest of places for a reunion with his father.

Wesley doesn't open his eyes, but deigns to speak: "Dr. Albert told me about your father. Sounds like a good man."

Felix nods. Feeling the burn behind his eyes, he looks away, determined not to let Wesley see him cry. He imagines Wesley has never cried in his life, not even when some madman apparently sawed off his ear.

Managing to swallow the pain and coming tears, he keeps his eyes averted nonetheless. "Did Dr. Albert tell you what happened?"

"His murder? I'm told RUF rebels came in and slashed everything to bits. Not very romantic." He shrugs. "Hey, man—Africa kills."

Felix has heard this before, and recently, but he doesn't

necessarily believe it. It isn't "Africa" that kills. He's sure of that, though he doesn't know how or why he's sure of that. Just that a reduction of this sort feels so *colonial*, a blatant racism that he cannot abide, a thing his father would never allow voice to. No, it wasn't Africa that killed his father. It was some disillusioned, wacko, drugged-up kids calling themselves revolutionaries who walked into a camp for amputees, a place where people helped other people, and killed indiscriminately—or something like that; he doesn't really know. Whatever the story, he does know this: he doesn't have a father anymore because of it.

"So what's your story?" Wesley asks.

"What do you mean?"

"You're thoroughly unsettled."

"My father was murdered."

"And?"

"And? That's not enough? Well, I just got violently ill, too."

"And?"

"Regrets, I guess," Felix says. "I have regrets." He doesn't know where this answer comes from, only that he knows he's suddenly desperate for someone to *talk* to.

But Wesley just laughs as if he's heard the most obvious utterance in all recorded human history.

"You, too?" Felix asks.

Wesley allows the smirk on his lips to fall and eventually disappear. "I wouldn't say that. Not regret, no. No use dwelling on those. Contempt is more like it."

Below them, the land narrows to a peninsula. The blue grey Atlantic is a long distance away. Here, the ground is a riot of green, stretching like a worn carpet. It has snags and pills, little pocks of brown, checkers of crops. But mostly it is green. Only a feeble squiggle of an unnamed river clawing at the land. And then the hideous brown grids of human civilization.

"The fucking savages don't deserve their cities," Wesley mutters.

He checks his watch. With a disdainful snort, he snaps his cuff and looks again out the window. He reaches over and pulls the window shade in disgust.

Another half hour passes.

"Freetown is pretty bad, huh?" Felix ventures, breaking the silence.

"A cesspool. But it's where I should be, I suppose. Both of us then. Course, for me a very different agenda. I should be slaughtering the savages."

"Savages." Felix says this flatly, the lack of inflection suggesting he is at once somehow both in agreement and appalled at such an assessment. He'd thought it himself, of course, but hadn't uttered it out loud.

"Though I do have to say, I do respect their dedication to the contaminated. We whites didn't invent the machines of war, of course. But we did perfect them. And we taught the blacks well. But the blacks are more elemental in their killing. More face to face, to feel the last breath of the vanquished. The whites try too hard for a sanitized version."

Wesley pulls a large manila envelope from his bag and leafs through the pages—dull mimeographed documents with impossible type. Felix looks over, trying to discern what it is, but recognizes only "Dr. James Albert" before Wesley crams the papers back in the folder. One page's corner creases as it's jammed inside. He doesn't notice. Or doesn't care. He closes his eyes instead and doesn't say another word.

If Felix could see what Wesley does, could understand the genesis of the images that haunt him, he'd try and scratch and claw his way out of that plane, pull the hatch at 20,000 feet and take his chances.

*The man's face is black. Actual black. His nostrils spread wide across his face. Two overturned bowls with scratches of pink on the undersides like a hippopotamus. The insertion of the knife. The widening eyes, open with recognition. The last breaths after pulling the trigger or plunging in the knife, finding the soft sweet spot between the ribs. The knife lunging deeper, being resisted—no matter how many times one does this, it's always a surprise, the resistance of so much inside the soft flesh.*

Wesley opens his eyes, smiles, fully awake now. Felix doesn't like the look of it and turns away.

The earth below had been fat and lush, but that is changing now. To the north, a serpentine river reflects the sun. Villages and half-tended crops lay nearby like a disintegrating patchwork. But to the south, the world is brown, dusty, unrelenting as far as the eye can see.

"We're probably four hours out of Niamey," Wesley says.

Felix nods.

The plane banks to the right and the river runs out of view.

Another small city flashes past. Like a kidney stone worming its way through Felix's manhood. A knot in his gut he hadn't even known was there tightens. Like a premonition of something terrible.

# CHAPTER TEN

Memuna Bright watches the girl—she will no longer utter her name—the tall girl, once her neighbor in the village. Watches as the tall girl smashes her baby sister's skull with a pestle used for separating millet kernels from their husks. There's that awful hollow sound; this will stay with her the rest of her life.

"Do it quickly! Do it quickly!" the mother yells. She wants it over now. Two soldiers hold her back. She watches, watches the whole thing, watches the skull separate, the brain leaking into the rice bowl. Why does she watch it? Memuna wonders.

A hand grasps Memuna's wrist and pulls her. But she twists away. Memuna is running now, her feet barely able to keep pace with the longer legs of her two older sisters. She sees that there are two more girls with them, villagers also, all of them between the ages of fourteen and nineteen. Memuna is six.

Their parents are already dead. The girls flee the village, slashing through the stubbled woods. Shins strike fallen trunks. Leaves slap their faces.

They don't get far before the RUF catch the older girls; Memuna manages to evade capture and throws herself into the elephant grass. The older girls are taken to an abandoned church and gang raped. While they kick and struggle and spit, Memuna hides in the bushes. Eventually, she sneaks up to the church and sits under the window listening. She hears the rape, and then she hears the smashing of the machete as the girls are forced to lay their hands on cooking stones.

She peeks in the window and screams when she sees the blood. The rebels hear her, see her, catch her, and then drag her back inside and put her arm on the same stone.

*Thwap!* Her arm almost all the way up to her elbow hangs from her body, attached, but barely, long threads of sticky black and red skin. She sees this, but she doesn't see it. Everything black, even though her eyes are still open.

She hears the English men when she comes to. There are bullets. Screams. Blood. Some of the blood splashes onto her face. One of the rebels falls on her and she tries to get herself out but her hand does not seem to be working. It won't listen to her brain. She does not remember that it's barely attached to her arm. She knows, but she doesn't know. Using her other hand, she wriggles her way out from under him. Once free, she sees that his eyes are open; they're looking at her.

She feels a strong grip on her arm, yanking her, pulling her away. Her instinct is to fight and gnash. But the English man is telling her that she's safe now, that she must calm down. But she fights anyway, and as she's pulled from the church, she takes in the dead rebels and the dead girls, one of them her sister. She sees this and she twists away and she escapes again into the tall grasses and she runs until she cannot hear their voices anymore. And then she falls. She lies down, listening to the sound of her own breathing, feeling her own breath against the grass, pushing the blades from her face and then pulling back toward her, where they stick to her before her breath pushes them away again.

Heavy footsteps approach. She wants to run, but she cannot. She stays where she is, watching each blade of grass, feeling them against her skin. But the footsteps get louder and then they stop. Directly in front of her she sees the dirty and bloody knees fold next to her face. She recognizes her sister's pinky toe ring.

Kadie doesn't hug Memuna. She doesn't cradle her into her arms. Instead, she grabs at her hand and she takes something from behind her back. "Look, there," she instructs Memuna. And the little girl does as she's told. And as she's looking away, Kadie takes the neck of a broken bottle from behind her back and she saws into the flaps of skin that still hold the hand to the wrist.

Memuna screeches. There is still one intact nerve and it hurts. But Kadie increases her grip and she hacks away at the last of the skin before the hand and forearm fall away completely. Memuna sees her sister and then she doesn't. White spots flash before her eyes and then that blackness again even though her eyes are open and she is still awake. She sees her hand on the ground, in the dirt. It is part of some other world now. It is a tin can, a flap of rubber. A thing apart from her.

Kadie lifts Memuna and they run. She reminds her sister to hold her arm up high and she does so. She listens and follows and runs, but she does not know how. Her body is acting on its own now. She is here, but she is not here.

Kadie and Memuna run. Kadie will soon be pregnant. But she does not know it. Pregnant from the rape that very day. The English men find the girls, shivering near the river bank. They take them to a field hospital. Kadie will be dead in seven months, when her body tries to deliver this child of the rape and she bleeds internally.

There are two uncles and a grandfather remaining. Memuna leaves the field hospital and is taken to an orphanage. But she runs away. She gets lost and it takes her four days, but she finds the ancestral village. When she arrives, her bandages have fallen off and she's dying of thirst. Her grandfather refuses to give her water, says that the rebels are still about. He retreats into the bush to hide, where the uncles already are, somewhere. The grandfather knows that taking in a little girl who cannot move quickly in the jungle, who will probably cry out, who will be slowed by her wounds, who will need more water and food, medication—he knows that bringing her means his own children will die.

So Memuna sits alone in her village. There is no one. She goes from house to house like a scavenging dog and waits for anyone to show up, she does not care who.

It is ECOWAS troops, arriving just ahead of the rebels. They take Memuna back to the hospital. The arm has become so infected that the doctors have to amputate, everything on her left arm gone now from the elbow down.

It is this that Issa Manzo thinks about, late at night, when the sounds of the desert are hollow ones—empty and hollow and all there is to do is think. In a world of awfulness, it seems, this is the worst. Thinking of Memuna; this is the only time in Issa's adult life he has allowed himself to cry.

But he must suck it up, remain the model of sturdiness to his men. *Men*—he laughs at this idea. But it is what he has to work with, and for the moment at least that cannot be helped. There is a plane on the way and capturing that will help in the fight, give a bargaining chip. He must focus.

# CHAPTER ELEVEN

The plane hits its discernible downward thrust. Outside, it's little more than brown dirt and the occasional stubborn scrub bush, some nondescript buildings, looking vacated, patches of grass, what looks like a small pond, well on its way to drying up.

"Why are we landing?" Felix asks.

Wesley is awake now, busy with his pockets, pulling this, stuffing that, assembling himself. "Relax," he says. "Just a refueling station, remember? We're in Diffa."

Yes, *Diffa*. The name arouses Felix. A real bush village. "Are we able to get out and poke around?"

"Why would you want to do that? This is just the airstrip." Wesley looks at his watch. "Besides," he says. "Diffa's a dung heap."

The pilot glides the plane to an easy and soft landing. He exudes competence—cool calculation behind shaded glasses. A man you want on your side. Made of the same stuff as Dr. Albert or Wesley, people who can uproot and place themselves in the world's hell holes and "dung heaps" and make a go of it. Felix wonders if his dad had become the same way, a "mensch," as he would call it, the type of guy who could go from his comfortable stone house in Baltimore to a makeshift camp crammed full with amputees and war-wounded. Did it faze him? Felix has no real idea; aside from one short phone call that got cut off, he hadn't heard from his father in the twelve weeks he'd been in Africa. He'd expected a bundle of letters but had to settle with the occasional report from his mom that she'd spoken to him and that "he's doing fine." She never knew the answers to any of Felix's questions about the day to day stuff.

The plane comes to a stop. The tall trees lining the strip are bare, tangles of empty branches, like wintertime. Except it's hotter than hell. The heat leaks through the plane's windows; a few decrepit buildings wilt in the rippled air. Nearby, several tall skeletal men—boys, really, as far as Felix can tell—wear body-length caftans and wordlessly carry rocks from piles and line them up in rows, a seemingly pointless exercise. They require no direction and seem to have a very practiced work routine. Behind them, half a dozen camels stand in what looks like a protective circle, all faces turned in toward one another, their lower jaws grinding straw and leaves.

Then, a commotion: men holding weapons come running toward the plane. The pilot looks out the window and yells, the cloak of cool off him now. In its place is something like panic. This ripples from the front of the plane to the back. There are murmurs, shuffling of shoes, general straining to see out the windows.

The pilot puts a CB to his mouth, utters some hurried French, snaps it off. He looks out the windows again, first the left, then the right, and back again. "What is this shit?" he mutters.

Everyone sitting on the left side of the plane gasps, creating a rush from the right. The pilot yells at the passengers to get back in their seats, without effect.

Wesley coolly peeks out the window.

"What is it?" Felix asks.

"A group of soldiers. They're armed."

"Can't we just fly off?" one of the passengers asks.

"They'll shoot us out of the sky."

*The pilot fiddles with the radio until he hits a station: . . . demanding higher wages from the government in Niamey. Troops sent from N'guigmi and N'gourti to quell the revolt have reportedly joined the renegades. In related news, Central African Republic president Ange-Felix Patasse, here in Niamey for the meeting of African heads of state, has received news of his country's largest airstrip in Bangui being commandeered by insurgents loyal to former Army chief François Bozizé. Investigations are under way to see if the events in Niger and the Central African Republic are linked.*

The pilot snaps off the radio. He and Wesley say "shit" in unison.

"What's going on?" Felix asks.

"Nothing to be afraid of," Wesley says.

Outside, the soldiers point their guns at the plane.

"Listen," Wesley says, turning to Felix. "I am your desert guide. That's why we're together, you understand?"

"Yes."

"If anyone asks, I am guiding you into the Sahara, a camel caravan route to Bilma in the Teneré. Understand?"

"Yes."

"Repeat it to me."

But it's too late. Issa Manzo thrusts his face close to the

window. He smiles, then taps on the glass. Motions everyone out.

The passengers comply, some holding hands in the air, others holding hands down, everyone mimicking the frightened faces staring back at them: rebel soldiers to hostages and hostages to rebel soldiers. Everyone frightened, it seems, except Issa Manzo and Wesley Nils.

Issa flicks his chin. *Allons-y*, he says to his men. The soldiers walk forward with their guns drawn. One of the soldiers positions himself in front of Felix. He's young. His scared eyes dart from side to side, not fixing them onto Felix's face. He wears a stars and stripes bandana and oversize olive pants cinched at the waist with a rope and cuffed above his feet, which spill out over flip-flops. Felix studies his toes, impossibly long and skinny, like earthworms. When he looks back up, he sees that the boy is staring him in the eye and that his own eyes are bloodshot. The soldier boy inhales quickly, a stab of breath, before letting it out through his mouth, something ammoniac, some toxic mixture of onion and anger. Felix realizes now that this boy also has an assault rifle trained on his chest. He tries to ignore this, to focus instead on the stuffed teddy bear strapped to the soldier's tattered backpack. But soon Felix cannot focus on the gun or the teddy bear or anything else really apart from the spreading warmth of urine soaking his legs, a thing he immediately tries to hide. But no one is inspecting Felix closely in any case, not in the presence of a larger than life figure.

The big man, alive and in charge, walks alongside the other soldiers.

"My name is Issa," he says. "I am the leader here." His English is the formal and dignified English of one who learns it not as a native but in some elite colonial school. There's an accent, but it's slight and difficult to place. Felix stares at the perfect V shape in the space between Issa's two front teeth.

"Welcome to Niger. We are experiencing problems just now. Unfortunately, you have become part of those problems, whether you like it or not. Just be attentive to what I tell you, you will be fine." He then repeats the speech in French.

The soldiers round up the hostages, forcing them into a small semicircle. A panicky commotion. Several soldiers yell at Wesley in their clipped Nigerois French. One of the soldiers standing behind him gives Wesley a sharp shove in his lower back. Wesley turns around and grabs the man's arm. Before anyone moves on him, Wesley takes the arm, places his own under the elbow, and snaps it. A sickening crack as the soldier slumps to the ground, his elbow joint pushing the skin on the opposite side of where it should bend.

The soldier starts to crawl away, stopping to pull his arm toward his body, stroking it with his other hand like a dog licking a wound. Issa kneels in front of him and grabs his arm. He surveys it like a prospector, running his fingers up and down the protrusion. In a lightning movement, he thrusts his palm onto the point and presses down as he pulls the hand toward the sky. The elbow snaps back to its normal position. The soldier sits there, in as much shock as he had been when his elbow was bent in the wrong direction.

Issa pulls a pistol out of his belt, points it at Wesley's chest. "Sit," he says.

Wesley complies with a grunt of annoyance.

Issa yells at the soldiers and they quickly disperse in separate directions. He turns to Felix and points him to the dirt with the mouth of his gun. Felix sits down next to Wesley.

"You two. Do not move." Issa storms over to one of the soldiers and rebukes him.

"What's happening?" Felix whispers to Wesley.

"It's a game. These kids are fucking amateurs. They're harmless."

"They look like they'd shoot us without even thinking."

"Who do you think you are?" Issa asks Wesley when he returns. "Just who are you?"

"I'm his guide. For the Teneré."

"The Teneré?"

"I'm his guide," Wesley says.

Issa looks at Wesley, looks at Felix, who returns the look with pleading, confused eyes.

"You are in bad hands, son," he says to Felix.

"Fuck you," Wesley mutters.

Issa smiles. A long pause, then he bends down until his nose touches Wesley's. Neither man blinks. Then Issa raises his pistol very slowly toward Wesley's head. Still Wesley doesn't move.

Felix turns away at the sound of the gunshot. He screams and turns to look: a puff of smoke twirling away from the tip of the gun, Wesley sitting in the same position, and Issa standing above him.

Both men are smiling now.

"It is a warning," Issa says.

A stream of bile shoots up through Felix's teeth and dribbles down his lips.

Issa rolls his eyes and takes them back to the hangar with the others.

When the sparse food comes, Felix doesn't eat; he can't.

Later that day, the soldiers commandeer a nearby radio station and order the staff to read a statement. Everybody, soldiers and hostages alike, listen to the broadcast on the pilot's commandeered radio. The transmission comes in clear and the French woman translates.

> We soldiers who have faithfully served our nation and our president demand the same living conditions that we believe all men of decency require. Until these demands are addressed, there shall be leveled the imposition of a nighttime curfew until further notice. Residents outside during curfew will be subject to search and further penalty.

A great roar goes up from the soldiers. Issa looks at his watch and gives the men a signal. The cheering stops. The men fall to the ground and begin their prayers. Issa, however, stands by, watching over them as a shepherd would his flock.

"Excuse me," Wesley says. "When are we going to be getting on our way?"

"You do not ask questions, *ajami*," Issa snaps. "Understand? Now everyone there."

Issa points to a dilapidated building that appears to be buckling under the withering heat. Everyone goes inside, where it feels like 120 degrees, and Issa instructs the hostages to sit. Felix scoops up dirt and sand and rubs it over his pants where he's pissed himself. One of the women dry heaves. Another cries. Wesley and the pilot look furious. After Issa leaves, Felix asks, "What's *ajami*?"

"Foreigner."

"Foreigner!? We built this place. It was nothing before us," a French woman says. She stands with her arms folded across her chest, looking very put out but defiant, too, somehow used to such things as being taken hostage.

"Just quiet down," Wesley says. "We'll get out of it."

Issa returns, standing with his hands on his hips, staring. Wesley chuckles. "Hey, chief," he says. "How about ending this little charade and letting us get out of here, huh?"

"Come with me," Issa says.

Wesley gets up and leaves the room with Issa, returning a few moments later, his face reddened from anger and, it appears, a slap across his cheek.

"Are you all right?" Felix asks.

Wesley doesn't respond.

"Are you all right?"

Again, he says nothing and instead grinds his knuckles into the palms of his hands.

The hostages remain in the blistering hangar for hours, wiping sweat off their faces and slapping their exposed skin for the biting insects until one of the soldiers, a muscular guy in cut off blue jeans with half his head in cornrows and the other half in wild, uncombed disarray, comes in and yells at everyone to get up, pointing toward the door with his AK-47.

On the way out of the hangar, the soldier grabs the French woman's ass. When she responds by smacking his hand away, he pushes her to her knees. He positions himself standing in front of her, but then Issa grabs the soldier's shirt, pins him against the wall, and viciously chews him out. The soldier slinks his chin into his chest and walks off, but not before Issa slaps him on the side of his head.

Then he addresses the hostages: "We are in negotiations with the central government for a fair and quick resolution to our problems. This is good news for you. Once we have come to a fair resolution, you shall be set free. In the meanwhile, think of yourselves as guests." He smiles. "But even guests are required to contribute."

The hostages are set to a slog through various chores, all without food and with relatively little water: sweeping the landing strip, replacing barrier stones, nailing pieces of sheet metal to a collapsing building. Working also are the three skeletal men in caftans Felix saw when they first arrived, still not speaking to each other or anyone else. One of them spends much of the day tending to the camels grouped within the makeshift pen just off in the distance.

During the workday, the sun pounding down on them, Felix is overcome by the sensation that he very well might die here, but this thought comes not as fear or anxiety, but as one in a series of possibilities—no more alarming than any other—where anything and everything is possible. The longer they don't eat or drink and the longer they don't talk and the heat continues to descend like a woolen blanket and the more nothing of any consequence happens, the more things become reduced to their simplest. Everything feels elemental. So he beats back any thoughts that try to form into something more than just a glimmer. Instead, he finds himself staring in fascination at the expanding wet spot between Issa's shoulder blades. As for his fellow hostages, they have only been together a day and have barely spoken to one another, but Felix already feels the kinship of those whose struggles are collective. They are in this together—except of course, they really aren't. There is a bit of a language barrier, for one, but more to the fact that their agendas could not be more divergent: these are tourists, intrepid types, seeing the old colonial expanse, paying a lot of money to throw themselves, voluntarily, into the harsh and unstable climate of West Africa. Felix, on the other hand, is there to get his father and bring him home. And he is not close to either.

There's a midday break to escape the sun's worst, and then the work resumes. Wesley is set to toil on a Jeep missing its tires, told to fix the water pump after one of the soldiers hands him a brand new one, newly arrived by pickup loaded with new soldiers, replacing a few bedraggled ones who set off once the rotation is complete.

At dusk, the new soldiers herd everyone back into the hangar. The hostages are given a few millet balls and water and told to go to sleep. But Felix can't. He wills himself to not think about his father. He passes the time playing geography games in his head. It's an old trick he used to do at home when he couldn't sleep. He would work from west to east, making his way around the world, moving from one country to another, their lines and shapes stuck in his head from hours of staring at maps. At home, he would invariably fall asleep by the time he hit the Middle East, but in Diffa, he goes around the world twice, and has already given up his battle with the mosquitoes when he figures he won't get any sleep at all.

He gives the country game a third attempt, only this time it sets off the thoughts he's trying so hard to keep at bay. He recalls the time his father gave him a globe on his sixth birthday. Its dimpled surface rose at the Rockies, the Himalayas, the Andes, and the Alps. A time plate sat on top, cutting off the tips of Canada and Greenland. Every country was one of seven different colors—except the United States, a conglomeration of fifty colored states.

His dad pointed to the jigsaw puzzle shape of Maryland, dwarfed within the gargantuan landmass of North

America. "Here is where we live," he said. "And here are all the places I've been."

He spun the globe and pointed his finger—in the purple, the green, the yellow, the orange. Hong Kong, Venezuela, Panama, overland on the hippie trail from Varanasi to Kabul. Though only inches apart on the globe, the exotic names he ticked off—Moradabad, Phnom Penh, Cappadocia, Oaxaca—were worlds away from Baltimore. Felix studied the globe, fascinated. The world extended beyond home and school and Brooklyn where his grandparents lived.

"And this is America?" he asked, pointing to the multi-colored area carrying red Canada on its back.

"That's right. When I was fifteen, Grandpa gave me a book. There's a scene where two people are talking. One is an American and one is English, and the English one, who's never been to America, says that she wants to visit Niagara Falls. And then she says that she wants to see the Woolworth building—that's in Manhattan—and then the Grand Canyon and the Golden Gate Bridge—that's in San Francisco, in California. Here." He pointed to northern California. "When I read that I decided that I was going to see those things, too. And I decided that I would see them by my twentieth birthday. And I did. I hiked from one rim of the Grand Canyon to the other. I hitchhiked to Niagara Falls and went to Toronto. And on my eighteenth birthday, I walked across the Golden Gate Bridge."

"What about here?" Felix pointed to Africa. So many colors, so many odd shapes.

"No," his father said. "I never went to Africa. After Asia, I met your mother. We went to Europe a few times. Then you were born." He put the globe on his desk. "Here, son. Happy birthday."

Now he had finally gone to Africa. And he hadn't come back.

Felix stares at the ceiling, waiting in vain for his eyes to adjust to the total darkness. Then, against every effort, the grief he's tried to suppress for so long bubbles to the surface, rising from his toes to his throat. Like a series of shocks through his chest, uncontrolled prods from something electrical. He swallows hard, full gasps of air and salt and mucus. He gets up to run away from it all, but as soon as he does, he steps on someone who hisses at him. Back on the ground, concentrating on breathing, fighting desperately to beat back any more thoughts of his father that try to take form.

He hurts, aches running through him like an omen.

Felix wakes to yelling and peeks out of the hangar. Despite the heat, already thick in the morning air, the soldiers play soccer on the airstrip, kicking a pile of rags tied together in more or less a sphere. Two pairs of sticks poking from the ground placed opposite one another constitute the goalposts.

Issa enters the hangar and yells for everyone to get up. "Who here plays football?" he asks.

Felix does, has since he was very young. Instinctively, his hand shoots up, but he pulls it back down hoping Issa hasn't noticed.

"Okay. You," Issa says. "You are on the skin team. Off," he says, pointing to Felix's shirt.

As he removes his shirt, he notices Wesley shaking his head and glaring at him. The fact that he has pissed off Wesley pleases him for some reason he can't name.

One of the soldiers walks over when Felix takes his place, his forehead decorated in streams of perspiration. He smiles, a perfect row of brilliant white teeth.

"*Jouez le football*?" he asks.

"*Oui.*"

The soldier sneers, lightly pushing Felix toward the pitch. He can't help but think about the Aztecs—the winners live on, the vanquished lose their heads. But as soon as he runs out, the rag-ball comes sailing toward him and instinct takes over. He traps it with his thigh, dekes to the left, pokes the ball through a defender's legs, pushes it to his right, and fires a shot that whizzes just inside the right goal-stick.

From the sideline, Issa applauds, smiling at Felix. He gives a thumbs up. One of the soldiers picks up the rag ball, tightens it, and throws it down again. He passes it to a teammate, who passes it to Felix.

Seeing a shirtless teammate making a run toward goal, Felix flips the bundle onto his toe and arches it over the defenders' heads. Great whooping and hollering follows—a teammate has headed it home for another score—but Felix doesn't see it.

Instead, he's lying face down in the sand, his head ringing. Just after he'd lofted the ball, one of the soldiers crashed his forearm against Felix's cheek and sent him spiraling to the ground.

Lying there, trying to collect himself, Felix feels pressure on his left calf. He looks up to see the guy walking across his leg. Laughter ripples across the field.

"Okay, okay, okay," Issa says, waving off the soldiers who've come to gawk at Felix's bleeding and swollen lip. Issa helps him up and walks over with him to the far side of the field.

"Do not show up a Nigerien," Issa says as they sit

down.

"I didn't mean to. I was just—"

"Just get yourself together."

And this is where the dam breaks. Felix dissolves into a torrent of tears, beaten down by the events of the past week, by the grief, the hunger, the thirst, by all the energy spent in trying to suppress it.

Issa looks stunned by this singularly unmanly display of anguish. "Get a hold of yourself. Do not let anyone see you like this. It is an embarrassment. You are a man, for goodness sake. If they see you--"

"I don't care about them. It's my father . . . my father." But he soon gets himself together. Issa is right. He manages to gulp down the tears and snot, running his hands across his face and collecting himself.

"What? What is wrong with your father?"

"He was murdered."

Issa doesn't say anything for a long while, allows Felix to pull himself together completely. "I am sorry to hear that," he says finally. "This happened while you were here?"

"No. It happened in Sierra Leone."

"Sierra Leone is a good distance from here."

"I know." Felix's voice breaks, but he catches it.

Issa clearly wants no more hysterics. "Get it together," he says.

Felix does so, composing himself by swallowing large gulps of air.

"So what happened with your father in Sierra Leone?"

"I don't know. I'm trying to get there so I can find out. So I can get him." He feels his lip and jaw, gingerly opening and closing his mouth, and then spits a gooey mix of blood and saliva onto the ground.

Issa chuckles at this. "He got you good?"

Felix shrugs.

"Come. It is time to eat. We will talk about that bad place, Sierra Leone, another time."

Issa offers his hand, which Felix takes. It's monstrous in size and rippled with hard calluses. "Let us go," he says.

The soldiers and prisoners follow Issa to a filthy tattered sheet covered with bowls of rice and tiny chunks of meat swimming in an olive green sauce. Everyone eats in silence as the soldiers watch, their weapons hanging loosely from their hips and shoulders. The taste of the food doesn't register to Felix; he eats it because it's sustenance and he's ravenous, but he eats mechanically, his eyes never leaving the lip of the dangling weapon a few inches from his face. Everything feels rudimentary. Eat, drink, walk if need be—grind jaws, contract throat muscles, shuffle feet. Nothing more and nothing less.

And yet Felix remains sentient enough to notice one of the skeletal workers in his caftan simply walk off toward the far horizon, his clothing trailing in the dirt, the skeleton occasionally grabbing at it and wrapping it around his torso. None of the soldiers seems to care, or even to notice—something Felix tucks into the back of his mind, for reasons that skirt the very edge of consciousness.

He rubs his swollen jaw. After a short time, a peculiar sense of something resembling contentment comes over him, a feeling that he is just temporarily caught in a strange paralysis of fear and surrealism, that dying out here like this is simply an impossibility, something that happens in movies and not to real people like him. It's been only a few days since Bangui and Dr. Albert, and yet that feels now like a scene from a different lifetime, inhabited by someone else entirely. Wesley, Dr. Albert—even his own mother and Lizzy; they all seem now to be just supporting actors, awaiting resurrection, a leading role, in a great drama being performed all around him, his inclusion very much against his will.

And this is how he gets through Day Two, through another day of work, speaking with no one, expecting nothing, believing less and less in these alleged negotiations and his impending freedom, which Issa does not mention, not once, during that day. It's hopeless. But what is hope anyway? An opportunity merely for dashed dreams, being cut down by a bullet as you ran like hell.

And yet that eventuality is no real deterrent, either. For once, dusk has descended and everyone is told to get to the hangar, Felix slides against the back of the building, moving swiftly but so obviously that if he is spotted he can simply act confused. But the soldier who herds them in looks so stoned and out of it that he doesn't notice a thing. Doesn't count his charges. Simply slams shut the zinc door where it rattles against its frame and tilts against itself, permanently ajar.

Felix stands there for five minutes, ten minutes, breathing heavily, sweating profusely, and then just takes off—off in the direction he earlier saw the skeleton go. There will be something, someone, out there, he tells himself, legs pounding the soft earth, taking off for everything he's worth. There will be no bullet in his back. He will make it, make it to wherever he's going. Why the hell not? How much more outrageous than anything else?

He doesn't know what he's doing, hasn't really thought it through at all. But he knows he's running, at the greatest speed he can muster, sprinting across the desert in the dark, only slowing when he senses he might stumble over something. But there's nothing, and so he keeps running. Only becoming conscious of the sound of another pair of shoes behind him and the attendant heavy breathing once it's right upon him. And then the meaty paw whacking him across his shoulder and hauling him to the ground.

"What the hell are you doing?" Issa needs only a few seconds to resume breathing normally.

Felix struggles for breath. "I don't know. I was scared. I'm scared."

"And so you think you would just live the night in the desert by yourself?"

"I don't know. I don't know."

"I would give you twenty-four hours at best."

Felix wants to cry again. His father is dead. He should have figured out a way to simply fly to Freetown directly, get him, bring him home. Instead, he's in the middle of literally nowhere, far, far from his dad, under the thumb of some Nigerien superhuman rebel.

Issa gets down on a knee. Despite the fact that it's thick darkness, Felix can see Issa's eyes, reflecting some far off sliver of light, some source Felix can't know and doesn't understand. "You are lucky I do not kill you here."

Felix opens his mouth to speak. Something. But nothing. Just a movement of lips with no attendant sound. But Issa seems to understand it. It is a thank you. But it could not be delivered without its being a concession. An acknowledgement of one man's power over another. And Felix won't concede that. Enough of the passivity, of being scared. He's pissed off. In some far-off part of his brain he hardly has access to, flashes this: let the fucking animals do with me what they will. In the other: complete submission. But apology is not in an American's blood. Not out here. And so it is just a silent, implied thank you—a moving of lips with no sound. That would be all. The best you'd get out of the American.

Taken back by the scruff of the neck, thrown into the hangar, alive enough to see the next dawn, Felix feels, for the first time in his life, like a man of action. No good result. But he can sit down, lean his back against the wall, ignore the stares of the others—he knows they are there, probing through the darkness—knowing that he's done something. Ineffective, yes, but action. He, for one, won't take it literally lying down.

# CHAPTER TWELVE

A large hand clamps down on Felix's mouth, waking him.

He struggles, an unconscious reaction, feeling as if he's suffocating, but Wesley leans his weight on him, bends to his ear, and shushes him. "Get up, follow me, don't make any sound," he whispers.

Wesley leads Felix to the far wall, where he peels back one of the corrugated metal strips. It gives barely two feet, straining against the next strip and the cheap fastener holding them together. It's just enough for them to squeeze through. Someone hisses, "*Vous faites une grosse erreur,*" to which Wesley replies, "Shut the fuck up." Then they are outside, in the hot night, Wesley holding both of their bags, standing stock still against the outside of the hangar.

They can hear the raucous shouting of the soldiers in the barracks floating out into the endless night and limitless black. Wesley puts a finger to his lips and points ahead. He walks away—no running, no sliding along the ground, simply walking, as if this is the most natural thing in the world.

Only once does Felix turn to look. He can make out the outline of the hangar, thinking of the people left behind. Someone is visible close by the hangar moving back and forth. But he's in front, with a view only of two sides, and no one, obviously, has thought to station behind. It's ludicrous how easy this is. Felix thinks of Wesley's assessment of these guys as amateurs. Perhaps he's right. They've covered the spot where Felix earlier ran, but haven't bothered with anywhere else it seems. "Your little stunt exposed a weakness," Wesley says. "Your stupid little stunt that could have gotten you killed. Good job."

Once they've walked for about ten minutes and all traces of the airstrip have disappeared, they run into one of the skeletal men in a caftan, holding a rope tethering three camels.

"This is Tombou," Wesley whispers. "Let's go."

Wesley and Tombou walk noiselessly. Felix hesitates a bit, trying desperately to understand. But within seconds, any weak ambient light has dissipated completely and he stands in thorough pitch. Terrified, he hurries to catch up.

When he reaches them, he hears Wesley and Tombou conversing, haltingly, as if they cannot understand each other very well. They are also no longer bothering to whisper, far enough away now from the airstrip.

"Wesley. What's going on?" Felix asks.

"Tombou's a slave. The Tuaregs keep slaves. You saw these boys at the airstrip, yeah? He's a Kesherda."

"But Issa's not a Tuareg, is he?"

"Issa is an asshole."

"Wesley, what are we doing? Issa said that they were dealing with the government, that we could probably go soon."

"He'll still be saying that in a month."

"So we're going to go into the desert and risk our lives? None of this makes sense."

"Isn't this exactly what you tried on your own?"

"But I didn't know what I was doing."

Wesley taps Tombou's shoulder and says a few words to him. Tombou stops and waits.

"Tombou will help us get to a bush village where we can arrange transport to get on our way."

"Why is he doing that?"

"I've given him money. In essence, I've bought his freedom."

"So now he's your slave?"

"For lack of a better word. But once we are free, he will be, too. You understand?"

"Not really."

"Well, I wasn't going to rot away back there. And I wasn't going to leave without you. I made a commitment to Dr. Albert and I intend to keep it. Now, keep up." Wesley tosses Felix's bag to him.

Imperceptibly at first, the sky begins to lighten and dawn creeps in, revealing a terrifying austerity. There are still a few patches of dried, yellowed grasses sprouting here and there—even an occasional acacia—but the men could very well be on Mars, soon passing only rock spreading to distant mountains, like the spent remains of a giant bonfire.

They mount their camels, Wesley with little difficulty, Felix needing help. While Tombou pulls down on the rope, forcing the camel to the ground, Felix hauls himself over the wide hump, needing to execute the maneuver three times before he gets himself steady. Then, they take off.

Tombou conducts himself as if he's been born on a camel, his body moving naturally to every sway and buck of the beast below him while Felix has to grip the saddle plank to keep from falling off. Wesley keeps his camel behind Tombou's and in front of Felix. Even though they have enough space to put most of Europe horizontally between them, they continue in a single line for reasons that elude Felix.

Aside from the whistle of small bursts of wind, the only noise that passes between them is the flatulence of the camels, so constant and repetitive that it seems as if they're engaged in a contest. The bursts are interrupted only when the camels release their bowels, a machine gun fire onto the sand. When his camel does it the first time, Tombou stops, hops off, scoops up the hard pellets, and puts them in his sack.

When the shadows on the far ends of dunes have turned from gray to black, Tombou stops the camels and ties their front legs. They protest with foul-breathed growling and sprays of snot and spit, but eventually all three camels are standing still in the dusk, ropes around their forelegs, while the men settle under a high dune.

Tombou pulls out the camel dung, dried grasses, and food from his sack. He digs a hole in the sand, wraps some bread, and buries it in the hole. At the horizon, the sky glows a deep orange, the sun sitting on the sand like a massive basketball.

Tombou lights a fire with the camel dung and grasses and spreads out yards of hay and areleshem leaves for the camels. Felix walks away from the fire. With his back to the flame, he lies down, puts his hands behind his head, and stares up at pure, unreflected sky. Flashes of light streak across the night in a swirl. It's a sky he's unused to. He's still in the northern hemisphere, so it's the same sky as at home, but it's one he's never seen without ambient light. The slope of the earth and sky sits like a giant bowl. Instead of mostly empty space, a vast void, the sky is instead a riot of celestial bodies, all moving and twinkling and very much alive.

Tombou, Wesley, and the camels disappear. Diffa disappears. Dr. Albert and Freetown disappear. The land, a series of ripples and waves like a great ocean at his back, lifts Felix, pressing against him until he's thrown into the sea of stars. As much as the sky has ceased to be a void, so too does the desert.

Felix is back home, in his childhood bedroom. There are metal bars on the side of his bed for his parents' concern that he might fall out during a restless night. Was this because he had actually rolled out once or his father's fear that his son had inherited his need to wander?

His father comes in and picks him up. He doesn't say a word. He carries Felix out of the room, down the stairs, and out the front door. Felix manages to ask what's going on, but his dad shushes him. He carries Felix to the backyard, where a ring of trees blocks the light from neighbors' houses. "Look up," he says, and he points at the dark night, punctured by a million blazes of light. It's the first time he ever really *sees* stars. There are a multitude of them, all winking and twinkling and darting like tadpoles. And it hits him like an anvil: *the world is bigger than you are.*

In the telling for years to come, when his father relates this story to party guests, for instance—even through the teenage years when Felix finds the story mildly embarrassing—he says that he felt a surge of electricity shoot through his chest from Felix's own, a synaptic connection brought on by the fact that they couldn't have been further from those objects in the sky and yet couldn't have been any closer, more attuned, to one another.

And now Felix is in a place where he sees those stars more brilliantly and more clearly than any night in his life since that one in the backyard. Gazing upon these things, lying within, without, on top of, below, a part of, and apart from—this is the first time in his life that Felix feels that he is truly a component of everything, every molecule on the planet. And for the first time, Felix has the sensation that his life is entirely his own. Wesley and his machinations mean nothing. It is him, only him, responsible for himself. He imagines it was how his father felt the moment he stepped onto that plane to Freetown and stepped out of their lives forever.

As he sinks into the wispy sand, Felix also rises above it, feeling at once grounded and weightless. He is so connected to everything that he has the sensation that if he dies at this very moment, the mountains will crumble, gravity will cease to exist, and whatever benevolent forces keep the earth spinning merrily through the atmosphere will fall away. Yet, it also occurs to him that the great engine in his chest could beat its last and the world will be utterly unchanged. Tombou would pack up the camels and go home. Wesley would go back and do whatever it is he does. First, there would be a call to Dr. Albert to tell him Felix is dead. Dr. Albert would call his mom and she . . . well, Felix doesn't want to think about that. He knows that in the grand design, his life counts for little, but his mother doesn't operate in "the grand design." So his flight of fancy is over. He slams back to Earth, pressed into the sand so that slight borders form around his knees and shoulders.

Tombou pours tea from one pot to another, back and forth, creating a protective foam over the hot liquid. Then he pours the hot ashes in a hole and covers them up. Next, he digs out the bread he'd earlier buried and passes it around, warm and fully cooked from the hot sand.

The men eat silently on opposite sides of the flame. Because of the position in which Felix sits, he can't see anything of Tombou except the sleeve of his caftan. Tombou has said at most two words since they've fled Diffa, and it unnerves Felix. But on the other hand he is content with silence; the desert seems well suited for quietude. And there is nothing to spoil it except the occasional snort from one of the camels.

Felix looks over to Wesley and sees that he's sprawled out on the sand, his bag strap looped around his forearm, asleep.

"Hey Tombou," Felix says. He doesn't respond.

Felix gets up and walks to the other side of the fire and sits down beside him. A flicker of flame dances in Tombou's face as he stares at the fire. Thin wisps of hair sweep down from his nostrils and jut over his lip. His skin is smooth and light brown. If he had to guess, Felix would say Tombou couldn't be a day over fifteen.

"I'm scared, Tombou," he says.

He looks at Felix. His head bobs almost imperceptibly as if he might be nodding.

"I have no idea who I can trust. I'm in the middle of the desert. I'm following Wesley. Is that foolish of me?"

Tombou turns again and looks at the fire, tugging the ends of his headwrap so that they pull tighter around his ears.

Felix picks up a pile of sand in his palm and lets it spill between his fingers. Tombou gets up and lays out his straw mat beside Felix's. He stretches out his bony hand and pulls the long end of his caftan over his shoulder like a sleeping bag.

Felix grabs one of the blankets they've brought, knowing the hot sand will not stay that way. He considers that falling asleep on a night and in a place where anything could happen is a bad idea. But he can't help himself, and soon he's drifting off to the sounds of Tombou's hypnotic Koranic chants.

Felix drifts peacefully until a great mechanical roar startles him out of sleep. He lifts his head in time to see a massive Peugeot truck coming straight at him, emerging from the shadows of an inky orange dawn. The sand grips his shoes as he tries to run away. The truck comes to a stop with a fearful grinding of gears and sheering of brakes.

A rotund man with a mustache that covers almost his entire lower jaw jumps from the car and yells at Felix, standing with his hands on his knees, his heart pounding away, too paralyzed with fear to run.

Several men jump from the open-backed truck. They get down on their knees and begin to mutter clipped mantra-like chants. In unison, they lower their bodies, hands first, into the sand, and then right themselves again. They repeat this several times and then climb back in the truck. The driver throws an insult at Felix and speeds off, spraying sand over the blankets that have kept him warm during the night. Just like that, the men are off, their presence betrayed only by the sullen bobbing of lit cigarette ends piercing the remaining darkness.

The departed truck reveals Wesley lying in the sand. When he gets on all fours, Felix can see it: Tombou face down below him. "Come on," Wesley says. "Help me with him."

"Is he all right?" Felix asks.

"He's dead."

"What happened?"

"I killed him."

Felix doesn't move. Wesley gives a snort of exasperation and then turns over the corpse with his foot. Tombou's arms thump onto the ground. His wrap falls off and Felix sees his head for the first time. It feels like an intrusion, like viewing something forbidden. But Felix stares anyway, at the little clumps of black hair studded with brown sand. Tombou looks even younger than he had the night before.

Wesley begins digging a hole, the sand flying in a fine spray behind him. Tombou's bony limbs splay in four different directions like a weather vane. For a second, it is Felix's dad, sprawled out, gunned down, left for dead in some squalid camp. But then Felix concentrates on the thinness and the blackness of his arms—it's Tombou, and not his dad, not in a thousand years.

"You gonna help me?"

Felix continues to stare. This is the first dead person he's seen who isn't in a neat coffin, worked over to look like some idealized version of what the body had once been. Is this what is in store in Freetown?

"Christ, man. A little help here!"

"Why? Why did you do that?"

"I caught him loading up the camels and starting off to Diffa. He was going to keep my money. Once he got to Diffa . . . we'd be hunted down like dogs."

Felix walks over and falls to his knees. Tombou's boyish face stares up at him. Granules of sand cling to his eyes. The greedy grains fill his nostrils and grab at the corners of his mouth. Felix wants desperately to clean out the eyes, but he can't bring himself to do it. Instead, he pulls the lids down. "I'm sorry, Tombou," he whispers.

"For fuck's sake, Felix!" Wesley explodes. "Your lover here was going to get us killed. Pull your head out of your ass."

Felix walks off and sits down in the sand.

When Wesley is done with the hole, he flips Tombou into it and shovels sand onto the body.

And then he's gone, just a beige mound and a small corner of fabric peeping through the sand.

"That's shallow."

"It's what it needs to be. Let's go." Wesley unropes the camels. He loads up two of them and smacks the third on its ass. It lopes over the nearest dune and out of sight.

He throws Felix a rope and they start walking.

"How do you know where we're going?"

"It's a day's voyage to a village."

"How do you know that?"

"Tombou told me last night."

"He told you this before you killed him?"

"Watch your ass."

Sweat drips down the back of Felix's shirt. He wraps his veil around his head. It could be the heat or that he has just seen a dead man, or a combination of the two, but he's numb. And empty—all he has is heat, and a dead man is ultimately what he's after.

"I don't feel good," he mutters.

Wesley takes pity. He stops the camels and pulls Felix's toward the ground so he can mount.

"Why don't you ride yours?"

"You should always keep your feet on the earth. As long as you can. Never give up natural advantages."

"Isn't the camel a natural advantage?"

"Damn thing makes me seasick."

Felix's head pounds. A thick, phlegmy film takes hold in the back of his throat and he pulls it to the front and spits. It drags along his lips and hangs from his chin.

"Don't do that," Wesley says. "You'll need your moisture." He fishes in one of his pockets and hands Felix a small, smooth rock. "Here," he says. "Put this in your mouth by your cheek. Stimulates the salivary glands."

The hours pass in dreamlike succession. Felix has the sensation that time has ceased altogether, alternated by feeling that days have slipped by. Throughout it all, Wesley keeps silent. Even when they stop for meals, when Wesley makes up the porridge of millet and dates from Tombou's store, he's quiet.

There are times when Felix breaks the silence, to ask about the weather, or if it had really been necessary to kill Tombou, but Wesley never answers. "Save your energy," is all he says, though Felix doesn't know what he should be doing differently.

He has a vision of Wesley eating his dead body to survive. No doubt he'll go before Wesley if they don't make it to safety. Aside from the truck that morning, they haven't come across anyone. And that drives it home for Felix: he's entirely dependent. So he fixes his gaze upon the horizon and reminds himself that it would be unwise to go crazy, a thing entirely within the bounds of possibility. The continued sway of the saddle, the blaze of the sun, the jackhammering heat, the silence of Wesley—all of it conspires to put Felix in a haze.

But the desert, when he allows himself to notice, is breathtaking, with its boundless play of light and shadow. The dunes rise and ebb with sensual, feminine curves. Thin lines of sand slither across them and shuttle over the tops in a fine spray. Occasionally, he spots a clump of grass and marvels at the possibility of it. How big are those roots? How far into the earth do they stretch?

It reduces Felix to the imaginings of a child. Mysterious worlds reside behind every dune, within every ripple of sand, in between each buffeted granule. When he was young, a small parcel of woodland promised his friends and him all the infinite wonders of the universe. But somewhere in the haze of passing years, that woodland became something knowable, even to be avoided, for it was populated with creatures that stung and bit and produced maddening rashes. These are places, if they had not been plowed over and paved, that no longer beckon the adult Felix, but loom much grander in his child's mind. Here in the desert, he is back to such a place, such a feeling, if only momentarily.

On the horizon, a thin mist of sand spreads over the landscape, darkening the air and obscuring the dividing line between sky and earth. The sand accumulates and rushes into large upward-moving patches. Giant brown mountains appear in the sky. An oppressive calm settles for just a moment before the entire sky darkens. There's a low growl, like an animal, then a roar, rising to a high-pitched shriek. The wind tears all around them. Felix wonders at the spectacle of such a thing, the amazing chain of events that leads to this splattering of sand against his face. Perhaps it's the crash of Atlantic waves in Mauritania that has sent this great gust dancing across the desert. Maybe it's come down from the Mediterranean through Tunis and is pounding its way toward Nigeria. But he has no more time for such flights of imagination. The sand is all around, encircling him in blackness and pelting his exposed forearms and face.

Felix dismounts his camel and crouches in the sand, holding his veil over his face. He moves into the promising protection of a towering dune, but this doesn't provide much shelter. The wind swirls in every direction, even from below, the air rising up over his body and spilling out over the top of his head. Through the darkness, he can just make out Wes-

ley trying to set up Tombou's portable tent. He screams out
to Wesley for directions, but it's pointless. The wind carries
away his words toward some outpost where doubtless an un-
suspecting villager will hear his ancestors on a gentle breeze.
There is nothing to do but wait out the storm.

He crawls toward his camel, which has gotten on all
fours, but it retracts its lip and barks, so Felix backs away. He
grabs his bag, makes sure all the zippers are secured, and places the loop around his leg. He puts his arms over his knees
and buries his head beneath them. The wind tears at his veil
and he has to constantly fight to put it back around his head,
tucking it in wherever he can manage to get it to stay before
it loosens again. Periods of relative calm alternate with vio-
lent gusts and hammering sand. Tiny exposed areas above his
wrists and ankles sting with the needling of the sand and he
tries desperately to cover them up. He shelters his mouth and
nose with his hands, but can't prevent the sand from getting
between his teeth. He waits for Wesley to come get him, to tell
him that he's set up a shelter, but Wesley never comes. Every
time there's calm, he looks around. But he can't see Wesley
anywhere.

When nighttime comes, with no moon and no fire,
Felix knows that he won't be able to see Wesley even if he's
sitting two feet away. So he covers his head with his arms and
thinks of Tombou, assuming his body has been fully exposed
by now. Eventually, Felix manages to drift off to sleep. Several
times during the night, he wakes and dumps sand off his veil
so it won't suffocate him. But he can't get his bearings. The
wind still whips, sand dances in funnels all about him, and
blackness envelops him on all sides.

By morning, the storm has stopped. Felix gets up and
dumps off what feels like acres of sand. It's ground into every

crack and crevice—in his eyes, between his teeth, in his hair and ears. Fortunately, it's acted as some insulation from the cold night. He wants to eat the small amount of food he has in his bag and suck the contents of his canteen dry, but he decides he better find Wesley first. He calls out.

No answer.

He walks up the great dune behind him, confident that Wesley will be waiting just below the ridge. He stands on top, his feet sinking gradually. The sight of his own footprints behind—and nothing besides—fills him with dread. An undulating ridge snakes out behind him, dropping off into a choppy plane of beige grooves. Beyond that, a massive dune circles a pit below it, the bottom leveled and smooth but rising to a valley that runs away from both the dune and the pit and flattens into a plane, stretching endlessly to the horizon. He is alone.

But he calls out again, sure that Wesley is around somewhere, perhaps gathering water at a nearby oasis.

Again, no answer.

Felix runs to ridge after ridge, climbing them in turn, hoping each will give him a different and more extensive view. Each time—only perfect cleaves in the mountains of sand, dark on one side and washed with sun on the other. Now, this void that he'd decided is not a void, that is full of life resting just below the surface, is in fact the emptiest, most forbidding patch of terrain on earth.

*So that is it. My guide and self-proclaimed savior, the one who kept warning me of Tombou's plan—this great man has taken the first opportunity to abandon me himself. It has been him all along who posed the greatest threat; not Issa, not that poor boy Tombou, that pawn in the great machinations of those who ruled his life, that boy who is at this very moment lying dead in the desert. And now I am going to die alone in the desert too, failing in the quest that brought me to Africa in the first place.*

It's been two days since Diffa. There's no way he can possibly walk back there. He can't even know what direction to go. He can sit and wait and hope that a camel caravan will be along. But searching frantically for any signs of tracks, tire or camel, he sees instead only an endless vista of rolling sand. Any tracks would have been obliterated by all but the gentlest breeze.

Every impulse says to get up and go. Don't just sit there, waiting, doing nothing. But he knows better than to keep walking. His greatest chance for rescue is to simply stay put and hope for the best.

So he sits—under the relentless, crushing weight of the sun. It feels like the sky has been rent in two, spilling fiery its contents in a steady molten stream on his back.

For now at least, there's no panic. He feels, instead, the crushing heaviness of utter doom mixed with the almost re-lieved realization that he cannot do a damned thing about it. So he sits and waits—waits for no one, for nothing, waits only for the grasp of death.

But then, under reactions that come solely from his physical body and its protest against dissolution, he gets up and takes off in a full sprint toward the horizon. His clothes and shoes drop from him one by one as he dashes through the empty desert searching for something he can't name, running only because running, because feeling his legs strike the sand, feels like the most alive thing he can possibly do.

And then he falls.

The sun pounds on the outside of his eyelids and sears itself into a fine point at the tip of his hairline. He wants to sleep, but he knows that he has few periods of sleep left that promise an awakening. He could just as easily slip off forever as wake in hours.

He gets up and follows his trail of clothing back to where he's started and gathers his bag. Inside, he knows, is a canteen of water and an orange. He also has a pair of socks, another t-shirt and pair of underwear, and a pad of paper and pen that he's brought along to sketch cities and jungles and sunsets, and which he's done none of.

He opens the bag and there's a note from Wesley on top of his clothes: "Stay put. I'll be back within a day. Just don't move and ration your water wisely. Wesley."

His first thought is shame. *Wesley is going to save me and I've been foolish to doubt him.* But if that's true, why didn't he simply wake Felix to go with him? *No, if I sit and wait, I'll die.* He has to get back to Diffa. Or find another village. If Wesley had been telling the truth, there's one within a day's walk. But if Felix chooses a direction and starts walking, he could just as easily be heading toward Libya. So, for his great decision, he sits back down in the sand and doesn't move, believing that it's his best chance. After all, Wesley did say multiple times that he was going to see through his commitment to Dr. Albert.

It will be dark soon. Not the dark that falls on cities, but uninterrupted dark, celestial dark, bottom of the ocean dark. And though the temperature is well over a hundred degrees, when the sun goes down, it will drop to about forty.

A gerbil scurries past. Felix thinks about chasing it— maybe it will lead him to an oasis or food. But it's too fast and he watches it flash out of sight. It enrages him. The damned thing has generations of evolution and adaptation behind it. Felix, by contrast, has had a paltry forty-eight hours. He doesn't stand a chance.

The sky lapses into shades of pink and orange, like a wash of watercolor spilled onto a palette. The sun grows less distinct, softening at the edges into a halo of lemon. The sky and dunes merge into one flaming color. When the sun finally slips behind the dunes, and night descends, giving up its pink to dark blue and then black, Felix steps outside of himself and regards his situation less with fear than with the neutrality of an anthropologist. He imagines sitting across from himself, taking notes on his pathetic condition, recording, for posterity, so that whoever comes across his body will have the record of the last few days or hours: *He knows that people die in wildernesses having never ventured more than a mile from where they set off. He sits in the gathering darkness, hoping that he will see the dull flicker of a nomad's campfire on the horizon. The temperature begins to drop. His eyes are open. But they do not guide him to what he seeks.*

Darkness. Blackness. Pitch. No stars or moon. Just endless sky and endless sand and increasing chill. He will never see his mother again. The heartache, the tragedy, in this for her. Her words coming back to him, "I will not lose my son the way I did my husband." The method is different, but the similarities are, indeed, probably too much to bear: her man and her boy go off to Africa and they don't come home. He can't bear it, can't ponder it anymore, the pain far too great. The regret and anguish too much, and so he turns inward, thinking of his own anguish, alive at this very moment. It's Lizzy. He misses her so much. Why had it been so easy to allow that relationship to dissolve? He'd never stopped loving her. Never once. But he'd erected an either/or: remain with her, being the dutiful and loving beau, or set off and see the world, slake the wanderlust. Of course he'd wanted both, but she was too grounded, too invested in starting a life. But she's a teacher. There are summers, plenty of opportunity to travel, to see the world. Why hadn't they even considered this? Because they were both on the cusp of adulthood, of freedom to choose, and why—for either of them—would one choose any stricture whatsoever? The answer now is simple: Why? Because what else is there? What is a moonscape over Panang compared to nestling someone you love? What is a circuit of the Giza pyramids against holding, touching, loving someone you love, the two of you cocooned in a bed you share while outside an icy rain pelts the windows, trying to get to you, but to no avail, your warmth and connection a bulwark against chill and discomfort?

He doesn't run through the usual: *when I get back, the first thing I'm going to do is go to her, tell her I love her, plead for her to come back, tell her I've been a fool.* No, he can't conceive of getting back. It's too much of a long shot. It's regret, pure and simple, and he wallows in it the whole night, shivering and cursing himself, Wesley, the world, everything in it. That most useless of human emotions, packed in with pity and jealousy and guilt.

When morning comes, Felix stretches out the aching chills and spaces out the meager cache of food and water so that he can at least give himself some chance, slim though it may be. Food isn't so much the problem; a man can go days, even weeks, without. Water is the issue—that relatively simple compound that flows in excess in the place he calls home, so far away. There's water here too—lurking deep under the sand, gurgling forward every so often, remnants of the Sahara's prior life as a floodplain. But around him now is only sand, nothing, death.

He pours some water into the cap of his canteen and downs it, careful not to have much more, unsure if this is even the wisest course. He does it again, and some drips over the cap's edge. He watches in horror as the paltry liquid evaporates almost instantly. He picks up the dark patch of sand and sticks it in his mouth, trying desperately to extract the moisture. It only makes things worse; he can't get the stubborn granules off his teeth and tongue.

He shivers through the next night, waking and dozing and then waking again, his teeth chattering. He knows he's in the most hostile of places, and if he lasts until the next evening, the indifferent twinkle of a star will be the only response to his pleas for survival. He watches, impassively, as the first streaks of orange paint the underside of the sky and gradually get lighter and yellower and then whiter and the day gets hotter and hotter and hotter, a cycle now with no time, an impossible turning of axes and gears that he no longer has any understanding of, all working its way around him, through him, without his consent and with nothing but indifference to his plight. Every so often, under powers foreign to his own waking mind, he gets up and walks. Then he turns around and goes back to where he'd been. On those occasions when wind covers his tracks, he spins on his heels and heads in a different direction. The landscape is the same no matter where he turns.

But then he finds a lake. He's sure of it; this is no hallucination. There are even clumps of grasses at the edge. The ground levels, spreading out in a fine bowl of blue water. But as he comes closer, the blue slowly turns to white, which spreads itself into patches, thinning more and more until disappearing altogether as he stands on the edge of what had been his salvation, in reality only wispy dried straw swaying in the breeze.

He keeps on for another day and a half, despairing when he finishes his water. He eats the bruised orange, each section in turn, unwilling to eat some and save the rest for later—he cannot be entirely sure there will be a later. He spends a full five minutes on each section, first sucking out all the juice, and then slowly chewing the skin. When he's done, he eats the peel. And then it's gone. He's out of food, out of water.

He comes to a concave pit surrounding a black rock and, scattering three mice, he sits down in it, gaining relief from the sun. Maybe it's time to give it up, to do nothing more than recount all the wonderful things he's done in his life, tell himself that it's been a good life after all.

But none of that is true; he hasn't done much really. He'd gone to college, made his way through, spent some months in Europe, and now here he is. His hero is dead. His mother will be shattered. His ex-girlfriend probably hates him.

There's space enough for one last series of cogent thoughts, here in the only time of day that isn't a punishment, just before dusk, in the coolness, still edged with patches of warmth: When Felix was ten years old, his dad drove him to the mall. They were heading to an athletic apparel store to get Felix an England soccer jersey for his birthday. It was all he'd talked about since he'd seen one of his club teammates wearing one. His dad was happy to get it for him; he just wasn't happy about going to the mall to do it. He drove all the way to the farthest reaches of the parking lot, where there weren't any cars. As they walked to the mall entrance, he bristled at the people circling in the closest lanes or idling while they waited for a spot to open up so they wouldn't have far to walk. His anger increased as he watched people pull into handicapped spots, slap a hangtag on the rear view mirror, and step nimbly from their automobiles.

Just as they were about to enter the mall, when a man in front of them failed to hold the door as they approached, his dad stopped. He ran his hand over his face and turned to Felix.

"There are villages in south India," he said, "Where the men capture hundreds of fireflies and put them into a net that they tie around their ankles. At night, when it's dark, the path is lit for them as they walk. Then, when they reach their destination, they open the net and let the fireflies go."

Felix wasn't thinking of India then, and he hadn't thought of India since his dad took him to see the movie *Gandhi* a few months earlier. But he did think to tell his dad that he appreciated living in Maryland and not India, and he meant it as a compliment to him, for providing a world where Felix got mostly anything he wanted, such as expensive England soccer jerseys. He was about to say I love you, but his dad looked to the sky and Felix could see the reflection of the passing clouds in his eyes before he closed them. His dad looked sad, and Felix didn't say anything. Even the jersey didn't cheer him up.

And it is now, just before sundown in the Sahara, when he sees what his dad meant in telling him those things.

He'll fight to the last, driven by a desire to see fireflies in India, driven by the same things that drove his father. He won't give it up so easily, just as he's sure his dad hadn't. So he gets up and walks, and the reward is immediate: something lying in a heap on the side of a nearby dune. He regards it as a triumph; he has walked and he has found . . . *something*.

A dead camel. It's covered in maggots. But there's still loads of flesh. This is a good sign. Someone has been here recently.

He sits down and waits. It grows dark. The smell of the rotting camel gets to him, so he walks some distance away and eventually passes out. The gnashing of a hyena as it rips at the camel's hock wakes him. He figures this is an omen of things to come—the fate that awaits him. But he still isn't ready to give it up, not yet. If need be, he'll figure out a way to cut open the camel's stomach and drink its water. The thought of it sickens him, and he decides to sit it out and wait again, assuming that he is at least perhaps near a caravan route.

He runs through survival scenarios he'd read about back home in Baltimore, snug under covers in his comfortable bed. The desert stories come to him clearly—victims of broken down transport vehicles surviving on urine until help arrives. People who attempt to survive on any liquid they can get their hands on—battery acid, radiator coolant—after their urine has turned a dull rust. One man who survived by killing another stranded person and drinking the liquid from his cranium.

These stories don't help. He walks away from the camel so that the animal is just a gray lump in the distance and then he drinks his own warm rust-colored urine.

Another night passes; another day beckons in the east. It's a day full of constant, tearing wind. It slams into him, then pounds far off dunes.

He watches the dunes smoke, shift, change. Then the

wind returns and he has to lower his head and shield his eyes. On one of those breezes, he smells the unmistakable scent of mint—it's strong and pungent. And then it disappears. He walks around inhaling deeply, trying desperately to find it again; he considers that mint the way a lost sailor might smell land. But it never comes back. His dead camel is his only hope, but he has lost it, too, somewhere probably near but just under the lip of a dune maybe, or camouflaged by zillions of grains of sand.

He moves his bowels, the first time in probably a week, burying the hard shit in the sand like a cat in a gargantuan litter box.

He sits down, holds on, watching the changes in his body—the singeing of the hair, the cracking of the lips, the slow wasting away—holding on now, on the edge of delirium, only so that he might see how the end plays out, all the time continuing to keep a watchful, detached, anthropological eye on the proceedings.

*He is reaching the ends of his limits. His throat is painful and the only relief is that there's nothing left of the salivary glands to swallow, to make the parched skin move again. The days are scorching, but he decides not to walk any longer. He will expend more energy that way than if he just sits and waits for a salt caravan or the occasional truck heading to Libya. But that will not happen if he is not near the "road." And in the absence of any discernible tracks, he cannot feel secure that he's anywhere near a road. But with the dull pangs of hunger having melted into numbness, the days are easier than the nights. It's at night that he feels the true expanse of the desert. For it is dark at night, and cold. And it's during the day that he at least has the hallucinations. He is at once aware that what he sees—whole towns, minarets, traveling packs of Bedouins—are mere figments, yet he delights in them anyway, having an argument with himself that runs thus: "Yes, I am aware that they are not real, but what if I wish to speak to them anyway? What if I wish to enter that city and lay my head upon some feather pillow?"*

*He believes that the Sahara sweeps fairy dust into the ear at night and produces magical moving pictures. It is on the fifth night that he has his final dream. He's walking through a desert. Dry lakebeds between parallel mountain ranges fill with floating prairies of wavy blue air, making mirrors of the reflected sky and the canyon walls, creating deep blue lakes. He walks toward the mountains. The heat claws at his bare back. The sun sits like a flower on the horizon. He is walking, alone, toward the crystal blue lake between the mountains. It feels as if the sky has some angry score to settle with his ravaged body. Then the sky begins to close up. Eyes, too. And soon sand is rushing up to meet his knees, his chest, his face. Darkness. Then he wakes. Dawn is arriving. Soon it will be hot again. But he feels a surge of life flow through him. An epiphany has come to him in this dream. He has done no less than figure out some of the great mysteries of the world. The Palestinian miracles which untold numbers have dedicated their lives to are nothing more than the recording of desert hallucinations. Jesus had not walked on water; it had merely been his receding image walking on the reflection of the upside down sky between mountains. And Moses' burning bush was just a thorn tree that had spontaneously erupted into flames in the desert heat. What a revelation! Judaism, Christianity, Islam: all began in the desert. Of course—how could it be anything else? When he leaves the desert, he will pay more attention to religion, will dedicate himself to one of them—to all of them.* Only God allow it! I promise! *Blackness again.*

Waking. For the first time since being in the desert, he feels alive again. All fear of death is gone. All panic at never being discovered has vanished. All the fright that has eaten away at him for the last five and a half days has disappeared. And so he greets the dawn by stretching his arms perpendicular to his chest until the first rays of the new sun warm his scaly face. Then he lies down and gathers the sweetness of freedom—such terrible, terrible freedom.

# CHAPTER THIRTEEN

It's unseasonably warm, a fact that at first escapes Rosemarie's notice as she wraps herself in several layers, as had been appropriate the previous few days, and steps out the door. She only realizes how uncomfortably warm she is as she starts her drive and feels the pinpricks of heat crawling all over her. She peels off her sweater while driving, an uncomfortable and somewhat dangerous maneuver, made worse by a sudden nagging feeling that she's forgotten to lock the door on her way out. Part of her feels the need to turn back around, test the lock. But another part of her regards this as futile, that in the end what does it matter? So what if someone breaks in—though it really wouldn't be a "break in" if she's left the door unlocked; it would be that someone simply walked in. In any case, what's the difference? The material stuff all goes away anyway. She had thought that many times, even before her husband was murdered. But now, it turns out, other stuff goes away, too. In the end, it all goes away. Besides, since he's been gone, the place had hardly felt like her home. So if her possessions have disappeared when she gets back, so be it. There are worse things. In some weird way, she thinks, tempting this kind of fate feels like a small liberation. One lives a life fearing things, results, bad consequences. And there's imprisonment in that. So if it comes to pass? Well, validation then, and at least the waiting is over.

Besides, she reasons, she's most likely locked the door

anyway. She's been doing that, by rote, for thirty years—same house, same door, same sturdy lock. Why should she have forgotten to do so this morning? It's just that she can't recall having done it. But she can't recall much of the last ten days or so, not since the call came. Instead, it has simply been a wash of odd, disconnected memories and activities. But they are largely gone now, the activities, that is. No more trundling down to C Street. No more phone calls, routed through labyrinthine circuits from one consular official to another. No, her son is there now, and he is retrieving her husband. Her dead husband.

She feels the tears returning but swallows hard, beats them back. She had initially suggested this meeting with Lizzy for her own sake, and at first, if she was honest with herself, to salve her own guilt over having initially rebuffed Lizzy when all she wanted was to help. But then it turned to something else. The idea had come in the desperate hours, that awful span after midnight and before 4 a.m. when she invariably woke; it was the same every evening: falling asleep, exhausted, the moment her head hit the pillow, but then waking not long after, the world at its darkest, the hours offering no reprieve of a place with function. Instead, just silences broken by house noises: a lonely faucet drip, a pop of hardwood, the poof of the hot water heater coming to life. She wanted someone to talk to, and while she knew that Lizzy's grief wasn't the same as her own, she also knew that she and the sweet girl were inextricably bound by their love for and attachment to the Laszlo men. That in and of itself was no easy thing. They were not easy, Francis and Felix. So alike in so many ways. So difficult to understand at times, so hard to make peace with their inner restlessness, always there simmering just below the surface.

So easy to see this restiveness as something directed outward, as something directed at you. *You* were the reason he had to go. *You* were not enough to keep him here, to satisfy him.

Rosemarie knows that Lizzy and Felix have more or less broken up, though it isn't entirely clear to her why or what form that took or was taking. But she has little doubt that Lizzy is feeling the same stabs of rejection that Rosemarie has for years now. Francis's need to go, to get out there—in this case to the most apocalyptic part of the planet. What did it say about Rosemarie that her husband felt he had to go *there*, of all places?

She feels herself getting furious again. She'd felt it before he left and had felt it every day while he was gone. Now that he is *gone,* gone—*really gone*—she feels it again. But this time it's mixed with grief, and the combination is the most nauseating thing she can imagine. And so during one of those awakenings, some time around 2:30, she resolved to call Lizzy when a more reasonable hour presented itself.

But now, as she makes her way to the little café where they've agreed to meet, Rosemarie regards their get-together differently than she had during the lonely hours. Now, in the broadness of the sun and the fact that people are scattered all over, moving this way and that, living actual lives, evidence that, in fact, the world still moves, grinds forward full of people whose immediate concerns are so wonderfully mundane—parking tickets; coffee served too cold, or too hot; *does she like me?*; I have this report due, that exam to study for—she can see now that this meeting is less about her needing to talk than it is about the comfort of providing a warm presence for Lizzy, that wonderful girl who Rosemarie has always regarded as perhaps maybe deserving of someone slightly better

than her son. Though *better* is not the right word. Her son is
a perfectly delightful person. She loves him thoroughly and is
proud of the man he's becoming. But he'd been infected—that
is clear—with that peculiar Laszlo restlessness. She sees it as
a simple lack of contentment. Though there is nothing simple
about it. She knows—she knows this in a way she wishes she
hadn't—it will manifest itself in ways that would wreak havoc
on a relationship. Either Lizzy has the itchy bone, too—and
that might be doubly disastrous—or she doesn't. And Rosemarie guesses she doesn't. Why else had Felix gone off to Europe without her? Why had she stayed behind?

But Rosemarie knows also that Lizzy must be suffering, too. For one thing, Lizzy loved Felix's father. They had
always gotten along so well. At first, Rosemarie observed, with
some bemusement, it was the obvious fact that her husband
was simply thrilled with his proximity to such a stunningly
beautiful young woman. He acted foolishly, cracking corny
jokes, hanging out with the kids as they watched a movie until Rosemarie would come in and shoo him away—to which
Lizzy would invariably say, "Oh, it's fine. No problem." But after he'd gotten used to her shining presence, Rosemarie could
see that they truly enjoyed one another's company, the way
they laughed easily, the way they could—and on several occasions did—sit with a cup of tea and talk of her interests and
dreams while they waited for Felix to get out of a shower and
get dressed.

Suffering also because she and Felix seemed to be genuinely in love. Who knew if that would lead to marriage, but
they were certainly old enough for the thought to have come
to them. Perhaps they had even had conversations to that end.
Who knew? What Rosemarie did know was that Lizzy must

have been suffering, too, and she must have felt all alone with that grief. So why should these two women, connected to one another in the way they were, suffer alone? Rosemarie can offer herself and her sympathies and finally, for a couple of hours perhaps, relinquish the tiresome role of victim. This, she reasons, will allow her to be the one dispensing comfort and in that way get a reprieve from the victimization of the universe.

When Rosemarie sees Lizzy sitting in the cafe, she feels a flood of tenderness wash over her. This is, she knows, in part because Lizzy is a proxy to her own son. Her son, out there in the wilderness, the blackness, the son she wills herself not to think too much about. When she does, the doubts come back to her: is she crazy to have sent him out there? What if something happens to him? She could literally not go on if such a thing comes to pass. There's Dr. Albert, of course—Felix is not alone—but Dr. Albert. She shrugs. She sighs. She despises him.

The wonders of youth: if Lizzy has had the same sort of troubled half-sleep Rosemarie has had, it's not visible. Her eyes look alive, as opposed to Rosemarie's sunken, raw, red-rimmed, exhausted eyes. Her blonde hair is shiny and silky-looking, nowhere near the victim of sun and product that afflicts women Rosemarie's age and compels them to chop it short. And her shirt: a canary yellow that few people would be able to pull off. On Rosemarie, she thinks to herself, it would make her look like a wilting buttercup.

When she sees Mrs. Laszlo, Lizzy gets up and goes to her. It's a tad awkward at first. How are they to greet each other? The last time they saw one another, now months ago, Lizzy was Rosemarie's son's girlfriend, at home in the Laszlo house.

Mr. Laszlo was still living there then. The last time they saw each other, Lizzy was finishing up school. Now she is a teacher in a school. And this is the way it is; Lizzy, at her age, can see the changes around her month by month. For Rosemarie, change is a slow and drawn-out process, observable only in the long sweep, the looking-back, the provenance of the aging and, eventually, the aged. Lizzy, by contrast, stands not far from the starting line.

Except change has come to Rosemarie now, too, ruthlessly and inextricably. And so they have, in this respect, swapped roles. And how to react to that? What to say?

Nothing, as it turns out. At least not right away. Instead, they simply embrace. Rosemarie feels Lizzy's hair on her cheek; Lizzy inhales Rosemarie's perfume, something suitable for an older woman, something sharply floral.

"I'm so sorry," Lizzy says as they sit.

"Me, too, dear."

There are the expected questions, the half-answers. Rosemarie tells Lizzy: "So Felix has gone to Africa so that he can identify Francis and then they can come home. I'm not certain when to expect him. He's with a friend of Francis's. I haven't heard from either of them, but I chalk that up to where they are, the difficulty, I guess, in making that call. Besides, in that respect—as you know—Felix is not the most reliable."

Lizzy offers a knowing, supportive half-smile. It's full of reminisce, and sadness.

"I tell myself he's fine," Rosemarie says.

"Of course he is."

"You're sweet to meet me."

"I was going to thank *you* for meeting *me*. I don't know what the boundaries are. I don't know how much I'm allowed to be involved."

Rosemarie places her hand on Lizzy's and gives it a little squeeze. This says that you are welcome, you are part of this. Lizzy squeezes back.

"Am I allowed to ask you?"

"Felix and I?"

Rosemarie nods.

"You're certainly allowed to ask. But the truth is, I just don't know. We were supposed to figure everything out when he got back from Europe. But now, well . . ."

Rosemarie nods.

"I just hope I can be of some comfort. To you, to him when he gets back. The rest of it, there's time. We'll figure it out."

Rosemarie wants to respond, but finds she can't. She knows that if she tries to talk, it will be gobbled up by tears. She realizes she has miscalculated once again; it is Lizzy who has provided the comfort, Lizzy who has said the right words, Lizzy who possesses the perspective. And it is herself, Rosemarie realizes, who needs to feel loved right now, she who needs to feel less alone. Her heart is so filled with gratitude for this person that she feels a sudden and surprisingly sharp irritation with her son. Perhaps it's his absence that brings it into sharper focus, just how much she feels for Lizzy, how much she truly adores her. She had always liked Lizzy, but now, thrust into a world where tragedies happen in places beyond the front page of the newspaper, where disappearances are as concrete as, well, concrete, the necessity of a person like Lizzy in their lives is thrown into great relief. Suddenly, Rosemarie can't fully imagine a life without Lizzy in it—somehow, some way. If only her son would get his act together, squelch whatever idiocy propelled him to foreign countries without his girlfriend, and rectify matters so that Lizzy will someday become Rosemarie's daughter-in-law and give her beautiful little grandchildren to fill her days.

Their meal complete—Lizzy even tries to pay, something Rosemarie dismisses as ludicrous—they rise and repair to the sidewalk. Before they part, Rosemarie only manages, "Well . . ." before she embraces Lizzy again wordlessly and the two of them stand there, immovable in the flowing stream of pedestrians forced to swirl around them, holding on for dear life as the seconds pass, edging to a full minute or more, before they part.

"I'll call you. Is that okay?" Lizzy says.

Rosemarie nods, wipes the tears away, hurries to her car.

When she returns to her house, its emptiness is expansive, a living thing, filling space. The way the chairs under the table look, sitting there all day doing nothing, inanimate objects, just waiting for her return. She imagines what their lives are like—these lifeless objects—in those quiet hours of disuse. But she quickly shakes these silly thoughts from her head. She stands there, doing nothing, thinking nothing. Just blankness. Blankness and darkness, even though a diffuse sunlight creeps its way through the sliding glass doors to the back porch. A place once full of use: barbecues and games of catch. Now, moribund. Lizzy swirls into Rosemarie's thoughts, and she smiles. But just as quickly she feels the girl's absence, more acutely than even her husband's or her son's. This empty house.

Against her will, she recalls the parties the Laszlos used to host—neighborhood people, mostly, the parents of

Felix's friends—when the house was filled. Those interminable and insufferable affairs—if she was honest—wherein she spent all day preparing food and cleaning the house and then spent the hours of the parties worrying about the state of the house, and then long hours afterward cleaning again, vowing she'd never do it again.

It was a point of contention between her and Francis. Every time. She wondered then and she wonders now why they kept doing it.

"Just leave it for morning and we'll clean it together. It's not going anywhere," Francis would say, edging up the stairs past midnight to go to sleep.

To this she would always reply, and this is why it irritated her to no end when he would say it, "I don't want to wake up to this mess. I just want to get it done now . . ."

He would sigh, trudge up the stairs, and she would stay downstairs, sigh louder, and start the cleaning ritual. She would never admit it out loud, but she had to acknowledge that she found something pleasant about having the place to herself in this way. And there was another thing, if she was honest with herself: when Francis did help her clean, she usually wished he hadn't. Inevitably, she would go back after him and do the job again, the right way. Even simple tasks like cleaning dishes; Francis just threw everything in the dishwasher, huge chunks of food still clinging tenaciously to the plates. She'd pull them out—there was no need to have the same argument again, she claiming that they wouldn't get clean, he claiming that they would, she explaining that all that food would get mixed into the washing and coat the other dishes, he explaining, in what she heard as his most condescending manner, the mechanics of drains. So she'd take them out of the dishwasher, rinse them off in the sink, and then put them back in the dishwasher. Of course, she'd have to do this far from Francis's eye, for he'd make the same comment he always did when observing this: "If you're going to clean them in the sink, there's no need to put them in the dishwasher." The argument just wasn't worth it. So she'd wait until he wasn't around, all the while burning with anxiety over the fact that she knew there were intolerably filthy dishes in the dishwasher, every passing hour getting harder and harder to clean, that disgusting leftover food digging its rotting talons deeper and deeper into the porcelain.

At the beach house they rented every summer, where there was no dishwasher, the ritual was even more maddening. Somewhere along the line, it had been decided that the dinner cleanup chores belonged to Francis and Felix. Francis would fill one half of the segmented sink with warm sudsy water. "Make sure it's hot water," Rosemarie would remind him while Felix would bring everything over and slip the dishes into the sink, one by one, watching them slide under the suds and disappear. Francis would then scrub each and hand them over to Felix, who was responsible for rinsing them in the other half of the sink and then stacking them to dry. All the while Rosemarie would sit on the nearby couch trying to read but never getting beyond a paragraph or two because she knew, just knew, what was really going on in the kitchen: the utensils with flecks of meal, the plates she imagined burnished with enormous swaths of grease down the middle, the glasses still possessing the clingy remains of grape juice or Aranciata. She just couldn't understand how these things slipped the assembly line, and how every time. It literally made no sense to her. So she told herself she'd do it all over, do it correctly, once everyone else was asleep. An added anxiety was in having to ascertain how many of the stacked dishes were "washed" this evening, how deep to go. To be safe, she'd decide, she'd simply do them all.

She hated being made to feel like a nag. Francis had often "joked" about her OCD. Well, shouldn't dirt be something one is supposed to be obsessive about? Shouldn't cleanliness, if nothing else, be the thing people should be compulsive about? She just didn't understand his flip attitude, the way he would thoughtlessly leave dishes in the sink at night. She recalled with a shudder his cavalier attitude the time she discovered a column of ants on the kitchen counter. "Sometimes, it's impossible to keep the outside world from coming in. This is a big house and there are lots of little cracks," he'd said.

"They're going to crawl all over our food," she responded, alarmed—alarmed at the prospect, alarmed that he didn't seem to care. "Our food, Francis, which we feed to our child."

"Where do you think these come from?" he asked, holding up a peach, an ant clinging to it with its back legs, its front twisting in the air as Francis swung the fruit around. "It grows on a tree. I am certain an ant or two, and quite a few other insects as well, have crawled all over this thing well before we got it." She flew out the door to the local pharmacy and returned with three different varieties and six total ant traps, which she placed over the counter. From the living room, where he was watching TV, Francis said, "That stuff is probably far worse to be around our food than ants are. At least ants are organic."

She would burn with anger and she hated the way those thoughts made her feel. It wasn't the way she envisioned herself. It wasn't the way she wanted to be. She could never recall actual moments of hatred before—not once in her life. While engaged in these late-night cleaning rituals after their parties, every now and again her path would take her just past the base of the stairs. There she'd see the dark, the light on her level swallowed midway up the stairs. She thought vaguely of snatching Felix and on the way down sprinkling some lighter fluid, setting a match, and fleeing to the front lawn. But the thought passed; she smiled at it, knowing she was allowed to think such things because they weren't real and no different from the juvenile thoughts little kids have now and again, when they get angry enough, that their parents would just die. They didn't really want those things. Or, more accurately, they only wanted them in that brief moment of irrational wrath. She loved her husband, dearly, during those chunks of time when she wasn't hating him.

Once again, she shakes off these nasty thoughts. Why is it, she wonders, that at this moment, her husband dead, murdered, and so far from home, does she remember the worst things about him?

She cries again, feeling absolute helplessness. It's something without a bottom, something separating her from herself. She feels her very core rent in two, a stew of anger, sorrow, and confusion coursing through her.

She gets to it, on her hands and knees, scrubbing with fervor, the only way she knows, at this moment, to deal with the terror of it all. She crawls along the hardwoods, shimmies herself into corners, pulls out dust and hair clumped into gray masses. She wipes down counters, disinfecting as if the disease of sorrow has perched itself along every surface. So long as she expends herself this way, exhausting the body to subsume the mind, the unbearable pain numbs itself, becomes in that way bearable.

Lizzy returns to her apartment after meeting Mrs. Lazlo feeling positively drained. She falls onto the couch and just sits there. Then, infected with a sudden burst of energy, she hops up and begins to clean the place. It was something she'd always done in times of distress, back to when she was barely a teenager and living at home in the expansive house where she grew up, a child of privilege. She's always found cleaning to be meditative and restorative. She figures it's the repetitive motion, the circular wiping, maybe, or the sweeping and swifting, eating up the space, transforming everything from dirty to clean, from intolerable to tolerable, from uncivilized to civilized. A place where she has control. Cleaning is, for her, the quickest and surest way of bringing a world of disarray into order. While it feels like little else in her life can be tamed in this way, she can stand in a room that's become disordered and within a matter of an hour or so, turn it into a space that offers peace and cleanliness and neatness. So this solitary exorcism of dirt soon enough takes on the feel of a ritual.

She pulls on the elbow length blue latex gloves, smiling at the satisfying snap of the ends as she pushes her fingers to the tips. She retrieves the bucket from beneath the kitchen sink filled with sponges, scrub brushes, various assorted cleaners—no-streak surface cleaner, anti-bacterial cleaner, lemon-infused general multi-purpose cleaner. Every surface with its own cleaner. A potpourri of cleaners.

Every lamp and light in the apartment burns brightly, a holdover from parties she remembers her own parents throwing before they split up when her mother, in her one bone throw to the domestic help, merrily waltzed through the huge house in her dressing gown flipping on every light switch on every wall and turning every switch on every table lamp. It was as if she was keeping at bay all the darkness of the universe, a darkness roiling in from the future to meet her in the present, a dark cloud she just knew was coming. Lizzy would trail her mom during this ritualized lighting, in her own mini-gown, and knew that not only was light the obvious way to make the world bright, but one more thing, one very important thing: we have light at our fingertips and one need only flip a switch or turn a knob and presto, no more darkness. Darkness, it turns out, could be defeated.

So as she cleans, Lizzy turns the dimmer switches to their highest point and keeps each lamp burning.

It's almost 1 a.m. now and the Laszlo house sparkles. Rosemarie will try for sleep. One by one she clicks off the lights. Darkness. Total, complete, full. She stands for some time in that darkness, soaking it in. To her surprise, she finds herself disappointed as her eyes start their natural adjustments. Darkness, sometimes, she figures, is good. Make a friend of it, for darkness, she knows—can just feel it—will be her constant companion in the days and weeks and months, perhaps even years, to come.

Part of this darkness, though, a part that nags at her, that won't loosen itself from her thoughts, is, she has to acknowledge, anger. Some deep recess, it's anger: fury at him, in fact. He left. And now he's never coming back. What a cruel thing to have done.

It's very late and one by one Lizzy clicks off the lights. Darkness. Total, complete, full. It was always there, haunting the corners, the default of the universe; a silly exercise to try and beat it back, she realizes. Lizzy stands for some time in that darkness, soaking it in. She's okay with it, to her surprise. She knows: darkness everywhere, and much more to come. May as well get used to it.

# CHAPTER FOURTEEN

Issa reminds the two soldiers who have accompanied him who they are looking for: the American boy, the Australian *emmerde*, Tombou, and three camels.

They're hardly a few hours in finding Tombou, only his left forearm, wrist, and hand still covered, the rest of him exposed, the skin already starting to peel away from his face. They discover two of the camels not long after, standing together on the edge of a high dune, stock still and dumb, just standing as if they lack the ability to think of anything better to do. As such, they prove very easy to corral and control, meekly following the soldiers back toward Diffa, while Issa takes the second Jeep they've set out with and carries on.

It's just before dusk when he sees Felix on the sand. Easy enough to spot from a good distance as his is the only form and only color that breaks the landscape's beige wash.

He's alive, and more than just barely. He's able to respond by shaking his head when Issa asks if he's okay. When Issa dribbles water in his mouth, Felix gulps at it, even shooting his hand up to grab the bottle. Issa rips it away. "You must drink it slowly or else you will—" He doesn't manage to get out, "Throw it up," before Felix is spitting it all over himself.

They try it again, and this time Felix manages to control himself. Issa helps by only giving him a little at a time. This continues for twenty minutes before Issa throws him over his shoulder and deposits him in the back of the Jeep.

Felix will remember the stars. That's what's prominent as he stares up and out of the back of the Jeep, telling himself that he's alive, and then not entirely believing it. Issa doesn't speak, so nothing can be confirmed for him. And yet the bounce of the truck feels real. The stars shoot across the dome of the night. They wink and twirl and seem to dance for him. Before, in previous evenings—he can't be sure how many there were—they seemed disdainful bodies, winking at him only to remind him that they were free and secure in their patch of sky, right where they were supposed to be, staring down and mocking him, the ephemeral stranger far from where he should be.

He reaches his hand up, touches the side of the Jeep. The metal feels real, impervious.

"You are a lucky boy," Issa says. And this confirms it for him. The man at the wheel is no figment. He has saved Felix's life. He puts his head back down, closes his eyes, allows himself to fall asleep—the first in some time that promises an awakening. Yet an awakening, not in any real sense, doesn't happen for another day and a half. Felix can faintly recall the thwap of the helicopter blades, the onrush of air. He'd earlier convinced himself that he'd dreamt that. But he realizes now it must have been real because when he opens his eyes he sees Issa sitting there, and when he asks, "Where am I?" the answer is in a hospital bed in Niamey, the capital.

Like a crude highlight film, he remembers the first sandstorm, the blackness, the inescapability of it, the feeling of isolation. Then he was waking up, wiping sand from every nook and fold in his body. Then, alone. What followed he had assumed was a series of hallucinations, such as the periodic ingestions of water, ladled to his lips by Issa. The understanding that no one is left, snatches of overheard conversations filtering through his delirium: the hostages have been allowed to leave, a combination of intercession from the Red Cross and the French government, and the fact that the negotiations with the central government have been successful. More accurately, he will later find out, the central government is no longer the central government. Control is now in the hands of the military. Men like Issa Manzo.

From his window, he can see steel and glass, not sand and mud. And there is the old sun that he knew so well, the one that had warmed him in youthful days when he would lie with his old dog, dead now, in golden patches on the carpet in the living room of his childhood home. He welcomes its yellow intrusion through the blinds. This is not the sun that had nearly killed him. It's familiar; he could be back in Baltimore. But Issa is no figment—and he is sitting at the end of the bed.

He focuses his attention on the IV drip feeding Felix's arm. He taps the line, cocks an eyebrow, and then sits down, apparently satisfied by this perfunctory examination. He gazes at Felix with something that looks suspiciously like compassion, sympathy, tenderness.

"I will get you to Freetown," he says. "I know what has happened there. To your father. I have called the American consulate. An official will meet you."

Felix nods. *Finally.* He closes his eyes.

His head pounds. His hands shake. His tongue feels like he's been eating the camels' straw and leaves. It will be this way for another two days, time during which Issa comes to visit and the two men sit as if old friends.

"Why are you doing this?" Felix asks, more than once.

"I have my sympathies," is all Issa says.

"But why?"

"There are times to ask questions. You are lucky. I have connections and you will get what you need, in the end."

"Wesley?"

"I do not know. Nor do I care."

When Felix is able to leave the hospital, he takes up temporary residence in Issa's modest house in the Rue de Maroc in Niamey's Abidjan neighborhood.

Issa's home is a modern one-story structure near the Grand Market and the main sports stadium. It sprawls like an American rancher and could easily be transported to Felix's street in Baltimore and fit right in, save for the locked steel fencing around the perimeter. The neighborhood is leafy, at least by Sahelian standards. Short trees sprout green, with roots that must stretch for miles underneath the sandy wash of the streets.

Inside are the same conveniences that Felix is accustomed to. A comfortable bed, a refrigerator, a TV with better reception than he could ever hope for in his apartment, thanks to the satellite dish on the roof.

Setting up his guest in a back room, Issa hands Felix a plane ticket to Freetown, good for a flight the following day, along with specific directions on what to do once he arrives, the name of a hotel, and directions to a Mr. Hank Peters' office at the American consulate in Freetown. Felix manages to say thank you, but little else, all of it so surreal to him: not even two weeks earlier he'd been in Bangui with Dr. Albert. Since then, Wesley, and Diffa, and the desert.

"Why are you doing all this for me?" he asks.

Issa doesn't answer, moves around the room instead as if he hasn't heard. It's an obvious avoidance tactic, so Felix doesn't ask again. Instead, he pockets all the documents and mutters, "Thank you."

Issa nods.

Felix places a call to his mother. She's not home and so he leaves a message. All is well, he says. He is with Dr. Albert, back in Bangui, he lies, hoping she hasn't called there and gotten a different story. He's on his way to Freetown now and will call again in a few days—when it is done.

"Come," Issa says. "I will show you a bit of my city."

They make their way along the orderly grid of streets lined with sand-brick houses. Painfully aware that he's the only white person around, Felix tries to remain as inconspicuous as possible. It isn't easy, considering what decorates his lips isn't the blue henna tattoos of the women he passes, but the hair he hasn't had the opportunity to shave. But the few people in the street, almost entirely women, regard Felix with little concern, even indifference.

Across the city, he can see the same tall buildings he'd seen from his hospital room, but here in the near distance is a world far, far away from anything he knows. He finds it thrilling and has no doubt his father would have as well. This area of the city is much prettier than he'd expected. Beautiful colonial houses stand flanked by sand and mud structures emblazoned with intricate patterns, their golden brown walls turning to orange when the sun hits. Spindly cracks run all over the dried baked mud, bits of straw poking out here and there. He's fascinated by the world before him, a world still fuzzy at the edges, like it's all a movie set created just for him.

A young dark girl in a red shirt passes by; there's a palpable air of confidence about her; this is her place, and she belongs here in this world. She passes two men. Despite the intense heat and gritty air, the men manage to look cool, even comfortable. One wears a stark white robe—somehow white—and a red-checked veil. White socks pulled halfway up his legs dip into a pair of black leather shoes. The man next to him wears sandals and a green and red robe and small white hat. A cane rests against the wall where the two men stand. They look like rare and majestic animals that manage to adapt to whatever harsh conditions surround them, like bighorn sheep facing a fifty mile an hour, bone-chilling wind while hanging on a tiny precipice.

Roving merchants sell salt pillars, animals, leather pouches, sandals, bags. It's clear from the shouts and stares that everyone assumes that someone who looks like Felix here at the end of the earth is wealthy. He doesn't have the ragged appearance of a Peace Corps type, and he's too young to be from some diplomatic corps, so he's a *touriste*. Silly—stupid even, and one who can be easily separated from his money.

"*Monsieur, monsieur*," they yell. "*Achetez, achetez.*"

He pretends that he doesn't understand, shrugs his shoulders, and keeps walking.

They pass a couple of banks and head toward the Grand Mosque, a lovely whitewashed edifice with Arabian domes and pillars and an imposing minaret inlaid with intricate tilework, set behind a squat stone wall and built, Issa says, with money from the Libyan dictator Kaddafi. They snake around several meandering alleyways before emerging onto a big courtyard. There are what looks to be about a hundred men on their knees, bent over with faces on the ground, the mosque looming behind them. The men rise and fall in unison, perfect rows of figures in robes, sandals in neat pairs in the sand near their heads. At the front of the rows sit half a dozen men on intricately woven blankets. A muezzin bellows a rhythmic chant through the four speakers atop the minaret. It cracks and buzzes across the landscape. Felix inhales, breathing it all in, loving it with an intensity that surprises him.

Issa clearly notices. "You like this?" he asks.

"I really do. My father would have loved it."

But just then the spectacle ends. The men slip on their sandals, linger with one another for a moment, and then head off in every direction.

"Come. I will show you one more thing before we eat."

"I can't help but notice that you don't pray with the other men. You're not Muslim? . . . Do you mind me asking?" Felix hastily adds.

"I am not anything . . . does this scare you?"

"No."

"You are Christian?"

"I'm not religious, but I'm Jewish."

Issa looks at him as if searching for horns or cloven hooves.

"You may want to keep that quiet," he says. "It is all the same bullshit to me, but many of these boys around here, they do not have education. They would be happy to kill you just for being Jewish. Being an American used to be enough to keep you safe, but that has changed too."

"Noted."

Felix inhales the sweet, musky scent of incense. Since they'd arrived in Niamey, all he's smelled is grilling lamb and hints of seas brought by strong winds over the sands. Incense seems wholly out of place. But there it is, wafting from behind a barely ajar door. Issa tiptoes over, sticks his head in. "There is a spirit communication going on," he says, emerging.

"A spirit communication?"

"Tandajar. She is famous the city over. She allows the spirits to possess her body. She can talk to the dead. People come from all over the desert to communicate with dead relatives through her. From Zinder, Agadez."

"Can I see?"

"Just be respectful."

Felix stumbles into the room. Into warmth and moistness like a womb. And yet it's blissfully cool. The cloying treacle incense jams the air.

A steady hum and buzz comes before him, somewhere in the full darkness, before his eyes can discern the messages of shape and outline.

He sees the dead body before the three live ones. He cannot make out the gender. A filthy sash pulled tight near the eyebrows covers the skull to the forehead. Half a dozen straggled hairs jut from above the lip and from the chin, but these are no giveaway of gender either.

The hands, gnarled with prominent veins, crossed upon the chest, the thin bones piled one on top of the other like refugees from an arthritic netherworld. The nails are filthy, caked and splattered with mud and sand. As if an understanding: that we are dirt and to clean it off now before becoming encased in earth and dirt and sand is an attempt to fool God.

The hum and buzz break into discernible syllables, an ancient language of stops and starts, some conjuring of spirits over the mists of time and place. Then chatter. Then cries, each burst punctuated by a man and woman, looking like children with streaks of tears on their cheeks, tugging on the robe of the priestess. Alternately tugging and rubbing her shoulders. Her head shaved completely bald. She rocks and hums and buzzes and exclaims, all of them oblivious to Felix's presence. Oblivious or indifferent to his intrusion.

Amidst the mumbled exhortation of the priestess's calls, Felix backs out into the searing sun. Back into the dead world of the living.

"Interesting?" Issa asks.

Felix is spooked. Yet, had he believed in such things, he would ask Tandajar if she could contact his father.

"It is not for everyone," Issa says. "Me? I think she simply takes people's money. But it helps them, so I suppose it is worth it."

They head for what Issa tells Felix is the old section of town, the Vieux Quartier, passing women dressed in indigo clothes, with little ribbons of white lace and heavy-looking silver jewelry around their necks. Painted stars decorate their cheeks and foreheads and a trail of black dots runs across the bridges of their noses. Following them are two young boys, each with a long braid in the back of his hair and a similar braid jutting from the forehead.

A merchant in a white robe flashes Felix a toothless smile as they pass another market. He sits on a straw mat in front of intricate weavings hanging on sticks, each one a swirl of colored fabric. Felix wants to buy one but thinks better of it: what would he do with it—lug it to Freetown? Issa isn't stopping anyway. He leads Felix to a restaurant—it's a snug room, with only four tables. The waiter walks over on limbs that hardly seem connected, like a skeleton that shimmies without the aid of tendon and muscle. Issa orders two Flag beers and *forah*, millet porridge mixed with milk and spices. He and the waiter speak for a long while. Then Issa turns to Felix: "He wants to know if it is true that all villages in America have rock over the ground."

"What?"

"Sidewalks."

He confirms; yes, he guesses it is true—American "villages," generally, have sidewalks.

The waiter explodes into a gleeful laugh; just imagine it: a place so rich that it pours rock over the ground for no other reason than to ease the effort of walking from one place to another and for the simple luxury of keeping one's shoes and pants clean. He's still laughing to himself and shaking his head when he walks into the back to make the meal.

While they wait for the food, Issa drums his knuckles on the table and looks around at no one.

"I was wondering," Felix begins. "I know it might be rude to ask questions like this, but I can't help but wonder where you learned English. You barely have an accent."

Issa lets the comment sink in and then says, "I earned my M.S. at Columbia."

"New York Columbia?"

"I also worked for the U.N. for many years in New York. I am working for them now."

"You're kidding."

"I am not."

"Wow," Felix says.

Issa looks at him; he looks for a long while, not saying anything, like he's trying to measure Felix once and for all. "The U.N. loves guys like us," he finally says. "How many Nigeriens you think they have over there? I am the shining example. You think there is no one more qualified to head up the place than a Ghanaian?"

"I suppose."

He takes a long slug from his beer. "In '98, Niger joined ECOWAS—the Economic Community of West African States—and agreed to stop the importation and manufacture of light arms into West Africa," he says in one long breath. "They started up in Niamey and N'guigmi. The way this thing works is that we give up the weapons and we get development projects and tools in return: sewing machines, bicycles, hoes. There is one village, between Aouderas and Sidaouet, a real rebel hotbed. They turned in a whole cache of weapons—the government had not seen anything like it. Now there is a school. So who better to oversee the program than someone who is from there?"

"Makes sense."

"You are here to get your father?"

Felix has no sense of the bounds of their relationship, so he just nods, then shrugs.

"That is the whole of your story then? Nothing else?" Issa asks after scooping the *forah* in his hand and shoveling it into his mouth.

That his father has been killed and, yes, he's going to retrieve his body, is a perfectly reasonable explanation, but he can't say it again. The inevitable questions will follow, about what kind of work his father was doing, how his mother and Felix felt about it, what kind of man he was—and Felix isn't sure he has the answers.

Felix looks at the bowl of food. He hasn't eaten any

and Issa isn't offering to share his. An open bottle of beer sits in front of him, and he lets it sit even though Issa drinks his greedily.

"You're in Niger. You landed in Diffa. That is the part that makes no sense to me."

"I have a friend, James Albert. Actually, he is a friend of my father's. He's a biologist. He teaches at Johns Hopkins University in Baltimore."

"I know where Johns Hopkins is."

"He's doing field research in the Central African Republic. When I decided to come to Africa, I stayed with him first."

"Not Wesley?"

"Dr. Albert introduced me to him. Wesley is his bodyguard, or something."

Issa shakes his head.

"It was his idea to run back in Diffa."

"I do not doubt that." Issa chuckles. "He is no one, believe me. A foolish fortune hunter with a much larger sense of himself than is warranted."

"I don't really know him. Back at home, we called Dr. Albert and he was getting ready to go back into the field. He's got his own plane. The rainy season was ending. So he flew to Bangui and I met him at the airport. I got pretty sick."

"The jungle is dangerous."

"Dr. Albert told me that insurgents in the jungles will shoot at planes just for target practice."

Issa gives a knowing laugh. "You going to eat?" he asks.

Felix dips his hand in the chunky mixture and scoops it into his mouth: a delicious hint of nutmeg and cloves.

"Dr. Albert flies out toward Cameroon," he continues.

"He told me it'd be better to die right away in a crash than to land and survive because there'd be no way anyone would ever find him."

"It is true bush."

"You've been?"

"I am a desert man. I do not go for jungles with their mini-elephants. Spider webs large and thick enough to trap a boy."

"That's what Dr. Albert studies—the elephants," Felix says, full of excitement now. "I can't believe it. Man."

Issa smiles. "I could tell you were different. The French tourists in Diffa with their *attitude supérieure*. I could see it as we have walked here: you have an interest in the world. Many people live their whole lives wishing for something to happen to them—too scared usually to *make* those things happen. But you . . ." He points at Felix and then shakes his head, happily bemused.

Issa waves over the owner. "This good man has a family to go home to." Issa produces a wad of francs, peels off a dozen bills, and hands them over. "Now it is time to get back home. You will tell me the rest there."

There is a surprising chill in the air, having stolen in so stealthily. The town is snugly cloaked within a clear and moonless evening. The stars blink in the black sky. It's quiet and dark. It's been a long day, and when they get back and Issa sets him up in the spare room, Felix begins to nod off, to flow into a ribbon of sleep that promises to be the deepest he's known in a long while.

"Hey," Issa begins. "Tell the rest."

"It's kind of a long story."

"Go ahead. Nights here last forever."

Felix pauses. "Well, I guess it really isn't a long story. There's not much to say. I don't know much. All I know is that RUF rebels killed him. Killed everyone."

"The Revolutionary United Front."

"You know them?"

"I did not know all that for sure, what happened."

"What?"

"Only that your father was killed in Freetown and that his body is at the morgue at Connaught."

"Who are you talking about?"

"The Americans in Freetown. The ones you will meet."

"I'm sorry. I don't---"

Issa is agitated. He begins pacing.

"I'm sorry if this is a problem for you," Felix says. "I didn't even know you were calling them. What is this Revolutionary United Front? I keep hearing the name, I know this is the 'RUF,' but I don't know who or what that is."

Issa stops pacing. A severe look comes over his face, one that causes Felix's heart to jump.

Issa pulls off his shirt. He turns and shows Felix a deep scar under his right shoulder blade. The skin is purple and raised in the middle, fleshy and rippled like a flow of hardened lava.

"This is my souvenir courtesy of the RUF."

Felix almost puts his finger out, wanting to run it along the skin.

Issa pulls his shirt back down.

"It's a terrible world, huh?"

Issa sits on the edge of the bed. "We are not helpless, Felix. We are men. We are responsible for what we do—and what we do not."

"I guess that's true."

"Do you know what I am to do in a few months' time?"

"No."

"I will be in Sierra Leone, where your father died, and do you know what I will be doing there? I will be recording the voices of the victims of the diamond wars. We go one of two ways: a Truth and Reconciliation Commission, like South Africa, or a war crimes tribunal. It is not for me to say . . . But *I* am not helpless. *I*, for one, will do something."

Issa abruptly exits but soon returns with two photographs. He hands one to Felix. There are two figures in the picture—a tall man, smiling and prideful, his hand resting on a young boy's shoulder. "My father," Issa says. "I know what it is like."

Felix gives back the photograph.

Issa hands over the other. It is of a little girl, her hair in tiny naps, a red barrette on the longest of them. She smiles, a beautiful big smile that shows all her small teeth. She has a tiny nose, just a bump on her face really, two little pinholes for nostrils. Enormous cheeks round out the face; she could be a baby model, an absolutely perfect face—all sweetness and innocence. But her left arm, raised toward the sky, ends just after the shoulder.

"Her name is Memuna," Issa says. "She is an orphan and lives at a group home in the capital." He runs the edge of his finger over Memuna's shoulder.

"Is she your daughter?"

Issa shakes his head. "No, I met Memuna when I did work in the amputees camp. Where your father . . ." He looks off into space. There is a vacancy in his eyes that makes him appear more hopeless and small than Felix would have ever thought possible for someone like Issa. But then he inhales and his back straightens. "Well, I am sorry."

Felix nods. Looks away, once again bites back the burn behind his eyes.

"I met her there. We became close and I promised to visit her whenever I was back. But by the next time I was able to visit, she had gone to the group home, where she is still. One day," Issa says, with great resolve, "I will adopt Memuna. Yes, this I will do."

Issa snaps his hands on his knees. "And you . . . you will go to Freetown tomorrow. And you will do what you need to do."

It sounds like an order, so Felix nods.

"And then so will I. Yes?"

"Yes . . . goodnight," Felix offers.

"Perhaps," Issa says.

Even though he's exhausted, Felix sits up awhile. He opens the window and lets in the cooling night breeze. The stadium nearby looks like something much smaller and inconsequential in the darkness. No one walks past. He's not sure who or what it is he's looking for, only that it's something.

It's late, and another long day beckons. He closes the window and goes to sleep.

# CHAPTER FIFTEEN

Hank Peters's small office is up five flights of stairs. A spotless desk occupies the middle of the room. Two trash cans, both empty, flank either side of the desk. The only object on the desk is a pen set, two instruments sticking up on either side of a miniature American flag. The office is stifling. But he knows better than to open the window. Even in the morning, it will only make things worse.

Hank stands at the window looking down: the same scene he has surveyed for years. He presses his forehead against the window. Perspiration from his nostrils fogs up the glass in a little circle. Below, a brown rutted road leads to the waterfront. A sickly-looking building rises above a house with a circular tin roof. Across the street is the white stone Law Courts building. Arches rise over every window with wrought iron balustrades underneath. A parade of four-wheel-drive vehicles snakes past, one of them stopping every so often to let someone out. Three men sit on the blue stone wall that rings the lawn in front of the building. They appear to be waiting for nothing, victims of the malaise and torpor that engulfs this land of heat and war and death.

Out toward the water, in the hinterlands of Aberdeen, is the camp where the murders happened. There, just a short drive away, the RUF tore the place to bits, killing the American doctor from Baltimore.

The phone rings. "Yes," he answers. A statement, not

a question. "Mmm-hmmm." He nods, twirls the cord around his finger, taking in all the details. It's 9 a.m. in Washington, D.C. He thinks of the six years he lived there. The ribbing he took when he went to Redskins games against his beloved Cowboys. He wants to ask the guy from State on the other end of the line how the Cowboys looked this year. He knows they lost in the playoffs. It's not like he can't get news. But he couldn't watch them play and so he has no idea how they looked.

He hears the details coming over the phone, but they only half register. A U.N. official from Niger. The kid from Baltimore. Had trouble in the desert. Is on his way from Niamey. *Mh-hmmm.* He stares at the brown of Victoria Park. *A park, by definition, should be green.* From his colleague's office down the hall, one can see the maze of Connaught Hospital, the lap of Kroo Bay behind, where the *USS Kearsarge* whisked him from trouble in '97.

The hospital: that's where he is, Hank is told, the doctor from Baltimore. In the morgue.

He turns from the window and walks to his desk. *Felix Lazlo,* he scribbles onto a sheet of paper.

"Okay," he says. "I'll be expecting him."

He hangs up. Outside the window, a simple fistfight between two men has escalated into something fierce. A woman has had half the hair ripped from her head. He turns. This is nothing. He knows what real violence is.

# CHAPTER SIXTEEN

Niamey's Hamani Airport is open-air and blazing hot. The departure is odd. Issa offers his hand and issues Felix a perfunctory goodbye. And then he turns to leave. Felix wants to stop him, engage him, tell him . . . something. He feels, almost ludicrously, that they have become friends. But he doesn't know what to say, and it is, finally, time to go. Anyway, Issa has turned and walked away. Felix assumes he will never see this man again, and his leaving now makes him seem almost like a figment, some odd angel who has shepherded him through a bad dream and dissipated back to the mental conjuring from which he has been born. An illusion. Gone.

So Felix rechecks his materials: air ticket, passport, the piece of paper with instructions to the consulate in Freetown and Hank Peters's name scribbled on it. Satisfied, he walks through the single terminal and heads to the front, past the understocked duty free shops, past shoe shine boys who beckon him even though he's wearing sneakers.

He spends the flight to Freetown imagining the sort of place where his father's body is being held. Differing versions of a filthy, insectivorous cave come to the fore. When he wills himself to see his father's body lying peacefully in a box, it morphs into Tombou covered in sand, or that camel being ripped to shreds by a pack of hyenas, or the deceased creature at Tandajar's communication. Dreams, but not dreams.

Below him, the accumulation of scrub quickly gives

way to thick jungle, interrupted only by small patches of open field and banana plantations. During the descent into Freetown, Felix looks for a bustling city, but there's none. The plane follows a palm-lined river running through brush and a few small villages. When the edge of the city finally comes into view, it's immediately swallowed by the harbor and a series of low radiating hills. Barely discernible slits run down the hillside like a staircase. At the airport, a helicopter rests on its helipad, a row of white tents and several blue United Nations APC's alongside it.

They land at Lungi close to the promised arrival time, taxiing past a large sign that reads, "Welcome to Sierra Leone. If you cannot help us, please do not corrupt us." Straight rows of palm trees, shimmering in the heat, line the swiss cheese tarmac. The hatch doors open and a refreshing, salty breeze fills the air. But a thick wetness follows, immediately descending over everything.

The airport is almost empty; Issa told him that it's been less than a year since international flights have resumed in Freetown. But gleaming new yellow tourism posters, emblazoned with palm-fringed beaches, tout the pleasures of the country. This war zone now a tourist destination?

At immigration, an officious man wearing a navy suit with red epaulets tells Felix he has to procure a landing visa. He points to a dingy office where a small man and a larger one behind a desk sit fanning themselves. Felix walks in and hands over the $100 for the visa. The big man takes it and then tells him that they will be holding his passport for checking because of his recent travels.

During his trip to Europe, after receiving his first passport stamp in Heathrow, his "Leave to enter the United Kingdom," he wanted an entire collection of stamps, each one representing to him another notch on his vaunted freedom tour. So every time he entered a new country, the first thing he did was go to a customs office and get the stamp. As a result, he had fifteen of them, plus two reentries into the United States, a Central African Republic stamp prohibiting "gainful employment," and now he was requesting Sierra Leone. All within six months. He explains all this to the officer, adding that he is only in Freetown to get his father. The large man smiles and assures him that it will be "taken care of" very soon. Felix sits around the office for three and a half hours, watching the smaller man run in and out no fewer than a dozen times.

Each time, the little man bows slightly when he comes in, and the big guy raises him up with a flick of his fingers. The little one delivers some message. The messages are greeted with, alternately, a grave nodding of the head or a bemused little smile. In both cases, the gestures don't seem to bode well.

*Just let me get on already, I'll pay you whatever you ask.* He wants to scream but instead, he sits and stews, mouse against the machine.

Eventually, the smaller man brings him a chicken sandwich and an orange soda and tells him that he can wait in the VIP Lounge. Felix waits for the punchline, but a VIP lounge actually exists, with a large window overlooking the runway and the Atlantic beyond. Heavy purple curtains, frayed at the edges, sweep the floor, stained in one corner because of dripping water from the barely functioning air conditioner. Still, he manages to get a little nap on one of the chairs.

After almost the entire day has expired, the big man explains that things are finally in motion. Once everything is cleared, they will make Felix's intentions known to the Americans at the consulate, and he will be able to proceed.

"Hank Peters?"

"I have never heard of him," the man answers, shrugging.

Another two hours passes, and Felix is told to come back to the office, where the little subservient man hands him his passport, says, "Okay," and does his little bow. Felix opens it and sees his visa and passport stamped. "We are sorry about your father," the little man says.

The day is gone now. The big man tells Felix to go to a hotel in town to sleep. He hands Felix a piece of paper and some leone notes in exchange for dollar bills. "I will have you driven there," he says. "This is a hotel run by my cousin. He will see you are okay."

The subservient man leads him down the hall to a waiting taxi. Felix hands the driver the paper and they set off, not realizing this means being driven only to a ferry terminal. The city proper sits across the harbor. But he's lucky, arriving just in time for the day's final ferry crossing.

He still holds out hope that he can run over to the consulate, make a connection, get the process going, despite the increasing hour and, as happens in tropical climes, with darkness coming on early. But all his rushing to get on board turns out to be a ludicrous exercise as the ferry simply sits interminably for reasons unknown. During the unexplained delay, not one soul on board registers displeasure or complaint, delays, apparently, as inevitable as breathing.

When they finally get on their way, the ferry moves so slowly that the ripples it makes in the water are barely perceptible. Felix pounds the metal rail and then explodes on some guy who asks him for money. He's immediately ashamed of himself and so he finds a place to sit down and keep his eyes on the floor. But a nearby goat keeps eyeing him with slitted eyes and soon it pisses gallons, the stream of urine snaking its way toward Felix. So he gets up and stands at the railing, watching, willing the perpetual approach.

The city presents itself across the water as a gathering of buildings hanging like tentacles from the foothills. Felix holds the rusty metal rail and watches Freetown approach, the boats in the harbor with their green, white, and blue flags bobbing lazily. He watches, and waits—waits some more, stops watching. It's an hour and a half across the bay, and fully dark by the time they reach the wharf. Going to the consulate is out of the question, so he resigns himself to the hotel and starting up the following day. He finds a taxi driver—the only one there—and hands him the paper with the address of the hotel on it.

They drive for approximately twenty seconds before the driver stops and drops him off at a dumpy one-story building—a spoiled American who can't even drag himself a hundred yards. "Ten-ten lion," he says. A few cents. Felix sighs, gets out, hands him the money.

Outside the hotel, a woman sits on the curb selling mangoes by candlelight. A yellow halo of light illuminates her and the fruit, everything cast in the same buttery glow. She wears a light-colored headwrap, turned brown by perpetual use. She raises her head and he sees the candlelight dancing in her watery eyes. He takes two mangoes, handing her a 1,000-leone note, not even a dollar, and heads inside.

There are half a dozen people lying on the floor, using their shirts and shoes as pillows. The proprietor stands behind a pockmarked desk, smoking a cigar and watching *Love Boat*.

"I'm Felix Lazlo. I was sent from the airport."

The man puts his cigar on the desk, ash side leaning off the edge, and comes over to him with a key in his hand. "Ivinin-O," he says. "How dee bodee now?"

Felix blinks at him.

"I apologize for this," he says, pointing to the people on the floor. "My wife's family from the villages is staying with me."

"I'm not taking anyone's room, am I?"

"Do not worry," the proprietor says, "They are not paying."

Felix follows him up a stairwell. Windows half-covered in peeled mesh screening shine weak lamplight on a stained welcome mat. Cockroaches scurry over it and into a hole in the wall. Standard stuff apparently, since the proprietor shows no embarrassment. Felix's room is small—a bed and a sink, one bare bulb hanging overhead, a long shoelace its on/off cord. Mosquito nets bunched with ropes hang over the bed. Long black smudges frame the window as if it had once caught fire. For a long time, he sits on the edge of the bed, trying to think clearly. He feels a tickle on his feet. A half dozen cockroaches dance across his toes. He crawls into bed and wraps the sheet, reeking of antiseptic, around his feet.

As if in response to a fervent prayer, the night passes easily and mercifully, a constant, cooling breeze coming in from the window. A blessing, for the next day promises to be one of the most difficult of his life.

In the early morning, Felix leaves the hotel and weaves through the crowd in the street. The sun is already intense—something dangerous and crushing, like it had been in the desert. Worse is the haze of diesel exhaust that settles in the thick humidity.

Already in the early hour, his eyes burn and his head throbs.

It's hard to move even in the shade. Simply walking down the street to a taxi stand is like wading through the shallow end of a pool. Felix asks to be taken to the American consulate. "*Le bureau d'États-Unis*," he says.

"What?" the driver asks.

Felix consults the explicit directions Issa had written down for him, puzzling out where he needs to be. "*Pres de l'arbre de cotton, je pense*," he says.

"We speak English here, *wetman*. Not French," the driver says. "The American offices at Walpole and Siaka Stevens Streets."

"Right, yes. Of course. Please."

They move onto the highway where they instantly come to a stop in a long unmoving line of traffic. The driver doesn't seem to mind; he sits calmly even while everyone around them honks incessantly.

Feeling utterly powerless, Felix leans up and asks the driver how long he thinks it will take.

"Never guess," he says. "Bad luck."

He sits back; nothing is in his control, so he stares out the window and wonders—not knowing one way or another—if he can simply walk to the consulate. He wonders, also, where it happened. Where is this camp for amputees where his father was murdered? He doesn't want to go and see it; as far as he knows, it's still a functioning place despite *Medecins Sans Frontieres* leaving, and the double shock—the place where his dad breathed his last, peopled still with amputees, and who knows how many—is too much even to contemplate, let alone bear. For now, it's a question of getting to the consulate, seeing Hank Peters, and getting the first, and worst, over with.

The morning fog has burned off from the mountain-tops. To the left, at the bottom of a hill, are palm wine sellers like in Bangui. And like Bangui, there's a rotten odor in the air. But a frequent breeze coming off the water carries away most of the reek. However, during lulls, it returns, oppressive and heavy, a raw tang of body odor and industry.

Below them to the right, the houses look thrown together. They pass several burned out buildings; each of these invariably has a gang of shirtless men milling around, pushing wheelbarrows or stacking pieces of wood.

The taxi rises further on the hill and the harbor comes into view below. A few tall buildings stand sporadically near the water. Aside from those, the city looks like a slapdash collection of one-story dwellings thrown together in every available space crowded by no fewer than two dozen modern banks and the occasional red brick church. Houses with rusty metal roofs, built on stilts and looking as if they're on the verge of collapsing, climb the hillsides. Freetown is lush, with green peeping through alleys and with forest on the mountaintops. The mountain "staircase" Felix had seen from the plane now reveals itself as a series of rice paddies. Far off, below them, red dirt spills onto a long beige beach where people move around in large crowds. The driver crawls through a series of massive palms and then pulls off the road and drives down Siaka Stevens Street.

The streetside houses are neat and tidy, several with stately balconies—Felix guesses these Victorians are the legacy of British colonials. They move toward a massive cotton tree and then snake through a zigzagged street and pull up to a beige building: The consulate.

Felix walks to the front door and finds it locked. He

presses the intercom and announces himself. The response is pure static. But moments later, the door opens and a grave-looking man in a business suit tells him to come in. "I will get Mr. Peters," he announces.

Felix suddenly wants company—anyone's. Even the taxi driver. Or Wesley. Just anyone. It's actually happening now. Up to this point, it has all been theoretical. His father is dead; he knows that. He's come to retrieve his body; he knows that, too. But so much has happened in between. What began as a simple plan—go to Bangui, see elephants, go to Freetown—has turned into Wesley and Diffa and Niamey and Issa. But all that is done now. He is here, in the same building as his father. And it occurs to him that it has been many months since that was last true.

A middle-aged man with a bush of salt and pepper hair, wearing a white cotton shirt and tan pants, walks down the stairs. "Hank Peters," he says, extending his hand.

"Thank you," Felix says, inexplicably.

"You have trouble getting here?"

"I almost died in the desert."

"Right," he says. "I heard something like that . . . your mother has been calling . . . a lot."

"Sorry," Felix says, but then he regrets the apology. He feels very defensive and protective of his mother suddenly. Up to this point, he'd concentrated on the foremost idea that he's lost a father, and that, on some level, it had been her fault, that she'd driven him away because she doesn't have much of an interest in the world beyond Europe or the South Pacific. So his dad lit out, but in the end he had every intention of coming back home and living out his years, faithfully, with his wife. But he needed to live a life with more exoticism than an occasional visit to an Ethiopian restaurant. It is, perhaps, unfair of Felix to think of his mother this way. He knows that. And yet he feels it anyway. He sympathizes with his dad's need to go.

He thinks again of Lizzy, of the patterns in life, of the women left behind. At least in Lizzy's case, he tells himself, she's probably better off without him. It's the only comfort he can provide himself and it is, really, no comfort at all. But as for his mother: she's lost her husband, and there can be no relief in that. Only pain, anguish, and questions with few answers.

"How did the Cowboys look?"

"What?"

"Dallas Cowboys. They lost in the playoffs?"

"I don't know."

Hank looks at Felix: is he really an American?

"Come on. I want to show you something." They enter a staircase—"Elevator doesn't work," Hank says—and walk up five flights of stairs to Hank's small, spare, and stifling office.

Hank walks to the window. "You see that building? That's the Law Courts building. It's the nicest in Freetown."

"It's beautiful," Felix mumbles, watching a couple of pickup trucks with their tops sawed off and soldiers holding automatic weapons clinging to the back.

"You don't understand what I'm saying to you. That building—that white one—that's the nicest building in the city. In the country probably. This is where I live." Hank presses his forehead against the window. "I just want to know how the Cowboys looked," he sighs.

Hank exhales. "During the coup attempt in May '97, this building was fired on. The windows were shot out. We all herded onto the seventh floor. The U.N. had 10,000 troops here, but they bungled it. Completely useless. Surrendered to the rebels without a fight. We were on our own. When we could finally make a run for it, we went to the harbor. The USS Kearsarge was there. It took us, a bunch of natives also. A lot of them wound up in refugee camps in Guinea. Fourekaria. Guekedou. When I came back, the U.S. government wouldn't let me outside unless I was in an armored van—it took me from here to my house and back. That was it. I look back— in some ways, those were the best times. They were exciting. Does that sound crazy?"

Felix doesn't know. He doesn't care. Actually, yes, it does sound crazy, and offensive. Since when is killing exciting?

"I'm sorry," Hank says. "Listen to me. I suppose you want to go to where your father is."

"He's not here?"

"Why would he be here? He's at the morgue in Connaught."

Angry, Felix follows Hank out of his office and down the stairs.

They head through a series of hallways and outside through a heavy steel door. Hank moves quickly down the street, past the Law Courts Building. Bird nests fill in the crooks of the building's upper arches. What at first looks like a design of peppered pinholes over and around the front doors is, upon closer inspection, clearly the remains of a spray of automatic weapons fire.

People walk by, but they are strangers. Cars and trucks move too, but these are heading to places Felix doesn't care about. These are places his father had never seen. Or maybe he had. He'd flown into Lungi before heading out to the camp, one of the first flights into the country after the war. Felix doesn't know if he spent any time in town. Maybe he—and maybe his lady friend, too—came in at night or on weekends. He has no idea how his father spent the last few days of his life. Had he seen these same boys without any shoes playing soccer in the street? Had he seen this parade of people wearing old t-shirts emblazoned with American sports teams? Did that giant orange Fanta billboard loom over the side of the road when he was here?

"That's the Ministry of Finance," Hank says, pointing to a burned-out hulk, black streaks painting the tops of every naked window frame.

A man sitting in front of the building holds a paint canister to his nose. Felix has seen this a hundred times in Baltimore, or at least some version of it, but this man holds the canister with the only hand he has left. What has happened to him that he is here on the street instead of in the amputees camp getting medical attention? Did Felix's father bend down and help people like this? Had he met this very man, extended his hand, asked him if he could help? This guy, sucking down inhalants on the streets of Freetown, saw his dad more recently than Felix has. He's sure of it. He thinks to ask this guy how his dad looked. Was he happy?

He's close now, and running out of ways to keep his father alive. And he is still alive to him—very much so. Because he knows damn well that even if these castaways on the streets of Freetown broke his father's heart, he was also excited by all of it. When he was here, he was in a very foreign place, and Felix is sure that sparked him like nothing else could. When he was home, in the last few years, he was plainly miserable.

His earliest memories of his dad are of a vigorous, powerful man—broad-shouldered, a thick mustache that drooped to his chin. Felix remembers him at his elementary school, telling his class what it's like to be a hand surgeon—the exciting things he did with knives. It made him proud; he loved it when the other kids asked Felix questions about him. He would make up what he didn't know, like the time he reconstructed a man's hand that had been crushed by a bus. "My daddy had to take out pieces of the hubcap," he said, believing it even if no one else did.

But while Felix was away at college, his father changed. Felix noticed it on those weekends and breaks when he was home from school. His shoulders stooped. He shaved off his mustache, and only the faint gray shadow of a beard remained. His hair thinned and grayed and he started wearing glasses. He moped around the house.

Felix was home for the summer before his senior year and as much as he tried to engage him in anything, his dad mostly sat around the house and read. At dinner, he chewed mindlessly, like a man present only in body; in thought, he was on the other side of the world. Usually the family would eat in silence until his mother couldn't take it anymore and would get up and leave the table. "Are you okay, Dad?" he asked once.

He ran his hand over his face and turned to Felix. He seemed to be reciting something from memory as he stared at an invisible point just above Felix's head: "There are villages in Africa where chiefs keep a hundred wives and feed them only pure cow's milk from a gourd until they grow so fat that they waddle around like seals." He looked back at his plate, speared

a green bean, and jammed it into the side of his mouth. Felix
didn't know what to say, and his father didn't speak for the rest
of the meal.

But then he got the opportunity to go to Guatemala,
and for a while, he was his old self. Dr. Albert had some connections with *Medecins Sans Frontieres* and he recommended
Felix's dad for work with Quechua Mayan villagers. For days
before his dad left, he floated around the house, humming
tunes and peppering his mother's neck with kisses.

When he returned, he told his mother and him tales of
noble, hard-working people whose hands he was busy saving.
But, he also regaled them with stories of beautiful beaches,
spewing volcanoes, impenetrable forests. He flung his arms in
the air, wild in the story of finding a waterfall in the jungles
near the Belizean border.

"You should have seen it. Thick, unyielding. We're
walking along and we can hear it—like the sound of an airplane, just this great crashing roar. We hack through and there
it is, pouring over like Eden. We stripped down and dove in.
Emerald green and beautiful. Just beautiful. Pure Shangri-la,"
he said.

Felix loved these stories and he loved seeing his father
that way, but his mother's face remained expressionless as she
sipped her scotch and soda. She didn't speak much in those
weeks before Felix went back to school. And his dad didn't
seem to care.

He spent most of his time looking over old photo albums, losing himself in the images of the other life of his, the
one spent in movement. He sat in the basement for hours and
stared at the pages of his many journeys, each one carefully catalogued by place and date. Felix watched him from the

top of the stairs, seeing him gingerly leaf through the albums. Seeing him like that, one would assume he was a man in love, looking at photographs of a beautiful woman smiling demurely at the camera, her hair whipped by wind.

Unfortunately for his mother, the thing his father was so enthralled with was no longer their steady stone house or the wife within it, but the lure of far off places. It would only be a matter of time before his father would be off to Africa. And once he'd gotten there, no matter how horrendous the circumstances, he would be thrilled by it. Of that, Felix was sure.

"Incredible how life goes on, eh?" Hank asks, breaking Felix's reverie.

He's making his way along the streets with such deliberation that Felix has trouble keeping pace. He wonders if Hank even sees the dropouts anymore. Or had he become immune to it all? Did he have to, for his own sanity? It's easier to look the other way—toward the Internet café; the hordes of people chatting into mobile phones; the man in a business suit hurrying past the double amputee; the young sellers shouting their wares: "Ah get de fry-fry," "Mina-ya. Mina-ya. Min-ya," "Ker-o-seen-ay." It's easier to see the others, the ones for whom the war seems distant, as if it hasn't touched them personally.

"You should've been here a year and a half ago," Hank says as they dart past oncoming traffic. "Anarchy. You could actually smell the fear—a thick cloud of it. These people now are all getting on with their lives, as I say. It's amazing how quickly they do it."

"I guess they have no choice."

"You're very smart," Hank says.

Felix doesn't see his facial expression when Hank calls

him smart. He thinks at first that the guy is being sarcastic. But no. He recognizes it for what it is. The simplest thing becomes the most profound. Here, all has been reduced to pure survival, to getting-on. *Everything* else is superfluous.

But not everyone is getting on. Looking back to the man holding the inhalant, Felix lets his eyes roam above his head, following the spider web design of cracks along the wall to a series of government posters, complete with official seal. "Allow Rebels Back Into Society—For Everyone's Good!" "Ask Rebels To Turn In Their Guns—For Their Good And Your Own!" "Give Us A Chance To Grow." Does this man, sniffing inhalants, his hand hacked off by one of those very rebels, presumably, have it in him to let the butcher back into society, to live with him as neighbors, to watch him clutch groceries with two good hands, see him walk by on two good legs, passing the rusted can that he uses to beg for money, the can that looks empty? Who besides people like Felix and Hank have any money to give this guy? But they are past him now and they haven't given him a thing.

A warm wind blows up, rustling the palm fronds. The man's can rolls over. Felix turns back to see one coin rolling out, circling the man's leg until it stops at his naked foot, his only foot.

"It's going to rain," Hank says. A giant black cloud rolls in off the water in the distance. Huge green plants with white flowers shake in the wind, some of the petals lifting off and landing at their feet.

People start rushing about to beat the rain. A man in a green and white British soccer jersey runs in front of them, turns around and says hello to Hank, and then walks into a World Vision office, under a "No Arms" sign. A sick joke—

there are thousands with no arms. Or is it merely gallows humor, a way to cope? The barely noticeable automatic weapon with the red line painted through it makes the meaning clear.

Next to the World Vision building stands a little video rental store, its windows plastered with Rambo posters. In front of the store, a young man who looks decidedly messed up on something stands with his empty palm upraised. A thin line of drool hangs from his bottom lip, almost reaching the pavement. He wears a Tupac Shakur t-shirt and tattered cutoff jeans.

"Is he one of the RUF?" Felix asks.

"West Side Boys. Part of the Sierra Leone Army that fought with the rebels. You can tell by his shirt. They love Tupac. Makes them feel like real American gang-bangers. Worst of the worst. They looted the city they were supposed to protect."

"And he expects people to give him money now?"

"What else is he supposed to do? There was a push for a while to try and forget everything, try and get everyone together. You see that place there?" Hank points to the Hollywood Haircuttery, a pink plaster storefront across Wellington Street. "They used to give free haircuts to amputees, but then people who'd lost limbs to things like polio or leprosy started demanding free haircuts, too. Of course some people recognized them and called them on it. So that ended real quick. The amputees camp in Murraytown used to house war-wounded also, but they had to separate them because the war-wounded got jealous of the amputees, thought that the amputees were getting all the attention while they got none. So fights started breaking out. The war-wounded would show up when the cameras arrived, ask for their fingers to be sliced off so they could go to America. That sort of thing. On the one hand, it's terrible. How can you condone a war-wounded beating on an amputee because one is getting more aid or has better chances of adoption? On the other hand, how can you condemn it?"

When they arrive at the hospital, Hank makes his way through the crowd of people milling around the front. They walk into the lobby, a sterile place smelling of pine solvent, and hurry past the front desk. They pass a poster that reads: "Sex Thrills, AIDS Kills."

There's a central courtyard to the left and a series of concrete walkways straddling the hospital buildings. Shade trees dot the courtyard, where groups of people sit around waiting, doing nothing. Black-and-white painted signs point the way toward ER, OR, and MORTUARY.

"Doctors here make seventy dollars a month," Hank says, though Felix hasn't asked.

They head into the basement. "Your father's coffin will go back to the States in an army C-130 transport along with the American soldiers who died in the peacekeeping mission in Gbaranga."

"Okay," he mutters.

Nothing left. Only humming opaque fluorescent lights above, bald, empty concrete walls on either side, and shining linoleum floors that reek of ammonia. "Wait here," Hank says. He leaves Felix alone and returns a moment later with a Sierra Leonean man wearing a loose black velour jogging suit and sandals.

"Do I want to see him?" Felix blurts out.

Both men look at him, their eyebrows arched high on their foreheads.

"What does he look like?" Felix asks.

"We have excellent morticians here, sir. Your father looks peaceful. They have done a wonderful job. He has been embalmed and he is in excellent condition."

"Probably looks a hell of a lot better than I do," Hank puts in.

The jogger tells Felix to follow him. Hank stays behind.

The room is airy and chilled. Felix's previous vision of a malarial sick-room infested with flies is way off. "Wait here," the jogger says. He opens a door and leaves.

The door opens again a moment later and the jogger wheels a gurney with the mound of body underneath a long white sheet. "I have to stay," he says apologetically. "You have to positively identify."

Felix nods. After all that has taken place to get to this moment, he suddenly wants them to have the wrong guy. He wants them to have screwed it up, have some old woman here instead. Or a little girl. He'll even accept a middle-aged man, but the wrong middle-aged man. Just not him.

But then the jogger lifts the sheet and exposes the face.

His hair is completely gray; gone are the prominent streaks of black. A thin gray beard covers his face. The eyelid over the right eye seems to have slipped and retracted toward the forehead. The blue pupil stares at him, but it has faded a bit, lost its spark. A faint smile rests on his lips, but it is not the smile Felix knows. It looks instead like resignation, like he had known in those last moments what was coming. Perhaps it had been a real smile at first, one that showed that he'd been happy because he'd gone out the way he wanted to, instead of without any dignity alone in some hospital room while his body rotted beneath him. But that smile had changed, had fallen into something sad. Felix hopes it's because his father realized at that moment that he'd never be able to tell Felix what he'd seen and done, and he'd never get the opportunity to hear what Felix had experienced during his trip to Europe, and summer nights spent swapping stories of their travels would never happen. In the end, Felix imagines, the smile faded because his father missed him, and because he loved him.

The pulled sheet also reveals his shoulder and forearm. The same gray curly hair runs from his wrist to his elbow, a thick carpet that never intrudes beyond those points. He had kept the hair off his industrious hands, away from the knuckle, by shaving once a week. And it never reached past the elbow, leaving a well-formed bicep clean and smooth like butter.

Felix puts his hand on his father's arm. A hot course of blood rises up in him and passes quickly through horror, sadness, joy, nausea. And then it subsides, taking all his energy with it. He wants to tell him about the amazing chain of events to get to this sterile room in Freetown, but only gets out, "You won't believe it, Dad."

"So this is your father?" the jogger asks. "You are sure?"

Felix nods.

The jogger pulls the sheet back over his dad's head.

"It's him," Felix says.

Then he's wheeled out—and Felix is alone.

## CHAPTER SEVENTEEN

Lizzy understands Felix's need to go, to retrieve him, as it were. Her father's abandonment of the family when she was just nine was the definitive event of her own childhood: when Lizzy thinks of those years after her dad left, the almost singular memory of it is of weekend mornings, when she'd stumble out of bed with the breaking of dawn, wrap herself in blankets, and trundle downstairs, her mother still asleep, and construct a fort of pillows to climb into, there on the deep carpet of the front room, where the early morning sun poured in. The room felt as if it operated in its own time zone, free of the strictures of chronometers and calendars and polar axes and the rest of it. With the sun like that, the rest of the house still bathed in the purplish gauze of early morning, the room was its own world.

As the sun narrowed and concentrated, she'd curl herself up in it, letting the rays bathe her face. Eyes closed, she'd watch the pulsing light show on the back of her eyelids, the sun beating upon the membrane and protective fluids of her eyelids. Whole new worlds, universes, every time she'd flick her pupils up, down, right, left. She'd drop the blankets off her, let the sunshine bore into her exposed skin or through her pajamas. She imagined it no less comforting than if she'd been back, somehow, in her mother's belly.

Then she'd shift, take her face out of the direct gaze of the sun, and open her eyes, watching the show of lunar dust dancing in the rays that she'd stirred up by moving. She'd imagine the journey, the sloughing off of cosmic particles from celestial bodies, floating and dancing and twirling, making what she imagined was a trek of thousands if not millions of years to visit her there in her house, where her father no longer lived, on a weekend morning when she had the leisure of being bored, of lying there all day if she wanted. There, she'd allow her mind to literally go blank, subsumed by light shows and lunar dust, a way of keeping at bay the thoughts that always threatened: that this wasn't right. That it should have been her and her mom and her dad, together. But it wasn't that way. Now it was just the two of them, the two females. And he was with another female, a different one, somewhere out west, far away, the only evidence of him the monthly checks he sent by mail without accompanying note. Before then, though, they used to do things, all three of them. But now they were only two and it seemed she and her mom never did things on weekend mornings anymore. Instead, those were the quiet times, times for contemplation or ignoring reality or whatever. During the week was easy; school provided the fill to the hours. But on weekends . . .

After her mom woke, she'd step beyond where Lizzy lay and retreat silently to the couch on the other side of the house with her newspapers and magazines and endless cups of coffee while Lizzy lay separated by sets of walls: kitchen, bathroom, a universe. When the split first came, Lizzy told herself it would be temporary. She did what all children do in such cases: convince themselves that their parents will be getting back together momentarily, that they will come to their senses, realize just how awful it is without one another . . . but as the days passed and the likelihood of that grew more remote, the next best thing was to go blank. And what better way than in a bath of sunlight? In this way Lizzy's chief memory of those days was actually non-memory, an insistent wall against memory-making, a willful vacuity.

So this is how she spent every Saturday or Sunday morning that wasn't overcast. On days without sun, Lizzy would create her own force fields: she would hold her breath and blow really hard, like clearing her ears, and imagine a giant invisible bubble spreading around her, widening to its limits, on the verge of bursting into oblivion. But just as it threatened to explode, she would need to inhale anyway and so there it stayed, perpetual protection, insulation from a world that could be cruel.

But on sunny days, in that front room, from the break of day until mid-morning, there she stayed, as the sun worked its way across the room, Lizzy moving with it, getting up and then plopping back down a foot over every twenty minutes or so, until it started its climb against the northern wall, and then quit the room, then the house altogether, splintered by trees and walls, before returning, weaker, late in the day to give its last announcements on the other side of the house before disintegrating into diffused colors piled one on top of the other behind the spider's-web of branches from the century-old sycamores just down the hill in the neighbors' yard.

On one occasion she could recall during these idylls, she heard her mother upstairs, the bathroom in the master just above the room where Lizzy lay. It was an odd muffled whimper at first, a foreign and indiscernible sound. Lizzy ran upstairs to investigate and discovered her mom on the bathroom floor. Lizzy could see her, through the crack in the open door: there she sat on the floor, a ravaged tissue box at her feet, the tears rolling down her face, strings of snot mingling with the tears to form a viscous trail across her mouth and chin.

Lizzy fled, back downstairs to the safe confines of her sun spot, where she tuned out the noises. Where she was safe and warm and alone again.

And as she got older, struck out on her own, moved into a place whose walls and earthly orientation didn't allow for the sweet intrusion of sun, she abandoned that habit of her childhood. Besides, the adult world, with its responsibilities and time crunches, didn't allow for it, either. But she kept up her bubbles, her imaginary force fields, a holdover from losing her father. And no one managed to break through. No one, really, until Felix.

She loves him, understands him, understands even now as he is far away, understands what it is he is after.

# CHAPTER EIGHTEEN

Hank Peters had told the hospital workers why Felix was at the morgue. The jogger, sympathetic, sends for Felix the following morning.

"I want to show you something," he says when Felix arrives at the hospital. "I am sure you are proud of your father. But I want you to see." He leads Felix to a long and narrow room where a doctor sits on a stool in front of a man missing both his hands. The doctor kneads his knuckles up and down the man's forearms. Next to him, a man smokes a cigarette held between the metal clasps of his prosthesis.

A pretty young nurse walks in and heads toward a cabinet. She unlocks it and pulls out some gauze and little wooden sticks, their edges coated in yellow wax. "*Therèse, amitriptylene, s'il vous plâit,*" the doctor says.

The nurse nods and hands the doctor some pills. He puts them to the man's mouth. The man opens and swallows—no water.

"Joseph speaks Krio," the jogger says, pointing to the patient. "But you may be able to understand. Joseph, this young man's father worked in the camp. He was a doctor."

Joseph looks at Felix, a slight smile on his lips. He nods.

"Do you think you can tell him your story?" the jogger asks Joseph.

"What a kin now," Joseph says. "If a bin no don pas."

Felix doesn't understand right away, but the jogger is
right. Without any sort of crash course, he soon understands
everything, and Joseph's story forever afterward—on those
many nights when it will come back to Felix—resonates in
clear English.

He tells how a group of RUF carried him along a jungle path, how they laughed about it, how, ultimately, he lost
his hands, and how he still feels them, especially at night,
when the pain becomes excruciating. "He-ah," he says, pointing at the ends of his imaginary knuckles. "A kin geh pain at
me fingers." He tells about the rebels' "joke"—"short sleeve or
long sleeve" they asked, meaning, "Do you want to be cut off
at the wrist or the elbow?"

Felix turns away. He can still hear Joseph tell his story,
can see the axe, hear the soldiers laugh, see Joseph run back
to his village with his arms in the air, hear the doctor explain
that once the tensed veins are cut, they retract into the arms
and so long as the arms are held high, the blood won't escape.

Here is a chance to ask about his father. But he can't.
Joseph's own narrative contains enough pain. So he thanks Joseph, and the jogger, and asks to leave.

Back downstairs, in the morgue, Felix sits at a desk
and watches as sweat rolls down the official's face. He keeps
running his palm over his forehead and the back of his neck
and then loses his grip on the pen. He doesn't ask Felix any
questions, but keeps looking at the report written by the jogger and uses that to fill in his own paperwork. On the walls of
his office are a poster of Miami Beach, a picture of the pope,
and the man behind the desk with his arm around Evander
Holyfield's shoulder.

He stops writing and slaps down his pen. He reaches

into the top drawer of his desk, brings out a rubber stamp and inkpad, and meticulously rubs the stamp along the surface of the pad—back and forth, back and forth, until Felix is certain the man's doing it to drive him crazy. Then he raises the stamp and slams it down onto the bottom of the paper—the exclamation point. "Give this to the consulate," he says.

"American?"

"You are not Sierra Leonean, are you?"

Felix takes the paper and leaves.

In the three days it takes to get out of Sierra Leone, Felix doesn't do very much. Tired of the cockroaches and other vermin that keep him awake at night, he moves to the Cape Sierra Hotel, and there, at night, stares at the garbage fires dotting the hillsides around town. He sits in the dark and thinks about the summer nights when he was young and when he and his father sat out on the back porch and watched the sudden exclamations of firefly, the quick yellow blinking out of nowhere and then the army of them lighting up the night. The dark humps of rabbits loping across the lawn and all was silent and empty and exquisitely alive. They'd sit that way, not talking, sometimes for hours, long past the first shift of yellow fireflies and into the second, synchronized purples of the later shift.

In many respects, Felix reflects, his life to that point had been defined—even determined—by his dad. It was his degrees from Georgetown that prompted Felix to go there, too. It was his travels that spurred Felix on to Europe. And it was his death in West Africa that has sent him here, too. But now he is gone, and it leaves Felix with the freedom to define himself. This is exhilarating, but also terrifying. As he carves his own path, he knows, it will be to his father that he would most want to turn to with his stories, his triumphs, his failures. And Felix knows for sure that his father would have wanted to hear them, and would only offer his advice if solicited, with all the confidence in the world that his boy would be all right in the end. Felix, too, knows he will be all right—or at least he thinks so. But now his dad will never see it. Felix wishes he could believe in it, but he just doesn't buy the idea that his father is sitting above somewhere, his feet dangling off the edge of a cloud, watching his boy make his way in the world.

The Cape Sierra is an improvement as far as vermin go, but it's infested with spiders. At first, this bothers Felix, but soon enough, he grows inured to them. He studies the spiders and blows at them in some sort of primitive test, to see their disjointed movements, their harried scrambling, their ignorance of the fact that this massive creature looming above and pushing wind is really just as scared of them as they are of him.

At night, Felix runs a hand over his leg or neck and realizes how incredibly filthy he is. It never registers during the day that he's getting dirty, but by day's end, he's streaked from top to bottom, his tan pants almost black. Then, he walks down the hall to the shower, a stingy, ice-cold trickle that takes half an hour to get everything off.

He calls his mother. Finally, a connection, after so many days. But the line is strained and has a delay and so they don't say much, communicating in hurried bursts that they often deliver at precisely the same moment so that neither can understand much. He does let her know that he has identified the body and that he will be home as soon as possible.

"Thank you," she chokes.

He doesn't tell her about the desert or Wesley or Issa, and it's obvious that she has no idea that things had gone drastically different than what he's told her. He concentrates on and hurries through the bureaucratic details: They will land at Dover Air Force Base and the coffin will be unloaded there. She can start making funeral arrangements in Baltimore once she confirms transport of the body from Delaware. The State Department is taking care of the transfer.

He obtains the consular mortuary certificate, which he needs to get back into the U.S. It's attached to a foreign death certificate, an affidavit from the funeral director, and a transit permit. He reads over all the documents, starting with the affidavit: "This attests to the fact that the casket contains only the remains of the deceased and the necessary clothing and packing materials. The remains have been embalmed (or otherwise prepared)." This is followed by an illegible signature and a government seal.

He knows now why his mother had been so angered by that language when she'd gone to the State Department in D.C. It's cold, so unbecoming a man who was on a mission of humanitarianism. It's general language, designed to cover everyone. But his father wasn't everyone; he was his dad, and he was his mother's husband.

Despite his anger, he keeps reading. The consular mortuary certificate affirms that "the deceased did not die from a quarantinable disease and the remains have been embalmed." The column just below, labeled "Cause of Death," is marked, "Homicide."

He falls into tears. Of course, he's known all along that it was a homicide, but this stupid legal language is just too straightforward, too simplistic. His father had been murdered. He wants to march back to the official office and scream the truth—he's been *murdered*.

But instead, he does nothing. And it occurs to him: he's done nothing *but* nothing, passive all the way, and in every case. Allowing others to take the lead for him, tell him where to go and what to do. He'd even have died had others not come for him, people of action. Like his father. And like Issa Manzo. Even that kook Wesley.

From here on, he determines, he will be a man of action, do his father and himself proud. He knows that Lizzy should be the first place to start. When he gets home, he will call her. Straight away. Even before he unpacks. No, he will go see her, won't even bother calling first. Even if it comes to nothing, then at least they will have a clean break of things. No more of this nebulous allowing things to simply dissolve, as if that is the easier and thus preferable way. Hard choices. It's what his dad undertook. It's what he will do, too.

It is, finally, time to leave, back to his old life that he resolves will be a new life, somehow.

He's soon back at the airport, standing at the end of a small line waiting to cross the tarmac to the military plane. His passport, ticket, and police clearance that he needs to leave Sierra Leone are all tucked into his back pockets. Physically, the rage has fallen away, leaving only his worn and aching body. All of it—the hostage taking, the desert, the death certificate—finally, and irrevocably, drains him of everything.

He leans against the gate that serves as the airstrip boundary. Beyond, he can see what once made this place beautiful. He hadn't seen it from the air coming in, nor had any of it occurred to him while his father was in that hospital, but now the serenity of the scene fills him with something that feels suspiciously like contentment, like hope. A low sweep of mangrove swamps, the white bobbing of fishing boats, the sun glinting off a piece of metal, a long crescent of sand, the men gathering their fishing nets: his dad would have imbibed it, just as Felix is doing now, hoping to sear it forever into his memory, one more deposit to the bank of beauty, something to serve as a bulwark against future regret. Within moments after takeoff, the hum of the four propellers makes him drowsy. He nods off a few times, twice landing on the shoulder of the army man beside him. When he wakes, the soldier smiles but doesn't say anything.

The engines drone. He stares straight ahead. He's going home, where there will be a funeral, a shattered mother, and hopefully an ex-girlfriend who, maybe, might still consider some kind of relationship with him.

Behind him in the plane, there are ten pine coffins, nine of them decorated with draped American flags for the dead soldiers.

The other contains his dad.

We need to look at this and see if this is a big enough time break to warrant this.

**PART II**

# CHAPTER ONE

There is something about the school bell that never fails to give Lizzy a pang. It's one more day, one more opportunity, but one more click of the wheel, one more spoke pushed toward an end: the day, the month, the school year. These kids will grow up and out, flail in an indifferent world, just as she did. Lizzy's a young woman; she wonders why she thinks such maudlin thoughts. She's too young for such rumination, she tells herself. But ever since the year started and Felix was still in Europe, she's felt each day tinged with sadness. Just nibbling around the edges, as if something is lost and cannot be regained. And yet there is always that hope that it will all be like it once was again.

But he'd gone without her. Then he'd come home, and left yet again. Without a word. It wasn't something she understood. Yes, he'd gone off to Africa to get his murdered father's body—no small thing, no easy trick. She could extend him that; she would hold no anger over that part. But didn't she deserve to at least be allowed to comfort him? His having failed to contact her meant that it was weird when she met Rosemarie. She came as a friend, as support. But having come instead as Rosemarie's son's girlfriend, those things would have been implied, all part of the deal. Instead, it was awkward, at least at first.

And so the bell, its shrill insistence each weekday morning, is like a terrible cock call from the first rays of dawn, some blaring announcement that this world, a world of work, is what separates her from him: he hasn't yet entered this world, one of school bells or water coolers or subways or rush hour traffic. He hasn't had to sit through interminable meetings, submit himself to the arbitrary whims of administration or the partners or whatever hierarchical structure exists in whatever world he will one day enter. No, he still operates in a more fluid place, a world of travel and movement and unsettledness. Africa—she can't even imagine it. And so the bell rings, and the boys and girls, almost all of them the ancestors of those same people a continent away, dragged here against their will across the Middle Passage, file into her classroom. He's there, and she's here, in Baltimore, herding children in after the bell.

What will she do after he comes home, after they sit down? Chart the contours of their relationship? Will she still be his girlfriend? Does she even want to be? If so, does he want her to be? These are the questions she plays out over and over in her head, night after night, knowing as the hours tick away how much closer that first bell is getting and resenting him for causing her to face that bell and a classroom full of children—often without breakfast, often without a stable home life, so many things stacked against them—when she will be weary, exhausted.

She had, for a time, taken to sleeping aids, but eschewed them quickly. She'd found them too effective, convinced that if she continued she'd never be able to go another night without them. Too young to start that now. So she stopped. And then tossed and turned. And resented him. Had he only called. Had they simply had a conversation, understood one another, put themselves on some firm footing.

She will go to the funeral. She will steer clear of anger and resentment. She loved him once, dearly. And she loves him still. And so let him go, she tells herself. Let him figure out himself during this time. She will be there for him, as difficult as that might prove to be, when he decides he needs someone to talk to. But that is all she can provide for him now. It's too much otherwise.

She needs her sleep. When that bell goes off, she needs to be present.

She needs to look out for herself, and for those kids.

# CHAPTER TWO

The rabbi, a woman from the local synagogue where, out of some vague sense of obligation, the Laszlos attended services on Yom Kippur and Rosh Hashanah, presides over the funeral service.

Friends and family from around Baltimore and down from New York attend. Doctors and nurses from the hospital come as well. A few people from *Medecins Sans Frontieres*, too. A doctor from that organization, a Spaniard working in New York, explains that MSF has reconstituted the camp after the attack, that they will not be cowed by thugs, and that in the final analysis, leaving would do a disservice not only to the people who are being served there, but also to people like Felix's dad, whose death, he asserts, will not be in vain. They will continue to work just as Mr. Lazlo would have wanted. Then he reads a letter of recognition and gratitude from the government of Sierra Leone, thanking Mr. Lazlo for his work there.

Lizzy attends; Rosemarie called her with the details. Her presence is sunshine and light, like a yellow dress on a foggy gray sand beach. The feelings churn inside him the moment Felix catches sight of her. It's as if she is the very life he'd been searching for during his trip. He can remember now that he'd seen her face as he lay dying in the desert.

But soon even these ruminations are subsumed by the attendant grief of the funeral.

Felix's uncle tries to add some levity to the affair, recalling stories from when they were younger growing up in New York, how Felix's father had always been bothered by cold and how his older and bigger brother insisted on keeping the bedroom windows open, even in winter. "I will never forget," he says, "The time that it had to have been forty below outside and I had that window open and I woke up at two in the morning with icicles hanging from my nose." Everyone chuckles. "I ran out of that room so fast and my poor brother, huddled up under his blankets, he was too stricken to move. When I opened the door, it created a vacuum and sucked in an Arctic wind. The little guy rose six feet into the air and screamed at the top of his lungs. It was a miracle he didn't catch pneumonia."

When it's Felix's turn, he's quick. With a composure that surprises him, he reads two lines from *Julius Caesar*: "Cowards die many times before their deaths / The valiant never taste of death but once." Speaking is easier for him than for the others—they had the shock of knowing this vital man and then hearing that he had died. They had seen him, had spoken to him, and he was very alive to them. Then he was dead—nothing in between. But for Felix, the shock has long since worn off. In some perverse respects, he is the lucky one.

Some three hours pass; the words of remembrance are endless and sincere and effusive. But Rosemarie doesn't say anything. She sits stoically, dressed in a dark purple dress and a black hat.

When the relatives leave the funeral home to go to the gravesite, a ferocious cold wind tears into them. Felix hasn't felt winter yet. Autumn had been unseasonably warm and that warmth had stretched into early winter. Then he left for Africa. Now it is almost February.

The cold wind is sharp as a razor. But it's good, a life-affirming blast that Felix would have given anything for in the stifling daytime heat of West Africa. He opens his sport coat and lets the wind knife through his tie and shirt.

At the graveyard, while the punishing wind tears through the little tent where the body is lowered, relatives take turns shoveling dirt onto the casket. The tent sides ripple so loudly at times that no one can hear the rabbi.

Felix looks at his Mom. She's staring at the hundreds of headstones, a small crop of granite planted in long, neat rows. Now, his dad's spot in this garden of death is just a mound of dirt. But soon his headstone will decorate the place where they will come for years afterward to put their pebbles. The tombstone hasn't been made yet, but they've seen the model. A simple one: his name and the requisite numbers—birth date, death date. Numbers that speak only of a span of time, they could not be more direct or simple. But they cannot be further away from denoting the depth of the man, and the reduction, to Felix, at least, is insulting.

They walk back to the limousine and get in. Felix touches his mother's forearm.

"Are you all right, Mom?"

She doesn't say anything. She isn't crying; she hasn't cried all afternoon. Sitting in the car, her face slapped red from the wind, it looks like any tears she might have had have been frozen to her eyes.

"He died the way he wanted to, you know."

She closes her eyes.

"You know what I mean. I have to think he was happy. He was helping people. He was a hero, Mom. The Sierra Leonean government sent a letter of gratitude. Not many people

can say they'll have such a thing read at their funerals . . .
Mom, say something."

She shakes her head slowly and looks past him toward
the gravesite. "The son of a bitch," she whispers.

Not more than a month after the funeral, Rosemarie buys a
place on the beach in North Carolina. When she was packing up, Felix went often to the Baltimore house—once their
shared home—to help. At the end of those long days, she always asked if he wanted to stay. He never did.

He didn't want to stare at those familiar walls, look up
at that same ceiling in his old bedroom where he had memo-
rized every tiny crack and discoloration. He didn't want to be
in that room where his father had come and picked him up
and taken him outside to show him the night sky. It was there
where Felix had dreamed of far off lands, spurred on by a geography book his father had given him when Felix was very
young: *Children Around the World*. All those children in the
book had presumably grown up just as he had, and he imagined that they too had to deal with crises just as unpleasant as
what had taken him into his childhood home to pack up so
the one remaining parent could move away, so she could be
rid of the memories that had turned from happy to excruciating in one quick rebel attack in a camp across the ocean. So
each night, he went back to his apartment, unable to face the
weight of staying, opting instead to watch the shadows from
passing cars create swirling sand and rising dunes on the ceiling as he lay in bed, each ready to swallow him whole and
finish him off.

In his apartment in the morning, he wakes alone. No
Mom and Dad downstairs, coffee floating up to him like the

smell of all that is adult. No Lizzy next to him, the scent of her a transition to adulthood. No Issa, no Wesley, no clatter of pedestrians in the street below a hotel balcony. Instead, just wanting more than anything to be a child again, for everything to be simple and explainable. Of course, this desire for childhood retards his manly desires: namely, Lizzy. He will, he tells himself. He just . . . can't now. For whatever reason, he can't. Doesn't feel up to the task required of him.

So the next day, he goes back to his mom's—it has ceased being "his old house" or "his parents' house"—and helps her pack again. When he had moved into his apartment the year before, he left behind all the useless junk that had defined his youth: jump ropes, board games, stuffed jungle animals—things that hadn't been thrown away and sat on shelves in the basement waiting for resurrection. Now, his mother instructs him to toss them out. "Unless you have a need for them," she adds.

He doesn't.

So, as a final severance from youth, he throws out his things, keeping only *Children Around the World*.

Each night, he remembers his resolve to see Lizzy, but he still feels paralyzed and tells himself that he will do it the next day, only occasionally coming to terms with the reality: he is terrified she will reject him once and for all. And then what will be left him?

But it must be done. He gathers up his courage and calls her. She agrees to see him, but she suggests a public place. So Felix drives to the diner where Lizzy and he have arranged to meet. It promises the worst.

Now, when he needs her badly, when there is nothing left for him in this world but her, he knows it can't be. And he can't blame her in the least. He'd been the one who'd run off to Europe, in part to escape from the crushing numbness of stability. Traveling had been an excuse; retrieving his dad had been a convenience in its own way as well. But now he's done those things, and now he doesn't want to go anywhere for a long time; he would be content to sit forever in front of a window watching snow fall and having Lizzy lean against his chest, her hair falling over both of their shoulders. But of course he's done nothing to that end since he's been home. Had there been any chance before, surely Lizzy has given up on the idea by now. And he certainly can't blame her for that. He's been stupid. Very. But it's the sort of blinding clarity that comes only in hindsight and only way too late.

When he walks in, he sees her sitting by herself at a booth, a cup of coffee and a dozen torn sugar packets on the table. A long swoop of blonde hair hangs over the right half of her face. She looks as beautiful to him as the very first time they had made love, exhausted and open, vulnerable but strong.

When he approaches, she looks up and manages a little smile. It's purely from her lips, which means it's forced. Otherwise, little crinkles would have formed along the bridge between her eyebrows.

"I'm sorry, Lizzy."

"For what?"

"Everything." He looks at her, and she turns back toward her sugar. She runs a pinky through the piles, separating each and then reconstructing them.

"Lizzy, I love you so much."

"Let's not make it hard, Felix. Please." She tears open another sugar packet and the granules fly out, covering the table. She sweeps them up with her hands, making a little mound that she pinches and puts on her napkin.

He thinks about the desert again, the dunes like gargantuan sugar piles, about the fact that he'd almost died. What does she know about hard? Repairing a relationship between two people who have feelings for one another isn't hard. It should be the easiest thing in the world.

"So, what do we do? Let it devolve to the friend thing?" he asks.

"Does that ever work?"

"We can try."

"Until the first time we end up in bed. Then it's all screwy again. It doesn't work."

He wants to get up and scream, throw the weight of everything he's been through against the closed doors of Lizzy's heart, let her see how much it has changed him, has transformed him into someone she can spend the rest of her life with.

Of course, he doesn't know if any of that is actually true.

He opens his mouth, but nothing comes except half-formed syllables. She looks at him as one does an incurable stammerer, trying desperately to draw the words out. He feels a terrible rising anxiety bubbling to the surface, feels a little pop of synapses. He needs to beat it back, to simply keep it together in that diner that suddenly feels more foreign to him than any place he's ever been. All around him, ordinary people engaged in ordinary conversation, and yet they all seem to be in on some big joke—only he is on the periphery and nothing he can do will ever shatter the wall that separates them. He feels on the verge of passing out.

Lizzy continues to play with her sugar. Pathetic as it is, he can't bring himself to fight for her. He feels that he just doesn't deserve her. Paralysis. He doesn't know where he is, who he is, what he can do.

In a sad little pantomime, an attempt at normality, he picks up a menu and scans it, but nothing registers. He feels tingles of heat prickling his face. "Did you order?" he mutters.

"Just the coffee."

"I'll get coffee, too."

"How's your mother?"

"She's moving to North Carolina."

"Your poor mom."

He's trying to keep it together, beating back the impending feeling of losing consciousness. "Do you know that my dad was found with some other woman?"

Lizzy slowly shakes her head; this bit of information seems to sadden her deeply.

He stares at the sugar piles, restraining himself from sweeping them off the table in a grand—and foolish—flourish.

"So, we're done, huh?" he says.

Lizzy shrugs. She looks away, out the window—a hope perhaps of soon being in her car and driving away, the nastiness behind her and a chance to start a new life without him. Finally, and for real. She turns back, takes in his face just for a fleeting moment, and then looks down at her hands. She nods almost imperceptibly.

To her obvious relief, it is over. The rest is just a slow unwinding. But in the absence of a declarative statement from her, he isn't ready to give it up so easily. He just can't muster the strength—or any good argument in his favor—at the moment. But it is not over, he tells himself. Delusion or not. It is not over.

For now, they delve into normality. They talk about her job. She loves it, she tells him, even though it's ten times the work she thought it would be. Tactfully, she doesn't ask him about his job, or lack thereof. Instead, she asks if he wants to talk about Africa.

He tells her about Diffa and Issa and Wesley. She listens with the requisite detachment and, yes, liberation of someone who is no longer intimately involved in his life, peppering his stories with phrases like, "Wow. Were you scared?" and "That's crazy," instead of things like, "I wish I could have been there for you."

"So what do you do now?" she asks.

He shrugs. "I thought about going back to Africa. See where my dad died." His saying this surprises him; he doesn't know where it's come from and doesn't even know if it's true.

"Maybe you should go," Lizzy says. "You never went to the camp, right?"

He shakes his head, angry that she seems to think this is reasonable, hoping instead that she'd demand he stay, no matter how foolish such a hope is.

"But I want to stay here now . . . with you," he says, aware of the contradictions, feeling dizzy again as if life is happening just a step ahead of him, he following along disassociated and powerless, a sensation he knows from his time in Africa.

"It might be nice to see where your dad actually was. Get some closure maybe." She tears open another sugar packet and adds exactly half to her coffee, measuring it, weighing each granule it seems. This is something about her that used to drive him crazy—a controlling urge that simmers just below the surface, deliberate and suppressed. He saw it if they made love after a few glasses of wine. It was a little thing here and there—a playful but firm bite on his lower lip, a darting tongue across his chest and stomach. Just when he figured he was in for something amazing, something he'd never experienced from her before, she would draw again upon that endless well of composure. The bite would turn to a soft kiss, the tongue would retract and it would be months before she would do it again. He sees now how stupid and selfish he'd been, that these were the things about her that he decided he didn't like. Incredible. How small, and how inconsequential.

"Of course, going there could also make you feel worse," she adds.

He bites back his anger, his disappointment, his overwhelming desire for her. "I thought about that," he says. "I still don't really know exactly what he was doing there. I really don't know what happened to those people he was helping." He sips at his coffee. "I met a man," he continues. "One of the victims. But I didn't understand it all. All I know is that they had limbs chopped off because some wackos wanted their diamonds. Or access to the diamond mines. I'm not even sure. I don't know if my dad even knew. I guess he did."

Lizzy looks at him for the longest uninterrupted space of time since he'd arrived. His chest burns at her eyes. "Felix, I have to go," she says.

He deflates. It's over, and he lets her slip away without doing a thing. Complete inaction, something he's sure his dad wouldn't have allowed. He lays a ten on the table and gets up. Lizzy leaves her purse on the booth and he grabs it for her, placing it over her shoulder. "Thanks," she says.

When they get outside, he leans in to kiss her, but she turns her cheek and he lands somewhere between her ear and neck. She puts her hands around his shoulders and gives him a hug, which he reluctantly returns. In doing so, he inhales the scent of her and shudders to his marrow. He tries to squeeze her harder, but she shimmies away, lightly puts her hands to his chest. "You can call me," she says. "Let me know you're okay. Just give it a while."

He watches her walk away. There is nothing left for him here, he decides. Perhaps he *should* go. It's back to life. Mundane, routine, purposeless life. Twice it happens: early morning and some boor outside can't bring himself to walk to someone's door and knock. So he honks. And he honks, then honks some more. Little toots at first, increasing until they're long insistences. This lasts until Felix hears a door open in the lobby of his building. It closes with its recognizable thud, followed by a series of little taps.

It only occurs to him afterward to curse this idiot's laziness. In the haze of waking, before he's opened his eyes but after the noise of the horn, he's back in Africa. In Accra. In Bangui. Freetown. Places where horns honk incessantly, a way of speaking. He's in shabby hotels, his eyes closed but ready to face the new world, a place that thrills and scares the hell out of him all at once.

But then he opens his eyes and what he sees is a paper representation of these places on the wall at the foot of his bed. He's nowhere near Accra or Bangui or Freetown. He's in Baltimore and the thought of it depresses him. He imagines this might be similar to what soldiers feel like after coming home from war. Who do they talk to? What do they talk about? *I've been shot at. I've killed people. And some asshole is bitching about his cell phone service?*

So when the phone rings, he doesn't answer it. He checks to see if it's Lizzy and when it isn't—she doesn't call—he lets it ring. He drinks coffee, sometimes skips breakfast. He sits in his room and looks at maps. Sometimes he drifts over to Asia; sometimes he goes back over the places he's been in Europe. He finally gets around to pasting all his Europe pictures in photo albums. But he always winds up in Africa.

He goes to the library; he goes online. He reads everything he can about Sierra Leone, that it ranks dead last on the U.N.'s Human Development Report—in essence, the worst place in the world to live. This is a country with a capital city that once earned the moniker "The African Athens" for its top-flight universities and hospitals. But Britain's pullout and a series of corrupt governors who exploited the country's diamond wealth and of course, the civil war, have all conspired to drag this small country to the worst spot in the world, right behind Niger.

When he was in Niger, Felix gleaned some sense of why it was so low. It was a pathetically poor place, a country plagued by a desert landscape that guaranteed a lack of progress. But Sierra Leone is lush and near relatively wealthy and stable countries, Ghana and Côte D'Ivoire. And it had been a fine place, once. Not a place that slaughtered itself.

He reads about how some RUF rebels got a $150 "transition fee" to help them back into society. It's all very well and good—quite noble, in fact. Forget retribution, which only makes things worse.

But it's not enough for him. What about all the people they killed and maimed? What about the kids they conscripted, the ones who were forced to kill their own parents so that they could then be "adopted" by the rebels, to become RUF children? What about them, these kids who were at once victim and perpetrator, the ones who could never go back to their birth families after what they'd done, but whom their rebel "family" subsequently abandoned? They are on their own, left to deal with their transgressions by themselves. What about them, these orphans?

And what about people like his father?

Driven now with some sense of purpose, he reads about the Kimberley Process meeting in Ottawa, which had been set up by several governments and the diamond industry to stem the tide of rough stones extracted by terrorizing the local populace—cutting off limbs and such, something that has, for him, long ago ceased being some theoretical thing that happened somewhere far from home, an article in the morning paper forgotten by lunchtime. Kimberley is a nice step, but mere window dressing apparently, for even Sierra Leone itself doesn't seem to care all that much. All of the diamond-producing countries in the world sent a representative except one: Sierra Leone. Outrage from afar, by people like him who can't do a damn thing about it, is nothing but bottled fury that eats away at him and changes nothing.

The Kimberley Process and the pacts ending the civil war in Sierra Leone mean only that the rebels could no longer emerge from the bush to sell their stones to dealers in eastern towns like Kenema and Bo; instead, they just smuggle the diamonds to neighboring Liberia where the stones make their way to Antwerp, Tel Aviv, and New York.

And the diamond dealers there complain that the problem isn't theirs to solve. "Go to the source," one of the dealers says. "Go to Africa. Install governments that aren't hopelessly corrupt. Once these stones reach us, there is nothing we can do about it. We certainly aren't breaking any laws."

He decides that he must go back and *do* something. At first, it had just been something to say to Lizzy, to draw her into pleading with him to stay. But perhaps this is the very thing he should do. No more passivity. No sitting and stewing from afar; instead, he will go to Africa as his father had done. Make a difference in someone's life, as he is sure his father had.

The first thing he does is try and contact Dr. Albert. First, by phone, which gets him nothing. And then by email, which does net a response, but only after a few weeks.

There have been more poachers, a real epidemic. Twenty-six elephants have been massacred at the Bai by seventeen men armed with Kalashnikov rifles and calling themselves part of CAR's transitional government force. After the slaughter, locals harvested the meat from the carcasses.

The killing began with a single incident a few months earlier, but had increased at an alarming rate. Dr. Albert has been back to the site. In recent weeks, he's also been meeting with government officials not only in Bangui, but in Cameroon and Congo as well, as those two countries share the tripartite border in the Dzanga Reserve, Lobéké in Cameroon and Nouabalé-Ndoki in Congo, begging officials in these countries for increased security and support. Then, he is to head to China and Thailand to lobby those countries' governments to increase anti-ivory efforts.

Felix offers his condolences, and in response, Dr. Albert remembers to do the same, explaining why he was not at the funeral and why he will not be home for some time—he

does not know how long. Johns Hopkins has been very gener-
ous in allowing him to stay in Africa and go to Asia, though—
he points out—he would be willing to bear the expense himself for these animals.

There are no questions about what happened to Felix
in the desert, about the kidnapping, about anything that took
place after Dr. Albert last saw Felix back in Bangui. It's obvious
Dr. Albert has no idea, and it's obvious, too, that Wesley hadn't
told him a thing—whether out of a feeling that he'd failed his
boss by not smoothly executing his charge or, more likely Felix reasons, he hardly thought it worthwhile to mention. And
Dr. Albert, with full confidence in Wesley, no doubt assumed
all had gone to plan. Having heard nothing to the contrary,
why wouldn't he?

At the end of this last exchange, Felix does ask about
Wesley, hoping to elicit some understanding to all these questions, but there is no reply. Dr. Albert must be gone, subsumed
by the crisis. Understandable.

His mother calls Felix and tells him she's coming to Washington to stay with friends for a week. They decide to meet for
lunch, at the same place they'd met months earlier when he
first got home from Europe.

Felix gets there first. He orders a beer and grabs a
newspaper, flipping to the "World Roundup" section: Sixteen
Guatemalans killed in anti-government street protests; Sus-
pected Taliban fighters killed while setting a bomb; Twenty-one migrant Albanians drowned; A blast in central Indonesia killed four and wounded three; Attacks by Philippine
rebels resulted in seven deaths. There had been a time when
his father's murder would have garnered the same pitiful page

20 paragraph. Now, nothing.

"Did you still want to wait?"

He puts down the paper and looks at the waitress. His mother is forty minutes late. But then he sees her coming through the door. She's wearing a bright orange dress with a red scarf and a matching red hat. She sees him, waves, and, smiling, moves quickly toward the table. When he saw her last, she barely moved; every motion was labored and looked pained. Now she looks like she's shed weight, years, and gravity all in one.

"Here she is," he says, getting up.

Rosemarie kisses him and they hug briefly.

"Been waiting long?" she asks. Before he can answer, she turns to the waitress and asks if the iced tea is presweetened.

"No, I'm sorry," the waitress says.

"Good. I'll have one." The waitress walks away and his mother removes her hat and scarf. "How are you, darling?" she asks.

"I'm well. You look great."

"The sun. It does wonders. Even rainy days on the beach feel like sunny days. Though to tell you the truth, I can only remember one day when it rained."

"I heard from Dr. Albert. He says he was sorry he couldn't make it to the funeral."

"It sure took him long enough. Well, what does it matter now? Is he back in Baltimore?"

"No. He's still in Africa."

She makes an indistinct noise—irritation, bemusement, something temporarily stuck in her throat—it's impossible to decipher. She grabs a menu. "I'm absolutely famished," she says. "Oh, I almost forgot." She puts the menu down and rummages through her purse. She pulls out an envelope and places it on the table. "Here," she says.

"What is it?"

"It's money. Your father's money. It's what belongs to you. There's more of that in trust funds. You'll get it when you turn twenty-five. We can go over the details someday. Just not now."

"Whenever," Felix says. He opens the envelope. It's a check for $86,712. He folds it and puts it in his coat pocket. The numbers don't fully register. They don't equal having his Dad back—a billion dollars wouldn't.

"He left a bundle of it to that organization, by the way."

"Doctors Without Borders?"

"That's right."

"That's admirable."

"You think so? What's admirable, Felix, is not running away from your family. That's admirable. Living up to your responsibilities. That's admirable. Living the life that you promised to live. That's admirable."

The waitress returns and places the iced tea in front of his mother. She takes a sip and lets out a long, satisfied sigh.

"Enough, Mom."

"What?"

"Stop trashing him. You act like you didn't know him at all. You married him. You knew exactly what kind of man he was."

"The man I married is not the same one who ran off to Africa."

"He didn't 'run off.' He was helping people."

"That was an excuse, Felix. Don't be naïve."

"I know he hurt you, Mom. But—"

"You don't know the half of it. Damn it, Felix. Stop defending him!"

"Forget it. Fuck this." He gets up abruptly, his chair spilling theatrically behind him. He doesn't bother to pick it up, but walks out of the restaurant and leaves her by herself.

A light drizzle has started. Through the condensation on the window, he can see his mother at the table, a lonely and dejected figure, completely deflated and beaten. One little action on his part has wiped away all that she's done toward healing since the funeral. A severe bitterness still simmers close to the surface, of course, but she's getting on with her life. How can he begrudge her that, in whatever form it takes?

When it's clear Felix isn't coming back, Rosemarie gathers her purse and walks outside. Without saying a word, she pulls a plastic head covering out of her purse and secures it to her chin.

"I'm sorry," he whispers.

She purses her lips, exhales audibly, and nods, acting as if the whole affair is behind them. She steps to the curb to hail a taxi.

"So, what are you going to do now?" she asks.

"I don't know. I suppose I should be getting a job, right?"

"Felix, if you're looking for me to give you grief for being unemployed, so you can pretend I'm pressuring you to get a job—"

"Forget it."

She puts her hand on his forearm. "Know that I love you, Felix. It's just . . . it's difficult. You are your father."

"Should I see you again before you go back to North Carolina?"

"I'll call you." A taxi pulls to the curb. She moves toward it. "So, you never said—what are you really going to do now?" she asks. "You're not through with Africa, are you?"

He realizes now that this has been no recent decision. Not really, anyway. It has been simmering all along, practically from the moment he got home. Giving anything to be back in the States, safe and sound, the minute he arrived he felt the pull to go back. That he hadn't seen where his father was killed—it gnawed at him, almost from the very second he got on that C-130 and it lifted off from Freetown.

"I don't know. I just don't know."

"Clearly not," she says.

He shrugs his shoulders.

"Be careful. Please," she whispers, and then slams the taxi door before he can respond. It might be the rain on the window, but it looks as if she's crying.

Felix thinks through how he can make this a possibility. Dr. Albert is not an option. Hank Peters? Should he simply fly back to Freetown, figure it all out once he gets there?

Then he thinks of one more possibility.

Back at home, Felix starts by contacting the United Nations, describing Issa (he doesn't know the last name, he explains), a soldier from Niger, used to work at the U.N. in New York. Lives in Niamey.

The United Nations cannot or will not confirm or deny the employ of those working in sensitive areas, for their own security, he is told.

He searches online and finds nothing. He thinks of a Niamey phone book, but none exists. Finally, after explaining the situation to the primary representative at State that his mother had dealt with, they are able to turn up an email address, one used when Issa Manzo communicated with Hank Peters in Freetown. Flushed with excitement, Felix fires off a message, one he labors over for hours. He doesn't really know this man. Their time together has a haze of surreality around it, and it visits him generally only in his dreams or on the periphery of his thoughts as his mind wanders.

How is he? What has he been doing? How is the weather? Finally, what are his thoughts about a visitor? Felix explains that he'd like to come back to Freetown, asking Issa if perhaps there is any way they can meet, remembering that Issa said he was doing work in Sierra Leone, a truth and reconciliation commission or a war crimes tribunal, something like that.

But there is no response.

So he lapses back into inertia, living life like a war-wounded himself—shell-shocked, riven with PTSD. He sits around and reads, takes long hikes at a nearby reservoir, avoids everyone and everything. He doesn't think about a job, even when he empties his bank account so that he can go grocery shopping. He subsists on spaghetti and canned tuna, and doesn't worry in any case. There's the check; he's just not ready to deposit it yet.

Then, finally, almost a month after he'd sent his email, the response arrives:

> Felix:
> It was nice to receive your message. I have wondered from time to time what has become of you and if everything went as planned back in your home. In fact, I will be going to Sierra Leone and of course I can have you as my

guest. Forgive the long time in my reply, but I had been in Israel, which I can explain. I will be at my home in Niamey the third week of this month and we can meet there. We will go to Sierra Leone by road and not plane, which I will also explain. In short and to answer your question, you are most welcome to come see me in Niger and we will go to Sierra Leone together. I am happy to have the chance to see you again. There is much I can show you.

Most Sincerely, Issa Manzo

## CHAPTER THREE

Niamey's Hamani Airport again, and it is, of course, the same: hot, full of loitering people, shoe shine boys, persistent and hopeful even in the face of Felix's sneakers.

But this time there is Issa, standing in front of a blue Jeep, leaning with his hand against the hood. A young woman, smiling bashfully and putting her hand over her mouth when she laughs, stands in the space between the car and the crook of his arm. Behind Issa and the girl, two men stride past trailing a camel with sacks of flour tied to its back.

The girl looks at Felix. Issa turns around. "Felix!" he exclaims. He sends the girl on her way. She stops smiling, shoots Felix an unfriendly look, and walks off.

"I didn't want to interrupt."

"Nonsense. I am glad you are here, my friend." He throws his arm around Felix's shoulder. Felix flinches, an involuntary movement that emanates from the fact, he suddenly realizes, that he's actually quite scared of this whole affair. In his zeal to do *something*, he now feels that this something might be very, very foolish. Fortunately, Issa doesn't seem to notice. He grabs Felix's bag. "You do not mind standing out?" he asks, putting the bag in the back of the Jeep.

"Powder blue."

"It is U.N.. One of the old ones. Powder blue used to assure safety. Not anymore. Just the opposite probably."

Felix nods. *What on earth am I doing? I barely even*

*know this guy.* Before he came, he'd looked at the maps again: a drive from Niamey to Freetown seemed insane—some 2,300 miles through unstable terrain, both physical and geopolitical. And yet it promised excitement, movement, a break from the crushing inertia his life had become. But now that it is becoming reality . . .

Issa fills the entire fifteen-minute ride into town with almost one long, staccato speech—he appears nervous, almost frenzied. Felix listens quietly, trying to take it all in, vacillating again between fear and relief, trepidation and excitement. First, Issa apologizes for the scare in the desert. "I am sorry about Tombou," he says. "That stupid boy. But he got his. He died after he left you there."

Felix looks at him, trying to gauge whether he's being straight. Tombou hadn't left Felix there, of course—Tombou had been killed. Doesn't he know?

"You remember your friend Wesley?"

"Not really 'my friend.'"

"He is very much alive, it turns out. He works for Executive Outcomes."

"Who?"

"A privately trained militia, for hire. I know because I used to work for them myself. It's what brought me to Sierra Leone in the first place."

"I think I remember my friend Dr. Albert telling me something about them. How do you know what happened to Wesley?"

Issa looks at him for a long moment. "I think there is a lot you do not know. And to tell you the truth, Felix, you do not need to." He slaps Felix's leg. "It is not a problem for you."

Issa continues: after Felix told him he was coming

back to Africa and that he might like to see the camp where his dad worked, Issa got in touch with Alexandre Grillet, a doctor with *MSF*. They would be expected there. Even if Felix hadn't come, Issa explains, he was heading to Freetown anyway to continue his U.N. work for the Truth and Reconciliation Commission.

"Israel?" Felix asks.

"Yes, that." He had been in Israel to check conformity of the Kimberley Process to assure that the stones coming into Tel Aviv were not blood diamonds. He ticks off the countries affected by the trade; it isn't only Sierra Leone, but also Angola, Congo, Liberia, Guinea. "It is good things are being done, but it is a sham, Felix. The procedures do little. I go to Israel. They show me the certifications. The stones are clean. But these do not account for the diamonds that are smuggled, the ones that never reach the certification stage. Four hundred million dollars through Brazzaville alone last year. Do you know that Liberia produces almost no diamonds? Yet last year, they exported 600 million carats. That is like Luxembourg becoming a member of OPEC." After telling Felix this, they spend the only silent minute of the ride. Soon, Issa is back at it, talking quickly, even a bit maniacally.

He'd had a terrible experience on the flight home from Israel, he explains. The plane barely crossed the Mediterranean and made an emergency landing in Tunis, where Issa had to stay for two days. He was sure he was going to die on that plane. "Me, Felix. The great African lion who cannot die. I was sure it was my time. No more planes for me I am afraid. It is the first time, since I was a child, that I felt truly vulnerable. I do not wish to repeat that." He took one of the crazed truck transports across the Sahara, back to Niger. It took more than a week, but sleeping under the stars had served to calm him.

"I understand that," Felix says.

Issa laughs.

He outlines the plan: they will spend a day or so together in Niamey and then drive to Sierra Leone. They have to go to various consulates and pick up their visas to cross into a whole host of West African countries, including Sierra Leone. That is a process that can normally take ages, but Issa had already been busy getting everything in order.

Issa prepares Felix for what lay ahead. Many days in the truck. Sleeping at checkpoints while guards come on duty three hours late, if at all. A circuitous route; coup attempts have taken place in Burkina Faso. "This time, though, it is outside forces mostly," Issa explains. "Nigerians. They are fighters. All the time. Fighting. And the corruption. We will avoid Nigeria. A straight line into Benin. And then west. Togo. Accra, in Ghana. Côte D-Ivoire . . . I hope it is okay we are driving. The plane . . . I just cannot take that chance again. I cannot explain the feeling."

"It's okay."

"We will go around Liberia, and into Guinea. Then it is Freetown, just an ocean from your home in Baltimore."

Felix smiles. The trip will be long, but they will see much. Despite his ambivalence, Felix finds the idea thrilling. After all, he reasons, he has no time constraints, nowhere he has to be.

"It will be a long trip. But we will make it to the camp. That is my promise to you," Issa says.

"I don't doubt you for a second."

"From there, I am off to the mines. And you go home."

This is disappointing to Felix, far off as it is. Issa is doing a lot for him and he doesn't want to impress himself upon him indefinitely, but he manages to meekly suggest that he might be interested in seeing the mines also.

"No," Issa says flatly.

"Why not?"

"The camp is bad. It is terrible, in fact. Enough to make a man cry. But the mines . . . no. The mines are the worst places in the world."

"But . . ."

"No."

Felix sits back, considers, thinks to protest, but the matter—at least for the moment—appears well and settled. He'll work on Issa another time, he reasons. They drive past the Grand Market and the stadium, all recognizable to Felix, and reach Issa's house on the Rue de Maroc. Issa throws Felix's gear in the spare room, offers him some water, and back out they go.

Felix is tired from traveling, but Issa is buzzing.

"I want to get you something," he says. "Follow me."

They pass men and women, camels and donkeys, merchants and craftsmen.

Massive pieces of cut up meat, hoisted and moved by chains and pulleys clangs behind an open door. But these aren't the sides of beef found in American slaughterhouses; ribs hold just the slightest bits of red meat, spine is visible, femurs protrude. Boys wait to carry away pieces of the carcass hacked into small bits by a man in a blood-spattered apron expertly wielding a large knife.

A boy sells cigarettes, by the pack and individually— VISA, Magnum, 555, Rothman's. Two veiny branches propping up a white cloth shade the boy and his wares. He's tall and angular, his limbs sticking out beneath his white robe. He smiles, revealing a perfect set of white teeth and sharp cheekbones. He nods his chin at Felix and smiles again. And in that one small gesture, Felix settles a bit more into a state of ease, remembering that this is a place he has been before, one that he needn't be scared of. It's a somewhat irrational thought, he knows, but he also tells himself that his father certainly wouldn't have been scared. And that makes a world of difference.

They come to the Grand Market, a place they'd passed on the previous trip but hadn't gone into. The boxed walls of the market rise up in arcs above them. The vaulted ceilings provide relief from the scorching sun, even as streaks of light shine through, falling on yards of light cotton clothes. Felix's sneakers slide across the sand-covered tile flooring. Away from the main gates, the modern buildings of downtown stand straight ahead on the Rue de Kalleye. Felix knows that somewhere in there is the hospital, the one where he'd been after the desert. The thought of it makes him shudder.

"Come on. I want to get you something," Issa repeats.

They walk to one of the enclosed stalls and Issa picks up a silver cross hanging from a black and tan chord. It's a beautiful and substantial piece, decorated with a circle on top and little clubs protruding from each end, a center diamond design etched with straight lines. "This is an Agadez silver cross," Issa explains. "The Tuareg give them as good luck in life and on journeys. It will become a memento of the better times that we will share." He puts it around Felix's neck and clasps it.

"Thank you."

The metal piece falls heavily against Felix's neck. Its

weight feels good, solid, substantial.

A place that couldn't have felt more distant from home in the first phase of his life, when he still had a father, suddenly feels like something, incredibly, close to home.

They're off by five the morning of their departure from Niamey, heading straight south, intending to arrive in Cotonou, Benin around eight p.m. In the beginning, the trip burns for Felix, hyper-aware as he is of everything they pass. The short, stubbed mountains of the Akatora range like his Western Maryland Appalachians, except no green reflective highway signs, no fast food pull-offs, no sleek black asphalt. A rich brown instead, a brown he imagines would chew them up had it been raining.

They cross into Benin on the way to Kandi, forsaking the river crossing at Mandaville. The place names are for Felix as exciting as the first dirty limericks he had learned as a kid; the incredible joy of being able to utter them: *Gogounou; Ndali;* conical huts dotting the countryside; *Parakou,* where they pass through the Marché International Arzeke, with women wearing clothing every color in a Crayola box and men on motorbikes with blazing lemon license plates; *Tchaourou; Kokoro; Savalou;* the slave coast outside *Ouidah,* where wall murals depict the trade in humans.

"It is still sad in Ouidah," Issa says. The dirt path to the ocean, where the captured were disoriented before being jammed into ships, the ancestors of the children Felix sees back home in Baltimore. Ouidah is a hotbed of voodoo; it is from here that it was exported to the New World, Issa explains.

Cotonou at dusk—the blue haze of exhaust in the air. The electric yellow shirts of the motorbike drivers. "*Zemi-*

*djan,*" Issa says, pointing. "Forty thousand of them." The wristwatch and cigarette sellers are packing up. Spots of neon. A hotel room with cracking plaster. From the open window, Felix hears drumming, sees pinpoints of firelight outside the city.

A weevil the size of his fist reposes near his head when Felix wakes in the morning. Even as Felix jumps back, only the thing's long antennae move. It sits on his pillow until Issa flicks it against the wall, where it smacks, falls onto its back, rights itself in an impressive gymnastic display, and scurries under the bed. Felix pours a tub of hot water over his head in the hall's one bathroom.

They are off again. West Africa's version of urban sprawl spreads all along the highway. Young girls offer themselves as Felix and Issa approach the border. Lines of vehicles wait to cross into Togo. Issa gets out and walks to the guard station. He shows I.D.; a man follows him back to the car and they move to the front, the man directing everyone else to move to one side or the other so that Issa's Jeep can pass—no one protests; this is the way things are done, apparently. Issa thanks the man, hands him money, and they are on their way. Country number three. It will be quick, this little slit of land between Benin and Ghana, a small claim to ocean like New Hampshire between its larger neighbors.

Passing through Lomé, looking like Miami's destitute stepchild. Beachfront. Helmeted bike riders. Hotels. A woman relieving herself on the beach. Police officers everywhere, directing traffic, looking as if they are just waiting to bust someone's skull. Traffic stops. People honk. Issa turns off, guiding through the poor neighborhoods—tin shacks and barefoot children—just off the beachfront blocks. Massive, big-breasted women nursing kids who look like they're easily five or six years old.

And then they are gone again, through an easy crossing into Ghana, this after a potential hassle averted on the road in Togo. There, when they stop at a police checkpoint, a man steps out of the booth, a rifle hanging lazily in his hand, and demands to know where they've come from and where they're headed. Absurd, really—there's only one possibility in either direction. His palm rests on the underside of his rifle butt. The end of the rifle peeps just inside the window, an inch from Issa's chin. Sweat pours from the man's face and his forearms glisten. "*Passage est 20,000 CFA,*" the man says. Issa reaches in his pocket, but he doesn't pull out money. Instead, he hands the man a laminated picture of himself with his name printed underneath. The man takes it, looks at Issa, back at the badge, and back at Issa again. "*Pardon. Je regrette, monsieur,*" he says, handing back the ID and placing the rifle over his shoulder.

"*Pas de probleme,*" Issa replies, and then hands the man some money.

"*Non, non, non,*" the man says, backing off.

"*J'insiste le sur.*" The man takes the money and shoves it in his pocket without counting. The two exchange friendly words, smile, clasp hands, and Issa and Felix are off again.

Ghana is a new world: sea breezes meet them through the open windows. Felix remembers his maps: this is the Gold Coast, the Ivory next, and the Grain after. They've left the Slave Coast, and the freshness in the air, the parting of the clouds above, seems divinely orchestrated. Felix buys a dozen oranges from a girl missing her two front teeth. She tells him her cousin in Tema sells mangoes, to look out for her. He promises he will.

Issa has no interest in staying in Accra more than a day; he explains to Felix that he is going to attend a conference with World Bank officials and then they'll be gone the next morning. Felix will be on his own, a welcome respite from the road and an opportunity to see some of the city.

During his one afternoon in Accra, he wanders the center of town, pulled by persistent hammerings, until he finds the source: an open-air workshop with men making coffins in myriad and incredible shapes: a Coke bottle, a chili pepper, a book, a Ghana Airways airplane, each, he is told, designed to reflect what the privileged deceased did in life: grocer, farmer, professor, pilot.

He stumbles upon the Timber Fetish Market. Emerging from a labyrinth of alleys—a place he wouldn't be able to find again in a thousand years—he gapes at the stalls in front of him. One table has two monkey hands, cut off at the wrists and clutching flowers. Behind the hands is a row of animal skulls, some with sunken faces, others with protruding muzzles and teeth that stick out at all angles. There are powders, charms, leopard skins, bowls of teeth, and row after row of juju figurines. He can hear his father's voice: "Enjoy it, Tiger. It's Africa."

"You want to cast a spell?" a lady at a booth asks.

A thought forces its way to the front of his brain—are there any potions for bringing people back to life?

"I don't think I need a spell," he says.

She points to a white powder. "I have used this to give my brother-in-law the head burn."

"What's the head burn?"

"Makes the scalp feel like it is on fire."

"What did he do to deserve that?"

"He was with a woman other than my sister."

The woman points to different bowls, each containing copious amounts of herbs and powders. "For impotence, to make someone stop gossiping, to make someone lose their hair." She shows Felix a neighboring kiosk where a row of medium-sized amulets hang from nails hammered into a plank.

"This one is so the woman can't resist you."

"I don't need any potions for that."

The woman laughs very hard, her entire body quivering in little ripples of flesh.

"Maybe," he says.

She grabs one and shows it to him. It is a little piece of wood with a tiny, hinged door on it. She opens the door to reveal a leathery piece of something that looks like a balled fruit roll-up.

"What is it?" he asks.

"Monkey fetus."

"Sorry?"

"Come on, boy. Do not be a little woman." She laughs again. "You make your wish for love—say it to the monkey, but not out loud. When you are done, close the door and the wish will come true."

"Then what do I do with it?"

"You take it home with you. It is your souvenir of Ghana, and when you are there with your love, you can look at this and thank it."

He thinks fleetingly of Lizzy, but says nothing to the fetus. He'll take it—why not?—and perhaps one day . . .

He thanks the woman, pays for the fetus, and asks his way back toward the hotel.

Passing Independence Square, he sees Issa through

a plate glass window in a restaurant, sitting with three white men in business suits. He waves, but when Issa looks out at him—Felix is sure he can see him—he doesn't react.

Issa is angry and sad when he returns to the hotel. The great finding of the conference, he says: Africa will not meet the U.N.'s millennium goals set for 2020, already extended because 2015 had been deemed a way too ambitious dream. The goals, he says, include cutting in half the number of people who live on less than a dollar a day and halving the number of people, in the many millions, who don't have clean water. It is simply too great a prospect, they realize now.

Felix doesn't tell him that he saw him in the restaurant, doesn't ask him who those men were. It feels to him like he isn't supposed to know. And Issa doesn't bring it up.

As they leave Accra behind, Felix doesn't bother to turn around. They are still three days from Freetown.

They follow the road out of the Ghanaian capital and into the Ivory Coast. Plantations of banana trees stretch out in every direction. Just outside of Abidjan groups of kids push rocks around holes in the roads and then demand payment for "fixing" the roads and making passage possible. Issa flips them coins. The kids scramble for them.

Further north these operations subside, replaced by joyous moments as they follow the paved highway up to the new capital, Yamoussoukro, where large groups of children wearing tattered Western t-shirts whoop and wave as they drive by. Issa honks as they leap about in the air, some of them turning expert cartwheels. They are only one night in Yamoussoukro, which lacks the stateliness and electricity of Abidjan, the old capital. Only the massive palace and basilica they can see from the hotel give off signs of life, people milling in large groups outside. A quick in and out; a total haze besides.

Onto higher lands, full of hill and thick forest, out to Danane, where lines of battered, struggling cars await passage into Liberia.

But they cut northward, climbing with their trusty vehicle into the mountains, making the pass into Guinea in the shadows of Mount Nimba to get the road south out of Nzerekore directly to Freetown. A crude roadblock at Guinea: a huge branch jammed into small posts with a sign instructing drivers to turn off their engines. They pass with only a small *cadeau* to the post man.

Tall yellow flowers. Soaring birds above, galloping goats below. Stopping at dusk as herdsmen let their cattle rest on the highway, soaking up the lingering heat of the day. That is when Issa and Felix sleep, the Jeep their moving hotel, kitchen, washroom. The food they took from Niamey has run out and all they could buy in Guinea was couscous and manioc, like eating a cardboard box. Plantains constitute dessert. Bathroom breaks are in the woods. Reclining seats for beds, blankets pulled tightly up to their necks.

During those increasingly rare moments when Felix manages to stay awake, he watches the little towns tick by with that old, familiar feeling that he recalls from trains in Europe: inconsequential places that had once been centers, justifying stops on the rail or bus line—little towns where real people live and work, love and die, but don't show up on many maps—places where the bus and the train no longer stop at night, gliding through instead in the darkness where diminutive name plates still trumpet the place—places that seem only to exist as figments, to lend authenticity to a set created for a young, wide-eyed American.

But his eyes are becoming increasingly closed, and the crossing into Sierra Leone doesn't distinguish itself as some goal reached, doesn't feel any more significant than anything else. Even the checkpoint guard is half asleep. He stamps the passports without any questions. Aside from the checkpoint, all that tells Felix that they have reached their final country is the increasingly strong signal of the Sierra Leone Broadcasting System.

Passing through the jungle, he sees quick twitches—a tiny red speck, a slither of green, a beat of black wing. But when he tries to fix on the object, it is gone, moving back into the jungle and out of his vision. Downcountry, the jungle recedes. Women and kids disappear. Instead, it is all barefoot teenagers and young men wearing tattered camo jackets and carrying rifles and bullet clips. A scene that becomes more and more surreal—a potential horror show that feels unreal to Felix, like he's watching it on a movie screen. Freetown is less than a day away and already the place feels sick. A country just emerging from war, with a tenuous hold on sanity. It feels like chaos might erupt at any second. Old farms left fallow, turned into huge mud pits, dotting the countryside. This is the general scene all the way until Freetown.

Beyond Daru, they come to Kenema, then Bo, large towns that barely register. Felix only remembers them as semi-familiar place names that he'd read about back home, places that mean little to him as they pass—simply more names, now in the hundreds.

But they will soon become the most meaningful places he's ever been. They will dwarf even Freetown, even the camp where his dad was murdered, where they stop at the end of this very, very long trip.

# CHAPTER FOUR

Felix was in college when his Dad called to tell him the news: "I'm going to Africa."

"Finally," Felix said, picturing him and his mother in the back of an open-topped Land Cruiser, khaki-clad with binoculars dangling from their necks.

"Freetown."

"Sierra Leone?"

"That's right," his dad responded, sounding impressed.

"What's in Sierra Leone?"

"I've volunteered to work with amputees at a camp run by Doctors Without Borders."

"That's noble."

"These are the people butchered in the civil wars, victims of the diamond wars. These are the people who lost their limbs. The result is that other people like me can buy eight thousand dollar diamond tennis bracelets."

Just a few months before this call, Felix had been home over winter break during the last weekend of Hanukkah. His mother was proudly showing off just such a bracelet.

"I returned it, by the way," his father said.

"I assume Mom was none too pleased."

"Your mother has a sense of right and wrong."

"How does she feel about going to West Africa?"

"She's not coming with me, Felix."

When his dad added Felix's name to a sentence, that

meant gravity. When he was a kid, it was "Tiger." Then, when Felix captained the team that won the Maryland state soccer championship three years in a row in high school, he was "Double S," for "Superstar." But since, his dad called him nothing at all usually. Maybe a "Son" here and there, but only in times of crisis did he call Felix by his name—only for such occasions as, "Felix, Grandpa died," or "She's not coming with me, Felix."

He asked if he could speak to his mother and, without explanation, his father said that she couldn't come to the phone. Felix pictured her sitting on the floor of the bathroom, a crumpled tissue in her hand, her elbow resting on the closed toilet seat, her usually perfect hair a mess in her hands.

The camp where he wound up was at Murraytown. This much Felix does know. But once his father had gone, Felix didn't hear from him afterward and all that was left him were terrible imaginings. But now he's close and able, finally, to see for himself.

Passing Siaka Stevens Stadium, they get the Main Motor Road toward White Man's Bay. The camp is on the outskirts of the city, past a collection of old Victorian clapboards, modern and destroyed buildings left to rot in the sun, and ubiquitous banks. Past the "power station," men on their haunches selling bags of charcoal and stacks of wood; vendors selling brown sandals and star apples; men dipping cloth into boiling vats of dye.

Felix steels himself for what's coming. But they arrive quickly, and before he can even register what's happening, they're at the entrance, marked by a large satellite dish astride a palm tree not far from the crude official signage: "Vulnerable Group Feeding Programme. Aberdeen Road."

Issa makes his way quickly to the entrance. But at the gates, he stops. He inhales deeply, puffing out his chest, and steadying himself as if ready to jump off a bridge. Sweat covers his face. With great agitation, he rolls up his sleeves, then rolls them back down, struggling over the buttons on the cuffs, before finally taking off his overshirt and wrapping the sleeves around his waist.

"Let's go," he says, and they step into the camp.

Felix had expected a swirl of activity. But few people move. A young boy missing one arm up to his elbow and four fingers from his other hand stares without embarrassment at the new arrivals. He has no doubt seen the likes of Felix before; he probably mistakes him for an earnest journalist or NGO person, people who file their reports and gnash their teeth at night because no one back home seems to really give a shit. Surely this boy can't know that Felix is at the camp because his dad has been killed here.

Beyond these few people, only the sides of the tents whipping in the wind move. But the wind isn't refreshing. Instead, it's brutally hot. Felix hadn't noticed it being so suffocating in town, even though there was more smog there. Here the entire atmosphere is suffused with oppression.

"All this for the diamonds?"

"Diamonds are essentially worthless," Issa says, organizing the contents of his bag. "They are only good for cutting hard things."

"What about all the jewelry?"

"Good marketing."

A man hobbles by on crutches.

"Amputations are forever," Issa says. He forces a laugh, but it's choked. He looks around nervously, so much so that

Felix has almost forgotten his own trepidation. "Are you okay?" he asks.

"Look, Felix. This is difficult. For me and for you."

"Yes."

"But this is not about me, no. This is not even about you. Is it?"

"I'm not sure what you mean."

"Just remember that these are human beings. Okay? People come here and they act like it is a zoo."

Felix nods.

"These are the people your father helped. You should be proud of that."

He is, of course. But it all still seems so far away from everything he knows about his father. He just can't see him here. This place is incongruous with a man who was rarely without his sheepskin slippers or his tweed cap, objects designed solely for comfort or fashion. Yes, he was willing—even desirous—of setting out to the world's harsh places. But he always enjoyed, even required, physical comfort.

They walk toward what looks to be the main tent. In front, a dozen or so children missing some body part or another play a game with stones in the dirt.

When they see Issa and Felix approach, the children come at them, either by their own legs or on the ground, dragged along with great speed by nimble knuckles. They shout and tug on the newcomers' clothing.

"You have to ignore it," Issa says, gently steering a small child off his leg. "You cannot help."

Felix follows his directions, looking away as the kids stare after him, away even from the little girl who looks from where he stands to be absolutely whole and intact, beaming an irresistible smile. Tiny braids stand out at every angle on her head. But when she turns to face him, he sees that her right arm is gone. Her smile turns to something shy, the eyes looking to the ground when Felix's catch hers. But it isn't shame or embarrassment in her eyes; she probably isn't old enough to know yet that she is all that different from girls elsewhere in the world. The eyes look away, but do they register any recognition before they turn? Does she see some of that older white man, the one who had been killed, in this young one?

The sun is relentless and punishing. Felix's arms have turned red, flush with sun and heat. He feels an immediate twinge of guilt, sorry for his easily-burnt white skin, skin that dictates that he was born elsewhere and not in Sierra Leone, guilty for having two long, unbroken arms soaking up the sun.

Issa taps his shoulder and motions forward. They enter the main tent, where a doctor tends to a man missing his left hand.

"Hello, Doctor Grillet," Issa says.

"Issa. *Bonjour.*"

"This is Felix Lazlo. His father was—"

"A good man." Dr. Grillet rubs his hands up and down the man's forearm, kneading his flesh like a masseuse. He looks at Felix. "Your father did a lot of good work for people like Mohammed here."

"You were here the day that it happened?" he asks.

"When he was killed? No, I was in town." Dr. Grillet points with his chin to Mohammed. "We can talk about this later, yes?"

Felix nods. "Yes, sorry."

Issa pulls a small tape recorder out of his bag. "You

think you can tell your story?"

Mohammed nods.

"Okay, we will wait outside," Issa says.

They walk out and sit down in the dirt. "It is important that we talk to people like him. It is for this." Issa hands Felix a miniaturized paper, laminated and stuck inside a little black wallet like what a private investigator might carry.

Felix reads it out loud: "Lomé. Article XXVI: Human Rights Violations. A Truth and Reconciliation Commission shall be established to address impunity, break the cycle of violence, provide a forum for both the victims and perpetrators of human rights to tell their story, and get a clear picture of the past in order to facilitate genuine healing and reconciliation." He hands it back.

Issa puts it back in his pocket. "You see how that is written? 'Victims *and* perpetrators.' The man who has his hands chopped off must welcome back the man who did it. 'Facilitate genuine healing.' This is a lawless society. There will be no genuine healing." He spits on the ground. "But we talk to Mohammed for more important reasons. As much as his testimony can be useful for war crimes later, it helps to show that we understand his story, that he has a voice. There is a lot of good work going on here. Men like your father, they are important." A distant look comes over Issa. "Me, too. I need to do this," he says. "I need to be better."

"I understand."

He snaps back, looking at Felix as if seeing him for the first time, the fog of whatever is gnawing at him distant now, suppressed.

"Did you see that man we passed in front of the mirror?" he asks, regaining himself. "He practices using the other side of his body. He watches himself so he can use a limb someday. A lot of them do not want the limb. It feels worse than the missing piece itself because they cannot use it. They prefer the hooks."

Mohammed comes and sits in the dirt. He has an air of restraint about him, nodding to all who pass without a gleam of anger or resignation in his eyes. They are alive eyes, in fact, ones that have not bowed under the weight of the world. Even Dr. Grillet's don't look as lively.

"Before the war, Mohammed was a barber in the east," Issa tells Felix.

"All of the men in the camp, they get their hair cut by me," Mohammed says. He smiles, the tremendous smile of one who is either utterly without a care in the world or doped to the gills. "I wanted to die after they took it," he says. "But now I can laugh and see the funny side of things." Mohammed's ability to laugh at things depresses Felix even more than if he had said the opposite. He pities Mohammed, and he immediately hates himself for pitying him.

From early on, his father had warned him off pity. He was a kid—maybe five or six—when it first registered to Felix that the man with the yellowed beard and wool cap who asked for money one day near the Inner Harbor didn't have any home to go to. He explained that he slept behind the walls of the Holocaust Memorial. "Some of the others used to piss there," the homeless man said. "But I remind them that it is a sacred place. Because you're living on the streets doesn't mean you have to lose all humanity." Felix's dad gave him a ten-dollar bill.

On the way home, he explained that we do things to make ourselves feel better, that a truly unselfish act is a rare and difficult thing to execute. But it doesn't so much matter why we do things, so long as the end result is a good one. "A lot of people would give that man money only if he promised to spend it on food instead of alcohol or something else. When you have your own money, Felix, and you want to help someone like that, don't give him instructions. There is nothing worse than losing your dignity. You should always have some pride in yourself. When you've lost that, all the other things don't matter so much. So if you want to give a man money, just give it to him. Do you understand what I'm saying to you, son?"

Felix nodded.

"Pity is patronizing. That means that it's not nice to feel sorry for someone else. If you feel that way, then you should help him. Otherwise, there is nothing you can do." As he told him this, they passed another man standing on the street corner. They didn't stop, didn't give him any money. And his dad didn't have to tell Felix why. You can't save everyone. You do what you can, and that's all you can do.

Still, it's hard to suppress. Felix walks a few paces into the path that runs the length of the camp. He tries to imagine his father walking into these tents, seeing where he could have slept, eaten, writing him the only letter Felix ever received from him in Africa—a terse, one paragraph note telling him that he'd started, paradoxically, to believe in God. A God who allows this horror, but who makes his plan known to men like his father, who finally, for the first time in his life, he wrote, knew exactly what he was on this planet to do.

Felix turns back to Issa and Mohammed and almost runs into a man who stands his ground in front of him. His hands are gone. He has no prostheses. He doesn't speak.

Felix stares directly at the stumps. It is no surgery, no clean cut. The shining skin is tough and loose, little folds and pieces hanging about the tightened sections. It looks as if someone has threaded the flesh with twine and then ripped it out before the wounds have had time to mend. Tiny spears of blackened bone puncture the skin. Instinctively, Felix reaches in his backpack and pulls out some leones. Felix hands the money over, but the man continues to look at him, not even twitching a muscle in his face. Felix drops the bills on the ground, picks them up, and stuffs them in the pocket of the man's shirt. Then he walks away, finds a place to be alone, breathes evenly, tries to hold it together.

Issa walks over and puts his hand on Felix's shoulder. "You cannot change it, Felix. You have to believe me."

He nods, opening and closing his fingers to guard against oncoming lightheadedness.

Up ahead, a man on crutches falls into a mud puddle. He struggles to get up before two nurses help him. The side of his head is caked with mud.

"Are you sorry you came?" Issa asks.

He is, of course, but he doesn't admit it. After all, he had asked to come. But the whole thing feels ridiculous to him now. What could he do in a place like this? He isn't his Dad. He isn't even capable of imagining him here.

"This is the worst place in the world," he says.

"You can go home. Any time." He shakes his head, tears shuttling down his cheeks in spite of himself.

"I can't pretend it doesn't exist."

"Come on. Let us go into town. Dr. Grillet knows where to find us. He can tell you what you want to know later. Unless it is too difficult."

"If easy is what I wanted, I wouldn't be here."

They walk toward the truck and the children set on them again. Felix remembers a candy bar he has in his backpack and he pulls it out and gives it to one of them. Stupidly, he says, "Now you share," but the kids are all over the one with the candy bar. Around his feet, the ever-growing mass of children writhing around in the mud look like eels in a barrel. Soon, a number of adults join the fray.

Three soldiers run over and whack several of the adults in the head with their rifle butts. The group scatters, leaving only the torn remnants of the candy bar wrapper half-covered in mud. Issa leads Felix away. "The sooner you believe me, Felix, the easier it will be," he says.

Issa and Felix order drinks at Paddy's Chinese Restaurant, a bar full of white people; local girls—prostitutes, Felix guesses; and with nothing Chinese about it. They wait for Dr. Grillet, who is almost an hour late.

Issa seems agitated again. "Do not ask Dr. Grillet too many questions about the attack. Okay?" he says.

Felix agrees, but it had been Issa who'd set up this meeting, he who had brought Felix there precisely so that he could ask the doctor what he wants to know.

"Sorry, gentlemen," Dr. Grillet says when he arrives. As he sits down, he asks for a scotch, raising one stiff finger in the air as he orders. It's a move to be executed in someplace like Milan or Biarritz or Rio. And the doctor seems better suited for one of those cities. Felix hadn't noticed it in the camp, but he is an exceptionally handsome man—well-tanned, dark hair gelled back, with loose crescent-shaped cords of hair swinging like ropes across his forehead.

"We had a problem with a little girl. She lost her lips and the gums are constantly infected. It seems the infection traveled to the lungs."

Felix wonders if the doctor has been dealing in euphemisms for long, for the girl hasn't "lost" her lips, as if they were keys. Her lips had been hacked off by crazed fighters, who did it for no other reason than to intimidate the local populace and smooth their paths to the diamonds—at least, that is what Felix understands.

"This is on top of the revision surgeries we had to do for the penciling on her arms. This is when the bones continue to grow through the skin into thin points. It's very painful and afflicts the younger children."

The waiter brings the doctor's drink. Dr. Grillet nods and hands him some leones. He puts a cigarette to his lips. Issa lights it for him and then snaps shut his lighter, an elaborate looking piece engraved with a chessboard knight. Felix is certain he's seen it somewhere before, but can't recall exactly.

"That's nice," Grillet says, pointing to Felix's Agadez silver cross.

Felix puts his hand to it. He'd forgotten about it. An amazing thing—so heavy and substantial and yet its presence had ceased to register, as if it had become a part of him.

"So you want to know about your father's work?" Grillet says, blowing out a stream of smoke.

Felix looks to Issa, who simply looks away and then fiddles with the clangy lighter in his pocket.

"He was with a woman," Felix says. "They were found together." He isn't quite sure why this is his first question, his first concern.

"He never let his relationship with Lauré get in the

way of anything here. There are strictures against fraterniza-
tion, but many people ignore it. We'd go insane otherwise."

"Lauré?"

"One of the nurses. She came from Paris. Very wealthy,
privileged. Came here, I don't know, to show she was more
than just that."

"I don't know any Lauré."

"She was your father's—how do you say it—*copine*? *Fiancé.*"

Something must be lost in the translation. Felix figures he means girlfriend, not betrothed. But he doesn't ask;
he doesn't really want the answer. The fact that his father had
taken a "fiancé" somehow isn't particularly shocking, considering where he was, but his parents weren't divorced.

"They died together," Dr. Grillet continues. "I suppose
if you have to go out under the assassin's gun, that's the way to
do it."

Felix assumes he meant they were in bed together, but,
again, he doesn't probe. He understands why his father had a
new woman, if indeed that was the case, why he had played at
beginning again, why here, in a place that was death, he had
searched for and found life. He understands all that. For his
parents had been married right out of college and his father
had to remain the man she married, to change and evolve only
in the context of their relationship, which, by the time they
were thirty, had already constituted a third of their lives. But
with this new woman, this Lauré, he could already be set in
his ways. He could leave the bed in the middle of the night, sit
at a lonely table, take a drink, and wonder at the magnitude of
the world and not have to offer any explanations, for this was
simply "his way," formed years earlier.

"This is a terrible place, son," Dr. Grillet continues. "We need people, each other, whatever we can get. When *Medecins Sans Frontieres* first arrived, we went north with the Red Cross and brought these amputees to the camp. We only got a quarter of them at best. The rest died. Even the ones we saved proved to be too many. We had to take a bunch of them out to Hastings.

"When CNN came, we sent them out there to photograph the kids with missing limbs. We figured once those images got out, countries would be rushing to get in and help. Back here, the scene was incredible. The women who had fled and come back, standing there just wailing with their hands on their heads, standing over the dying men, some of them with 'R-U-F' carved into their breasts."

Issa emits a strange grunting sound. Dr. Grillet and Felix look at him, but he stifles the noise inside his glass as he raises the last of his beer to his lips.

Dr. Grillet takes a drink as well, retracting his upper lip after gulping down the scotch. "I did thirty operations that first week. The people who came through, the ones who lived in the end; they came out with no desire at all. Without hands, they could not work. They could not feed themselves. Try to imagine that. No hands at all. You are totally useless. You cannot even go to the bathroom without someone helping you. Some of them cursed me for saving them, for not letting them bleed to death back at their villages. Now that they are here at the camp, I help them best I can. That was what your father was doing."

"What happened the night he died?"

"Excuse me." Issa gets up and slides his chair across the floor behind him. He walks over to the bar and orders another drink, choosing to stand there.

"I was in town, but I heard all this from the survivors," Dr. Grillet continues. "It was a regular day, like most others around here, people doing their work, and the RUF came in and shot up the place. That's why you see the soldiers at the camp now. They're Nigerians mostly. Until then, we had no protection. We didn't need it. No one figured we'd be targets. Killing foreign nationals working for an international aid organization—it doesn't make sense. All it does is bring international heat. To that point, no one was really paying much attention."

Issa comes back, carrying three drinks, looking a bit steadier. "They wanted to send a message," Issa says. "I understand they believed that the camp was harboring ECOWAS troops—West African alliance soldiers—but they were mistaken. It was all a mistake."

"No one would doubt your authority," Dr. Grillet says.

"That is what I understood at the time."

Felix looks at Issa, unsure what this exchange means, but he thinks of the scar Issa has on his back.

"Massacring six aid workers only brings international heat," Dr. Grillet repeats. "That's the last thing they wanted."

"But by that point, they probably knew that their cause was a lost one," Issa says. "The RUF wanted to oust the corrupt government in Freetown. That was how it started. And it was a legitimate cause. But it turned into something far less just. It turned into madness. Just for power. Butchery."

"Taylor saw to that."

"Charles Taylor. President of Liberia. He worked with the RUF, protected and supplied them," Issa explains.

"Why?"

"He was trying to gain control of Monrovia during Liberia's civil war. ECOWAS troops were using Sierra Leone as a base for missions in Liberia, so Taylor wanted to destabilize Sierra Leone to better his own chances.

"After I was through in Sierra Leone, I went back home to Niger. I needed time away from this place. At the airport in Niamey, a Liberian diplomatic aircraft landed. It took off loaded with weapons and military vehicles. Then it went back to Freetown. The very next day—that is when the madness started." Issa turns his watch around his wrist, revolving it again and again as he speaks.

"They called it Operation No Living Thing," he continues. "Many people killed. Girls raped. They used to spread tubes of Tenovate on their skin to lighten it. Now they were caking on mud to make themselves darker, less desirable. Many who survived had run to the cemetery and pried open the vaults to hide there. In Freetown, the Nigerian peacekeepers came and killed everyone they thought might have been a RUF rebel. This included small children. But to be fair, the rebels could have been anyone—even small children. These same Nigerians. They are the ones who are left to protect the city. You can imagine how the people in the city felt about that. I learned a lot about Sierra Leone at that time. I learned a lot about myself, too."

"Children?" Felix asks.

"Most of them were forced into the RUF. They were easy to recruit because they were no longer in school. The government in Freetown couldn't afford to pay teachers anymore, so those teachers began charging the parents of the students. Only the wealthy could pay. The rest went out to the street. Easy pickings for the RUF. And once they are in, the RUF becomes family. Killing becomes normal. Cutting off your own father's hands, drinking other people's blood—"

"But the RUF came from Liberia, you said. What about the government of Sierra Leone? Couldn't they do anything?"

"Completely impotent," Issa says. "At first the government said they would not be cowed by the rebels and asked the people to 'join hands' in resistance. The next day, the rebels drove up to the presidential compound and threw a bag of severed hands over the fence. The government was too gutless to do anything further. Besides, the soldiers in the Sierra Leone Army who were supposed to be fighting the RUF, many of them actually fought *with* the RUF. Called them 'sobels.' Soldiers by day, rebels by night. It was very difficult to know who was fighting for who. Those were confusing times. People often had to question which side they were on and why—and that answer could change from morning to evening."

"Kabbah became Sierra Leone's president," Dr. Grillet adds. "When he was running for office—this was a free election, by the way. There were some irregularities, yes, but it was called free and fair." Dr. Grillet takes another drink, somewhat fiercely. "It certainly was not bad by postcolonial standards. It is true, some rebels did try to disrupt the voting, but the people wouldn't have it. They refused. The election went on; the rebel soldiers were actually cowed." Grillet smiles. "So Kabbah won in a runoff. He had a slogan: 'The future is in your hands.' So once again the RUF chopped off hands and told victims to ask their president to provide them new ones. They've actually a good sense of the ironic, these RUF thugs." Dr. Grillet raises his hand for another drink.

"But you see, this is why people like your father are so important. That is all anyone can do, come here and help the people who are already victims. Prevention is impossible."

"How can that be? This sort of thing can't be prevented? Ever?"

"Felix, do you know how the war ended?" Dr. Grillet asks. "They brought in the rebels, the very people who did all the killing. They're now in the government. Foday Sankoh—he was the RUF leader. He was made chairman of the Commission for the Management of Strategic Resources, National Reconstruction, and Development."

"Diamond czar," Issa says. "This was the result of the accords. This is why the U.N. was here, to help implement the conditions. Lomé was what provided the blanket amnesty, but it was appended so it did not include genocide or crimes against humanity. That is part of what we are doing here, taking Mohammed's story. This is why I have come back here. It has to be decided: was this a crime against humanity?"

The amputee girl in the camp, maybe three years old at most: Crime against humanity? Was there any question?

"I say prevention is impossible," Dr. Grillet says. "I suppose there are ways to fix it, but these ways allow the killers to go free, encourage the victims to forgive and forget, to live side by side again. You cannot imagine what that must be like. So we come to help them now. That is all we can do."

Felix nods. The disbelief obviously remains on his face because Dr. Grillet adds, "I am a doctor, son. I have to believe in the power of healing. I could not do this job otherwise. But sometimes even I think there is nothing that can be done. When that first convoy arrived with the amputees needing medical care, I had little hope. There was one man—his stumps were bloated, infected, crawling with maggots . . . the rebels laughed at him when they found him on the road.

Kept him alive so that he could die the slower way, from an excruciating infection. This man told me that he pleaded for them to shoot him. But he could not afford the bullet so they wouldn't do it. Imagine: paying for your own bullet. He had utterly given up. He asked me not to perform the surgery, but to give him something to die quickly." Dr. Grillet takes another drink and slams the glass on the table so hard that a crack snakes through the base. "But I did the surgery. I ignored his wishes, and hoped I was doing the right thing. The last I heard that man was in London being fitted for a prosthesis. So . . ." He unfolds his hands and shows his empty palms. They are working hands, etched with lines of industry. "This is why we are here. Why we stay. Your father, too."

"I understand," Felix says.

But that is only partly true. Dr. Grillet's reasoning perhaps explains why he is there, why the rest of the aid workers are too, but it doesn't fully explain his dad. All he can do is guess at the holes. He'd probably fallen in love with the idea of Africa—even the Africa a cosmos away from the tourist trails—and with saving people. It was a guard against the inertia of home. But it was all temporary madness, an escape like a narcotic.

There is not much else to see or do; there is no reason to go back to the camp. Nothing there can tell Felix any more about his father that he doesn't already know—or doesn't want to know. He tells Issa and Dr. Grillet as much and excuses himself. They look at one another, don't say a word, and watch him leave.

# CHAPTER FIVE

Felix is sitting on the bed when Issa walks in.

"I thought I knew my stuff," Felix says. "I've always been up on current events. I've always paid attention to the world. I don't remember any of this. Amputations. Civil wars."

"This also is when the war was going on in Bosnia. Your country is still very European. It is not unnatural to focus attention there instead of Africa."

"I still find it sad."

Issa looks out the window for a long time, his hands clasped behind his back. Finally, he turns around, grabs the bag he's brought in with him, and hands Felix a stack of papers. "Dr. Grillet thought you should have these," he says, placing the papers on the bed. There are yellowed newspaper clippings, scraps of notebook papers, and receipts and medical forms written in French and English, tied off with a silk red cord.

"These are my Dad's," Felix exclaims.

"He found these papers not long ago and the rules are very clear; they are to be turned over to your government. Only when they are through with them do they get sent home. Dr. Grillet can get into trouble."

"But these are my Dad's. They'd get sent home to me."

"To your mother, eventually. Look, Felix. There are rules. Your father is a special case for you, of course. But do you know what? Something you do not want to hear? It is not special to government channels. Or to anyone who lives around here. To them, it is just another man, a *tubab*."

He knows he should be grateful. But he's furious. Perhaps it's a simple shield for what he assumes will be the excruciating next step: communing, at last, with his dead father. And while he does that, he doesn't want a renegade soldier, U.N. worker, hostage-taking African with a diamond wristwatch hovering over him.

Felix starts leafing through the papers. The newspaper articles are from American and British publications, chronicling the diamond wars, a few of them with accompanying photographs—kids on beaches with no legs or arms. He assumes the children without noses and lips and ears would have crossed the line for those wanting to digest their breakfast as they read their paper.

The article on top is from the *London Times*: "Finding diamonds at Bombona is dangerous business. Ironically, the commodity that everyone searches for, the rough stones that men break their backs for, ten hours a day, seven days a week, can get them killed if they find a good stone. They can try and hide the stone immediately, act as if nothing has happened, and slink out of the mine site and get into Kenema to unload as quickly as possible. But the reality is that the men seldom find anything. A few specks here and there are the best they can reasonably hope for. And when this happens, they often hide it in their mouths, careful not to swallow it before they get a chance to trade it in town.

"But what keeps the men coming back, day after day, are the tales of the rare jackpot. Huge stones do turn up. Their finders will enjoy the spoils; this usually means moving away from Kenema, perhaps going to Freetown, where they live in the relative luxury of the upper lower class. Just last week, a man found a twelve-ounce stone in the middle of the street in Kenema. He had been cursing a passing lorry driver who had sideswiped him and his bicycle. As he got himself off the dirt road, his eye caught a sparkle. He dug and there it came. Enough rain and enough passing lorries had exposed the rock. And this man's good fortune, to be the one within inches of getting run down, would deliver him a ticket out of Kenema, perhaps out of Sierra Leone altogether."

Felix puts the paper aside and leafs through the rest of the pile. There are several letters, a few of them to Felix. A surge of heat runs through him; his cheeks flush. Little white spots flash before his eyes, temporarily blotting his view. He sits back and takes a deep breath.

Felix hears Issa ask if he is okay. He manages to nod. Wordlessly, he waves Issa out of the room. When he hears the door shut, he takes a few more deep breaths and turns back to the letters. He picks up the top one, a "Dear Felix" scrawled atop the page in that familiar, barely readable script of his father's.

Dear Felix: I know you respect me, and not in that bullshit way "respect" means for grade A assholes who demand complete subservience from their sons, even after they've grown. I'm talking a sincere and genuine respect, an admiration. I appreciate it. But there's a point, and you'll know this with your own sons should you have them, there's a point at which you get afraid of being found out. You become petrified that your son, the boy who looks up to you as a hero, will come to realize that you're little more than a fraud. The stories, Felix? All the travel stories that you loved so much? They're true, yes, but rather exaggerated, some grossly, if I'm honest. Nothing intentional, but just the natural progression of memory and inflation so that your boy will look up to you. That time I almost died in Central Asia? Looking back on it, it probably wasn't near as dangerous as I made it sound. Who knows for sure. The question, Felix, is that a man be there for his son in every way possible, to show him the way without pressure, without smothering. "That's what you did, Dad," Felix says aloud. Your mother often said that all my maps and photos and nonstop stories of all these places would send you out to do the same things, but the world is a different place now. It can kill as easily as it can amaze. And sending you out there, she always said, that wasn't the thing to do. I'm thinking now that she was right. Getting you the Eurail pass was the compromise. Send him to Europe, she said. Safe, easy, let him get the bug out that way, be like his daddy by going, but to the safe places. But a Eurail pass is hardly a compensation, Felix, for not having told you about the dangers in the first place. Making the danger seem more like adventure than danger at all. The Tashkent incident? It was dangerous. But I made it <u>less</u> so by telling the story as if it was <u>more</u> dangerous than it was. Does that make sense?

Felix flips the page, but there's nothing on the back. When he thumbs through the pile to find the continuation of this letter, a small scrap of paper falls to the floor. He reaches down for it, stares at it, at the writing on it, more indecipherable than usual. It's only a few words, scribbled across the top. He turns it several ways, slanting it so that the letters are almost vertical. Perhaps this is the last thing he'd written, an attempted note to someone, to Felix, to Felix's mother, as the rebels bore down on his tent.

He turns it a few more times, squints, traces his fingers over the letters, and then it comes: "*I wish I was a mole in the ground. If I was a mole in the ground, I'd root that mountain down . . . But I'm only a man.*"

He remembers it now. His father had been obsessed with American roots music. Bascom Lunsford and Mississippi John Hurt and Uncle Dave Macon and Dock Boggs. Felix can recall him singing those old tunes around the house. Every now and then, when he was in moods that were probably mournful and doleful, but that Felix thought at the time were cheery because he was singing, he would sit on the edge of his bed and play his guitar.

Seeing that piece of paper with the opening lines to the song, "I Wish I Was A Mole in the Ground," Felix is back in that same place, that odd stretch of time of which he can recall precious little, when he was very young. His father used to sing that song to him. It was a funny tune, and he used to sing it with comedic flair, pausing at each new verse before plucking away at the strings. Felix would picture it all as his father sang, the same way each time: "*I wish I was a mole in the ground. If I's a mole in the ground, I'd root that mountain down.*" He would see his dad with two shrewish teeth, burrowing beneath a massive mountain. He'd see the thin cartoon line, denoting the tunnel slicing the mountain in half, his mole-dad emerging on the other side, flexing his little biceps as the mountain tumbles into the sea.

"*Rosie wants a nine dollar shawl, Rosie wants a nine dollar shawl. When I come over the hill with a forty dollar bill, she says, 'Baby where you been so long'?*" His mother smiles, enjoying this rare usage of the shortened version of her name—in fact, he never hears his dad call her anything other than her full name, "Rosemarie," or the occasional "Honey," except when he plays this song. They all smile at this, at the playfulness of it. Felix especially.

"*I been in the pen so long, been in the pen so long. I've been in the pen with the rough and rowdy men.*" Now, Felix sees his mom wearing an apron, wielding a rolling pin, menacing but still smiling, cannot stop herself from smiling, asking his dad where he's been. Because his dad has told Felix that the "pen" is jail, Felix pictures him there, inside with the "rough and rowdy men." His envisioned cartoon mother continues: "*Don't like a railroad man.*" His cartoon mole-dad responds: "*If I's a railroad man, they'd kill me when they can, drink up my blood like wine.*" Here, Felix pictures the mole wearing an old-fashioned train conductor's cap, way too tall for his little rodent head, holding onto the side-rail of a steaming locomotive, slicing a mountain again. The train bellows and emits a cloud of black steam and then disappears into a mountainside tunnel, his dad waving his cap before he disappears.

"*Wish I was lizard in the spring. O, I wish I was a lizard in the spring. If I's a lizard in the spring, I'd hear my darlin' sing.*" Now his dad loses his mole body and morphs into a slithering green iguana, the little mouth studded with teeth, the forked tongue singing his wish to hear his darlin' sing. This darlin', of course, is his mother, who returns to the scene when his dad sings, "*Rosie, let your hair roll down. Rosie, let your hair roll down. Let your hair roll down and your bangs curl around.*"

Then, back to the beginning: "*Oh, I wish I was a mole in the ground . . .*" and there can't be a happier family anywhere in the world, no boy in any place on the planet who is more content than Felix is at that moment.

Holding the paper in his trembling hand, he realizes that he'd forgotten it all these years, had buried it somewhere that hasn't been cracked open in almost two decades. But for his dad, it was still there. Felix wonders if it always had been, or if in the darkness and misery of that camp where he'd spent his last days, the sweet memory of singing to his only son came back to him, warmed him, made him get up the next morning, convinced that this was the way to prove to his son that he wasn't a "fraud."

Did he know, those many years ago, when he took the guitar out of its case, pulled the humidifier from between the strings, loosed the pick from below the neck, and started away on "The Mole Song," as Felix called it, that it would come to mean to him so much more than some little ditty that his boy clapped and sang along to? Did he realize, sitting in the family living room, plucking away with those hands he needed to protect and preserve for work, that there would be a day when they would both be brought to the most terrible place on earth, each for his own different reasons that suddenly seemed so similar—did he know what role that song would play in pulling them both there?

Even if Felix didn't know it himself?

# CHAPTER SIX

The waves hardly earn the name today. Instead, tentative pushes onto the sand, and then quick retractions back out to the briny depths—ephemeral and timeless all at once. Small, inconsequential, deflated. No hiss, no roil. No foam to speak of. It's a cold and blustery day and no one is on the beach apart from Rosemarie. This makes her happy. She wants this place to herself. She'll stay here as long as she can take it, dressed as she is: inadequate for the surprising nip in the air.

Oceans. Literal, metaphorical. Distances. Wide as oceans. All that. Francis dead, and Rosemarie with a feeling that in some ways she never really knew him. Not really any-way. But does anyone ever really know anyone else? Any more than they know themselves? She doubts it. Who, exactly, is her son, now across this very ocean somewhere, engaged in something Rosemarie wouldn't even have had the capacity to imagine when he was just a boy, when he was that little kid running to her with arms wide open, unembarrassed, because he loved his mama. Now, a grown man, following after his dad. Only in a way she is sure he could never have imagined, either.

Rosemarie feels a sudden need to gather him in her arms again, squeeze him down, make him a child again, press him back through the years into infancy, spare him all this, the terrors of human life. But she may as well ask these ocean laps to reverse themselves, too, for all those thoughts and desires are worth.

She wants to gather Lizzy as well, bring together the both of them, explain that love between human beings is an incredible gift and that union is the warmth we all want and need in a cold world. But what they don't tell you, what can never be known to the young, to those just setting out, is that the future is so fraught and you are forced, after enough time, to live beholden and prisoner to the past, to try and convince yourself that, yes, you *can* go back there one day. But it's never to be.

*Felix, Lizzy will one day no longer light up when you walk through the door. She will resent you and your dirty laundry and your failure to pick up your socks, and she'll convince herself that you aren't doing enough to help with the child. And you, Lizzy, you must know that he will not forgive you the extra pounds that will inevitably come. The sagging skin. He will hold you in his mind's eye forever as the beautiful young woman you are now. And he'll resent your inability to defy aging.*

It's a futile game in the end, she knows. It hadn't been so long, after all—on a beach just like this one, barely two hundred miles up the coast. There the three of them were—happy, healthy, on public display with no pretense. It was true happiness. Real and true. Before the itches and the discontentment and the need for him to leave. The *need*—she can't get over it.

Felix was barely five years old on that day she now recalls so clearly. He *was* five, she knows. Because at six he could swim. Even in the ocean. And she can see him now and he's too large to be just four or three. There he is, on his father's shoulders, Francis leaning into the waves while behind them horseshoe crab carcasses deposit themselves on the beach. When particularly large waves come, they brace themselves,

Felix holding on and leaning in, hands over his father's face. No matter; he can't see anyway, his eyes closed as the wave swallows him, knocking against Felix's chest. The boy tenses, panic in him—she can see this, she, his mother—but he holds on, rights himself as the wave passes, tenses again as another one comes in quick succession. He's a brave boy; she can see this, too.

On the beach later, Francis points to the horizon while Felix, towel draped around his shoulders, hair still damp and mussed, stringy and knotted from salt and sand, follows the course of his finger, listening as his father tells him of France and Portugal and all the wonderful things there.

Rosemarie smiles, nodding at the recollection of their honeymoon, before Felix completed their family, the Eiffel Tower and how the elevator to the very top stopped momentarily, clattered and bucked, and how several people gasped and how she was grateful afterward to not know that this wasn't normal, that it was supposed to be an uninterrupted push toward the tip, that it was not supposed to act like a Ferris wheel and stop at intervals. But then it started up again, and they made it to the top, silently taking in the view of perhaps the most beautiful city on earth. The way Francis slid his hand onto the small of her back and held it there. And it felt more solid, that hand, than the edifice upon which they stood. What is mere steel and girder compared to flesh and bone?

It's a losing proposition in the end. You do your best. You can tell yourself that you have it better than 90% of the world's population. Probably far more, if you really think about it. Look where you are after all, she tells herself. Just look around you. A beautiful beach, a home just a few blocks away. Decades of the "good life," hosting parties and having a healthy son and a husband who was better than most. A surgeon. Thoughtful. Good-looking. So why does she think so often these days of his shortcomings, she asks herself. Perhaps this is part of being human, too. Or maybe something in her own makeup that prevents her from simply being content. And if so, is this any different from the man she now condemns for that same fault, for failing to see her and their home in Baltimore as enough?

Condemned—condemned to live in the past. To fail to absorb the beauty around her now but rather to have her mind float back to a simpler time that, she must concede, probably didn't feel so simple then. It's just that the daily difficulties of sleep deprivation and fevers and aloneness as Francis spent long hours at work while she stayed home, day after day, with a colicky infant—well, those days are gone now and so mundane she hardly remembers them. Instead, she is doomed to remember only the best of those days and then lament their passing. What a cruel mental fate.

She gets up, brushes the sand from her bottom, walks the two and a half blocks back to the cottage. She hasn't yet changed the decorations, left by the previous owners—moving to Colorado, they have no need of these objects anymore. She will, someday, remove them; they're not her taste. The dried starfish, the sea dollars, the plastic crabs, each perched with glue or nail to the walls. It seems yet another front, a human need to present an illusion of happiness. Yes, this is a beach house, the decorations say (there is even a painting of the cottage with the letters, B-E-A-C-H H-O-U-S-E stenciled on the bottom) and as such you should remember the privilege of that. And yet . . . it all seems so phony to her.

She reaches for the starfish closest to her, ripping it off

the wall. Only it's been there for some time, and the glue has adhered it so thoroughly that half the disgusting thing breaks off in her hand, leaving the other half on the wall. The half in her hand immediately starts to shrivel and flake as if it's still a living creature, a sea animal suddenly exposed to cold and dry and retracting in on itself in some kind of desperate biological defense.

She tosses the thing in the trash, resolves to attend to the rest later, and scrubs the dried flakes of the creature off of her.

She walks to the guest bedroom where a dozen boxes remain still unpacked. She kneels at the one nearest her, rips the packing tape, and opens the cardboard flaps. She sees immediately that this is not the one she's looking for. But the second box contains the picture; she spots it right away, there on top in its silver ornate frame.

She pulls it from the box and blows on it—the dust of moving. She can still recall the woman who took the picture; Francis had asked her in his passable French. She smiled, was happy to oblige, shattering that unfair reputation of Parisian snobbishness. One stereotype she did uphold, however: she was stylishly dressed, and rather beautiful, managing a middle-aged grace that seemed so effortless for so many women Rosemarie saw on that trip. She expressed that sentiment several times, articulating her misgivings, before Francis declared that she was the most beautiful woman he'd ever known and always would be. Her eyes misted and they clinked wine glasses and made love in the hotel. They were young then. The woman snapped the picture, handed back the camera, and instructed them in beautifully accented English to enjoy Paris. It was only weeks later, after having the roll developed, that they realized that the kind photographer had cut off the tip of the tower. They had it framed anyway. What else was there to do? They never went back to Paris, as they often said they would, to correct the shot. The picture hung in their foyer for many years. And here it was—resurrected.

Rosemarie places it on the little stand next to her bed. The last thing she'll see at night and first thing in the morning.

Living in the past: perhaps that isn't the most terrible thing to do after all.

# CHAPTER SEVEN

Felix buys a flashlight and batteries from a vendor on the street. When the lights go off for the evening at 8 p.m., he goes into the hallway and leans against the wall to read the rest of his dad's papers.

Dear Felix:

We went to Kenema today. Remember when we would drive around Baltimore or D.C. and I would insist that we not skirt the rough parts, that we see the desperation and the blight because this was the real world after all, not something that we should turn from. Your mother would give me hell for it, claim I was endangering us for no good reason. Maybe she was right, though I'm not sure there was 'no good reason.'

Well, if I really wanted to implant you with some lesson, an appreciation for what you had, I needed only take you to Kenema, Sierra Leone. It is a brutal place. It wasn't destroyed by the rebels; in fact, it's fairly nice by Sierra Leonean standards. But that's precisely what makes it so discouraging, I'm afraid. What's been destroyed there is humanity, something that is utterly destructible and irreplaceable, not mere concrete and steel. Children run the streets begging for money. They all insist on selling diamonds. Everyone has diamonds, and they're utterly worthless because that's all everyone has. Even worse than worthless, they're worth more than the people themselves. And they know it, Felix. There is no humanity . . .

Another letter, crammed between two newspaper clippings:

Felix – I cannot even begin to describe the pathetic scenes. One of the aid workers took us out to the mines. It's like nothing I've seen – even more terrible in some respects than the camp. Men in murky water – up and down, digging, digging, digging. These people were inflicted with something. You could see it in their eyes. They don't blink. They are mechanical. They hack at the earth, mud up to their necks like piles of shit. For the diamonds. It's despicable. And these are the lucky ones. These are the ones who do it voluntarily. These are the ones who have lost their houses, their wives and daughters and uncles and brothers and sons. But they live here in the village. They don't see me at the camp. They are the lucky ones – they should be dead if they were so lucky. It's enough to drive a man insane. And why? So some schmuck in Baltimore can buy his wife a bracelet. The idiots at the store, the ones who schmooze him, assure

him it's a great choice, a beautiful piece, do
they know the price paid to get it? Did I think
to even ask? It's easier to turn a blind eye. Let
the world turn a blind eye – I wish I could.

Felix wants to go there—both Kenema and the mines.
This is undoubtedly why his father had never sent these letters; he knew they would have this effect, that Felix would naturally want to follow him there, as he had been following his
interests since he was a boy. His father knew Felix would have
insisted on joining him in West Africa, seeing what he saw,
and he knew that Rosemarie would have lost her mind. That
was not something to put Felix in the middle of.

He walks to a little windowed alcove above the lobby. Moonlight bounces over the tiny ripples in the filthy pool.
Palm trees shade the scene, crowding out the unpleasantness
beyond and socking Felix in a world of comparative luxury,
the insects and intermittent air conditioning excepted. But
he knows what is beyond; he knows those people are just a
few streets away. He knows that they are using one hand—or
none—to climb into simple, wooden beds in dirty, tattered
white tents. He isn't going to complain about the thick heat in
the room, the blanket of humidity that makes sleep impossible after the A/C shuts off for good.

Felix stacks the papers and places them gently in his
bag. He goes downstairs and finds Issa sitting in the lobby
reading a magazine. Felix sits down next to him. "I'm sorry,"
he says. Issa puts the magazine aside and places a hand on
Felix's shoulder.

Felix lets himself sink into the couch, numbed and
without any discernible compass point left. He slinks slightly

toward Issa, feeling the proximity of his broad shoulder. And then he finds himself, against his will, sinking into Issa's chest.

He misses his dad, and Issa is the closest thing he can get.

"Will you take me to Kenema?" he asks. "I want to see the mines."

Issa blinks and stares wordlessly. Then he nods.

They get the highway out of Freetown, crossing a brown wrought iron bridge over a river studded with huge jagged rocks. A threadbare version of urban sprawl: the gradual descent of tall buildings, an easing of traffic, flat rows of squat dilapidated houses, a result of poor building materials and heavy rains.

Issa explains that when Nigerian soldiers beat back the rebels and prevented them from taking Freetown, the rebels fled east along this same road, torching villages and villagers along the way. Here, the war reached its cruelest zenith—the spots along the road with massive piles of debris used to be villages where women were raped, kids were conscripted, limbs were hacked off and tossed to the buzzards. Now what remains are thick stands of vegetation, helped along by the decay of human casualties.

The woods thicken on either side of the road, interrupted now and again by buildings with rusted tin roofs, sitting side by side with thatch huts. They pass the steel shell of a car with elephant grass growing through. All the parts are gone. Just beyond the dead automobile stands a bridge spanning a wide, flat river. Beyond the river is only green. The road is still paved but spotty and decaying. Then the jungle closes in almost to the road's edge.

Occasionally, they pass through breaks in the foliage,

untended fields, bare except for a few trees. In one of these fields, a woman with a baby strapped to her back stands ankle-deep in water and pulls tall green stalks out of the ground. Felix can't imagine where such a person lives. It's misery. And yet . . .

Pretty hills rise and fall in the distance. Palm trees line the road and tip their fronds over the rest of the jungle, catching breezes and turning over. It's exposed and raw and gorgeous. Felix inhales deeply the scent of deep earth, affirming even through the dense humidity.

The tarred road degenerates into a dusty red track, first chunks of pavement then dirt. They finally reach a few towns, passing through Waterloo and on into Bauya, where people are busy erecting thatch roofs and spreading mud walls like plaster.

Felix tells Issa of his dad's description of Kenema. He responds that things are not as bad anymore. It is still a dangerous place, but now that the war is over and things have relaxed a bit, Kenema is once again enjoying its status as one of the wealthiest places in the country. The biggest problem now is the Russian Mafia, which comes in a couple of times a year to buy stones. Everyone but the biggest dealers have to close up shop during that time. It puts everyone on edge.

"You know," Issa says. "Not long before September 11, some of Osama bin Laden's men were in Kenema buying stones. It is probably what helped finance the operations in New York and Washington."

This bit of information would have been enough to startle Felix, to wake him from complacency had he been dropped in Kenema unannounced and unaware. But the connections between this wretched place and tragedy has already been well established for him. And this is the effect: the fact that he is heading to a place that may have played an instrumental part in the single worst attack on American soil doesn't register now as much more than a curiosity.

They cross another large river and the road opens up. Fields, crisscrossed with weak streams, spread out on either side. Clumps of trees are scattered about. Rusted tanks line much of the route, many of them overtaken by weeds. They cross the Jong River and into Mano, a decent-sized town, before passing a bunch of villages where a sea of white tents front crumbling and bullet-ridden buildings. Clearly the same route to the diamonds that the RUF had taken after sacking the capital.

Issa says they will stop in Bo. He points up and though Felix hadn't noticed before, it looks like it's going to rain. Large arms of the jungle have been crowding the road sporadically and the gray shadows have turned to black. Considering the red dirt track that passes as the road, it's obvious why Issa doesn't want to stop during a rainstorm.

They don't move quickly enough, however; between Mano and Bo, the heavens open up. It beats so fast and hard against the truck that the wipers on their highest speed can't keep the windshield clear. Issa keeps driving, slowly, sure that if they stop on the rutted, muddy road, they'll be stuck.

It's a slow ride, but paralleling some defunct railroad tracks, they reach Bo just as the rain lets up. Bo is little more than a collection of one and two-story structures between cotton and palm trees and looks as if its buildings have been dropped randomly from thousands of feet. In the distance, the gray, jagged outline of mountains form the horizon.

The bulk of the town is off the main road, hidden

within chunks of unmolested jungle. They go directly to find a place to stay, passing diamond stores—nothing like what Felix is told to expect in Kenema—but a concentrated collection in what looks to be Bo's downtown: a few storefronts huddled at the corners of a crossroads and wide packed dirt heading off in every direction. The diamond stores sport elaborately painted signs, airbrushed with the store's name: "Big Mac Diamond Office," "Good Luck Diamond Office," "Moon Diamond Office."

Even though it is only afternoon, once they get a room in the Premier Lodge, they stay inside. The rain starts again and continues past dark.

Nights usually offer a reprieve and have often been able to cheer Felix somewhat. No matter where he is—Bangui, Niamey, Freetown—he can look out of a hotel window when the sun has gone down and see the fires, hear the drumming, and take in a city alive with the night when the heat has subsided. But in Bo, just silence and darkness.

He keeps dozing off while watching British comedies on TV, often muted by punishing rain on the roof. By morning, water covers almost the entire floor. Only a few inches of one raised corner is spared. The plan is to leave early, to go and not come back. But before they leave, Issa tells Felix that he wants to show him something. They walk to a two-story rust-colored building set off from the main road. They take the stairs, complete with an intricately designed steel rail, and pass the "Boys Dormitory."

A bearded white man wearing a panama hat comes out of an office. "Can I help you with something?" he asks in an unfriendly and suspicious tone.

"My name is Issa Manzo. This here is Felix Laszlo.

We work for the United Nations, collecting accounts for war crimes tribunals." Issa shows the man his ID, which he studies for several long moments, turning it in several directions, up to the sunlight, and scratching his finger across the laminated surface, before handing it back to him. Felix waits for him to ask for his ID, already settling on a story that a local official has confiscated it and he is awaiting its return. But the man doesn't bother with Felix; taking Issa's ID is enough legitimacy for them both, apparently.

"Can we see what takes place here?" Issa asks.

"I do not want these kids to talk," the man says.

"No," Issa agrees. "I only wanted to show my associate here."

The bearded man looks at them both, his arms folded across his chest.

"We need to see some good," Issa adds. "It has been difficult. I want to show Felix that the kids here, that they are not beyond redemption."

The man nods, his face relaxing, and he drops his arms to his sides before raising one hand to shake. "Of course," he says. "I'm sorry."

He introduces himself as James Connoy and leads Felix and Issa to a courtyard in the back of the building where about two dozen boys and girls—five or six years old up to late teens—chase after a soccer ball or sit in circles talking. Three older girls, teenagers, it appears, sit on swings and chat like old ladies, their feet lazily sweeping the dirt as they rock back and forth. Everyone looks reasonably well fed and happy; they all wear clean clothes. Six boys sit in the middle of the courtyard getting dirty with a game of marbles.

James takes his visitors inside, to a classroom decorated with pictures on one wall. They aren't displayed the way such pictures, scrawled with crayon, are usually displayed in American elementary classrooms—a showcase, something to brag about. Here the pictures are within a square close to the floor, a special place cordoned off just for this purpose.

On one painting, the figures have well-defined shapes and are decorated with a kaleidoscope of color, each within a firm line. Had this in fact been in a classroom or post office back in the States, this same painting would have been a rendering of a bouquet of multicolored balloons, perhaps, each a perfect sphere, none of the colors bleeding beyond the boundary line. There might have been a family, some birds, a doggy, a park scene, little curlicues of smoke rising from a red brick chimney. But this one in Bo is instead a series of panels with captions, such as, "Two killed his friend." In the picture, a man in green stands off to the left, watching. A red boy is on the ground, already dead. Next to him, another boy holds up his hands, a plea for mercy. But it's futile. To his right, an intricate and well-detailed machine gun is already spraying bullets at the boy's legs. Below this scene is written, "The rebel is chasing this boy." A psychedelic car speeds toward a running boy. Below the boy's feet, to the right, hovers a purple building where people run. And next to that is another building, but this one is engulfed in red streaks, next to the caption, "He is burning the house." A man sprays the house with bullets and the two figures in the door are caught between the bullets and the flames. But this one has a "happy" ending. The last caption, in black, reads, "We killed the man with a ni-knife." The killer man is now small, and he looks at the sharp end of an enormous knife held by a smiling boy.

James explains: "Mostly they show themselves as victims—and of course, they were. But you see, they are not missing limbs, like the victims in the pictures. It's their way of empathizing, of seeing themselves in the victims' shoes.

"You see how this story ends? 'We killed the man with a knife.' This is the good guy, the hero, killing the rebel. Of course, you have to remember that the artist of this picture was the rebel. In other words, he knows he was 'the bad guy.'" Felix looks around at the kids playing—one of those kids shooting marbles a killer? "We don't discourage that thinking," James continues. "They need to first come to terms with what they did. Only then can they be absolved. We spend a lot of time convincing these kids that it wasn't their fault. But we keep the pictures here. They must not forget. Or else it will come back to them at the wrong times. They must face it, come to grips with it. Their own families fear them, you know. They will only take them back after they've gone through here. Eliza, one of the girls you see out there on the swings, killed her baby sister with a pestle. Smashed her in a rice bowl while her mother looked on. This Eliza hears at night—her mother screaming, the hollow sound of that baby's head . . . She cannot go back to her village obviously. They won't have her."

A great burst of noise and energy rattles the floor. The kids run into the room and scramble into their chairs. Then they notice their new visitors. They flip their chairs and run over, pawing at Issa and Felix and asking for candy and money until James quiets them. "Where you from?" they ask Felix. They seem to be totally uninterested in Issa.

"America."

There is a spontaneous eruption, almost a round of applause, as if Felix has come bearing all the wealth and gifts of his nation. Next comes a chorus of shouted names: Michael

Jordan, Bill Clinton, Britney Spears, Arnold Schwarzenegger. James quiets them again, just in time for one unlucky kid to yell out, "Osama bin Laden," which elicits laughs from the others. James grabs the boy by the elbow and steers him to the corner, where he makes him face the wall. He drops his head and sulks. This is the same kid who'd chopped off someone's arm? Had terrorized whole villages, maybe his own parents? He seems too small, too weak, too terrified of being thrust into a corner. He takes the punishment without the slightest resistance. Felix stares at him, this tiny creature standing there with his chin on his chest.

"Come on, Felix," he hears Issa say. "Let us leave James to his work."

Felix thinks James will insist they stay, but he just nods. It is time to start math lessons, and their presence, obviously, is a big distraction.

On the way out, Issa pulls out his laminated picture of Memuna from his wallet.

He shrugs, sighs. "It is very possible that one of these kids did it to her," he says. "I try not to hate them, Felix. But when I look at her . . ." He runs the edge of his finger over Memuna's shoulder.

"How can you stand to come here then?"

"I have always meant to come. I need to if I ever hope to understand . . . I am not such a good man, Felix. But I am trying." He looks off into the distance. "One day," he says, "One day, I will adopt Memuna, as I have told you. When I have stopped moving around."

"When will that be?"

"When we are done here. When you go home, I will go

home. For good."

The rain gives way to hazy sunshine by afternoon, floating tiny prisms in the air. When the clouds break entirely, the sun is intense. The jungle returns to its impenetrable feel, but a decent roadside buffer has been hacked out and successfully staves off what has become for Felix increasing feelings of impending asphyxiation. But soon thick vegetation crowds the road again and his anxiety returns. For Issa, too, evidently. He warns Felix against opening the windows in the jungle, that any spirits that wish to could easily leap in. It's the closest he's come to anything spiritual in all the time Felix has known him, but he remembers Issa having told him that he doesn't like jungles.

Despite the sporadic closeness of the surrounding thickets, it isn't lost on Felix that they're driving over paved roads, relatively free of potholes. This, he imagines, is due to the wealth generated by the diamonds. They pass a rusted tank. This too, he knows, is from the diamonds. The sightline of its large cannon points directly at them, seeming to track them through their entire transit.

The faint echoes of some strange sound floats to meet them: a steady cadence of swooshing and banging. In the field ahead, women pound tie-dyed sheets of cloth onto stones and large pieces of plywood. Up go their arms, twirling behind their head, and smashing down again. Up, twist, untwist, down—BANG! whoosh, swish, swish, BANG!

Ahead, three small figures run back and forth on the road. They are boys, naked except for white cloth around their groins, standing together on the right side of the road. One darts across, trailing a tail of string, which one of the other boys holds onto. They pull each of their ends taut. Issa stops the car. The two boys continue pulling the string. The third comes over to the driver's side window and holds out his hand. Issa drops three coins into his palm. The boy waves at the two holding the string and they drop it. "I cannot drive through their string," Issa says. "These boys are entrepreneurs."

This is the beginning of "civilization," small collections of dwellings, alternating between brick, nylon, and thatch. All along the road, women work the fields. Felix wonders if the men have been killed off, or if they're sifting gravel in the rivers and mud-filled lakes Issa has described as the mines. There are no animals. None, anywhere. Felix had seen the occasional mongrel prowling the streets in Freetown, half-crazed and looking as if rabies had set in. But out here in the fields, where animals should be, there are none. Even in Niger, packs of animals, though bedraggled and appearing close to death, loped alongside undernourished villagers prodding them with scrawny sticks. Here, just the backbreaking thrust and pull of women in fields.

There had been more life in the poorest places in the hills of Guinea. There, even the reserved women smiled, a hand perched on the side of whatever was on their heads. Men held out goods: watches, cigarettes, mangoes and plantains, animal skins. Further south, along the road toward Yamoussoukro, boys leapt in the air at the sound of Issa's horn and the sight of Felix's waving hands, like he himself had done as a kid peering out of his parents' car rear window when some truck driver, responding to his pulling elbow, let his whistle bellow. But here, nothing.

Rolling hills buckle over the horizon. Fields choked

with low-lying and veiny carpets of green and dotted with mid-size trees dominate the landscape. Then the fields give themselves over to little square plots in scattered rows full of rainwater. One building squats on the far end of the field. A gray hill rises just behind it, standing in front of where Felix can see the brown ruts of the road running and then disappearing behind the hill.

"Just beyond there," Issa says. "There is Kenema. Here is where we can see the progress made on halting the blood diamonds."

"How can you tell which are blood diamonds and which are clean?"

"They are all blood diamonds."

Issa swings the truck onto a muddy ridge and the back tires skirt away for a moment before gripping the road. They are headed, finally, straight into town.

"The diamond merchants are Lebanese," Issa continues. "There are many Lebanese in town. Even a Lebanese school."

The road very suddenly turns to flat and uninterrupted pavement, a straight line of tar delineating civilization. Then Kenema proper begins: a series of one-story houses all with matching burgundy roofs. Men walk along the roadside with axes and shovels slung over their shoulders. In the distance to the left, the white tents of what Felix can recognize as a refugee camp spread out into the hills.

"Kenema is lucky," Issa says. "It was spared the war damage. The rebels only got to the edge of town. The Kamajors—spiritual hunters from the Mende tribes—beat them back."

They soon hit "downtown," the road still paved, lined

with palm trees and pastel-painted clapboard houses. A series of power lines has been strung alongside the main road, looping from one utility pole to the next, just like any modern city anywhere.

They slow at what appears to be Kenema's main intersection. A BP gas station sits on the corner and the pavement spreads out beyond it, the second paved road in town.

They pass the intersection and turn off the pavement onto Kingsway Street, where Issa says the diamond dealers congregate. Felix's first impression of Kenema is that it's nothing like the seedy underbelly of conflict that his dad had described. Kingsway, in the center of town, isn't such a bad place either—a little run-down, but nothing terrible. Shops, each painted in bright colors, line the streets. Atop each storefront run balconies where clothes hang on lines, electrical wires are strung back and forth, and big satellite dishes point toward the heavens. One of the stores is closed, its red gates shuttered, but in front sit two men selling knockoff watches and waiting, it seems, for nothing and no one. Several other tables have been set up here and there, each offering something that looks semi-useless and very cheap. Then a diamond store, easily identifiable by a painted shark, tail waggling, with a massive stone in its jaws. But this place is shuttered, too.

People in the open storefronts sit around not doing much of anything. It's as if they all have the same thing to sell and thus no one to buy. Piles of red coolers; cans of gasoline, the red banners exhorting customers to "Top Up Here." A red painted store, curb painted to match, a bored-looking man sitting out front among the bicycles and cheap electronics, the store's address number painted all around on sparkling white diamonds, cut into perfect cones. A blue painted storefront, doors open to the sidewalk, trumpeting "General Goods, IC Center, Electrical, Power Saw, CD/DVD Plates, Robin Machine, Electronics, Tiger Generators."

Issa stops and he and Felix get out. Men asking if they want to buy diamonds barrage them—*you should follow; you can get the best price in town!* Small scuffles break out between the pitchmen and stop only when Issa waves them off and tells them they aren't interested. The men, deflated, walk back to their storefront positions. But one boy isn't deterred.

"Hey, wetman," he says. He's maybe thirteen, in baggy blue jeans and a Liverpool football jersey. He's been sitting on a bike under a pink and blue patio umbrella in front of the Kenema Photo Studio. He lets the bike fall to the ground and hops over to Felix.

"You want rent my sist-ah?"

"Pardon?"

"She's good boom boom."

"No," Issa says, steering Felix away and toward a storefront. "Go home, young man."

"Shit. I am home, suh." He thrusts his hands in his pockets and walks down the street, favoring his right side. When he bends his left leg, what should be a corresponding motion in his right is more like a straight swing, as if nothing in that pant leg bends—just a long, steel rod instead.

A green balcony with the sign "Yamaha Store. Alie El-Alie & Brothers Diamond Dealer" creates some blessed shade on the sidewalk and curb below. Two of the four steel gates are retracted, one revealing a white countertop, the other a series of decrepit bicycles leaning against one another. Three men sit idle on the green curb, hands clasped between their knees, leaning against the shop's walls. A gold shovel painted below the "Diamond Office" sign appears to spear one of the men in the back of his neck.

As Issa and Felix approach, a young light-skinned boy—one of the Lebanese, Felix guesses—runs from the store and crawls onto one of the black man's laps. The black man cradles him to his chest while the boy squeals with delight.

"The dealers here wait for the stones to come from the bush. They buy and then resell to people like us," Issa says as they walk inside. A fan churns slowly on the ceiling; a row of three fluorescent lights buzz and snap nearby. There's no evidence of diamonds anywhere; instead, the shelves are stocked with cheap plastic radios, clocks, cans of shaving cream and shampoo, a motor-scooter, and a bunch of electric fans.

The merchant, clad in a loose plaid shirt and sandals, doesn't get up. He returns Issa's "hello" with only a barely perceptible nod of his hairy chin.

"Diamonds?" Issa asks.

The man points to a door behind the counter. Felix expects the man to grill Issa, to ask why this odd couple wants to see the diamonds. But there's nothing, just a walk through a door to a room where an overweight Lebanese guy with a goatee and no shirt sits behind a large slab of plywood supported with cinder blocks. He wipes his forehead and asks Issa and Felix to sit down. Beyond this, there are no courtesies. A security camera points in their direction from the corner, but from where Felix sits it looks like the camera is aimed way over their heads, toward an ancient air conditioner held together with duct tape.

Felix turns around, expecting to see a dozen faces crowding in, a nod to the illicit business they're undertaking, but it has the feel instead of getting a car loan or playing a game of checkers.

"Can I see your best?" Issa asks.

The fat man reaches behind him and pulls out a piece of cloth. He opens it and twenty or so diamonds tumble out. He pulls a small fluorescent desk lamp toward the pile and lowers the light onto the stones. Had someone told Felix he would have witnessed such a scene, in his imaginings the diamonds would have been like all diamonds he's seen in stores and on fingers back home—cut, polished, gleaming, translucent, prismatic; instead, these are unpolished and milky. But their unspectacular appearance makes them more extraordinary somehow. Here are the stones as the Earth has made them.

Felix feels a surge of electricity shoot through him. All that wealth, there for the taking. There they sit, not behind lock and key in a glass case, but in a pile on a dingy table guarded by a man who looks as if he wouldn't even be up from his chair by the time Felix has grabbed the rocks and beat it halfway out of town.

Issa runs his finger through the stones, halving the pile. "These are from Tongo?" he asks.

"Kono."

"Can I get certification?"

The diamond seller pulls out several sheets of paper as Issa plucks the largest stone off the top of the pile.

The Lebanese man smiles. "A good choice," he says. "That is seven hundred American."

Issa places the stone on the table, pulls out a wad of American dollars from his pocket, peels off five one hundred dollar bills, and hands them over. "I will give you five," he says.

"Six."

"Five hundred dollars. The prices have dropped everywhere up and down the street except for here?"

The diamond dealer snatches the bills and thrusts the paper toward Issa. He takes a small steel pincer, plucks the stone Issa has chosen, and puts it in a piece of white cloth. "Here," he says, handing it over and swatting at the air with the back of his hand, to show the way out and the contempt he has for his niggling visitors.

Outside, Issa shows Felix the official paper, complete with a Liberian government seal certifying that the diamond is clean and has been mined in Liberia under the auspices of government overseers.

"It's that easy?"

"The paper allows me to get through customs, government inspections, whatever. The way it works is that someone would buy the whole lot, transfer them to Liberia, or Guinea, and get certification there by paying off a government official. But for just one stone, I can buy the certification here."

"What if you tried to get into the U.S. with that?"

"It is no problem. I have the certification."

"Wouldn't people know it's a fake?"

"How would they know? It is the same paper that certifies clean diamonds. I can take it directly to Antwerp if I wanted. Besides, I stick the diamond in a sock in my bag. There is no smell. No trace. I could walk through customs with a cigarette box packed with a million dollars' worth of diamonds. Untraceable."

"So what do you do with that diamond now?"

"Turn it into the U.N. offices. Show that the embargo has no effect. That Kimberley, for all its good intentions, does very little. The man who sold it to us was not truthful either.

This stone came from the Tongo field, a rebel held area. There the diamonds are crinkled and cleaved. Kono diamonds are smooth, full of good color and shape. They are premium diamonds. But less likely to be smuggled.

"The rebels still control many of the mines," Issa continues. "They trade the stones to Liberian officials who certify them as clean. The rebels get arms in return. They get machetes. Even now, even as they are officially part of the government, they continue to keep control of the mines through intimidation and massacre. And it's just for money, for power. They are no longer fighting the government. Do you know what the end result of all this is?"

Felix nods; he does know. People like his father buy diamond bracelets for their wives, they give them as gifts, somewhere along the line they get an education, take back the gift, cause rifts, fly off to Africa to redeem themselves, get murdered in amputee camps.

Issa's story differs, of course, though not by much:

"The end result is a young man—he does not know; he is innocent of any malice—he goes from his home in Baltimore. He goes into a classroom, he gets to a knee in front of his pretty teacher girlfriend and her students and he proposes. He gives her the diamond that comes with amputated hands. But he does not know. The children do not know. They cheer; they go home and tell their story to their parents, who smile and laugh. No one knows."

Felix's heart jumps. Does Issa know that Lizzy is a teacher? Had Felix told him? Is he trying to implicate him in the terror? The scene Issa describes is uncannily similar to one Felix used to imagine.

And as for his father: it's obvious why he'd returned the

diamond bracelet. He couldn't live with the fact that he'd been an unwitting party to it all. He probably couldn't even look at his wife, couldn't see those shiny stones dangling from her wrist, probably couldn't help but imagine the wrist with black skin, held against a tree stump, seeing the axe come down. THUMP! He probably heard it in his sleep.

And his poor mom. No doubt she thought it was insane that her husband would give her such a beautiful gift, that he would then read newspapers, look at atlases, trace little paths through West African jungles, and demand to take the bracelet back, explaining all the while why the both of them should have been ashamed of themselves. And there he was, in the dark of night, deciding he would go to the camp and help the people who were already victims. This would be his great penance for having bought the bracelet in the first place. This is why he came to this godforsaken place.

"Come," Issa says. "Tomorrow, I will show you the mines. We need to keep going."

"Okay," Felix whispers.

"It is all I can do now . . . I am not a good man," Issa says.

Felix doesn't argue with him. Everyone has his own demons to exorcise.

They aren't long for Kenema. And even though it is arguably the most prosperous place in the country, it's also a gleaming and apparently unstoppable example of the great dichotomy: the very thing that should have brought some measure of comfort to the majority of Sierra Leoneans is traded and thrown around here, obstinately remaining the very thing that is the cause of so much of their misery.

Lodging is a place just outside of town, near the craft

market. On the way there, Issa and Felix pass a hulk of a building, wires and beams exposed and naked like a man with bone poking through the flesh. An overpowering stench of human excrement emanates from the building. Patches of grass and weed sprout along the roof and each of the three levels below it as well as on the crumbling balcony. Every window gapes, framed only by rotting wood, like the open hungry mouths of abandoned chicks. An inexplicable cinder wall sits on one balcony—only a quarter of it actually, beginning and ending with no purpose in a place where it seems to have been dropped from the sky. Below the next level is a hopeful and miserable reference to better times: painted images of cake, fish, baked turkeys—little legs wrapped in white bows—manioc and mangoes dancing in a Mediterranean blue sky, ending their conga line at an orange sun sliced by a thin cloud and the reach of a palm tree, reminiscent of all that is carefree and beautiful, massive palm fronds shading the perfect triangle of a sailboat, floating lazily to a place where people aren't massacred.

Five men sit in the very middle of this building, like the center square on a tic-tac-toe board. They rest comfortably on benches, as if this is their home. Felix wants to imagine that this is merely some hangout, nothing different from the forts his friends and he used to build in the woods behind their houses when they were kids. But he is sure that this is where these men live, and the desperation of it, the crushing poverty of it, is almost too much to take.

And yet Felix will go deeper. As if he has no choice.

# CHAPTER EIGHT

For the next few days, they drive around what Issa calls the "Wild East:" Kailahun and Koindu near the union of the Guinean and Liberian borders. There's the slow march of Sierra Leoneans walking back to what had once been their villages, kicked out of Guinea and kicked out of Liberia, Issa explains, by citizens who are tired of hosting the refugees; these Sierra Leoneans and their camps are a blight on the countryside. People attack them.

So the Sierra Leoneans march back, possessions on their heads and in bags on trucks so overloaded that they have to stop at the bottom of hills, unload, and then reload at the top. Back to the scenes of devastation, to the places where they were terrorized, their relatives dragged off, conscripted, scarred, gang-raped, turned into amputees. Despite the assurances that their homes are now safe, they are obviously resistant. Felix certainly can't blame them.

When he was growing up, a family down the street had a daughter who hanged herself in the attic. Within the month, the place was for sale. The parents never went back into that house. It made perfect sense then, and Felix can see it in the eyes of the Sierra Leoneans now, walking back home along the highway: Home will never be home again.

There's Kono to the north, then the twin towns of Koidu and Sefadu—brown shacks and red dirt streets, people wearing camouflage t-shirts and flip-flops. This is where the rebels forced the villagers to dig for diamonds, even pulling up the earth in their own homes. There had been better days, of course. Before the terror. Issa tells Felix about the "Koi-du Crouch," the way of walking with one's head toward the ground, better to spot a diamond. Rain is the best for this; it forces a man to bend his head and it washes away the dirt from the stones.

Now, in Sefadu, the asphalt falls off in huge chunks, tumbling to the side of what still functions as the road. Many of the houses look as if they have been halved with gigantic chainsaws. The tops are gone—just frames and foundations, empty hulks. There are only a few structures that are more or less intact; one can see right through the open windows. Where the floor should be are now massive pits. People mill around, but Felix can't imagine where they live. They whistle and lick their hands as Felix and Issa pass, a come-on to buy diamonds: one need only to swallow and then simply walk through customs and retrieve the diamonds later, the actions suggest. This is it, the only thing resembling commerce left. The town looks like what Felix imagines Hiroshima did a week after the bomb.

But if he wants a terrible scene like his father had described, an orgy of pathetic men, the massive Koidu-Yengema diamond field, a ring of forest around mounds of neatly piled dirt, is a welcome disappointment. It's an orderly affair, with cranes dipping their pulleyed buckets into holes and pulling clumps of mud. The operator opens the jaws and dumps the dirt, creating larger and fresher piles. At the far end of the muddy fields and pits is a crisscross of conveyor belts shuttling loose dirt and gravel. It is dirty work, true, men covered in wet mud, wearing nothing but pants cuffed below the knees, but they don't look unhappy. They talk while they dig, smiling occasionally, and sing rhythmic songs like a satisfied chain gang, their archless feet and long toes slapping and gripping the mud.

A large contingent of relaxed Namibian and South African peacekeeping soldiers chat amiably with the workers. Issa stops and talks to the head South African, a white man, and they speak of soldiering and camaraderie. The South African tells them about the diamond field at Zimmi south of Kono along the Moro River, where rebel factions and old splinters of the Sierra Leone Army are still fighting it out, where huge yields of diamonds just below the surface wait for extraction. If only he could get the go ahead to bring his boys down there, the South African explains, "We'd wipe them out once and for all. But lots of foot dragging. Almost like they don't want this thing to end." Who the "they" is, Felix isn't sure.

Before Issa and Felix head off to Koidu to get gas and food, Issa and the South African say goodbye, shaking hands in the stylish West African way: an intricate combination of several quick motions, an arrangement of varied grips ending in a finger snap.

Everything is so quick and uncomplicated that it's hard to imagine that this was a site of devastation and massacre only a few years earlier. But this is also a mining operation overseen by international peacekeepers; this is not a RUF mine. That, Felix imagines, will be a very different thing. And that is where Issa is taking him.

"Outskirts of the Tongo Field, in the jungle," Issa says. "There you will see what your father wrote of. These are still dangerous places, but I know someone. His name is Marc and he currently heads up the Ministry of Mines and Natural Resources. Otherwise, we would not be going."

Koidu is a dusty town, a way station on the road to nothingness, sculpted like a pock out of the jungle. Lines of laundry hang on balconies. Merchants set up their movable shops on crude kiosks of ratty wood tied together with rope. It's clear that Koidu doesn't have the relative wealth of Kenema. They pass a shop adorned with the words, "Mohammed Barrie, Trader." The men who mill in front of the shop watch Felix and Issa pass, their eyes never leaving them, but they don't exhort the strangers to come inside.

"The diamonds are gone from this place," Issa says. "The people who were able to have moved on. You see that there," he says, pointing to an abandoned building with chipped white paint and empty window frames. "That is the old school. The pit mine runs from underneath it all the way to the jungle."

Felix remembers another grim statistic he'd read back home: barely ten per cent of the population is literate; in Koidu, it's easy to see why. And even now, with the war ostensibly over, the kids aren't back in school. Groups of them sit around the streets in tattered clothing, doing nothing.

Issa stops in front of two of them, a boy and a girl, who stand idly on the sidewalk. They don't run up, don't ask for money, don't wave, don't smile. They stand there instead in their filthy white shirts and stare—big, wet, unembarrassed eyes that don't flinch. The boy wears a pendant at the sloping collar—it looks like a simple gray rock like any Felix could find in the woods at home. The girl's shirt hangs on one side to the middle of her arm, a little black nipple peeping above the swoop of the collar. She wears hoop earrings and several brightly colored necklaces. Her eyes betray something angry, as if she's seen way too much of the world and blames all of its miseries on whomever is on the other end of her gaze. Felix will come to know this look as the stare of the war affected—pure vacancy, a disassociation from their bodies so that they don't have to be themselves. Koidu, almost instantly, gives him the creeps.

"Once we hit the mines, you will be wanting to come back here," Issa says.

Felix supposes Issa is right; the orange Fanta he buys at the gas station is something he's sure he isn't going to get out there. He sips and thinks it over: Turn back? Call it off? He has to do it, he decides, unpleasant as it will be. Still, he can't ever imagine wishing he were back in Koidu.

They leave the Jeep at the station, Issa giving instructions to fill it up and check the axles, hoses, pumps, and filters. The trip into the jungle promises to be murder on man and machine.

On the way out of town, the beauty of the surrounding countryside cheers Felix somewhat—little ripples of tree-studded hills frame the horizon while close in they pass a dizzying spectrum of colors: flowers of red, blazing lemon yellow, bluish-purple, pink stems jutting from paler pink petals; tiny black and white butterflies shuttling between flowers in lazy arcs; huge stands of elephant grass swaying like fields of green wheat.

The rusted tin roofs of Koidu disappear, and then soon after, the open spaces of country materialize. They are in the jungle, back in the thick, bumping along at ten miles an hour over the rutted road. Issa curses each pothole as if it's a rebel. Brown dust swirls all around, covering everything inside the truck.

They barely speak. Issa concentrates on avoiding the biggest holes, lurching this way and that, sometimes driving right into the fringes of the jungle, the tall grasses and short shrubs an easier traverse than the pits in the road. Each hole is like a warning, an admonition that they're moving deeper and deeper into a place they shouldn't be. Felix doesn't even know if this is where his dad had gone; he thinks not, that this mine, wherever it is, is way too deep and way too far from Freetown. But if he visits the most inaccessible, the most horrid, he reasons, he can absolve himself of any lingering feelings of guilt for not having gone as far as he could. And every pitch and rock of the Jeep feels one step closer to the horror.

But this is no death wish. There's been a cease-fire, and while things are still not as they should be—the rebels still control the area—this trip is not suicidal. It's just damn scary. But Issa has said he knows someone on the inside, a prospect that puts Felix less on edge.

When the sky begins to darken as the sun falls behind the thick canopy, Felix wonders if they've made any real progress. It feels as if they're barely twenty miles outside of Koidu. Hell, in a long day, they could have walked it. He has no idea how much farther they have to go, either.

Regret again, and ache, a feeling this is all a mistake.

But soon, a gray sheen forms over the foliage, and eventually everything glows white like a fine layer of snow, like hell frozen over.

A gargantuan moon rises alone in the black sky. Out of nothingness, a beacon, like the lighthouse at Alexandria must have looked to sailors approaching Egypt. Felix can see the craters, the pocks, the falling lines along the surface. He raises his hand and stretches his fingers, sure he's going to scratch the underside. But it sits just out of reach.

They eat some bread and lamb they'd brought from Koidu and drink their warm sodas and then try and get some sleep. But Felix is awake the whole night. The screech of monkeys seems synched to the precise moments when he dozes off. Every time he jumps up, at first startled and then merely to shift his body in the seat, he looks over to Issa. It appears as if he's awake too, moving back and forth on each side, like he's haunted by bad dreams.

When dawn arrives, it does so slowly, as if unsure of itself. There is only an almost imperceptible lightening of an unseen horizon, a hazy delineation between earth and sky before spreading itself across the land and punching the darkness away until the faintest light peeps through the slits between the leaves. Felix is thrilled when he hears the engine start, more than ready to move again, to get away from where they are, as if sitting still makes them targets for something. It's still a bit dark, but soon, and with great acceleration, the entire world brightens and the accompanying heat comes on quick and thick.

Despite the heat, the day starts blissfully clean. No diesel exhaust, no burning garbage. It is jungle and life and it moves around them as they step out to pee and then hop back in the Jeep to take off. Within an hour, when bursts of humidity break into a light but steady rain, they flank a river. Issa pulls the Jeep to the side and tells Felix to get out and follow him.

They walk ten minutes down an overgrown and muddy footpath, silent the whole way. Felix is overcome by a very sudden but unmistakable surge of panic, moving deeper and deeper down this jungle path, feeling immensely vulnerable. The silver cross around his neck feels like dead weight, something dense and heavy, banging against his chest like a warning. Trying to control himself, to tell himself that Issa is a friend, a guide, someone he can trust, he continues on, slapping at tree branches and mosquitoes and slipping twice in the mud, the cross clanging against his jaw. Each time, Issa stands ahead waiting for Felix, but he doesn't offer any help. Things have changed. The deeper they go, the more distant from Issa Felix feels. He pulls himself out of the mud while Issa just stands there, quiet and withdrawn. More silent panic now—Felix can feel his heart thumping. He tries to find the words to say that he wants to turn around, get back in the Jeep, he's seen enough even though he's seen almost nothing, go back home, crawl inside of Lizzy, call it all off . . .

They emerge onto the edge of the river where six men sit around an old compressor belching black fumes. A dugout canoe bobs lazily at the water's edge. Two long planks jut into the river, which is the color of coffee. The planks end where a plastic tube that runs from the compressor drops into a wide section of river; there, wooden boards sit in tenuous criss-crosses. Felix takes deep breaths; the opening allows his chest to uncoil. The jungle path has induced a paranoiac feeling of suffocation. He's relieved by this realization—it is not Issa he needs to fear. But when he gets his breath back and then is able to ask Issa how he knows about this place, he remains unresponsive, replying only, "I know."

They move closer to the men. One of them jumps up and bounds toward the new arrivals. Felix flinches, but the man is full of smiles and hand slaps.

"Is it the devils' river today?" Issa asks.

"Down the way at Sewa," the man answers, "Three get

up caught up in the lines. They die under. They go on Friday—no-no." Just then, the plastic tube bobs up and down on the water's surface. The men sitting on the boards spring to work, pulling on a rope. They tug until the black dome of a man's shaved head pierces the surface of the muddy water. When the rest of his face follows, the rubber tube in his mouth becomes visible. The men help him climb out and then uncoil the tube from around his legs and crotch. He's wearing only white muddy briefs.

The man who's emerged from the river looks around. His hands are clenched in fists. He sits on the riverbank, looking dazed. Everyone crowds around him, so Issa and Felix walk toward him, too. The river man opens his palms.

Several of the men gingerly rake their fingers through a pile of rocks and mud while the man forms a ridge with his thumbs so nothing will fall out. While they inspect his catch, Felix concentrates on the man's face. His bloodshot eyes are puffy and look like they may burst in his head. Little flecks of dirt and sand stick to every spot on his face and in his ears. It's clear from the lazy positions of the men when they'd first arrived, looking like they were waiting for fish to bite a line, that he'd been under a while. And now he's come up with a handful of worthless pebbles and dirt. The last of the rocks spill over his hands and he lets them fall to the ground. The men around him offer condolences by patting him on the knees and shoulders and head. He just sits there, more dazed than dejected.

This man had gone under, blind, attached to life only by an orange tube from which he sucked dirty oxygen. He'd groped around the river bottom holding onto whatever might feel like a diamond. And now, for risking his life, what he has to show for it is nothing but a puffy face and what Felix imagines is an unspeakable headache. He tries to suppress his pity, remembering his father's dictate against the uselessness of pity, but has trouble stemming it as another of the men strips off his shirt and pants and wraps the hose around his legs, pulling it so that it sticks tightly in the crook of space between his thigh and testicles.

They say their goodbyes and as they walk back to the Jeep—somehow the trip back feels like mere seconds compared to the walk to the river—Issa explains: "It is either this or become a rebel. This is the only job they can get. They do not hurt anyone this way."

The rain begins to fall a bit harder. Back in the truck, their going is slow but steady. They soon pass the village where these men have obviously come from. Thatch huts line the road, villagers sitting in front of them.

"Do you see these people?" Issa asks. He is clearly agitated again. "Do you see what they are doing?"

They aren't doing anything but sitting outside their houses getting rained on.

"The first time I was here, many years ago, they were dancing. They should be dancing now. The rains coming is a big event. It means the farms can be useful again. The rains used to mean drumming, singing. Now there are no farms. Left to rot and turned into mud pits for digging diamonds. Those men should be farming. Now all they can do is sit on a river bottom for hours pulling up sand."

Even when Issa stops the truck, no one moves. Felix stays behind while Issa walks over to a pot-bellied man in a red Chicago Bulls tank top. They exchange words, shake hands, and talk a bit. Issa kicks at the ground; he looks nervous. He points at the road, the village, the trees above. Then he folds his hands and listens to the man, nodding every few seconds. When they're done, they shake once again and Felix sees Issa surreptitiously handing the man some money before he comes back to the truck and gets in.

"Village chief. I ask his permission to pass. It is a sign of respect that the RUF ignored," he says. "He wants to show us something." Felix gets out of the truck and moves into the back seat for the chief. For the first time in a while, Issa smiles, obviously appreciating this show of respect.

The rain picks up and the once dusty road turns to mud. The further they move, the less "road" the road becomes. Instead, it's merely a swath cut out of the jungle, strewn with huge rocks and sluiced with rainwater.

"During the war, the RUF made sure the road stayed this way," Issa says. "It allowed them to ambush people easily."

The chief mutters something and points to the woods on the right. Issa gets out of the truck and Felix follows. The chief stays behind. "All that Doctor Grillet and I told you back in Freetown. All of that cannot make as much sense as what I can show you—here," Issa says. He points to the woods, his eyebrows raised as he looks back to the chief. The chief nods. Felix can't see anything beyond the same grasses and shrubs that have been framing the road since Koidu.

He follows as Issa moves down a barely discernible path, a thin groove in the grass that winds around trees and ends at a concrete structure swamped by foliage. They push away some branches.

"What is it?"

"A rebel killing house. Here is where many died."

Felix feels a sickness rising in his chest, but he doesn't turn around and go back to the Jeep. He doesn't tell Issa he's not up for it. He doesn't protest. Instead, he walks inside. Somehow, without thinking.

Grasses and weeds coil among the entranceway. It takes Felix a few moments for his eyes to adjust to the darkness. But when they do and he looks at the walls, he sees them breathing. He's sure he isn't hallucinating. He looks closely; the walls ripple and pulsate. He steps closer and examines the ripples: a mosaic of reddish-brown spots and streaks.

It looks as if something on the floor has exploded, spraying the walls all the way up to the ceiling. The base of the wall is almost black from the clotted stains. Felix feels sick. He wants to run away, but Issa stands silently in the corner, running his eyes up and down the walls.

Felix follows Issa into an adjoining room. It's bright there, with a large window in the middle of one wall. All around the window, swirls of dark red like fingerpaint run from edge to edge, ceiling to floor. Rainwater drips from cracks in the ceiling and spatters in little puddles at their feet. It smells of rot and mold, but there's something else, a sharp, metallic tang like dead earth, putrid soil mixed with body, animal, sweat.

The final room looks burnt. An old rusted and gutted filing cabinet stands in the middle of the room. A stained gray pillow lay beside. A pillow—something manufactured for the express purpose of human comfort.

Under the right side of the window, there's a dark brown stain so deep and so big that it looks like a pile, a fresh puddle of congealed blood. Felix turns around and throws up, his meager breakfast splashing to the floor.

All that has flowed from veins in this very room is so far beyond his piddling nausea and subsequent stomach ache that he feels stupid and ashamed. He wipes his lips and bucks up. He wants out of there and begins to leave, but he looks once more at the far wall on the way out. There's a face in the middle. It looks like the face of a creature—half man, half lion. White locks run from its head, cutting through the mottled splotches of red. Three teeth form a crooked row at the top of a gaping mouth, screaming, roaring in agony. There is a perfect bridge of nose, perfect cheekbone, perfect neckline all stabbed in the middle of an explosion of dried blood. Felix points it out, but Issa can't see it. He runs his fingers along the facial contours, showing Issa where to look. But Issa still can't see it, even as he turns and tilts his head—it's like one of those hologram posters that only some can see, and only at certain angles. Felix runs his fingers over it again, over the swooping hairline. It dawns on him that he's tracing his fingers in some-one else's dried blood—in dozens of people's blood, maybe hundreds. It feels only like a poor spackling job, a pre-sanded matte of grooves and bumps.

He looks at his fingers, but they're clean. No blood has come off—and of course not. It has been dried on, plastered for years now.

He waits for something else, a sense of the dead—waits for their spirits to tickle his hair and spine and run their fingers on the back of his neck. But he feels nothing. There are no spirits hovering, waiting for eternal peace. No, that killing room is the farthest thing from it. It is only death. Stillness and heat and darkness and death.

They walk back toward the truck in silence, Felix car-rying a dim pang of shame that he's left some piece of himself in there with the pieces of them.

Issa starts moving more quickly. Felix hurries to catch

up, but Issa moves with incredible speed and deftness. Felix begins to run, meeting Issa only when he stops somewhere between the killing house and the Jeep.

He watches as Issa grabs the watch off his own wrist and flings it as far as he can into the woods. Felix watches its arcing flight, its path traced through a tangle of vines and the sweeping fingers of palm trees.

# CHAPTER NINE

After seeing the chief back to his village, Issa and Felix take off again and embark upon a long, wordless lurch along the rutted jungle track, the silence broken only by one pronouncement: "I do not like jungles," Issa mutters.

The rain and the trees cloak them in darkness. A slow and steady buzz rings in Felix's left ear. He feels a sensation like he's falling, only to be jerked up at the last moment. Even when the jungle breaks, when they drive through a little clearing that runs off just to the right of the road, leading to a small concrete, tin-roofed shack, it still feels like they could slip into the mud and get swallowed up forever. Felix knows that perhaps he should be scared. But he feels little beyond the faint nagging of dizziness lying just below his consciousness.

They pull in front of the shack: satellite dish on the roof, a clothesline with wet and grimy shirts strung between two trees, three dogs milling around in the mud. When they get out of the truck, the dogs run over and jump on them.

"Marc?" Issa calls, pushing the dogs away.

"Issa? Come inside."

Marc is a pot-bellied, dark-skinned man in a pair of Speedos sitting in front of a television, a half-eaten banana in his hand. The rain on the roof makes a terrible pounding sound. The TV is turned to an earsplitting volume. A generator bleats and sputters in competition. "This stuff makes me laugh," Marc yells, pointing to the TV: A pissed off Skipper hurls a barrage of coconuts at a fleeing Gilligan. Marc laughs again, a massive hearty growl that shakes his entire body, wiggling his flesh from neck to calves. Then he settles down and draws a contemplative sigh. "He is such a fucking idiot—this Gilligan." Marc eats the rest of his banana in one gulp and gets up.

"You are late," he says.

"We had some trouble on the roads."

"Of course." Marc slips into a pair of gray pants.

Suddenly the noise on the roof stops. Both Issa and Marc look up and then look at each other.

"This is Felix," Issa says.

Marc shakes his hand. "Welcome, welcome," he says.

"Marc heads up the Sierra Leone Ministry of Mines and Natural Resources," Issa says. Since he has already told him this, Felix figures the announcement, so Marc can hear it, is perhaps Issa's way of ingratiating himself.

"Uh, uh. Second in charge," Marc says.

"Sankoh is in Pademba, yes?" Issa asks. The two men laugh knowingly, and Marc's flesh starts quivering again.

"Come. They are expecting us."

They walk back outside. Shafts of sunlight splinter through the tall trees and reflect off puddles. The three men get back into the truck and drive off, bumping and lurching along at a tortoise pace.

"These roads are improved, can you believe?" Marc says. "It was worse with last year's rains."

"Rains" elongates, drawing out of Marc's mouth like he's been pushed to the ground. The Jeep pitches into a massive hole and comes to rest there, one tire dangling over the pit while the others spin uselessly. They get out. Felix helps to try and free the Jeep—to no immediate effect—and then steps off into the woods to relieve himself.

He finds a slight clearing in the bush. Small trees have been hastily chopped down, their stubby trunks pointed like spears. Grass barely covers the ground; spots of dark brown still shine through the green. It looks as if the area has been heavily trod. He starts to pee and sees a stump in front of him that's cleanly cleaved, unlike the others, and pocked with slim chop marks. The razor thin slits are darker than the rest of the wood. He guesses what those stains might mean and he thinks of Joseph, the man back at the hospital in Freetown. This could have been the spot for all Felix knows. The tiny bones of his fingers could very well be lying nearby. He spits and looks away, concentrating on the stream of urine pounding the brown earth.

Its hammering on the mud slowly reveals a whitish tip. It doesn't sparkle or shine, but it sticks out in such great relief from the mud that there's little question what it is. Not bone, not in this case.

He continues to pee on it, washing away most of the dirt. He finishes and then picks up the stone, wiping off the remaining mud. It's almost as big as his pinky nail, its coloring clear with a hint of white.

"Felix," Issa yells.

He doesn't know what to do. Should he stick it in his pants, his mouth, his rectum? Should he tell Issa? Should he tell Marc? Smuggling a diamond is ridiculous. They're going to be subjected to a thorough search when they leave the mine camp; Issa has prepared him for that—"Enjoy it," he'd instructed. "Close your eyes and imagine a woman."

"Felix," Issa yells again.

Felix thrusts the diamond in his boot, where it wedges against his ankle. He can feel its ragged edge against his bone as he walks back to Marc and Issa.

"Were you searching for it?" Marc asks. He laughs again, his whole body convulsing. Issa looks at him and smirks. Felix stands, dumb, until he realizes it's an innocuous joke, a dig at the supposed smallness of his penis. He tries to force a laugh, but manages only choked titters.

They finally free the Jeep and head off for the mine camp. Felix is silent for the rest of the drive, the diamond against his ankle scraping away like a knife. He finds it hard to breathe again, and his ears buzz more than before. He resolves to get rid of the diamond first chance he gets, knowing how stupid it was to have taken it in the first place.

The mine camp emits a horrendous smell, like an overturned port-a-potty baking in the sun. The opening of the camp does nothing to ease Felix's feelings of claustrophobia. Enormous black piles swarming with huge flies fill several clearings in the woods. They drive on a bit further until they reach a series of decrepit buildings. There, two scraggly roosters chase each other in circles.

Several muddy men cradling AK-47s sit in a circle with tattered playing cards. As Issa, Marc, and Felix get out and walk toward a long, flat building with cheesecloth in the windows, it becomes immediately evident that the men playing cards are the liveliest inhabitants in the camp. Most of the others lean against the walls of the decrepit shacks, staring vacantly with bloodshot eyes.

Piles of food wrappers and beer cans litter the whole place. That same horrendous smell when they'd first arrived hovers over everything. And then Felix realizes what those piles are—of course there are no flush toilets.

A naked baby crawls out from behind one of the buildings. It has to be a fake, a wind-up toy like a robotic dog. They haven't seen a woman since the last village, hours earlier. It simply *can't* be. But a man sitting nearby grabs the baby by its arm and cradles it in its lap, where the baby rests without moving.

A shirtless man emerges from one of the buildings. He has a massive purple scar stretching across his entire torso, from shoulder to belly button, a strange protruding thing that resembles a tiny thumb.

"Issa," he exclaims. "Such a long time." He comes over and gives Issa a big hug. Issa hugs back but does not smile.

"How are you?" Issa asks.

"Could not be better. Look at this world. It is paradise, no?"

The man smiles, revealing shards of cracked teeth, some of them chiseled into points, obviously with intent, like wolf fangs. He tells Issa and Felix to follow him into the building.

"Patrice," Issa says, addressing him, "Should we get our bags?"

"Leave them. I will have the men put them in your sleeping quarters. You will have that barracks all to yourself." He points to a zinc-roofed building. "It is the luxury suite," he says. "Marc, you will stay with us."

They start toward the building. A man holding a rifle sidles over and steps in front of them. He looks with great intensity into Issa's face, his eyebrows making a severe V across his forehead. Then a look of recognition comes into his eyes.

"Hey," he spits. "What the fuck you here for?"

Issa sputters, but Marc intercedes. "He is with me. Do you have a problem?"

The man smiles, something malevolent. "No," he says, his eyes still on Issa's face. "I don have no problem." He backs away and spreads his arm in mock welcome.

A heavy, oppressive feeling comes over Felix. He wants to leave. He determines that he'll speak only when spoken to. He'll ask no questions, show no curiosity about anything, and he'll tell Issa that he wants to get the hell out of there as soon as possible.

They enter the main building, where there's a long table in the middle of the room and half a dozen men sitting around drinking beer and looking at maps. Piles of broken glass sit in the corners, and the wood paneling on the walls is bowed and split. It's filthy and rundown, but a veritable paradise compared to outside. Patrice introduces Issa and Marc and then points to Felix. "Who are you?" he asks. Nothing comes. Sweat drips down Felix's forehead and his armpits. He feels like he's going to puke again.

"Is he dumb?" Patrice asks.

"This is my assistant Felix," Issa says. "He has been unwell. He just needs to sleep."

"He looks like the last white man I ate. A missionary. Ate his heart," Patrice says. He looks at Felix, a smile slowly breaking over his face before he throws his head back and laughs toward the ceiling—a rolling laugh, coming from the bottom of his feet and rippling, gaining strength like a wave, working through his torso, and then pouring out of his mouth like hellfire.

Patrice comes over and rubs his hand on Felix's head

like he's the coach's son who's made a tough outfield catch. Issa laughs hard—a little too hard, it seems to Felix. Issa is supposed to be scared of no one; he is also the man who is supposed to save Felix from these lunatics. But now Felix doubts he could, or would.

Worse, Felix can feel the diamond against his ankle, sucking the life out of him. He needs to tell Issa, but he can't peel him away. So, as the men play cards, he excuses himself to the barracks so he can get rid of it.

The floor is swept clean and their bags have been stacked neatly in a corner. A hot wind slithers through a hole in the glass in the window. There's no one out there, so Felix takes off his socks and shoes and the diamond tumbles out. He rolls it between his fingers, feeling its nubby edges, its surprising lack of heft. He could give it to his mother, he reasons, some recompense for his dad having taken away her bracelet. She deserves it, after all. And this one he could justify. He found it; no miner toiled for it. No little girl lost her arm because of it.

But then it looks like a rock—nothing more and nothing less. A stupid milky piece of compressed carbon. No more valuable than lead.

He throws it out of the window and watches as it skidders under a pile of dead leaves.

His heart leaps when he sees a figure leaning against a tree nearby. He hadn't seen him before; the man had blended into the tree like a walking stick on a branch. But Felix can see him moving now. His head lolls, his woolly hair matted and unkempt. His bony knees are drawn up all the way to his chin, and he unfolds himself and lets his legs fall to the ground. His eyes, seemingly too big for his face, look Felix's way, but then the lids close over them. If he's seen what Felix has done, he registers no reaction.

Feeling a bit safer, Felix lies down, cocooned in the barracks where he can finally try and salve his spinning head and buzzing ears. The monkeys in the trees and the men playing cards provide a distant soundtrack, far off and faint. When he closes his eyes and gives in to the exhaustion, he can just as easily be in his bedroom in Baltimore or in a hammock at Deep Creek Lake in the mountains of Western Maryland where his parents and he used to go when he was in elementary school. He could be dozing in that hammock, the sun lighting the backs of his eyelids, summer heat leaving him lazy and content. He could hear the faint whine of a lawnmower or a chainsaw far off in the distance, maybe some voices floating out from a television in a nearby cabin or the pleasant and mellow strains of a radio broadcasting an Orioles game.

But then he falls away from the dream and he doesn't have to open his eyes to remember that he isn't back at home and it isn't a decade earlier; he's in West Africa, in a jungle. The temperature isn't one to induce mere laziness, but lethargy instead—a sick sort of malarial stupor. The heat is oppressive and thick and it smells like disease.

He lay like that for hours, unable to get up and move, every now and then opening his eyes to see a deep wall of green outside the window, feeling alone and scared and waiting for Issa to come back, thinking that he'll never return.

Then he hears Marc's and Issa's voices over everyone else's, distinctly at first, though he can't make out what they are saying. Their voices soon mix with the eerie mechanical tones from a distant television or radio, the same one he'd heard when he floated back in time and space to Western Maryland.

A low motorized buzz wails incessantly, somewhere far off. He hears the roosters crowing and he opens his eyes expecting dawn, but it's night black.

He falls into a deep and exhausted sleep and doesn't wake until morning. Issa tells him that when he came in to check on him, he was fast asleep and in the same exact position as when he went to bed, sometime after midnight. "I saw cockroaches crawling over your face. You did not wake up even then, so I let you sleep." Felix wants out of there and he tells Issa so.

"But this is what you wanted to see," Issa reminds him.

"I just have a bad feeling."

Outside, someone pounds on our door. "Hello?" Patrice asks, and then enters. "Come on," he says. "Breakfast. Then we can go to the mine."

Felix implores Issa with his eyes, but Issa ignores it, snapping to at Patrice's insistence.

Under watchful eyes, they are given a breakfast of roasted corn and groundnut stew. After they eat, Patrice and two armed men parade them first around the outskirts of the camp and then lead them along a narrow footpath to the mine.

In front of them sits a massive lake of brown water, ringed by the tree line. It's like walking over a sand dune and seeing the ocean, or running toward a cliff edge only to realize that you've come to the Grand Canyon. The mine is a gargantuan wound scratched out of the jungle—torn up earth, mixed with sweat, piss, and rainwater. The smell of rawness is overwhelming: acrid and almost sulphurous, burning his nostrils.

About a dozen men stand in the water in front of them, the brown liquid up to the middle of their thighs. They are all barebacked and wearing torn cut-off pants. Several wear wool caps despite the intense heat. Each man holds a circular wire-bottomed pan, which he keeps at water level, shaking it back and forth and in little circles. Other men carry shovels of dirt and drop them onto the pan, at which point the man holding the pan shakes again until all the dirt sifts through and he's left with a pile of stones. Then the two men, together, run their fingers through the stones with incredible care, caressing the surface like they're petting a malnourished kitten. What remains, invariably, are rocks, pebbles, and more pebbles, the little remaining water sifting through. Finding no diamonds, they dump the stones into huge spent piles and repeat the whole process over again. The only break in uniformity comes when some of the men kiss the tips of their shovels before plunging them. In this way, the lake expands, minute chunks of earth gobbled up further and further and deeper and deeper, the entire landscape churned up one row of shovels at a time.

To the right, another group of men digs at a different pit. They're even more orchestrated, their routine and practiced flicks of wrists spraying the dirt into graceful arcs behind them. They're all muscular, but they look undernourished—sinewy and lean. They wear the same miner's outfit: no shirt, cut off shorts or jeans, no shoes. They're covered in flecks of reflective dirt, like they've been tossed by ocean waves and have just emerged from the sand.

Despite his earlier promise to himself to remain quiet, bide his time, and just get the hell out of there as soon as possible, Felix can't help himself and asks, "Do they ever find anything?"

Patrice laughs. "Of course. Why else would they be here?"

"Because they have no choice," Felix offers, in spite of himself. For a moment, his own impertinence scares him. However, *I owe this to my dad*, he thinks. *I am here, so I may as well . . .*

Issa flashes a stern look, but Patrice just laughs. "I do not know where this idea comes from. Look at these men. Do they look unhappy? They can leave whenever they like. When they find diamonds, they do go—they go to Freetown and buy fancy motor cars."

Issa is quick to concur. "All it takes is one big stone to change your life," he says.

"They love this—thrill of the hunt, you know," Patrice continues, nodding. "In Kono and Koidu, they eat, sleep, drink, and think diamonds. Wherever you go, what they talk about is only diamonds. In the nightclub. In the restaurant. It is diamonds. All the time, diamonds. You go to the market, they talk about diamonds. Everywhere. It is their life. What they know, what they love."

They'd been to Kono, that look-alike Hiroshima. The people there didn't seem to love the diamonds; the diamonds had destroyed them. More to fact, thugs like Patrice had destroyed them in their thirst for the diamonds.

Felix walks toward two men working together, up to their crotches in water. With the exception of a freshly created rivulet running behind them, banked by tall green grasses, they're completely enclosed by mud. "Today will be a lucky day," Patrice says, pointing at the men. "Today, this is the lucky spot."

"Can I talk to them?" Felix asks.

"Of course."

They climb out of the mud and offer Felix their wet

and slippery hands.

"Any luck today?"

One of the men sticks out his tongue to reveal a tiny white stone on the tip.

"How much is that worth?"

"Around 35,000 leone."

Fourteen dollars.

"That's not much," Felix says, feeling immediately ashamed of himself. Maybe fourteen dollars is a small fortune. But the man doesn't seem to take offense. "The big one come," he says.

"What will you do with the money when you find it?"

"I will buy a house for me family."

"I will buy a motor-car. I will move to America. I have a brother there."

"You don't want to stay in Sierra Leone?"

He shakes his head as he jumps back into the water. The other man grabs the shovel and they get back to the sifting.

"That is often how you count wealth in Sierra Leone," Issa says. "How many relatives you have living in America or in Britain."

Felix takes one last look at the sweeping orgy of activity—the constant thrusting of arms and shovels, the sprays of dirt, the glistening backs of the hunched men, the incongruous gentleness of the sifting. He's ready to go home.

That evening, Felix packs up his things. Going through his bag, he notices that his journal is gone. It irritates him, but it isn't a huge deal. He's hardly written anything in it, and he decides not to even ask for it back. But obviously someone has rooted through his stuff. At least he'd gotten rid of the diamond. He'll tell Issa about it when he gets in from drinks with Patrice and the others.

But he falls asleep while waiting and wakes up to a hard smash against his head. His right ear goes deaf on impact. Before he can collect himself, another kick falls across his head. He backs away best he can, attempting desperately to extricate himself from his sleeping bag, all the while trying to shield his head. A hand yanks at his hair, getting a piece of the Agadez silver cross's string and pulling upward, cutting off Felix's air supply before the string snaps and the cross skitters across the floor. Then the hands are off him and he gets a momentary reprieve. In the dim light from the outside generator, Felix can make out the outlines of someone coming at him, his foot raised and poised to deliver another blow.

"Okay, okay. Enough."

He looks up to see Marc holding back the man who'd been beating him. Felix's head spins. His ear buzzes.

"What is it?" he asks. "What? Where's Issa?"

"What is *this*, you motherfucker?" Marc holds a diamond between his fingers. "You stole it from the mines."

"I didn't. How could I do that? How could I?"

The man gives him another kick, this time across his shoulder. An explosion of pain tears through his arm. Fortunately, he falls with the kick or his shoulder surely would be broken or dislocated. Blood trickles off his upper lip and drips down his face.

The door slams.

It's light outside when he wakes. When he stands, the blood that has not dripped out of his mouth and nostrils rushes to his head. Dizzy, he sits back down. But he isn't quick enough. Soon he's on his hands and knees, retching bile and blood.

The door opens and Issa comes tumbling in.

When Felix touches his shoulder, Issa jumps back and winces. "Is it broken?" Felix asks.

Issa coughs in response. His left eye is swollen shut. There's a chunk of hair missing just above his forehead, a startlingly pink patch of skin in its place.

"What happened? What's going on?"

"You should have told me, Felix."

"The diamond? I didn't--"

"You cannot keep those. We are in trouble now."

"I found one in the woods, but I threw it away. I swear . . . Issa, I'm sorry." He reaches out to touch him again, but Issa retracts. He doesn't say anything else and instead hands Issa his blanket to rest his head.

They sit for what feels like hours, Issa's pained coughing the only noise between them.

The door opens. Someone throws sorghum balls onto the floor and then slams the door. Felix hands half to Issa. He eats gingerly, keeping each bite on the same side of his mouth.

"I'm sorry, Issa. I didn't know."

"It is not all your fault."

"Of course it is."

He shakes his head.

"There is a lot you do not know, Felix. You may not understand." Issa steadies himself against the wall. "It is a hard life in this part of the world. A man must do what he needs. To survive. To feed his family. He digs in the mines. He sells the diamonds. He cuts off limbs."

"I don't understand."

"I was born in Niger. I do not wish that upon any person. It is hard there."

"But you got out. You went to America. You work for

the U.N. . . . Don't you?"

"I first went to Sierra Leone as a mercenary. Hired . . . for pay . . ." He looks away. "By Charles Taylor."

"But—"

"Those men in Accra. The ones you saw me with? Drinking beer?"

"Yes," Felix says, realizing now that Issa *had* seen him.

"Diamond dealers. And the men with them were U.N.."

"So?"

"It is in the culture. We are all a little corrupt out here. If we are not a little corrupt, then we are a lot. It is those of us who do get out, who do get opportunity. How do you think we get it?"

"So you're involved in the diamond trade?"

"Was. That is why I have been beaten. RUF rebels working here at the mine . . . when they found the diamond."

"I don't understand. Tell me."

"I used to run their diamonds into Guinea and then take a percentage. It was innocent at first, just a way to make a living. The rebels said they were only giving the diamonds to Poppy—Foday Sankoh. They would get the diamonds to him, people got money and arms in return. They started it all for the people. Save them from the corruption in Freetown. But they got too much power, became drunk with it. I saw what they were doing in the villages. Children. Drugged up, illiterate. They could not be stopped."

"So you stopped working with the RUF?"

"I backed out on a deal. I gave the diamonds back, but they claimed I stole some."

Felix thinks of his diamond. Obviously, that zombie

had seen him. Or maybe they had just planted it. His bag was gone. Who knew for sure? It was done now.

They sit in silence. Felix reviews the events, tries to make sense of it all. It's been merely six months since he'd first come to Africa, a span between dental checkups, a basketball season, a time in which so little often happens in a person's life.

"Are we going to die here?"

Issa doesn't answer.

"Why did you come back if you knew this might happen?"

Again, no answer.

It slowly grows dark in the room, the silence heavy like rotting fruit.

"Issa—why did you come here? You came back to the very people you broke with to record stories for a tribunal against them. Why?"

Issa pulls out his picture of Memuna. He rubs one finger over her face, then traces the finger over her left arm, reattaching an imaginary appendage there.

"Absolution," he says. "But I should have left you out of it." The picture falls from his hand. He turns over and coughs. "Your father, Felix . . . I am very sorry," he whispers.

"What happened. What happened to him. I am sorry."

Felix nods. "Thank you," he says, at a loss to say anything else.

Issa coughs, sputters. "You don't understand."

Felix has come all this way, done all this, just to understand his dad. But he doesn't ask Issa anything else. At this moment, he thinks he knows all he ever needs to know—his father is gone, and nothing will change that. Nothing anyone says or does.

He leans in and looks closely at Issa; his eyes are closed and he's breathing very slowly. Felix takes the picture and puts it back in Issa's hand.

They sit in these positions for almost the entire day. The first interruption comes when one of the rebels opens the door and throws Felix's backpack at him. When it lands on the floor, little pieces of civilization scatter from it: a handful of American and West African coins; two pens; a keychain—all things that are useless to him in this place. They are mementoes of another world, one that Felix complained used to bore him.

He quietly stuffs his belongings back in, retrieving his silver cross from where it had been sitting on the floor, and shoves that in, too.

When the door next flings open, Felix recoils. Issa doesn't move.

"These are the thieves, huh?"

Felix can't believe it. He recognizes the voice instantly—how could he not?

"Wesley?"

The guard, brandishing an AK-47, looks at him, then looks at Wesley. "You know each other?"

"Never seen him before in my life. What are you doing to these boys? You starving them?" It is Wesley for sure, but he's lost his accent. He speaks now like an American. He smiles at the guard and then looks at Felix. He narrows his eyes and gives a barely perceptible shake of his head. Felix gets the subliminal message.

"So you'll have me take the American? Believe me, you don't want him here. You get the Americans involved, it's a pain in your ass. Those agency sons-of-bitches are already sniffing around in Freetown."

"They know about him?"

"I heard them talking all the way in Accra."

"You CIA?"

"I'm Canadian. Those boys are good to get drunk with, though."

"Take him."

"I'm doing you a favor."

"But the African stays here."

"Do with him what you will."

"We have some things to settle."

"Have fun," Wesley says. Looking at Felix, he says, "Come on. Help me load the wood. Leave your things here. You'll come back for them when we're ready to leave."

Felix gets up and follows Wesley, turning to look at Issa before he leaves the room. As the door slams, Felix hears Issa say, "You do not know—"

The guard charges back into the room and slams Issa with the butt of his rifle. Felix hears him yell. He doesn't know what to do. He imagines putting up resistance, telling Wesley that he won't leave without Issa, but for now it is all he can do to get his feet to follow his brain's instructions.

"Grab that end," Wesley yells. Next to Felix's feet sits an enormous hunk of tree trunk.

"You loading up?" a guard asks Wesley.

"Yeah."

"You need to take some of my boys to Kolahun."

"How am I going to do that?" Wesley asks. "I'm full here. I already have the banana coffin."

A huge wooden banana with a hinged midsection fills

much of the back of Wesley's pickup. Felix recalls the coffins he'd seen in Accra. Apparently, a fruit vendor has died.

"That is not my problem," the guard says. "You need to take my boys."

"But I spoke to Songay."

"I do not care who you spoke to."

Wesley puts his hands on his hips. "Three of my guys will be here in the morning. They were held up in Freetown getting the documents for the hardwood transfer. Your boys can go with them."

The soldier lowers his gun and it falls at an angle that leads directly to Wesley's crotch. "They go with you."

"Fine . . . When my boys get here, you tell them to take the wood." Wesley reaches inside the driver's side window of the truck and pulls out a bottle of liquor. "In the meanwhile," he says, slowly shaking the bottle back and forth.

The guard smiles. He takes the bottle from Wesley and puts his gun back on his shoulder as they walk toward the guard station.

"Hey," Wesley says. "You gonna put this guy back in the pen?"

The guard takes Felix back to his room, where Issa is still inside sitting against the wall.

"I don't know what's going on," Felix says when they are alone again.

"What is going on is that Wesley is saving your ass."

"I still don't see how."

"I cannot say that I like him, but perhaps I underestimated him."

"He's driving a pickup truck with a banana coffin in it. He says he's picking up hardwood for a shop in Accra."

Issa manages a little smile and shakes his head.

"Is that ridiculous?" Felix asks.

"Accra coffin makers get their wood from Sierra Leone and Liberia, yes, but there is no way a fool like Wesley would be working for them. Coming all the way out here, with a coffin already made, too. And these idiots believe him." Issa rubs his shoulder.

"You all right?"

He waves off Felix's concern.

"He says that he has more people on the way with more trucks."

"You have to give him his due."

The door bursts open. It's Wesley.

"Grab your shit," he says to Felix. He scurries over to Issa, who does not flinch. Wesley bends down until his nose is almost touching Issa's, a reverse scene from the Diffa airstrip. "This is your lucky day," he says. "When you hear me sneeze, get up and run to the truck. The coffin will be open. Jump in and close the lid. When we drive and you hear three taps, count to fifty and jump out of the coffin."

Wesley hurries out and Felix follows, adrenalin coursing through him. "Get in the truck," Wesley orders. He walks over to the guard station and just as he enters lets out a monstrous sneeze. This is followed by a chorus of good-natured yelling from inside the station. As the station soldiers and Wesley erupt into a high-pitched song, Issa comes running toward the truck. He runs hunched over, holding his shoulder, and when he reaches the truck, he sidles in the back and slides into the coffin. He lowers the lid and smothers a grunt of pain.

Wesley walks out of the guard station with three guys whose arms are locked around each other's shoulders. Each has a rifle hanging over his chest. They pass Wesley's bottle of liquor back and forth. One of the guards hands it to Wesley, who refuses. He puts out his hands in a pantomime of a steering wheel. The guards groan, and Wesley grabs the bottle. He takes a slug and hands the bottle back. The guards, zigzagging along the path, shout their approval.

They jump into the back of the truck and sit on the ledge, their feet resting on the coffin. Wesley gets in and turns the truck around, heading away from the mine site. Felix is ready to burst from the excitement and tension. He's sore from the beating, but intact, and most of it has subsided under waves of adrenaline.

He bites back his questions, anxious but knowing better. Wesley fiddles with the radio until he gets a barely discernible station playing American and British pop tunes from the Eighties. The guards continue to drink and sing songs of their own.

Soon they quiet down. The truck bumps along the roads, the high beams revealing a thick canopy of trees. Felix thinks about Issa bouncing around in the coffin, wondering if the jarring is exacerbating his injuries, wondering also if he's able to get enough air. Wesley turns down the radio.

"Where do you boys need to be dropped off?" he shouts.

"We stay with you, driver," one of the guards shouts back.

"We're going all the way to Accra."

"Then that is where we go."

"But I was told Kolahun."

"You will stop this car when we tell you. We will search you for stones. If you are clean, we go to Accra. If you are not, you die here in the jungle."

Wesley stops talking. Felix barely breathes. The guards are no longer laughing, no longer enjoying themselves. Felix looks back and sees that they're staring straight ahead, solemnly smoking cigarettes and looking like they're steeling their nerves for some particularly nasty job.

"This damned radio," Wesley shouts. "It keeps breaking up." He bangs the dashboard three times. This is the signal. After a count of fifty, Issa is going to open the lid and he'll get his head blown off. Felix doesn't understand it.

He starts the count in his head—*eight, nine, ten— twenty, twenty-one, twenty-two—thirty-three, thirty-four, thirty-five—forty-seven, forty-eight, forty-nine—Fifty!*

Nothing.

He looks at Wesley. Wesley looks at Felix. No movement. Has Issa suffocated?

High-pierced shrieking comes from the back. Wesley steps hard on the accelerator as the soldiers leap from the truck, tumbling and rolling in the dirt as Wesley speeds away. They keep shrieking, wailing in half-formed words. Wesley continues to floor it, swerving masterfully around the holes and rocks in the road. Issa is sitting up in the coffin, watching the guards collecting themselves in the distance.

"Get down," he yells.

A loud crack of gunfire echoes through the woods. Felix ducks. Wesley steps even harder on the gas and they fly over holes, logs, rocks, veering into the jungle edge, and then cutting hard to the middle of the road, a virtuosic performance. Two more gun blasts sound, but they can no longer see the guards. Soon the only sound they can hear is the trio of hoots that Wesley, Issa, and Felix let loose into the West

African night.

"Goddamnit!" Felix screams. "Holy shit!" His heart is thumping so hard that he feels the pulse in his hands and feet.

"These local boys don't mess around with death. They see someone coming out of a coffin, they flee. Superstitious isn't even the word," Wesley says.

Felix looks into the back of the truck, where Issa is now straddling the tip of the banana. He reaches back and Issa grabs his hand.

After another few miles, Wesley pulls the truck to a stop. "All right," he says. "I gotta piss. You two probably do too if you haven't already soaked yourselves."

They all laugh. "Let's make this quick," he says. "We're approaching the border. I need to get our papers in order. Grab those out of the glove compartment," he says to Felix as he gets out of the truck.

"Whatever you say. You are the man." Felix hears Issa get down from the back of the truck. Wesley walks around to him.

The glove compartment is empty except for a few oil-stained napkins.

"Wesley, there's nothing in here."

He doesn't respond.

"Wesley?" Felix gets out of the truck and circles around. Issa pees in the woods. Wesley stands behind him. Issa turns around and the two men face each other, Wesley with his back toward Felix, the headlights directed on the both of them.

"Listen," Issa starts. "I owe you. For my life."

"Don't worry," Wesley says.

"We started bad. But, this time, well . . ." Issa raises his hand and puts it on Wesley's shoulder. "Thank you," he says.

In the bright light, Felix sees Issa's eyebrows rise. The smile on his face slowly melts away. He looks down just in time to see the pistol Wesley holds to his stomach.

Then he looks up, at Felix, and their eyes lock. A silent goodbye and then Issa looks away. It is then that Wesley pulls the trigger.

He is already shot, and is on the way down. But that isn't enough for Wesley. He catches Issa, grabs him by his head, props him up to full height, and shoots him again.

# CHAPTER TEN

With Issa dead on the ground, Wesley rifles through his pockets and grabs his ID badge. Then, he kneels down beside him and, almost tenderly, cradles his head.

He pulls out a pocketknife and deftly saws off Issa's right ear, placing it in a small white piece of gauze.

Then Wesley gets back into the truck. Felix can hear Wesley tell him to get in, too. It is distinct and without any accompaniment—a steady voice filling the vacuum of silence trailing the aural path of that gunshot. It floats right to him, like a whisper that finds its mark from a thousand miles away.

Then he feels Wesley's hand grabbing his arm. Felix twists away and kneels down over Issa. A perfect hole disrupts the smooth plane of Issa's forehead. A small trickle of blood runs from the opening, where it bubbles into pearls between his eyebrows. One eye stares past Felix into the mystery of what had been life. The other reposes behind its lid. Felix manages a sweep of his fingers across Issa's sweat-soaked forehead before Wesley's hand is back. On Felix's neck this time, pulling him to the truck. This time no nimble escape, no easy release. Now the wind is being sucked out of him. His throat constricts. He sputters, but then a slight loosening on his windpipe sets in motion a mechanical gasp, an unconscious bodily protest against death. This is easy—a few quick coughs, a shove into the car, a slamming door, and they are off. This is no bullet to the brain.

"He was a cheap gangster," Wesley says as he starts the truck. Felix has no snappy retorts. Instead, he looks back to the crumpled heap that had once been his friend. That is where it would end. Someone—probably the rebel soldiers—will stumble upon him. Realizing who he is, and that he has just escaped their clutches, they will probably make some game of desecrating what's left of him. There will be no proper burial, no tributes like Felix's dad had.

"A RUF gangster, a cheap diamond runner. People like your friend Issa are responsible for the misery in this stinking hellhole of a country. You know that?"

"Those days are over," Felix screams. "You fucking asshole!"

Wesley keeps driving, eyes steady on the road.

"Issa was a different person. He didn't do those things anymore. It's the very reason we were even at that mine camp in the first place. Don't you know anything?"

"I know plenty." He repeats that Issa is a RUF thug, a two-bit charlatan who was probably setting Felix up to have him killed in the mine camp. "There are a lot of people who wanted Issa Manzo dead—not least of which is Charles Taylor, the president of Liberia. Your friend and hero was hated in some high places."

"Taylor wanted him dead because he'd stopped working with the RUF. He was in the same shack I was. Didn't you see how he was beaten, you asshole?!"

Wesley only repeats the story.

"And so . . . what? Charles Taylor hired you to kill him?"

"That's right." He jiggles the ID and ear in his front

pocket. "I just made a lot of money."

"He was going to be killed by the rebels back at the camp. Why come all this way?"

"I only get paid if *I* do it, you know. Besides, cherry, I made a commitment to Dr. Albert that I would see you safe to Freetown. Much longer than I had anticipated and under very different circumstances, but I will make good on that, too. You see, I always keep my commitments. I have a reputation to maintain." He smirks, self-satisfied, vainglorious.

Felix lunges at him, pounding away as hard as he can on Wesley's neck and face.

The truck stops with an abrupt jerk. Wesley opens the driver's side door, grabs Felix's neck with his right hand, and flings him out. Felix lands on his injured shoulder and cries out in pain. He doesn't have a chance to get up before Wesley's boot is on the back of his neck. Felix squirms, kicking and clawing. He feels the air being squeezed out of his chest. "Let me know when you're through," Wesley says. And then he feels the warm splatters of piss as Wesley relieves himself a few inches from Felix's head.

"You fucking asshole," he manages to winch out of his constricting throat.

"He killed your father," Wesley says.

"Bullshit!" Felix screams, now out from under his boot and gasping for air. "Bullshit. You're a liar."

"You're so fucking naïve. He was a runner for the RUF. He admitted that to you, right?"

Felix doesn't answer.

"Did you ask him if he was with the RUF the day your dad was murdered?"

"He wasn't with them anymore."

"How do you know that? How do you know that Issa Manzo himself didn't give the order to go into that amputee camp?"

"Because Issa wouldn't do that."

Wesley laughs—laughs like he's never heard anything so funny. "That's a pretty flimsy rack to hang your hat on."

"And you're some fucking hero? A savior? You left me to die in the desert, you prick."

"In fact, I told you to stay exactly where you were, and had you done that I would have been back for you the very next day, which I was, incidentally. I was busy getting us to safety and you were doing nothing but slowing us down."

All Felix manages is to tell him to shut up.

"You're a very, very small cog in a very large wheel, Felix. Do you understand that? Do you understand anything that goes on around here, in this godforsaken shithole of a place?"

He doesn't answer; there's nothing Felix can do but agree with him—it's a recognition he's made long ago. Felix realizes that he doesn't know a damn thing, and suddenly everything and anything seems possible.

## CHAPTER ELEVEN

Felix is supposed to fly home with Wesley. That was the plan, anyway. Out of Freetown, they'd do the long one: stops in Conakry, Nouakchott, Paris, and then Washington Dulles.

But there isn't any way he's keeping that date.

When they arrive in Freetown, Felix gets out of the truck at the first light, slams the door, and walks away.

"You're free to go. My job is over," Wesley yells at him.

Felix doesn't turn back.

"You're welcome," Wesley screams.

His flight won't be leaving for another two days. So he passes one day at Lumley Beach watching the water spread like a tentative lover over the gray sand. It's a lazy beach, protected from ocean force by a crescent cove. He lets the sea wrap around his naked toes and thinks of his boyhood days, of the first time he ever went in the ocean. His father held him steady on his shoulders while the brackish water completed its interminable march to land, causing him to lean into the throb of each wave. Behind them, pieces of horseshoe crab littered the beach. Ahead of them, eternity.

When the larger waves came, his father held Felix up so it only slapped against his chest and sprinkled his face. Off on the horizon, beyond cresting whitecaps, was Europe. His dad had been there and had told Felix about it. "It's France out there," he said. And he told Felix about Paris, about wine country, about a place where naked ladies danced, about holes

in walls where men saw it all, until his mother told him to
stop it. And he could imagine it out there, just beyond where
his eyes strained to see it—sure if he looked hard enough, he
could see the tip of the Eiffel Tower, the same steel structure
where his dad had his picture taken. Felix had looked at it in
one of his dad's many photo books. It was one of his favor-
ites. He's a young man in the picture; it's a windy day and his
hair is dancing over his head—a wild mane of hair that looks
nothing like the way he wears it later in life, when he's Felix's
dad. And then later, there is the picture back at that place, but
this time he's with his wife, Felix's mother. Less hair, less of the
tower, too, cut off at the tip.

He tells Felix that you can't see France from the ocean,
that the ridge you see from the shoreline continues to be a
ridge even as you travel close to it, for a long, long time until
finally you'll be able to see land. And that would be France.
"Or Portugal, actually" he says. And then comes the geography lesson. Portugal: the sailors, Lisbon's old section, Algarve,
the cork trees. Felix loves it, all of it. Not only is this water a
blast to play around in, but it leads to exotic places.

From that summer on, he's a water bug. Every chance
he gets and in every place he goes, he dives and splashes
while his poor mother looks on horrified because she's never
learned to swim. Felix can only imagine now the feeling she
must have had when he emerged from the ocean, coughing
and sputtering after having disappeared in a tumble of white
foam and brown sand, having been slammed and crushed by
a wave he didn't catch.

Felix walks further on, away from town to where the
sightline stretches beyond the protection of the cove. Here the
sand is warmer and beige and he sinks his feet ankle deep.

He thinks again about those boyhood trips to Ocean City, the longing for spits of land on the other side, way off over the horizon, unable, then, to fully grasp the magnitude of what lay in between. Then, he'd pictured France and Portugal. Now he's far south—with men not in berets swigging wine and nibbling croissants, but men knee deep in blue water tugging on long nets, pulling in a haul of flipping fish, their scales reflecting the sunlight. Yes, he's on the other side of the ocean, but in a place he could have scarcely imagined back then.

The men smile at him as he passes, as if the war is a distant thing to them. They are engaged in the business of life, on this beach and in the capital city behind it, and even up-country in the jungle. Perhaps it will all be this way again; he won't know, for he is sure that once he gets on that plane to Niamey—for that is where he decides he's going—he will never come back to Sierra Leone. Probably he won't go to West Africa at all. He has no desire to stay even one night in Niamey. He will go to Issa's, and then he will go back to the airport—get out of there as soon as he can. Go home.

But he has to go to Issa's. He has to see, one more time, the house where he lived, so he can be sure that Issa was an actual human being and not some hallucinatory amalgam of Felix's dreams and nightmares.

Ludicrous is how Felix regards Wesley's assertions about Issa's role in the murder of Felix's father. The idea does nag at him, it is true, forcing itself into his consciousness despite his efforts otherwise. But that is yet another reason to go to Issa's home, to put to rest such ridiculousness. Felix is sure he will find something there, something that will confirm the fact that Wesley and his silly, hurtful pronouncements cannot be trusted.

Felix has to pass one more day in Freetown before he can get on to Niamey, however. Lumley has been beautiful and peaceful and it gives some semblance of legitimacy to the tourist posters in the airport. But he wants out. So he heads to the airport to wait there. He goes to the VIP lounge, where he'd gone the last time. This time, the rule limiting it to Business Class travelers is being enforced, so he can't go in.

A Welsh aid worker tips him off to the "presidential suite." Head out on the strip and go into the building about 100 yards along, he says. Felix does as suggested, looking around furtively when he steps onto the strip. But no one stops him. In fact, it only takes a few thousand leones to get in, where he shares a long and comfortable couch in the air conditioning with a pastor from Burundi.

The flight passes uneventfully and before Felix knows it, they are swooping down on Niamey. Residents wash their clothes in the Niger River, with its great brown islands rising every twenty feet or so. Felix tells the taxi driver to drop him off at the stadium. He will know his way from there. When he stops on the Rue de Stade, he pays the driver and gathers himself for just a second, remembering where Issa's house would have to be from where he's standing. He can see the Place de la Republique in front of him. His house isn't in that direction. Felix turns around and things become familiar: the strip of low trees and brown buildings, stocked with millet pounders in a pile five feet high. He makes his way past the persistent hawks of children asking for *cadeaux*; past street vendors; a litany of "Non, non, non . . ." and waving hands to indicate he isn't interested. He wants only Issa's house.

He isn't on the Rue de Maroc but a minute before he finds it. Of course it looks exactly the same; it hasn't been so long since he'd been there. Away from the busy downtown, away from eyes that stay on his face without embarrassment, he feels emboldened. He approaches the locked front gate. He grabs the lock and steps on it, using it as a hoist. Putting his hand on top of the steel fence post, he throws his leg over, dangling a leg on either side. He swings the other over and lets himself drop to the ground, where he falls hard and rolls over. With the wind knocked out of him and his shoulder throbbing, he sits with his arms on his knees until he catches his breath. There's a boy staring at him with wide eyes, a trail of snot glistening his upper lip.

Felix can forgive him. The sight of a white guy jumping a fence and landing in the front yard of a house that obviously doesn't belong to him is a strange sight. But apparently not enough of one to excite any reaction. He continues to watch as Felix gets up and goes to the windows, cups his hands to them to see inside; watches, finally, as Felix takes a small rock and taps at the glass above the lock in the window on the west side of the house.

He chips out a small, diamond-shaped hole just above the lock spring. He picks up a few leaves and wraps them around his fingers, tying them off with the stems. With his fingers protected from the glass, he reaches in and snaps the lock. It recoils as if it had been on the verge of bursting. The window springs about three inches and it slides easily the rest of the way. He climbs in and falls to the floor.

The first impression is of heat—a thick, encompassing heat like the humidity of the jungle. He gets up and slowly makes his way through the house. He's not precisely sure what he's expecting, but he finds himself disappointed when he realizes that it's just as he had remembered. But of course it's exactly the same; Issa last left this house with him and had never come back. But it holds the smells of someone living, cooking smells that permeate the whole place, something like a tomato paste mixed with garlic plus something acidic and strong, like lemongrass or dill.

He decides that he's in the house because he wants to take something. It will have to be something that Issa himself would have given him. But here is a house full of things, surprisingly crammed for a man who's always on the move—closets full of nice shirts and pants; stacks of books, movies, and papers; bulky and sturdy furniture.

The small, framed picture on Issa's desk at first doesn't register as anything terribly important, just a photograph of someone who's a stranger to Felix. The little girl in it wears a pretty pink and black dress. She's smiling the smile of someone who hasn't a care in the world—wide and pure and unaffected by anything.

Felix looks more closely, at the way she holds her arms. Both are behind her back, like she's clasping hands. He can just make out the uninterrupted space of background between her left arm and her torso and realizes that her left arm is gone, chopped off above the elbow. This is Memuna, the little girl whose picture Issa had laminated and carried around in his wallet. This is the same girl that Issa had shown Felix the picture of in Bo, the one he was going to adopt as his own daughter. He turns the frame over, carefully twisting the little screw, and removes the glass from the wooden slate. The picture falls face down on the table. He scoops it up and reads the back: an address for the orphanage in Freetown. It does occur to him to go, get her, save her. But just as quickly: No, he must get home. Home, already. He puts the picture back in its frame, and stuffs this into his bag.

And then he sees a beret on the bedpost, black like the one Issa had with him when they first met, tilted too like he always wore it. He stuffs it, too, in his bag.

He walks into Issa's office and leafs through a pile of papers on his desk. It's mostly correspondence with people Issa knew in various parts of the world—Sydney, Bangkok, Chicago. He'd never spoken to Felix about any of these people, and for a fleeting moment Felix feels a slight sense of betrayal, as if he'd been the only friend in the world Issa had. Or at least, he was the one Issa would have referred to as "my American friend." But here is someone in Chicago. And of course, he'd worked in New York and probably knew a hundred people there.

The letters strike Felix as tragic documents—each unsent, each awaiting the postage that will never come. On the other side of each one, a person waiting and wondering. Someone who will eventually give up, perhaps become angry or exasperated after so many months, or years, of silence. He feels a strange sense of purpose, as if he's instantly become the sole executor of Issa's legacy. To that end he considers writing to each of these people, to tell them of the man Issa had been, how he'd met his end, and how he'd acted as something of a surrogate father to Felix, in some crazy and ultimately inexplicable way. Next to this letter is a stack of pay stubs from Executive Outcomes, each embossed with a chessboard knight, a thing that confuses Felix. Wasn't this the outfit that Wesley belonged to?

Then Felix spots the letter addressed to him.

"I am so very sorry," it begins.

This is the world we live in. But that is no real explanation. It is no excuse. I hope only that my taking you to the places you want to see will be in some small way a compensation for the grief that you will have to live with for the rest of your life. Grief that is my fault. I will tell you everything when you are here. I have just responded to your email inviting you back, so now there is no changing it. You are on your way, and the thing is to be done. It took a lot for me to do this, Felix. I cannot expect you to understand it.

I came to Sierra Leone with Executive Outcomes. We were to defeat the RUF. But I changed my mind. It was an easy thing to do. I looked around. All of the soldiers were whites – mostly all South Africans. Apartheid guys. There were Australians, too. And some Scots. One Canadian. And even though I was there and one other – a Kenyan named Jomo – so many had that apartheid attitude.

And then there was the RUF. And they were fighting for the people. They were fighting against the corruption in Freetown. The short story is that I changed sides.

This is what he'd been telling me at the mine, Felix thought. But the answer to why he hadn't sent the letter:

I was not at the camp. But I was convinced that there was more going on there than the doctors claimed. So I gave the order. I did not know what the result would be, not before. I can tell you that your father had involved himself. In retrospect now, I see it for what it is: a good man trying to make good change. But that is not how it came to me then. Then, he was an ajami meddling where he should not have.

I am sorry. I was a different person then, too. Perhaps I can explain. Perhaps I can do something. I do not know what.

Responsible for his father's death? Issa? Is that what he was saying?

A surge of bile shoots its way to the back of Felix's throat and then dribbles out from between his lips. He spits, and then finds he is on the floor next to the small puddle, on his hands and knees, his head a vortex, his mind whirling.

He rolls over and tries to collect himself and when the pinpricks and stars cease their dance across his field of vision, when the pockmarked ceiling of Issa's home comes back into focus, he considers it again. This is what he was trying to tell me, he thinks. This is why he did everything he did for me. But, my father . . . my father.

Felix hauls himself up onto a chair.

He sits for a very long time, his hands between his knees, the blood struggling to pump itself back to his brain. It's inconceivable. All of it. Somehow responsible for the death of his father? No. Couldn't be. Worked for the same organization as Wesley before he switched sides and paid for it with his life? No. Not Issa.

And why not Issa? Why not the possibility? Because that would have been the biggest betrayal of all. It would have been the ultimate pinprick to the fragile bubble of ignorance and innocence that stands between Felix and a final collapse, here in a dusty West African city. He has to have and retain faith in the things he needs to believe. There can be no other way. And yet . . .

In a rage that shocks him, that removes his consciousness and leaves behind only an animal fury, Felix leaps up and smashes everything in sight: picture frames, furniture, the television set. He overturns the desk, tosses and tears Issa's papers. He kicks, he thrashes, he screams, until he is back on the floor, heaving, spent, reduced, finally, to emptiness.

After a time, Felix gets up, surveys the damage, and then simply opens the front door and walks out. He doesn't look back at that house. And when his flight leaves, he doesn't look down at Niamey either.

# CHAPTER TWELVE

During the first few weeks Felix is home, he has dreams about diamonds. Not diamonds that kill people, that fuel civil wars, diamonds steeped in blood. These are instead glamorous stones. In these dreams, he sees hundreds of them spilling out over a table like water from a pipeline. He sees the Lebanese dealers smiling at him, imploring him to take what he wants. He picks them up, lets them fall through his fingers, picks them up again, over and over like sand at a beach.

It is only in the morning, when he wakes, that he sees the long, bony fingers of the miners inspecting the gravel on their sieves. He sees the amputees in the camp, and the desperate men sniffing inhalants in Freetown, and the crazed fighters at the mine camp, the kids at the Bo school, Issa's knowing eyes coming to understand—in that very brief moment—that this is the last moment of his life.

He doesn't need the darkness to see it all again, the same scene that won't leave him: it is the eyes, the sad look of resignation on Issa's face. He doesn't need to close his eyes to see it; in the weeks to come, the vision comes often and without warning. It can be when he's watching TV, or while reading the paper, or sitting on the subway; it makes no difference. He sees the smile fade, then the eyes looking downward for just a moment, maybe to the gun, maybe to the ground, but away from him, full of understanding that this is where it is going to end.

There are occasions when this remembrance makes Felix happy, satisfied. Issa had murdered Felix's father. Indirectly, perhaps, but still. It was true. Issa had implied it himself, and so he got what he had coming to him. But then other times . . . well, he didn't actually murder anyone in that amputees camp, did he? He wasn't even there. The responsibility for what happened doesn't fall on Issa. Right?

In the end, Felix doesn't know. Best he can divine, Issa had been embroiled with the RUF at the time when the attack against *Medecins Sans Frontieres* took place. And while he was not there, Issa, by his own admission, did give some kind of order. Things got out of hand. Felix's father was murdered. There are consequences to decisions and orders.

So maybe he did share the guilt. But to try in some way for absolution, Issa, upon realizing who Felix was and his relationship to the white doctor who had been killed, then tried to deliver to Felix the understanding he sought. If Issa could not bring Felix's father back to him, he would do the next best thing—or so the thinking went, Felix supposed. Issa was dead now, too, so Felix couldn't ask.

One thing Felix could do is he could retain his fury; Issa lacked the courage to tell Felix to his face. It was, instead, in a stupid letter he never sent. Then again, he had sort of said as much when they had been imprisoned together, back in the mine camp, before Wesley arrived to "save" them. And Issa had resolved to adopt Memuna, give her a life beyond an orphanage, give her a parent, give her access to all the things a little girl should have in this world. That was a mark to the good on the balance sheet.

In the end, it was all too much to think about for too long. Follow the mental threads down their respective rabbit holes and your head would explode. Issa operated in a world where stark delineations of black and white existed only in Saharan dune shadows. But Issa the human being, Felix knows, functioned solely and deeply ensconced in grays. And now, blacks and whites, absolutes, were a luxury long gone for Felix, too. And so he would carry on, best he could, and allow Issa to be many things at once—killer, savior, surrogate, superior, deeply flawed, at once the strongest and yet most fragile person Felix had ever known. There could be no other way, no alternate path out of the madness. After all, Felix reasons, while we are all innocents, we are all also guilty as hell. His father, too, leaving his family behind, leaving such grief in his wake. We cannot run from our sins, none of us. All we can do, Felix knows, is grapple with them, find some way to try our best to make amends. This, he decides, finally and at long last, was what Issa was trying to do.

And so, despite a perpetually swimming head, Felix wills himself into some semblance of normality. He resolves to be there for his mother as much as he can and promises to drive to North Carolina when he gets everything settled.

With his mom, he leaves out all the rough stuff. But he doesn't hold back a thing with Lizzy when he finally sees her. He doesn't call her, but instead simply shows up at her apartment. He forces himself up the sidewalk, then turns around, then goes back. He knocks, inhales, feels his heart pounding inside his chest.

The door opens. After a fleeting look of surprise, she takes his hand and wordlessly leads him in. It's the look of him, no doubt—a wasted man with nowhere else to go.

He pours himself out to her—mostly just snatches of impressions at first, but then growing to encompass the thickness of the jungle, the miners, the amputee camp, the sneaking suspicion that the entire enterprise has done little more than emphasize the worst stereotypes of a massive and diverse and extraordinary continent to people like him, people who are born in luxury and can scarcely even recognize it until in its absence, how people like him see the whole of Africa as nothing but hopeless. But it is far more than that; it has to be. It is, after all, from where we all come. It is the cradle of humanity—for better or for worse. This is what he realizes, what he tells her. "It's hard, to think, to convince yourself, that 'those people' need saviors like me, like my dad. I was useless there." He pauses, swallows hard. "It's all so complicated. So confusing."

Lizzy strokes his hand and hugs him.

He tells her about Issa, but only up to the final moments. "I watched him die," he says. He leaves out the letter, leaves out the rest. He reminds himself that if he wants any kind of normality in this lifetime, he has to leave it alone, push it away, own it in the deepest recesses of himself, but disallow its bubbling forth, a task he reckons carries with it something of the impossible. But if he wishes to stay sane? He must, he must, he must.

Lizzy slowly shakes her head.

Felix shifts gears and tells her about the desert. "I saw your face," he says. "In the last moments before I died—or thought I was dying. I could feel things collapsing. Like turning off a series of switches and motoring down. I saw your face. I was making an accounting of what was the most important thing to me."

She begins to cry.

"I'm sorry, Lizzy. This isn't fair of me. You have every

These two pages need to be worked on to get rid of the time elapses. Use strong transitional sentences instead.

reason to hate me."

"Of course I don't hate you."

"I only remember this now. I'd forgotten it. But I'm sure of it. I saw you. I guess . . . I wanted to be with you when I died."

She kisses his forehead, his lips, through the salty film of her tears.

"I'm changed, Lizzy. I will never, ever take you for granted again."

She nods, hugs him, tells him she loves him. And he tells her he loves her, too—more than any solitary thing in this world or any other.

A few days later, when he goes to see his mother in North Carolina, Lizzy comes. They spend the week lazing around, walking along the beach, hanging out, talking, practicing at being normal human beings again living normal human lives.

One afternoon, the three of them sit together on the sand and watch the soft lap of the waves. The thrumming of the ocean is muted and calm. Felix heads inside to his mother's to fetch her book for her. There, on her nightstand, is the photograph of his parents in front of the Eiffel Tower from many years earlier. He smiles; she hasn't tossed it. And now it's displayed, at the place where she closes her eyes each night.

When Felix rejoins her and Lizzy on the beach, he puts his hand on his mom's shoulder and then gives her a long hug. She's taken aback at first, cradling her drink so it won't upend. But then she hugs him back, and from over her shoulder, he can see Lizzy smiling at him.

On the last night at Rosemarie's, Lizzy goes to bed early because she has a headache. Felix and his mom stay up late talking. A cool breeze circles the veranda and they listen to the silky swoosh of the trees in the wind. They sit through long, comfortable silences and longer periods of rapid fire discussion, about life in North Carolina, about politics in Maryland, about inconsequential things. Then, the important stuff.

"Mom," he says. "I think I'm going to ask Lizzy to marry me."

"You think?"

"That's stupid. No, not 'think.' I'm going to."

His mom puts down her soda and lime and wraps her arms around him and kisses his cheek. She smells faintly of sun and sand and seawater, a wonderful combination that exudes health. "I think you should," she says. "You would both be very lucky."

He agrees—and so does Lizzy when he asks her.

He has no ring. He supposes he should have—it was a bit cheesy to ask the way he did, he knows—more a suggestion than an actual asking. And her response fit the informality of it all: "I think that would be nice," accompanied by that irresistible nose-crinkling smile.

He has an idea about the ring. He thinks that she realizes it, too—a tacit understanding that all his sincerity is there, and the rest, the accoutrements, will come later. After his descriptions of the diamond mines, she doesn't expect a diamond ring, of course. It isn't her style anyway. Twenty-three years old, she is still the very essence of youth, a girl who would age a decade with a diamond ring slipped onto her finger.

First, they will move in together. They will share living space, share a life, play at being together again without the interruptions of college classes, and continents, and wanderlust. They will learn to live the normal, mundane lives that are the due expectations of those who are healthy, and young, and privileged.

One night, Felix receives a large envelope from Dr. Albert. In it is a newspaper clipping and a short note telling him what he's been up to. He's no longer in the Central African Republic. He has retired from Johns Hopkins and has started freelance consulting for zoos. He's just gotten back from Oiji Zoo in Kobe, Japan and he's going next to Kabul, where officials hope to reestablish the zoo that was destroyed during the Taliban's reign. Loads of donations had flooded in after pictures of Marjan circulated worldwide. Marjan was the lion that had half his face blown away by a grenade tossed by the brother of a Taliban fighter whom Marjan had eaten.

The old adventurer is still doing his thing—and Felix still admires him for it.

Also in the envelope is a photograph. In his letter, Dr. Albert apologizes for not having gotten the photograph to Felix earlier, but he'd forgotten he had it and only found it recently when he was cleaning out his office at Hopkins. It is of Felix's dad at the MSF camp. The inscription on the back reads: "James – thanks again. Everything I hoped. We'll have stories back in Balto." It's dated the day before he was killed.

In the picture, he looks happy. There's a smile on his face—not too wide, out of place as it would be in a location with so much misery. But it's the same look he used to get when he completed something—or, more accurately, just before he completed something. It could be a relatively simple project—replacing the security light in the backyard, for example. He would do the wiring, run the cable, and just as the pole was settling into the hole he had dug, the look would cross his face: accomplishment, satisfaction, an appreciation of his own competence. It was the same look Felix imagines he got when he completed surgeries, the same he got, most probably, every time he touched one of those amputees and made them feel human again. The photograph is a fantastic gift, one that Felix plans to have framed and keep above his desk.

Last, he reads the newspaper clipping:

MONROVIA, Liberia (AP) – An American citizen arrested on June 14 in Kakata, Liberia has been charged with impersonating a CIA agent and will be returned to the United States for trial, according to embassy officials here. The man, identified as Wesley Nils, also is under investigation in the deaths of two National Patriotic Front of Liberia (NPFL) rebels associated with the former government of President Charles Taylor, now in exile in Nigeria. Mr. Nils was arrested by U.S. agents with the aid of Liberian army soldiers.

Felix slides open his dresser drawer and places the paper inside, another memento from the most extraordinary trip he's ever known.

Later that evening, Lizzy and Felix lay in bed together. He's quiet for a long time, and it's obvious that his silence is something heavier than just a post-coital contentment.

"Are you okay?" Lizzy asks. He sighs, shifting his arm under her shoulder, inhaling the scent of her hair. "I feel impotent," he says.

"It didn't feel that way to me."

"Thank you. It does wonders for me. But I'm talking

about Sierra Leone, and I'm sorry to worry this subject again. But, it's just—the kids. My dad did something and he did it in a very respectful way. Me? Nothing. I feel impotent. What can I do?"

"You do everything you can, which, unfortunately isn't that much. Take comfort in the fact that your dad did enough for the both of you, for a hundred men."

"It's not that simple."

He leaves the bed and goes to the closet. He digs out a shoebox into which he had placed his Agadez silver cross, Issa's beret, and the photograph of Memuna. "Look at her left shoulder," he says.

Lizzy's eyes mist as she takes the picture, holding it just at the very edge, careful not to get a thumbprint on it as if that would be the final insult to this little person. "Her name is Memuna," he says, as Lizzy slowly shakes her head. "Issa was going to adopt her."

"Where is she?"

"An orphanage in Freetown."

"Do you know where? How to get to her?"

Felix removes the picture, flips it over, shows Lizzy the address of the orphanage scrawled there.

Lizzy sits up and places the photograph on the bedstead next to the picture of the two of them hugging at a party.

"Let's save her, Felix."

This idea has been incubating in his brain for months, but he has never said it out loud; it seems too extreme, too much beyond the position he is in at this moment in his life. He is very much a kid himself after all—one who has grown up in a hurry, for sure. But a young man at best. Could he care for a child? Especially one who isn't even his?

But the other question, too: Could there ever be a more lasting and more appropriate tribute to his father?

Lizzy looks once again at the picture. "We can do it," she says.

# CHAPTER THIRTEEN

The first trip is to the Sierra Leonean embassy in D.C. There, Lizzy and Felix speak with a Mr. Caulker, who applauds their intentions and promises his aid. But he also warns them that adoption can be difficult. He has, in fact, spent much of the week working on a case where a group of families in New York tried to adopt amputee victims who had come to the U.S. for treatment, and that there were great battles going on because these kids were in fact not orphans at all.

"Until the war the concept of adoption was totally foreign to Sierra Leoneans," he explains. "There is no Krio word for adoption; the people use 'men' instead. *Men* is a common arrangement by which a child is raised by someone other than the biological parents. But never, under any circumstances, are actual rights transferred. So what we have been seeing is situations where some kids, dispersed by the war, are now being reunited with family members by complete accident. A mother or father, believing that the child has been dead, shopping at a market in the city or on a special trip to the capital from somewhere in the jungle, sees that child also out on a shopping excursion buying supplies for an orphanage."

"And they didn't know the child was there?" Lizzy asks.

"They had gotten separated during the war. A very common occurrence and often done deliberately, to spirit away a child for safety reasons—maybe send them uplands to relatives, say. There have also been a string of cases where

birth parents who claimed to have left their children with or-
phanages for foster care returned to find them adopted out
of the country. So now the government is making exhaustive
investigations into the allegations and is putting much tighter controls on the entire process. That is made even more
difficult by the fact that the American government does not
recognize any registered adoption agencies in Sierra Leone.
So adoption has to be initiated through an American service
operation, which furthers suspicion on the part of the government of Sierra Leone." He fixes Lizzy and Felix in the eye: "In
short," he says, "It won't be easy."

Felix and Lizzy visibly sag, which Mr. Caulker takes
note of.

"I want you to be aware of the obstacles. But this does
not mean there is *no* reason for optimism. If Memuna is still
in this orphanage, that means she has been more than two
years there, which lessens the hope of a family member coming to retrieve her. Plus, if your friend Issa had been talking of
adopting her for years, and it was something Memuna and the
orphanage workers knew, then your chances are even better.
You two can go as something of his emissary."

Felix's jaw tightens. His feelings surrounding Issa have
not fully unwound themselves. But those feelings, and everything else swirling around his head, are soon subsumed
when Mr. Caulker calls the orphanage and immediately gets
through to a social worker from Wisconsin named Cecilia.

There is a long pause, which Mr. Caulker passes by
turning a pencil over and over in his hand. But, finally: Yes,
Cecilia confirms, there is a Memuna at the orphanage. In fact,
there are four Memunas. But only two of them had suffered
amputation of the left arm. And only one of them was the ap-

proximate age of Issa's Memuna. The other had just celebrated her nineteenth birthday the day before.

"If your couple is truly interested in adopting her," Cecilia explains, "They will have to come and see her in person."

Felix and Lizzy have a one-day layover in Paris. While there, they go to *Goutte-d'Or*, Paris' Little Africa, and make their way to the *Marche Dejean*, an open-air market teeming with hundreds of Africans from various ex-colonies. Lizzy stops at a jewelry stall. She inspects a gray metal ring, carved with serpentine designs and interlocking lacy snowflakes. While Lizzy moves off to another stall, Felix surreptitiously buys it. When Lizzy returns to him, Felix gets down on one knee and slips it on her finger.

The day slips seamlessly into evening, time suspended. They remain in a celebratory mood, even after a sumptuous dinner and two bottles of wine, even as the suggestion of daybreak appears in the east. They catch a flight to Conakry, Guinea, and take an eight-hour bush taxi from there. When they arrive in Freetown, they stay at the Cape Sierra—same pool, drained now, the same cockroaches—but it does the trick. While Lizzy sleeps, Felix goes to the U.S. embassy and asks for Hank Peters, but he's told that Mr. Peters is in Bissau for the opening of the new U.S. consulate there. Then he is headed back home to Oklahoma. His time in Freetown is over. In fact, it appears that the entire staff has turned over; Felix doesn't recognize anyone in the building, nor does anyone recognize him. It is as if, now that relative stability has reached Sierra Leone, the excitement is over and people have gone home. A new crop, ones who appreciate the lack of "excitement," have taken their places.

Lizzy and Felix head to the orphanage early the next morning. They pass the stadium, the Cotton Tree, the American embassy, the Aberdeen Bridge, the turn off to the amputee camp. But Felix doesn't narrate. Even when Lizzy remarks about the grandeur of the Law Courts Building—it has been freshly painted since Felix had been there last—he doesn't respond. They are mostly quiet, the taxi heavy with anticipation. This is a long trip, in more than just distance, and what is on the other end of it is heavier still.

When they arrive, a deferential man in a royal blue shirt greets them and then tells them he will get Cecilia, bowing as he walks away. They wait, taking in the collection of wood buildings built up around a dirt courtyard. Distant mountains and electric green encircle three rows of neat, bursting crops. The orphanage workers wear royal blue shirts and are distinguished less by this outfit than by their intact limbs. The orphans are mostly young children, and like young children everywhere, they play, yell, squirm, adapt. The ones who are capable run in chaotic circles in fields and within the crude outlines of a soccer pitch drawn in the dirt. Those missing legs sit on the side of the pitch beside their crutches and cheer. One among them gets up when the ball sails toward him. Balancing himself on his crutches, he gives the ball a hearty kick and sends it sailing over everyone's heads and into the bushes. Some of the workers who witness this cheer. The players, retrieving the ball, scowl.

Momentarily, a young woman approaches. Her face is full of freckles and framed by straw-colored hair.

"Cecilia?"

"Yes. Come." She shakes their hands, and leads Felix and Lizzy to the main office. They pass an open shed where eight young women—looking somewhere between sixteen and twenty-five—are busy working ancient yellow sewing machines. A woman in the same royal blue shirt walks to each machine, checking on the girls' progress.

They settle into the office and Cecilia hands them bottles of water. "I've sent for Memuna," she said. "She'll be here when she's done washing up from the game."

Felix looks to Lizzy and can see a fresh course of blood rising in her cheeks. It's all happening so quickly. At any moment, the girl who someday might be their daughter is going to walk into the room. What will they say to her? How will she react? Will she feel threatened by these two white strangers? Will there be indifference? Has she even been told that they were coming?

"No," Cecilia answers to this last question. "We don't tell them, in case someone then doesn't show. But Memuna's very smart," Cecilia continues. "She'll understand why you're here."

"When we met with Mr. Caulker, he told us how it isn't a foreign concept for Memuna to be cared for elsewhere— even somewhere across the ocean—but if any of her relatives appeared, they would expect her back."

Cecilia nods.

"I mean, what if she herself decided she wanted to come back? That this is her home?"

"I would never dismiss that as a possibility. But I reviewed Memuna's intake form for the orphanage after I learned you were coming. This form includes the conditions of her arrival, a birth certificate, and the parents' death certificates. We also have copies of reports by the police and the Ministry of Social Welfare, Gender, and Children's Affairs detailing the search for relatives, in Memuna's case unsuccessful. If a relative should happen to pop up, well, I've been doing this for a while and I can tell you that nine times out of ten in such a situation, they will say it is the will of God. In their view, her losing an arm was the necessary price to pay to get to America. It's worth it. As for her wanting to come back, well, that's something you'll have to figure out with her. But you can expect that she'll get used to being in America. She'll be a new person because she's only nine years old. I'm guessing she won't ask to come back here."

"Will she understand us?" Lizzy asks.

"English is the official language in Sierra Leone, as you know, but Memuna would have grown up speaking Krio. We make English part of the curriculum here at the orphanage, however. When children get adopted, it is almost always to the States or to England. We want them to be prepared."

At that moment, Memuna walks through the door. Lizzy has the picture of her in her bag; she and Felix had all looked at it many times, holding it between them at home, on their laps during the flight, on the hotel bed in Freetown the night before. The girl who walks in looks little like the one in the picture. Of course, she has aged almost three years, no small number in a girl so young.

But there is something different, a serenity that adorns her face. In the photograph, the smile is infectious and beautiful, but if one looks very closely, there's something else—expectation, some confusion, a plea to the camera for help. It's in the eyes, which stare ahead unflinchingly, asking for something even in their silence. But this person, this beautiful little girl standing before them now, holds the understanding in her eyes of someone ten times her age. She knows why they are here. Her eyes fall directly on Felix and Lizzy and don't move. In that one look, she tells them that she can stay in Sierra Leone if she needs to, that these two strangers are her hope for leaving only because they are sitting here, but if need be, she can turn right around, go back to her games in the dirt, and never see them again.

"Hi, sweetie," Lizzy says.

"My name is Memuna."

They all laugh, a letting out of tension that is palpable. But Memuna doesn't laugh, or even smile; she holds her gaze steady. Felix wants desperately to reach for her, cradle her in his arms—as Issa had so much wanted to do. But he holds back, unsure of himself.

"Memuna," Lizzy starts, getting off her chair and crouching onto a knee in front of the unfazed girl. "Do you think you might like to come home with us? To America?"

"To live?"

Lizzy nods. "I am going to be married to this wonderful man here and we would like you to come live with us. His name is Felix and he was friends with Issa."

Memuna's eyes widen. She looks at Felix. "Is Issa with you?" she asks.

Felix hesitates. He'd forgotten that no one had told her that Issa was dead. How do you explain death to a nine-year-old girl, someone who was, he had to remind himself, a stranger?

But of course Memuna knew death, in ways far more profound than Felix or Lizzy did.

"I am very sorry to tell you that Issa died."

Her chin drops and a fat tear splashes onto the ground. She stifles a few sobs.

"I am sorry, Memuna. But I can tell you that he loved you. He told me that, many times. In fact, he is why I am here. He is how I knew about you."

"I think Issa would have wanted you to come back with us to America," Lizzy says. "What do you think? Do you think you might like to come live with us in America?"

Memuna looks at all of the adults in turn, holding her gaze with each until meeting Lizzy's again. She then nods, almost imperceptibly. Lizzy's eyes well with tears and the two shake hands, an oddly formal gesture but one that seems somehow appropriate, a seal of the deal.

Memuna then gives a little curtsy and walks out.

In private talks with both Cecilia and with Lizzy and Felix, later that day and the next morning over breakfast in a Freetown restaurant, Memuna repeats that she'd like to go with them. She has been at the orphanage for more than two years. She has seen the kids who left, the ones heading to America and England. The event is always treated as a reward for all the suffering, a reprieve from a life without a proper family. So now that her time has come—and she always believed that it would come some day—she accepts it without hesitation.

All that is left is the paperwork, but this consumes months.

Memuna accepts the long delay. Back at home in Baltimore, Lizzy and Felix call every two weeks to make sure she is still okay. She is fine and she will wait, she says. Memuna has the patience of someone who has lived three lifetimes, or a short one packed with enough horror for three. "I am ready to go to America," she says. "But now I wait."

The American Embassy in Freetown initiated the necessary investigation into Memuna's situation. Once that was complete, the American Embassy in Dakar, Senegal, received the documents and scrutinized them. To keep the Sierra Leoneans in the loop, however, everything was done in conjunction with the Ministry of Social Welfare, Gender, and Children's Affairs in Freetown.

The official investigation into her case winds up taking more than six months. When it is complete, the finding doesn't change anything: Memuna's parents were murdered and there is no indication of any family member searching for her or having attempted to retrieve her. A judge then signs off on the adoption. That step complete, the documents are sent to Dakar, where a consular official confirms that the child is in fact an orphan. The officials in Dakar send Felix and Lizzy pre-interview forms and instructions on how to apply for final adoption.

In the meanwhile, Felix and Lizzy go to the State Department in D.C. with their birth certificates, passports, and official papers asserting their desire to adopt. Finally, after almost eight months, they get the call: It is time to get Memuna. Only one last trip to the U.S. embassy in Dakar, and then Felix, Lizzy, and Memuna can officially be recognized as a family.

Dakar is hardly a delay. They are there just overnight, though with the excitement of everything neither of them gets any real sleep. Memuna has already been confirmed as an orphan, and the necessary preliminary forms are all on file, along with the High Court certification. Felix and Lizzy hand over the remaining documents: Memuna's birth certificate, a signed medical exam, Memuna's Sierra Leonean passport, a 2x2 inch photograph of Memuna, and the twelve dollar immigration visa fee.

By the time Felix and Lizzy arrive at the orphanage, they've been exhausted by the trip—ragged by the voyage that had started twenty-six hours earlier in the U.S. But all that is forgotten when they see her. They spot her through the window of her residential building, but she does not see them. A breeze is blowing the curtain, and when it falls back against the window to reveal Memuna, there she is sitting on a bench. She wears a pink dress. Her legs hang off the bench, crossed at the ankle. She swings them gently while humming a steady rhythm. They listen closely. It's a song she has no doubt learned in childhood or here in the orphanage, a song that they wonder if they will hear back at home. Or will it be something she will abandon, some part of her from another life and world that she will leave behind? Is this the last for her, the humming a way of saying goodbye to everything—the things she loves and the things she hates? Is she scared to leave this place, the only country she has ever known? She has never been more than thirty miles away from where she is at this moment. How will she do thousands of miles away, in a brand new country?

If there is fear in Memuna, she hides it. When they enter, Memuna hops off the bench and runs over to them, no hesitation. She wraps her arm around Felix's leg and buries her head in the crook of Lizzy's lap. This is their daughter. It is time to leave Sierra Leone, perhaps the last time for any of them.

At the airport, Memuna sucks in a deep breath as she crosses the threshold to the plane. And when it rumbles to a start and taxies across the airstrip, she looks out of the window just once. She runs one finger across the window, and then settles back in her seat, inhaling deeply again.

"Are you okay?" Felix asks.

Memuna nods. Lizzy places her hand on Memuna's chest and slowly rubs back and forth. They are going home, and Memuna will become a citizen the moment her little feet hit the tiles of Baltimore-Washington International.

# CHAPTER FOURTEEN

For the first few months, Memuna doesn't speak about her life back in Africa. The closest she comes to any of it is when she has dreams that she has both her arms and both her hands. But these aren't reasons for renewed sadness. In fact, the dreams buoy her. She tells Felix and Lizzy all about them, how she saw herself doing laundry or carrying buckets of water in both hands. They make her happy for the rest of the day and while it breaks Lizzy's heart every time, she soon comes to appreciate the dreams the way Memuna does, as visits from old friends. It is clear that Memuna cherishes her reunions with her whole self, with the little girl she had been.

Memuna's favorite place to go is the grocery store. It is a matter of true and wondrous amazement to her every time they go—there, on the shelves, are dozens and dozens of the same item. They sit in rows of three, ten or so deep. Take one and there's another behind it, just waiting. And there are thousands of such items in the store. It took Felix some time to appreciate grocery stores again after his time in Africa. They seemed plastic, fake places. He hated the sanitation, the tidiness. He longed for the central market, where everything was bare and open and real.

Memuna once asked if they shouldn't buy a hundred of something, so that they'd have it when the day comes that there aren't any more to buy. Felix tells her that people in Baltimore only do that when there's the threat of snow. He and

Lizzy laugh, but she doesn't get it; she's never seen snow. That will come soon and when it does, she'll have another wonder to change her life.

Once Memuna has settled in, Felix takes her to his mother's in North Carolina while Lizzy stays home and tries to get caught back up with her professional life; Lizzy hates to see them go, if even for just a few days, but she agrees that seeing the beach will be a great experience for Memuna. Even though she has lived her entire life within a hundred miles of the ocean, she has never been there.

Felix recalls the first time his mother had seen Memuna. When Rosemarie entered the house, Felix saw the quick look flash across her face: horror, fear, pity—contempt even. After all, this girl's presence was the direct product of some circuitous journey that had radically altered, even shattered, Rosemarie's life. But she quickly swept the look away, scooping Memuna into her arms and onto her lap, unable to completely look away from the end of the stump where the skin looked waterlogged. But like everyone else who met Memuna, Felix's mother was quickly won over by her smile—the same innocent, unashamed retraction of lips that seemed to swallow her whole face.

By that afternoon, the two of them were great buddies, Memuna clinging to her as if this was her long lost grandmother.

Now at Rosemarie's house at the beach, she insists on taking Memuna by herself into town to buy her ice cream. They are gone for a couple of hours and when they return, Felix opens the door expecting to see happy faces. But neither one is smiling. Memuna doesn't look unhappy, just indifferent. But Rosemarie's sadness is unmistakable. She gives Memuna a little pat on her head and, with a cheerless little smile, pushes her gently toward the living room. Memuna runs there and Felix can hear the television go on moments later.

"What happened?"

Rosemarie plops onto a chair and opens her mouth. But a cascade of tears comes first and it's several minutes before she can collect herself. It's a torrent unlike any Felix had ever seen his mother loose—more, even, than over his dad. Alarmed, he asks her again what happened.

Between sobs, she manages to get it out: "She asked me if, now that she's in America . . . if her arm would grow back."

Felix sits down. As far as he knows, Memuna has never asked that. He wonders now if this is the beginning of it, the realization finally that she is different. The old sickening thought comes back to him: maybe they've done her a great disservice by bringing her to America. At least back in Sierra Leone, she wasn't different from everyone else.

"We are not helpless," Issa once said. Of course not; this is no easy world, no unruffled life. But anything worth something rarely is. Memuna knows that, and of course, Felix had learned it long ago. He only hopes that now his mother would understand it, too. It can't have been easy for her. This little girl will always be a palpable reminder of what she lost when his father left.

But Felix has to hope that maybe his mom finally understands. Maybe she realizes—perhaps even appreciates— why his dad went. When Rosemarie picks up Memuna and only one hand grasps the back of her shoulder, maybe she will also understand why her husband never returned, why her husband's life was sacrificed. Felix could never ask her to say that it was worth it—he doesn't believe that himself—but he has to think that in those moments, she understands. She understands everything.

Memuna comes back in the room. Seeing Rosemarie crying, she crawls onto her lap. With the one good hand stroking the back of Rosemarie's hair, Memuna smiles. And so does Felix. And so, finally and genuinely, does his mother.

# CHAPTER FIFTEEN

Memuna has rounded out Felix's strange affair with Sierra Leone. The country has begun a slow transformation, finally, into a good place. While Sierra Leone will never cease to be the place where his father was ripped from his life, it will now also be the place where he gained a daughter, a place that will forever bind Lizzy and Felix in ways that would have been unimaginable to either one of them at the beginning of their relationship.

It is morning. Memuna wakes. Last night was good, only soft exhalations while Lizzy and Felix hovered near her bed. She sleeps now without the night light. She wants to be a big girl, she says. Felix and Lizzy would let her sleep with one if she wanted because they want her to be a little girl again; she had been one once, though she doesn't remember. But she's almost ten now. She doesn't need a light, she says.

She kisses them both on the cheek. She fixes cereal for herself, deftly moving everything with her right hand, what remains of the left arm bobbing in exact rhythm with the right. It's a remarkable scene, one that would inspire pity in those who don't know her. But Felix and Lizzy only marvel at her, this little model of efficiency and self-assurance. They let her dump in spoonfuls of sugar. If this child had been born to them, here in the United States, they wouldn't let it go. But Memuna can have sugar. She can have anything they can give her.

They spend the day at a local park. The first time they went there, the kids—and the parents—stared at her. Some of the bolder parents asked what had happened to her. Felix and Lizzy told them. They had never heard of Sierra Leone.

This time no one stares. They know her by now. She's a little beauty. And she's sweet and innocent, still damaged somewhere deep inside, but that seems to melt a little each time she runs under the monkey bars or plays the second partner to someone's seesaw ride. They no longer stare, no longer see only what isn't there. Instead, like her parents, they see the person who is there—whole and complete.

One night, just before bed, Memuna leaves Felix's office with the photograph Dr. Albert sent him.

"Who is that man?" she asks. "Where is he?"

It's a long story, Felix tells her.

"Just start," she says.

"He was in Sierra Leone," Felix says, stroking her head. "He was a good man. A very good man," he continues. He can see out of the corner of his eye, Lizzy leaning against the doorframe, watching.

"That man is my father," Felix says.

Memuna studies it for a few moments, then puts it down, apparently satisfied for now. But she will no doubt have more questions some day. And Felix will do his best to answer, to tell her everything.

Eventually, she will discover Issa's effects also: his beret, the silver cross he gave Felix. She will certainly ask about these things as well. And when she does, Felix will tell her all about Issa, too. It is only what to leave out that he will need to decide.

But isn't that the way with everything?